ODELL'S CHARGE

Odell saw the Comanches riding toward him at about the same time Crow did. Just seconds before, the horse had seemed worn out, but now he fairly pranced along the ground, pushing against the bit. It was plain he sensed the coming fight or flight.

There were four Comanches spread out in a long line and trotting right at Odell. He knew nothing of Indian fighting, but he tried to calm himself and remember the advice that a seemingly endless number of Texans had given him. Common sense told him that he stood little chance against such long odds, and from what he'd heard his flintlock rifle was going to be little help in a horseback fight out in the open. The Indians were too close and his horse too used up to turn and outrun them. He spied the brush-choked gully just behind and to the left of the Comanches and decided to make for it if he should survive the charge.

A wild, shrill shout went up from one of the Comanches, and it was answered all down their line. Odell took a spare bullet from his pouch and put it in his mouth for a quick reload. He cocked the hammer on his rifle and kicked his horse forward at a run just as the Comanches did the same. He charged forward with his teeth gritted and the wind folding the broad brim of his hat back against the crown.

THE
TEXANS

BRETT
COGBURN

BERKLEY BOOKS, NEW YORK

THE BERKLEY PUBLISHING GROUP
Published by the Penguin Group
Penguin Group (USA)
375 Hudson Street, New York, New York 10014, USA

USA I Canada I UK I Ireland I Australia I New Zealand I India I South Africa I China

Penguin Books Ltd., Registered Offices: 80 Strand, London WC2R 0RL, England
For more information about the Penguin Group, visit penguin.com.

THE TEXANS

A Berkley Book / published by arrangement with the author

Berkley Books are published by The Berkley Publishing Group.
BERKLEY® is a registered trademark of Penguin Group (USA).
The "B" design is a trademark of Penguin Group (USA).

For information, address: The Berkley Publishing Group,
a division of Penguin Group (USA),
375 Hudson Street, New York, New York 10014.

ISBN: 978-0-425-26533-8

PUBLISHING HISTORY
Berkley mass-market edition / September 2013

PRINTED IN THE UNITED STATES OF AMERICA

10 9 8 7 6 5 4 3 2 1

Cover illustration by Robert Hunt.
Cover design by Diana Kolsky.
Cover images: Guns © James Daniels/Shutterstock; Texture © Vectorkat/Shutterstock.
Interior text design by Laura K. Corless.

ALWAYS LEARNING   PEARSON

This book is dedicated to
the members of the U.S. Armed Forces—
patriots present and past—sacrificing dearly
and serving their country in harm's way.

Hats off to you, and thanks.

Chapter 1

Odell Spurling knew he ought to shoot the Indian. It was an easy shot from where he lay in a bois d'arc thicket, but he hesitated. Three years on the frontier was more than enough time to instill in most folks the axiom that the only good Indian was a dead one, but sometimes it seemed that Odell wasn't ever going to make a proper Texan. He quietly wallowed himself a more comfortable spot for his belly and readjusted the double-barreled Bishop rifle against his shoulder. He looked out over the rotten log he lay behind and gave careful study to the young warrior watering his horse at a gravel shoal fifty yards down the creek.

The Indian had come up the creek bed, traveling quietly and leading his horse. That in itself seemed suspicious, but Odell wasn't even sure what kind of redskin he was looking at. Any number of the old frontiersmen in the area could have told you what tribe the young brave belonged to at a glance. However, Odell was new to Texas, and it was safe to say that the country was chock-full of more kinds of

Indians than you could shake a stick at—Tonks, Kronks, Cherokees, Wacos, Wichitas, Caddos, Apaches, Kiowas, and others too numerous to name. His neighbors claimed that there would be no doubt about it when he saw one of the dreaded Comanche, but the young brave watering his horse didn't seem especially threatening to the casual glance.

Odell was just seventeen, and the Indian he was looking at couldn't have been much older. No war paint decorated his smooth face, and by his trappings he seemed quite the dandy. The top of his forehead was painted red at the parting of his black hair, and a single, brown feather dangled from one of his double braids. A veritable stack of copper rings encircled each of his upper arms, and long, silver earrings dangled almost to each shoulder. A bison-tooth necklace and red-wool breechcloth completed his dapper getup.

The French trade musket he held in one hand looked oversized against his slight frame. But while small in stature, the native's brown hide popped with lean, hard muscle beneath a liberal coating of bear grease, like ropes stretched taut underneath wet burlap. Odell was a very big young man, but the little Indian seemed to have muscles where there weren't even supposed to be muscles.

The Indian squatted down beside his drinking horse and cast a wary look around the brush before scooping up a handful of water. His eyes passed right over Odell, but the young frontiersman was sure that he was well hidden. He might not know much about Texas, but he did know the woodlands. Half of his life had already been spent hunting and running traps in the mountains of Georgia, and the timber along the creek bottom provided him with terrain to his liking. Anybody who could sneak up within spitting distance of a whitetail deer, or shoot the head off a gray squirrel in the top of the tallest tree, ought to have nothing to fear from a lone Indian boy.

Gnats and mosquitoes swarmed about Odell's head, and

some other kind of crawly thing was working its way up his britches leg, stopping periodically to sting the hell out of him. He willed himself to be still and weather the insect assault on his tender flesh. He was a hunter by nature, and was enjoying the excitement he felt over seeing his first, honest-to-goodness plains warrior in the wild.

The Indian continued drinking one handful at a time, as if afraid to set his musket aside. The little bay gelding he was leading had drunk his fill and pulled against the rein of his war bridle in an attempt to pick at some water grass growing along the edge of the creek. Odell was quite shocked to see that the horse was saddled, considering that he had always been told that Indian men rode bareback. A buffalo-hide shield hung from the wooden horn of a Mexican saddle on the off side of the horse, and a long, hoop-iron-tipped lance was tucked under the stirrup leather. A water bag and a beaded set of saddlebags were tied behind the cantle.

When the brave had quenched his thirst, he shifted his weight over onto one leg and grimaced for a moment before farting loudly. His horse spooked and pulled hard against his rope, jerking the young Indian onto his back and dragging him several feet along the rocky bank. He just managed to hold on to his mount and roll over onto his belly. The horse stopped spraddle-legged and crouched low in the front end, his eyes wild and little ears pointed forward. The gelding blew loudly out his flared nostrils as his master eased to his feet and worked his way up the rope. A soothing hand along the horse's neck quieted him somewhat, but the white showing in the horse's eyes and the high carriage of his head showed that he was still looking for the booger that had made such a noise.

Ignoring the stirrup, the brave leapt astride the frightened horse with one fluid swing of his leg. He gathered his horse-hair rein and smiled down at his mount and rubbed his neck again just ahead of the withers. With a mischievous look spreading across his face, he shifted in the saddle, lifted his left knee a little, and farted once more. The sound reverberated against the seat of the saddle, amplifying the crackling baritone to monstrous proportions.

If the horse had been scared before, he was positively beside himself then. Something was about to eat him, and he scrambled wildly on the creek stones beneath his feet. He crow-hopped twice to throw whatever thing had snuck onto his back, and then bolted off in a dead run. The little warrior laughed aloud and had no trouble pulling the horse back down.

Odell couldn't help but laugh himself, and the brave's head whirled around at the sound. His eyes locked in on the clump of brush that concealed his observer. The trade musket was up to his shoulder in an instant. He sat his stomping, crazed horse and searched the thicket carefully.

Odell tucked his cheek tight against the stock of his rifle and squinted down its long barrel. He found the blade of the front sight, and the Indian's chest danced around before it. He normally couldn't miss at such close range, but his calm seemed to have left him in an instant. He had the hammer cocked for the .60-caliber right barrel, and a load of number six shot in the left shotgun barrel if that big round ball didn't do the trick. The little chunks of charcoal that were the brave's eyes focused in on Odell's hiding spot, and Odell wasn't at all sure that he was well enough armed. For the first time, the handful of scalps dangling from the bottom of the brave's shield registered in his brain for what they were. The Indian didn't look like a boy to him anymore.

Despite his study, the Indian couldn't make out Odell's form in the thicket. However, he did recognize the black, double eyes of the Bishop rifle peering at him over a log for what they were. He thumped his heels into his horse's belly and clattered down the edge of the shallow stream in a dead run. He cast one last look over his shoulder before he darted off into the timber a hundred yards down the creek.

Odell watched him go with more than a little relief. The

wild look on the Indian's face just before leaving gave Odell a little notion of just what his elders had been preaching about around the fireplace at night. His size had always made him confident where physical danger was concerned, but for a moment he wondered if he had taken that Indian far too lightly. Something told him that had he not had the advantage of cover, his scalp too might have been hanging on that shield before sundown. And another little voice was yelling loudly in his ear that the stout warrior was undoubtedly a Comanche.

He considered the fact that the Comanche had entered the brush on his side of the creek. There was a good chance that the warrior was right then circling his position, either to lay in ambush or to sneak up on him from behind. While the farthest thing from an Indian fighter, common sense told him to move somewhere else, and to do it in a hurry.

As quietly as he could, he rose to his feet, and stooped to avoid the thorns on the low-hanging limbs above him. His backwoods upbringing served him well, and he slipped quietly through the tangle of brush until he reached a cow trail paralleling the creek. He turned down it in the opposite direction of the Comanche, and his long legs churned in a ground-eating run. After several hundred yards, he ducked off the trail and headed away from the creek. He then moved more cautiously, never taking more than a couple of steps at a time before stopping to look and listen.

The belt of thicket and timber along the creek bottom was at no point more than a quarter of a mile wide. A half-mile stretch of prairie lay between it and a low ridge of cedar and rock, just beyond which was home. He crouched at the edge of the timber and peered out through a clump of sumac bushes at the open expanse separating him from the next cover. He was once again well concealed, and nobody could cross the prairie to his front without him seeing them first or come up behind him in the brush without his hearing them.

He wished more than ever that he still had a horse, and remembering how he had lost his just reminded him how much he had to learn about the new country he was calling home. A week earlier, he had forgotten to hobble his horse, or to at least make sure he was securely tied, while going afoot to where his hounds had an old boar coon treed. He had to go home and tell his cranky grandfather that the horse the old man had given him had wandered off. There were a lot of miles between neighbors on the frontier, but the news traveled amazingly fast that he was a kid tenderfoot who couldn't even keep track of his own mount. Seasoned pioneers had clucked their tongues and shaken their heads at the latest folly of Pappy Spurling's overgrown grandson.

The old man was already mad enough at him for losing a valuable mount, and now Odell was going to be either chased home by a Comanche or late for supper because of one. Either way, it seemed like Odell's standing in his household and community was about to suffer more damage. Texas just seemed bound and determined to embarrass him.

The smart thing would have been to lay low until nightfall and then cross the prairie to home, but there were other matters to be weighed. He valued his scalp as much as the next man, but the wild call of a young man's hormones ruled out any chance of rational behavior. He was sure Red Wing would be finishing up her evening's chores before too long and going out to sit on the porch to stare at the stars. If he didn't get there first, he'd have to play second fiddle to that damned Prussian lover boy. He tugged impatiently at the floppy brim of his stained and ill-shaped felt hat and considered risking the open. Odell couldn't help it if he was wildly in love.

He conjured up an image of Red Wing's pretty face and weighed that against the risk of being killed. It was not even a fair contest, and he took one last look around him before lunging out into the open. While he might not outrun a Comanche pony, he figured he could hold the Indian at bay with his rifle if it came to that. He was fifty yards out on the prairie before it came to his mind that the Comanche might get him with a lucky shot from that smoothbore before he even had a chance to fight. His back felt twice as wide as normal.

Now Odell was a big, long-legged rascal—six foot three in his socked feet, when he had any socks—and he put those bullfrog limbs to proper use and fairly flew over that patch of Texas sod. He was halfway across the prairie before he realized he was running scared. His breath was already coming in ragged gasps, and his heartbeat throbbed in his ears. Ashamed at letting fear overcome him for a moment, he slowed to a walk. He kept a careful watch behind him while telling himself that a skilled marksman on foot had the advantage over a mounted attacker. Common sense didn't provide the calm and comfort he had hoped for. He stumbled more than once, because he couldn't pay attention to where he was going for looking over his shoulder for Indians. The cedar ridge looked impossibly far away.

Chapter 2

Odell's home was dark and lifeless, and for a minute he contemplated bypassing it entirely and going straight to see Red Wing. However, the glowing coal of his grandfather's pipe brightened and dimmed in the darkness in some strange symphony with the lightning bugs' pulses as they flitted about the yard. The old man must have drawn especially hard on his pipe when Odell neared the porch, because for an instant he could plainly see the seamed and cracked lines of his pappy's face.

"Where've you been, boy? I was getting worried about you." Years of smoking and corn liquor had made Pappy's voice more like a growl.

"I got to hunting and ended up farther away than I planned." Odell leaned against the corner of the house at the end of the porch.

"The moon's damned near full tonight, and you ought to know by now that the Comanches like to ride by the light of the moon."

"I saw me a Comanche . . ." Odell had intended to impress, but he regretted his words just as soon as he let them slip out of his mouth.

"You saw a Comanche?"

"Yeah, I saw him over on that little creek just across Mustang Prairie. I was fifty yards from him and he never even knew I was there." Odell thought recounting his prowess in getting the drop on a Comanche might help his grandfather forget the folly of his losing the horse not so long before.

"I didn't hear any shots," Pappy said.

"Aw, he ran off when he finally spotted me."

If there was one thing Pappy Spurling could do exceptionally well, it was cussing. He got up so fast that his rocking chair almost tipped over, and he let out a long string of the vilest, most imaginative profanities while he stomped half the length of the porch and back. "Dammit, boy, that Comanche buck could be prowling around here right now waiting to steal our stock or scalp us in our sleep. Ain't you ever going to get a lick of common sense? If you see a Comanche, you shoot the sonofabitch and don't give it any more time nor thought than you would killing a rabid dog."

"I reckon I spooked him off, and he'd be scared to try anything around here now with us knowing he's around."

"I swear, sometimes you make my ass want to dip snuff. Comanches ain't scared of nothing. You don't shoo them off like chickens under your feet."

"It was just one Comanche buck, and not much more than a boy at that."

"Comanches are like fleas. When you see one, there's bound to be more around. And besides, one Comanche can raise more hell than ten of any other kind of Injun I ever knew."

Pappy was pulling at his long, white chin whiskers like he did when he was worrying over something and reached inside the front door and pulled down his old Kentucky rifle from its pegs, his practiced hands finding it quickly even in the dark. He sat back down in his rocking chair with that long rifle across his knees and rocked fiercely while his pipe worked like the furnace on a highball locomotive. He had fought the Creeks with Andrew Jackson in Alabama, and his eyes strained into the dark around the cabin looking for Comanches sneaking up on him.

While Pappy rocked, he considered the long shadow of his grandson beside him. Odell was a good kid, but the fact that he was a kid was half of what kept Pappy put out with him. There was a seventeen-year-old trapped in a man's body, and Odell's teenage mind couldn't understand why he wasn't treated like the man he appeared to be. Pappy figured that maybe time and patience were the only things that would ever make a man out of Odell, but those were two things that Pappy had little of. His old bones had just about run their life's course, and he'd never had much patience even when he was younger.

A stubborn stump that had to be dug out of a field, a cranky mule that needed shod, or any other kind of hard work was something he could butt his head against until the job was done. He didn't mind things that got in the way of his plans, as long as he could lay hands on those problems and bend them to his will. He was sure he would eventually carve a good farm out of the brush, but he was by no means confident where anything concerning raising children was concerned. You could butt heads with kids all you wanted and not get anywhere for your troubles. He felt he had done a terrible job with his own children, evidenced by the fact that his only son was so inept as to be unable to even travel from Georgia to Texas without getting himself killed, thus leaving Pappy with Odell to raise.

"You turn in, but sleep light. I'll wake you later and you can relieve me on the porch," Pappy said.

"I was planning on going over to the Wilson place." Odell thought Pappy was getting all shook up over nothing.

"You're going to do what? Are you out of your mind?"

"Somebody needs to warn the Wilsons." Odell was instantly proud of himself for thinking up such a quick and commonsense excuse to leave.

Pappy grunted begrudgingly. "You go ahead, but hurry back here as soon as you've given them word."

"Can I take your horse, or at least one of the mules?" Odell asked. It was four miles to the Wilson place.

"No, you'd just lose whatever you rode," Pappy said. "Anyway, those long legs of yours are about as fast as any saddle horse can walk."

Odell knew there was no sense arguing and started along the trail that led up the river. The moon was bright enough that he could see his way as plain as day.

"Don't you get to mooning over Red Wing and forget to come home," Pappy called after him. He chuckled to himself after the boy was out of earshot.

Odell would have mumbled some smart-alecky remark but thought he had better not risk it. Pappy was hard of hearing if you were trying to get his attention for something you needed, but sure enough, if you were a hundred yards from him and mouthed off in a whisper, he would hear you. Odell spent the first two miles grumbling to himself about that crotchety, cantankerous old coot. He was danged near a grown man, and it was high time he left home. He was bigger than any Texan he'd ever met, and he didn't need anybody bossing him around like he was some snot-nosed kid.

His temper and his desire to see Red Wing put wings on his feet, and it took him just half an hour to reach the Wilson place. His mood brightened when he came within sight of the house. The moonlight was so bright he could even make out somebody on the front porch. His heartbeat quickened. She was waiting on him like she had for most nights during the last month.

His lifted spirits were short-lived when he noticed the

horse tied to the corral beside the house. The Prussian had beaten him there, and his hopes of stealing a kiss would have to wait for another night. He stopped in front of the porch and studied the shadows of Red Wing and the Prussian sitting side by side with their feet in the grass.

"Hello, Odie." Red Wing always called him that.

"Herr Odell, it's good to see you." There was something about the Prussian's strong accent and buttery voice that made Odell envy him. It was smooth as a kitten's purr.

"It's good to see you too." Odell thought nothing of the kind. For some reason he always felt belittled in the Prussian's presence. He was pretty sure he could lick him, but then there was that damned sword that the Prussian always had at his side.

"I'm glad you came," Red Wing said.

Even with the moonlight, Odell couldn't see her in detail, but he knew that face just the same. He thought about smooth brown skin and those soft doe eyes. Her hair was as black as the darkest night, and she would be wearing the red ribbon he'd given her to tie it back.

"Herr Odell, what brings you on such a long walk in the night?" the Prussian asked.

"There are Comanches about." Odell was sure that damned foreigner knew good and well what he'd come for. The Prussian was just rubbing it in that he'd gotten there first.

"Comanches? I hope there will be a time when we've rid the country of those thieving, killing devils," the Prussian said, or at least that's what Odell thought he had said. The Prussian's accent was so strong that Odell couldn't always understand him, and half the time he mixed his native German tongue into what he said.

"I did a little scouting and crossed the trail of one this evening." Odell saw no sense in giving his story any more detail. It wouldn't do to have the Prussian know he'd let a Comanche pass through his sights without firing a shot.

Odell had come to learn that most Texans were pretty much of a similar opinion when it came to Comanches.

"By *Gott*, those gut eaters are probably stealing my horses and burning my house right now." The Prussian stood angrily with his sword sheath rattling against the porch.

Odell thought it rude and highly insensitive for the man to be talking so harshly about Indians in Red Wing's presence. While true that she wore pretty dresses, played the piano, and sang beautiful folk songs, the blood in her veins was Comanche. Colonel Moore had captured her on a raid against the Comanches sometime around the Battle of Plum Creek. He had given her to the Wilsons, and half the white pioneers along the Colorado River had curled up their noses at them for taking in a savage child.

The Wilsons were about the richest folks in the country, but their money never had been able to buy them a daughter, and Mrs. Ida Wilson wanted one more than anything. They took Red Wing in and started raising her like a lady. Four years later, very few who didn't know her would have guessed she had been born a Comanche. Her adaptation to the white man's ways had been remarkable in such a short time, and she was nothing if not beautiful. Most folks had conveniently forgotten her heritage, especially the overabundance of bachelors in a land short of women. She spoke better English than any Texan was expected to and had already read more books than Odell ever knew were written. The only sign of her former life was the fact that she insisted on keeping her Comanche name, even if a roughly translated Texas version of it.

"Do you think the Comanches will come here?" There was no hiding the terror in her voice.

"There was just one of them. I don't think there's anything to fear."

"There will be more of them," she said quietly.

"Don't worry, Frau Red Wing. I will stay here to fight

for you if need be. There are enough of us here to stand off many Comanches," the Prussian said.

Odell didn't like that at all. If anybody was to do any fighting for Red Wing, he intended to be the one to do it. The Prussian had his left hand on the pommel of his sword just like he always did, and Odell couldn't help but wish he had one too. He had to admit that the weapon made a man look far more impressive than a Bowie knife or just a plain old butcher knife stuck in a belt. The Prussian cut quite a figure in his fancy coat and ruffled shirt and with that sword rattling against his leg. Supposedly, he had killed two men with that blade. That might have just been talk, but what was indeed a fact were the two Lipan Apache skulls stuck on top of fence posts at the Prussian's corral. The two Indians had made the mistake of trying to steal his horses.

"What's this about Comanches?" Israel Wilson stepped out on the porch, followed by the rest of the clan.

"Odie saw a Comanche," Red Wing said.

He wished she would quit calling him that in front of everybody. "There was just one."

"Why didn't you shoot him?" Mrs. Wilson asked.

"We'd best put the chain and lock on the corral," Israel said. They had built a tall picket pen to enclose their stock at night. "The dogs will smell them out if they get close."

"Bud, go fetch me my pistol gun," Mrs. Wilson said to her oldest son.

"Honey, you don't need your pistol. Me and the boys and Major Karl have enough guns to protect you." Israel Wilson put his arm around his wife's waist.

The old lady shoved him away gently and took the pistol her son brought her. "Ever since I saw what those Comanches did to Jenny Wilbarger, I vowed I won't be caught without my gun when Indians might be at hand."

Odell had always been pretty impressed with Mrs. Ida, if in fact a little intimidated by her. She never failed to have something to say to him, or anyone else for that matter. She had a sharp tongue and a low opinion of most men's ability where any kind of thinking was concerned. Life had taught her that men did little but suffer women with babies, scratch themselves, and wander off to play at the least excuse. She had birthed and raised two sons in a one-room log cabin without another woman within twenty miles to comfort her and felt that she was more than a match for any man who liked to puff himself up by making pioneer talk. While she often sounded as cranky as a wildcat with its tail being twisted, she wasn't near as mean as she let on.

"Mama, quit being so dramatic. None of us are going to believe you'd shoot yourself to keep the Comanches from getting you. You couldn't stand the thought of missing out on scolding them a little while you had the chance." Bud was already ducking out of her reach when he said it. He was the joker of the Wilsons, if a little on the slow side, and always willing to risk his mother's wrath for the sake of fun.

"Lord, no, you ornery devil. Even if I was in a pinch and down to my last bullet, I wouldn't use it on myself. I'd shoot me a Comanche to get a little even for what they've done to some good people I've known."

"Mama Wilson, if those Comanches knew half of what I know about you they wouldn't come within a day's ride of this old place," Israel Wilson said, but it was plain that he was a little nervous himself and trying to soothe her.

"What about your grandfather, Odell? Is he by himself?" Mrs. Ida asked, and the accusation in her voice was plain.

"You'd better get back home," Israel said sternly. "He might need your help."

Odell wished he'd never seen that Comanche, or at least had kept his mouth shut about it. He had nothing left but a long walk back in the dark while the Prussian got to stay with Red Wing. He picked up his rifle and started home. The last thing he heard before he was out of earshot was the sound of a piano and Red Wing singing.

His pace was much slower on his return, and he made

the journey in a brooding daze. Red Wing would soon be of marrying age, and he could see no way to compete with a fancy, foreign gentleman like the Prussian. Folks said the man was a baron or something back where he came from. Odell thought if his foolish Pappy would just give him another horse he could at least look more the part of an eligible suitor.

He had just sworn to himself to get out from under Pappy's thumb when he rounded the bend in the river and saw his house lit up with flames. He stood gut shot in his tracks and watched the embers and sparks floating all the way up and across the face of the moon.

Chapter 3

His home was a burning hell, and he could do nothing until morning light. Daybreak finally came and the sun showed over the horizon like a raw wound, soaking through and saturating the dark clouds until the sky was bloody red. He sat on a stump under the blood bay sky, staring into the smoldering pile of coals and ashes until the heat scorched his face. Pappy wasn't to be found, the stock was all gone, and their good dog, Blue, lay at Odell's feet with his throat cut and an arrow wound in his guts. Odell ran the poor, blind old mutt's fur through his fingers and thought about Indians and Texas. He knew he was to blame for it all.

Come full daylight, he found Pappy not in the charred ruins of the house, but in the woods along the river. They had drug him there and tied him to a little piss elm sapling. Odell couldn't tell if they had shot his belly full of arrows before or after they tied him there. Pappy's empty eye sockets stared at him, and he turned away and fell to his knees, crying.

He was digging a grave under Pappy's favorite cypress tree when a party of men rode up with the Prussian leading them. One of the men started to get down and help him dig, but Israel Wilson stopped him.

"We've no time for that. Those Comanches are putting miles on us while we sit here," he said.

"Help me bury Pappy and I'll ride with you," Odell said.

"What are you going to ride? The Comanches have taken all your stock," the Prussian said.

"Somebody can go back and fetch me a horse."

There were five men in the party, and all of them looked at Odell with hard, cold eyes. He knew they blamed him for Pappy's death just as much as he did himself.

"No, we can't wait. Those Comanches hit the Youngs' place and ran off with their baby girl before they came here," Israel said.

"What about the rest of the Youngs?" Odell asked.

The men passed a look between them before Israel answered. "They killed them all right inside their house, except for that oldest girl. We found her about halfway between their place and yours."

Odell didn't need an explanation, and none of those who had seen her body were ever going to give one. People want to forget those kinds of things.

"I'm coming with you. I'm going to kill them for what they did to Pappy."

"Boy . . ." the Prussian started to say.

"I ain't a boy." All the hurt and anger began to well up in Odell, and he was ready to fight somebody, anybody. He needed to hurt another like he'd been hurt. He cocked his right fist and started for the Prussian.

Israel shoved his horse in the way and looked down at Odell with a contemptuous smile. "Odell, this is a job for men."

Israel wheeled his horse and charged off before Odell

could take a swing at him. The others followed, leaving Odell alone with the Prussian.

"Odell, maybe you are still a boy. A man wouldn't have left his grandfather alone with Comanches about," the Prussian said.

Odell leapt at him with both fists swinging wildly, but the Prussian shoved him down with a booted foot and spurred his big Kentucky gelding after the rest of them. Odell lay on his back and watched them all ride away. Dust, soot, and ashes caked his face, and he felt dirty outside and in—the kind of filth that he could never wash away. He would rather have died with Pappy than feel like he did right then.

He stood and took up his pick again. He swung the tool with hard, fast licks, liking the feel of the impact jarring through his arms and shoulders. The packed earth gave way in big, pleasing chunks as he found a temporary victim for his wrath. It was slow work, picking some and then stopping to shovel out what he had broken loose. By the time he'd managed to dig down three feet he was heaving, and he sat down with his feet inside the grave. His labor had milked him of whatever feeling he had left, and he could once more think with some clarity. A cold, vicious seed of vengeance began to sprout within him.

Once his strength had returned to him he rose and went to his grandfather. He tried not to see the man as he was, but instead as he had been. The slashed and hacked body was not the man that he loved. He wrestled the tortured, bloody hull to the grave and laid it there. The sound of the first shovelfuls of earth falling on Pappy's body quickened his heart like cold water hurts your teeth.

He took up his Bishop rifle and stood long over the fresh mound of earth, studying the wagon seat spring he'd driven at the head of the grave to mark it. It might be a long time before he came back, and he didn't want to forget where it was. The man lying underneath that Texas sod had taken him in and finished raising him when there was nobody else left that an orphan boy could call his own, and he knew nothing was ever going to be the same again.

He said his good-byes and headed west along the river in a steady jog with his rifle clutched in his right hand. His meager supplies consisted of a half-full powder horn and enough bullets and shot to load his gun a few more times. He'd salvaged some dried ears of corn from the charred remains of the crib, and he carried them in a burlap tow sack slung over his shoulder.

Odell was a traveling man, but even his long legs were no match for a Comanche on horseback. Nobody ever had much luck riding down a raiding party when it knew it was being followed. The Comanches traveled light, and when unencumbered by plundered stock or a village in tow, they could sometimes make better than eighty miles in a day. His only chance was to borrow a horse, and a good one at that. He had no money and could only think of one place where he might beg himself a mount.

The Wilson place came into view as the trail he was on entered a clearing where Massacre Creek emptied into the river. Red Wing was stirring hominy in a lye pot in front of the house, and she shaded her eyes with one hand and watched him come. He stopped before her, not quite sure what to say. Something about the look on his face must have told her all she needed to know. She stepped forward and wrapped him in a hug. She squeezed him tight while he let his arms hang at his sides, feeling startled and surprised at her actions. He'd often thought about what it would be like hugging her, and now that it had happened he wasn't sure what to do about it. Tentatively, he placed his left hand on the small of her back and pulled her tight into him. He could feel the quiver of her body beneath his palm, and warm tears soaked through his shirt where her face rested against his chest. They stood like that for a long moment, and he felt strength return to him, as if he fed from her concern.

She finally pulled away from him and held him by his shoulders at arm's length. She made no attempt to hide the tears that ran down her cheeks. "We saw the smoke coming from your place this morning."

"If I'd been there, Pappy might still be alive," he said.

"Or you might be dead."

"I almost wish I was." Odell was looking over her head at someplace far, far away. "I still remember when he showed up to get me in San Augustine. He didn't ask about my mama or my daddy, or try to pump me for information. He just said, 'I'm your grandfather. Come on, boy, let's go home.' Now that I think about it, he never asked near as much from me as I thought he did."

She knew how great his loss was. His family ties had been almost as shifting and traumatic as her own. His parents had started west from Georgia with everything they owned in a single wagon. They had stopped in Louisiana to resupply before crossing the Sabine River, but they never made it into Texas. His father had gotten trapped in a crooked card game and stabbed to death with some tinhorn gambler's Arkansas toothpick. His mother, weakened by the loss of her husband and ready to quit, fell victim to the typhoid fever epidemic that was sweeping the settlements. At thirteen Odell was stranded in a strange land, and the only family he had left was a man he didn't know and had never seen before.

"The men left here at daylight," she said.

"I saw them."

"What about the Youngs?"

Odell couldn't meet her eyes. "They're all dead."

"Is Father on the Comanches' trail?"

"He is."

She bit her lower lip and tried not to start crying again. The fear of losing another family was so great in her that she almost couldn't bear it. She took a deep breath and tugged at Odell's sleeve. "Come on up to the house, and I'll feed you. I feel better with you here to watch over me and Mama."

Odell didn't budge out of his tracks. "I need a horse."

"You need to stay here. Those Comanches are probably long gone, and even if you could catch up to them, you'd just get yourself killed."

"I have to try."

"If there's any chance of catching them, Father and Karl will get it done."

"You mean we should leave it to the men while I stay here and tend to the butter churning," Odell said bitterly.

"I meant nothing of the kind. I just don't want to lose anybody else I love."

It took a moment for what she said to register with him. He could have sworn she said she loved him. "I thought you were falling for that Prussian."

She smiled at him the way parents smile at foolish children. "No, it's not Karl that I love."

"I'm glad to hear you say that." His words sounded foolish and inadequate to his own ears.

"Are you?"

He was torn by the need for revenge seething inside him and the desire he felt for Red Wing. He tried to ignore that soft, sweet face lit up by the sunshine and seeming to stare into his very soul. That was the one and only thing about her that disturbed him. She never seemed to lose focus, and when she wanted something from him her attention could be quietly intense and a little discomforting. Odell knew his own mind never stayed on one thing too long. Most days, it flitted around like a grasshopper jumping from one blade of grass to another.

"I need to borrow a horse," he said.

Over the course of the three years he'd lived close to her, he'd told her things he told no others. They were both orphans in a way, and bonded by those scars of loss they shared. They had walked the riverbank and made each other laugh long before she could even speak good English. She knew his stubborn nature, and that her words would hold no sway with him once he set his mind to something.

"You can take Crow, but you'd better bring him back." She turned away from him, more hurt by the lack of effect her admission of love had on him than she was willing to let him see.

Crow was her good black gelding, and she babied and petted the horse like a spoiled child. Colonel Moore had bought the Comanche buffalo runner from a Mexican trader days after the fight in which he captured her, and used it to carry her to the Wilsons. Odell knew that the horse was more to her than just a pet. It was a last link to her former self and the people that she no longer called her own.

The two of them went to the corral gate and she whistled to Crow. The horse came to her in a trot, and put his head over the gate for her. She rubbed his face and played with his forelock. "Crow is the fastest, toughest pony in Texas, but Father won't agree. He thinks nothing can match Karl's Kentucky horse, but he's wrong."

"I can't take your horse," Odell said.

"He's the only one left on the place, and if the Comanches are raiding, he may be the only horse left in the settlements for miles and miles."

"You'd never forgive me if I let something happen to him."

"No, I wouldn't. But you'll take him anyway, won't you?"

"I have to go. Can't you understand that?"

"I understand you think you can make up for some bad thing you think you've done by killing others, or maybe getting yourself killed. Maybe you think a few Comanche scalps will make you forget Pappy's death."

"You don't know how I feel."

"You're wrong, I know that much. I was basically already an orphan before Colonel Moore captured me, and I know about loss. That was the one thing I already knew when I came here to the Wilsons. Death doesn't fix anything for the living. We just have to patch up our lives and try to forget the bad things."

"It ain't about bringing Pappy back or me making up for failing him. Those Comanches need to pay for what they've done."

She started to reply but got hung up. She was proud of her English, but sometimes when she was upset or excited the words wouldn't come. At times like that she couldn't seem to speak at all. She couldn't find the proper English words she needed, nor could her mind grab hold of the Comanche she still dreamed in but hadn't spoken aloud in years.

"They need to pay, or you need them to pay?" she finally managed to ask.

"You don't know what they did to Nellie Young."

"I was a Comanche once and know more than you ever will about just how cruel they can be."

Odell went through the gate and caught Crow. He saddled the horse with the spare rig that was resting on top of the fence. It was a bare-bones Mexican saddle with huge tapaderos covering the stirrups, a fat saddle horn, and a hair-on, tanned deer hide to cover the seat. He unlaced the stirrup leathers and adjusted their length to fit him. He cinched up and climbed on and off a few times to readjust the stirrups. She handed him a hitched horsehair bridle and he slipped the Spanish bit into Crow's mouth.

"You hold on for a minute." She turned and ran for the house.

While he waited, he stuffed his sack of corn into the long Mexican saddlebags that were tied behind the cantle. By the time he finished she was running back to him with something clutched in both hands against her skirt. She stopped, panting in front of him with a small bar of lead in one hand and a wadded-up piece of cloth in the other.

"You take this, Odie. There's a bit of powder in that rag, and if I had the time, I'd mold your bullets for you," she said.

"Thanks."

"You mold those bullets good and grease your patches carefully. I want you to shoot straight when you have to, and come back to me."

There was nothing left to do but ride, but he hesitated anyway. "Maybe you don't think I'm man enough to do this thing I'm setting out to do, but I promise you I'll be back."

"I know the kind of man you are, Odie. I know it better than anyone else, and that's what scares me. When others might turn back, you'll go on, because that's the way you're made. Vengeance has a hold on you, and you've always been half wild and more like the Comanches you hate than you know."

"I'll come back to you, I promise." He wasn't as sure of that as he tried to sound.

She was so, so near to him, and her lips seemed to be begging for him to kiss her. She was only fifteen, with her willowy body only starting to take on the curves of womanhood, and perhaps too young for a man to court. But Odell was a young man himself, and he loved her. She had always been his woman, even if only in his mind. What that meant was only a vague, shy concept fluttering around inside him, but he did know if there ever was anything he should do, it was to kiss her. He'd never kissed a girl, although he'd thought about it enough. His body wouldn't seem to obey his will, and he stood flat-footed and clumsy before her without a trace of anything on his face but awkward and handicapping shyness.

Mrs. Ida had walked outside and was watching them from the porch. "Where are you going with her horse?"

Odell threw one look at the old lady and took Red Wing in his arms. He kissed her clumsily but long. She yielded to him softly and passionately in one last effort to keep him with her.

He pushed gently away from her and shoved one big foot into the stirrup and swung aboard her good horse. "So long, Red Wing. Maybe I won't be gone too long."

Mrs. Ida was starting down to path to the corral with a frown on her face, and he waved to her as he rode out of the gate and set old Crow to a high lope toward sundown. Red Wing shaded her wet eyes once more and watched him disappear in the distance. He never looked back, not even once.

"What's that boy doing with your horse?" Her mother said behind her.

"I loaned Crow to him. The Comanches killed Pappy Spurling and the Youngs, and Odie's going to hunt them down."

"That fool boy will get himself killed, and maybe your father too. You shouldn't have given him your horse."

Red Wing gave her a wistful smile as she passed by her on her way back to the house. "You don't know him at all."

"I won't have a daughter of mine mooning over the likes of Odell Spurling. Where do you think you're going?" Mrs. Ida asked with a halfhearted scowl. "That hominy needs tending to."

"I'll tend the hominy pot, but when I get done I'm going to start sewing on a wedding dress. That fool boy is the man I'm going to marry when he gets back."

Chapter 4

The tracks left by the Comanches driving their herd of stolen horses and those of his neighbors following them were plain, and Odell stuck to them like a cocklebur tangled in a mustang's tail. Crow was as tough as Red Wing had said he was and they rode the sun down and kept on traveling by the light of the moon. The trail he followed seemed to be going up the river to the northwest, and though he lost it in the dark, faith and feel kept him moving and he picked it back up again at sunrise.

He traveled hard for two days, only stopping to sleep for a few hours at a time. He had nothing to eat but mush made from the hard corn pounded into coarse meal between two rocks, but vengeance fueled him and gave him strength. The trail veered west from the Colorado to follow along another river he presumed was the San Saba. All of the country was new to him, and when the trail turned north again and crossed the Colorado a second time, he slowly began to leave behind the low, rocky ridges and stands of oak, cedar, and mesquite. The country began to open up into grasslands with only scattered timber along some of the drainages. The brown summer grass was thicker and healthier than the rugged country he had left behind.

He dreamed one night of his mother. It bothered him that he couldn't exactly recall anymore what she looked like in his waking hours, but her face was plain in the dream. His father didn't appear to him, but Odell could feel his presence just the same. He wanted to ask them just what it was he had done that had cursed him so, but he awoke beside the cold ashes of his little fire alone. He closed his eyes and tried to summon the ghosts again but couldn't. The dream had felt so real that waking was like losing his parents all over again. The stars were already fading in the gray morning light, and he finally got to his feet and went to saddle Crow.

He passed the Prussian and his neighbors on the third day when he saw where they had lost the Comanches' faint trail. Although he considered himself no tracker, he trusted his own eyes and went where his hunch told him. Somebody in the party of white men had been a fair hand at reading sign, and Odell had simply followed them up until that point, hoping they would lead him to his quarry. When the Comanches gave them the slip Odell wasn't sure just how he could stay on the raiders' trail alone. However, the Comanches seemed to be traveling with a goal in mind. He found that if he kept to their line of travel that he usually came across some sign of them later on. Every time he was sure he had lost their trail he stumbled upon it again.

Somewhere north and west of nowhere, he crossed another dry riverbed and came out on a wide expanse of prairie scattered with prickly pear and yuccas. To the north was a line of rocky little hills and he spied a gap between them. He spent no more time looking for Comanche sign and aimed for that pass.

The sun was in his eyes and the dry grass crackled under Crow's feet. The heat coming off the ground threatened to jerk them both like strips of buffalo meat. The black horse had lost some weight and his former sleek and shiny coat was caked with dried sweat and dust. He was still willing but needed a long rest. Odell couldn't afford to give him that and knew he was pushing the limits of riding him to the point of ruin.

Crow stopped and lifted his head high with his ears erect and forward. Odell strained to find what the horse was looking at in the distance. Finally, he saw the slim finger of smoke coming off the hills. The odds were it was an Indian camp making that smoke, because no white man with any sense would build a fire so plainly seen in a land where that was liable to get him scalped.

"You've smelled smoke or Indians. Either way, you might just be the best horse in Texas." Odell rubbed Crow's neck and booted him forward.

He had no plan how to proceed next, so he just rode straight for the smoke. He'd hung his rifle by a string from his saddle horn, and he freed it and rested its butt on his right thigh with the muzzle pointing skyward. He checked his knife in its sheath, weighed his powder horn, and jiggled the bullets in his shot bag to make sure they were still there. It was at least a mile to that smoke, but even at a walk he was going to get there pretty quick.

L ittle Bull squatted by the fire with a chunk of greasy meat clenched in his teeth and hot juice dripping off of his chin. He glared at the Jersey milk cow tied to a tree at the edge of his camp. She wallowed her cud in her mouth and looked back at him in dumb contentment, with her tail switching flies and her fat, full udder almost dragging the ground.

If it hadn't been for that stolen cow slowing him down, Little Bull would have been almost back to his band's camp far to the north. As it was, most of the war party had left him behind, and he was still far south of the Antelope Hills. He knew the Tejanos were sure to be following him, but he couldn't bring himself to leave the cow behind. He'd stolen her two days back, and he was bound and determined to keep her.

Little Bull's belly bothered him terribly sometimes, and his chest ached liked something was hung there. By accident on an earlier raid he had taken a drink of the white man's cow milk. He had found that it cooled his burning stomach and settled the bile that rose up in his throat. His intent was to take the cow to his camp for his squaws to milk.

Tejanos traveled far too slowly to catch Little Bull at any other time, but the cow went even more slowly than those hated white men did. He threw down the bone he'd picked clean and moved to where he could watch the plains south of the hill. There were two separate dust trails worming their way toward him, and neither one was very far away. He knew the closest for the three warriors who had stayed behind with him. They had split off from him two days before to try to steal more horses from a Wichita village to the east. They were originally from one of the Honey Eater camps, and were far more familiar and at home in the land of timber and little mountains they had raided in the past days. Little Bull himself was Kotsoteka Comanche, the Buffalo Hunters, and his home range was the Canadian River Valley to the north.

The three Honey Eaters weren't especially good raiders or fighters, but any allies would be welcome help at that moment. The second cloud of dust had to be Tejanos, either on the trail of the three Penatekas coming to join him, or following his own tracks. Little Bull gathered his weapons and mounted his horse. From the size of the dust, the Tejanos were few, and he knew four Comanches were more than enough to whip them.

He left his hobbled bunch of stolen horses in camp with the cow and rode out of the pass until he reached a bare ledge of rock providing a better view of the prairie. He waited there for the other warriors to join him while he watched the Tejanos' dust grow nearer. He sat his horse with his long lance across the animal's withers, and his short, squat body was as still as the stone. He scratched at a sand flea on his muscular arm and his black eyes strained to make out his prey.

He laughed to himself when the rider came into view. It was just one Tejano, and he was almost sure that it was the long-legged one who had almost ambushed him on the little creek far down on the Colorado many days ago. He had watched him flee across the prairie that day and would have known him anywhere. He hated white men even more than Apaches and Mexicans, and the one coming his way had shamed him by stalking so near him.

The three Penatekas had reached the foot of the slope and stopped there to look up at him. They pointed toward the Tejano and made excited sign language, as if they thought Little Bull was so dumb as to have not noticed pursuit. Young as he was, he knew he was worth all three of those warriors in a fight. He started slowly down the hill, reaching them just as the long-legged Tejano made the edge of an especially open section of the prairie two hundred yards away.

The Penatekas fanned out to one side of him, angling for a long dry wash that ran in the direction of their quarry. He gestured angrily for them to follow his lead straight toward the Tejano. It was only one white man, and there was no need to sneak up on him. A quick charge and some bloody war whoops would unsettle the Tejano's aim and they would make quick work of him.

He fitted his buffalo hide shield to his left arm and made sure his bow and quiver were secure on his back. The buffalo tail that hung from his lance and the scalps dressing the edge of his shield whipped in the strong south wind. His heart throbbed deeply in his chest as he anticipated killing another of the hated breed of pale men who had taken his family away from him.

In his fervor to kill another Tejano, Little Bull failed to see the third dust cloud a few miles to the south.

Chapter 5

Odell saw the Comanches riding toward him at about the same time Crow did. Just seconds before, the horse had seemed worn out, but now he fairly pranced along the ground, pushing against the bit. It was plain he sensed the coming fight or flight.

There were four Comanches spread out in a long line and trotting right at Odell. He knew nothing of Indian fighting, but he tried to calm himself and remember the advice that a seemingly endless number of Texans had given him. Common sense told him that he stood little chance against such long odds, and from what he'd heard his flintlock rifle was going to be little help in a horseback fight out in the open. The Indians were too close and his horse too used up to turn and outrun them. He spied the brush-choked gully just behind and to the left of the Comanches and decided to make for it if he should survive the charge.

A wild, shrill shout went up from one of the Comanches and it was answered all down their line. Odell took a spare bullet from his pouch and put it in his mouth for a quick reload. He cocked the hammer on his shotgun barrel and kicked his horse forward at a run just as the Comanches did the same. He charged forward with his teeth gritted and the wind folding the broad brim of his hat back against the crown.

If the Comanches were surprised by his charge, they didn't waver in their attack. They whipped their ponies wildly and shouted like crazed animals. Odell rode straight for their middle, and waited until he could see their painted faces before he veered sharply to his left. He ran Crow straight toward the last warrior on the left of the line. Two arrows sailed close past him and he shouldered his rifle and strained to steady his front sight on the Comanche not twenty yards in front of him. The brave fired one more snap shot from his bow and started to drop off the far side of his horse to pass by on Odell's left. Odell pressed his trigger a little too late to get the Comanche, but the shotgun pellets hit the brave's horse square in the face. Shadowed bits of blood and bone rained through the sunshine, and the horse went as limp as soft rope and melted into the ground in a cloud of dust. Its rider scrambled on all fours to get away from the wreck.

Odell leapt Crow over the dead Comanche pony and kept on toward the gully. The Comanches to his right were circling back to him and a musket ball from one of them clipped his sleeve. He made the edge of the gully with them right on his heels. The bank was too high and the brush too thick to leap down among it, and he bailed from the saddle at the lip of wash. An arrow struck Crow in the shoulder and he shuddered violently and almost went down. Odell pulled at the single rein he held while the black horse fought to steady his buckling knees.

One Comanche and then two passed across Odell's front, firing a single arrow apiece, then dropping on the far side of their running horses. The third Comanche still mounted

came head-on at him with the sharp point of his lance lowered. The weapon looked impossibly long and wicked bearing down on Odell's chest. He cocked his last barrel and
took aim at what little he could see of the warrior's head
behind the shield.

His aim was off, and the .60-caliber bullet struck the
cured bull-hide circle and ricocheted into the pony's neck.
The Comanche was only twenty feet away when his mount
crashed under him. The warrior rolled to his feet and struggled to unlimber the bow on his back. The other Comanches
were coming back and Odell's gun was empty. He let go of
his rein and leapt down into the plum thicket that filled the
gully.

The little thorns on the plum bushes and the limbs ripped
at him as his weight bore him through them and to the
ground. He scrambled to a sitting position and tore the plug
from his powder horn. He spat the bullet from his mouth
into his hand and dumped a big enough mound of powder
over it to just barely cover it. He poured the powder down
his rifle barrel with his cupped palm and then started the
bullet. His ramrod seated the charge home effortlessly without the resistance of a patch. The low-growing brush was
too thick in most places to walk upright, and he crawled on
his belly to the edge of the gully while trying to get the
flintlock pan primed and ready to shoot.

He stood and peered over the lip of the bank several yards
from where he entered the dry wash. Crow was standing
pitifully with the arrow sticking out of his shoulder and two
of the Comanches were passing back and forth some seventy
yards beyond the wounded horse. There was no sign of the
two dismounted warriors. He looked to the far side of the
gully behind him but could see nothing for the thick brush.
He was sure that the two that he'd put afoot were probably
sneaking through the thicket to poke him full of arrows.

One of the warriors on the prairie spotted him and both
of them were soon zigzagging back and forth toward him.

They had loops of rope tied around their horses' necks, and they used their mounts to shield them from his rifle. With one arm in that loop, their heel and calf over the horse's back, and the bow or lance in their other hand hooked against the near side of the horse's neck, they hung suspended on the offside of their running horses. As they came ever closer to him his only chances to shoot them were the brief instances when they swapped from one side of their mounts to the other. Despite what many a windy old frontier blowhard swore, the only good thing was that they couldn't shoot their bows while hanging in such a manner.

Odell started to take an iffy shot but willed himself to hold his fire. When they turned and raced away from him at the last moment it dawned on him that they wanted him to shoot. With an empty gun he would be at their mercy, and their antics had already distracted his attention away from anything coming up from behind his position. He set his gun butt-first on the ground and carefully loaded the shotgun barrel with powder, wadding, shot, and wadding. It was more time-consuming to load the shotgun barrel, and there was no quick way to do it. A sloppily charged scattergun was more dangerous to the shooter than to what he was shooting at. By the time he was finished loading it, streams of sweat were rolling off of him. It was hot, but not that hot. He could feel the Comanches sneaking up on him, and he was as scared as he'd ever been.

Staying where he was would get him killed quickly, and he took one last look out of the gully to check the positions of the two Comanches on the prairie. They were keeping their eyes on the spot where his head stuck up above the bank and trotting their horses in a wide arc just out of easy rifle range. He dropped back to his knees and crawled along a rabbit run. The gully was fifty yards wide where he was at, and he found a deer trail running down its center. He rose to a crouch and ran twenty yards down it until he heard something in the brush and ducked off the trail. He shielded himself behind the base of a clump of bushes where he could see a few feet either way down the path. Flies buzzed about his head, and the heat of the thicket made it hard to breathe.

It seemed like an eternity before the Comanche showed himself, but in actuality it was only a few seconds. Odell heard him coming at the last second and had his rifle aimed at the sound. A war-painted face peered out of the brush twenty yards away and he pulled the trigger. He didn't take the time to shoot carefully, or his unpatched bullet flew wild, because his shot only kicked sand into the Comanche's face. Odell hustled to move his position in the thicket.

The sound of Odell's rifle was followed by Comanche war cries, and the three of them he hadn't just shot at made enough racket to sound like a whole tribe. He crawled farther down the gully and stopped just before it choked down to a narrow pass. A buffalo crossing had beaten down both banks and trampled away the brush in a wide swath. Two of the Comanches sat their horses on either bank. Only Odell's shotgun barrel was loaded, and he couldn't get into killing range without them seeing him. Their bows' range matched a shotgun charge, and he had no desire to take an arrow in his guts.

He assumed that the warriors on foot were still somewhere in the brush behind him, but that was the direction he had to go. He worked his way quietly to the far bank and crept along it. He found a place under an exceptionally thick stand of shinnery oak about eight feet tall and decided to wait things out. He couldn't see the Comanches if they were coming, but they couldn't see him either. He had no water but hoped he could slip away in the night.

Digging a place for his hips in the sand, he prepared himself for a long, hot day. He had barely begun his wait when he smelled smoke. In a matter of minutes a cloud of it was rolling up the gully toward him. The dry grass in the bottom of the wash was sparse and choked back by the shade of the brush, but there was enough of it and other dead, dry

fuel to give him a bad scorching. He crawled to the barest
spot he could find under the shade of an overhang in the dirt
bank. The Comanches had him trapped and intended to flush
him from the thicket like a covey of quail, or else roast him
alive.

The low wall of flames moved with the wind until it was
only a couple of yards from him. The bone-dry mass of
branches on a dead clump of brush burst into flames like
they were soaked with kerosene. The heat from the fire was
unbearable, and he shielded his scorched face with his forearm. When he could bear no more he scrambled up the
sandy, crumbling cutbank.

No sooner had his feet hit the prairie above than a cry
went up and a Comanche started his horse toward him. The
brave was fifty yards away and coming fast with his bow
ready to draw. Odell took five running steps straight for him
and then dove headfirst back into the gully. He had traveled
just far enough to clear the advancing wall of flames, and
plunged through the sooty limbs of the thicket. As soon as
he untangled himself, he lunged forward on his belly with
the Comanche stopped on the lip of the cutbank just above
him. An arrow buried itself in the ground beside him, and
two more glanced off the limbs above him. All three pro-
jectiles came in the space of that many seconds.

Odell clawed his way a few more feet and rolled over on
his back. He pointed his gun between his knees at the Comanche above him and fired the shotgun barrel. The black
powder smoke and the smoldering cloud from the fire kept
him from seeing if his shot had any effect. Another arrow
careened off the brush in front of him, and he knew that he
had missed, or at least failed to deal the warrior a death lick.

Most of the Comanches were probably upwind of the fire
waiting for him to show, and he hit the deer trail down the
middle of the gully running like his pants were on fire—
which by coincidence they really were. If there was one
thing Odell could do well, it was run. A jackrabbit flushed

under his feet and if it hadn't veered away, there was a chance Odell would have passed him.

He intended to get across the buffalo trail bisecting the wash and hide himself farther down its course. When he reached the crossing, he found that the other side only contained a thin line of brush and was bare past that. He could hear the sound of hooves thumping the ground behind him and knew he wasn't going to have time to reload even one barrel. He turned up the buffalo trail toward the opposite side of the gully from where the last Comanche had been shooting at him.

He cut a beeline across the prairie, hoping that he could at least reload his rifle barrel on the run. He fumbled at his bullet pouch and dropped the first two bullets he could lay his hand on. The sound of a running horse was right behind him, and he ducked behind a huge clump of prickly pear. He looked wildly behind him at another mounted Comanche circling around the cactus with his lance leveled like a jousting knight.

The circle Odell kept to around the prickly pear clump was small, and he could just stay ahead of the horse and that lance in such a tight turn, at least until he ran out of wind. At the pace he was keeping, it didn't take him long to burn out. He waited until the lance was almost sticking him in the kidney and then ducked and dove backward under the horse's feet. The lance passed over him, but a hoof thumped him between the shoulders and rolled him in a ball. The air was driven from his lungs, and he lay where he had been struck for a brief instant while he gathered his wind and his wits. That was just long enough for the Comanche to double back.

The lance was bearing down on him again, and there was no way he was going to be able to dodge. He could already feel the sharp bite of its steel piercing his chest when it was still several feet away.

Chapter 6

Some mighty force struck the warrior in the chest and he tipped over the back of his horse as gunfire cracked from behind Odell. The frightened Comanche pony passed over him again, and another hoof clipped him on the head. His vision was blurred and his mind was swimming dizzily when two more horsemen thundered by. He could just barely make them out, and they were well past him before he recognized the Prussian racing away with his saber brandished above his head.

Odell propped himself up and watched the Prussian and Israel Wilson take the fight to the Comanches. Both men had emptied their rifles, and Israel pulled up to reload while the Prussian kept up the charge. Two of the Comanches burst out of the gully riding double on a single horse. They headed for the little mountain, but their pony was no match for the Prussian's Kentucky horse on a short run.

The Comanche riding behind twisted and snapped an arrow at their pursuer. The shaft seemed to strike home as the Prussian reeled in the saddle for an instant. However wounded he might be, he straightened and closed the last few yards on the braves. His saber flashed and the rearmost warrior's head toppled off his shoulders and bounced along the ground beside the running horses, as if it were no head at all and nothing but some childish toy. The headless body still clung to the warrior in front of it for several strides before it slid slowly off the horse.

The remaining Comanche rider parried the Prussian's next blow with his shield and tried to veer away from the saber's reach. The Prussian knew he had to stay close to keep the bow out of the fight, and he clung to the Comanche's side like a mesquite thorn buried in his flesh. He feinted at the shield and then changed the arc of his stroke to strike the Indian's bare leg just above the knee. The shield dropped and a backhand slash in passing took the brave across the chest and cleaved him from the saddle.

The Prussian pulled up his lathered horse and turned broadside to the fallen Comanche. The bloody warrior had risen on his one good leg and was fumbling weakly with his bow. The Prussian calmly pulled a pistol from his belt and shot him dead.

Odell tore his attention from the scene and staggered past the dead Comanche at his feet. The warrior's horse was standing just a few yards away, and Odell tried to ease up to him. He needed a mount badly, but the animal shied and blew at him loudly in fear. It took off in a run with its head canted to one side to avoid stepping on the rein of the war bridle trailing from its mouth.

Odell didn't have the time to cuss his rotten luck before he heard Israel scream. He turned to find the settler wounded and on the ground. The warrior standing over him looked up at Odell with hate and pleasure smeared across his face as plain as his war paint. He smiled a wolf's smile and ran his knife around Israel's head. He jerked a handful of the old man's gray hair away with a sickening snap that was audible even at a distance.

Odell grounded his rifle and rushed to reload it. The Comanche tucked the bloody scalp behind his breechclout belt and jerked two arrows from his victim's body. He took up Israel's rifle, powder horn, and supply bag. Before Odell's shaking hands could ram another ball home, the warrior swung astride Israel's horse and let out a mad whoop. He whirled away and headed for the hills.

Odell capped his gun and leveled it to his shoulder, but the Comanche was a hundred yards away and a dim target in the dust and smoke. He tried to steady his weakened muscles and will a good shot home, but finally lowered his gun without firing.

The look on the brave's face was etched into Odell's mind as if with a sharp chisel into soft rock. It was the face of the Comanche he'd snuck up on along the creek days before. Thinking back, that moment seemed much farther in the past, as if years and years ago.

"You just keep riding, Mister Injun. You ride as fast and as far as you can, and I'm still going to remember you," Odell said.

The Prussian rode up with two Comanche heads in one hand and an arrow sticking out of his thigh. He dropped the heads and slid off his horse to sit on the ground. "Herr Odell, come pull this arrow out of me."

Odell crossed over to him, avoiding the heads. The Prussian wasn't that much shorter than him, and even broader. The arrow was buried deep in the massive thigh. Odell tried not to look at the severed heads or Israel's body while he examined the wound.

"I don't know about this. It's in pretty deep," Odell said.

"Pull it out," the Prussian rasped.

Odell knew that the longer he waited, the harder it was going to be to make himself do it. He grasped the shaft of the arrow and pulled as straight and hard as he could. The first tug didn't free it, and the Prussian shouted his pain and pounded the ground beside him with one fist.

"Lucifer's balls, pull it out!"

Odell jerked the arrow again and it came free without the arrowhead. He pitched the shaft aside and pressed his hand to the bleeding hole in the Prussian's leg. The pressure must have moved the arrowhead within the punctured hole, and the Prussian shouted his pain again. Odell had nothing to bind the wound, and when he let go of it to find something, the blood poured in a steady, percolating pulse.

He ran to Israel's body and removed the rough cotton shirt. He cut two long strips from it with his knife and folded one of them into a large square. He returned to the Prussian and pressed it against the wound while he tied the other strip firmly around the leg to hold the compress down.

"The odds are the wound will get infected if that's a hoop-iron point in your leg," Odell said. All the Indians in Texas gathered barrel hoops and other scrap iron from the settlements and ground out blades and arrowheads from them.

"I'll probably bleed to death first." The Prussian tried to laugh but didn't quite manage it.

"Where's the rest of your party?" Odell asked.

"By *Gott*, they turned back home yesterday when we lost the trail for a while." The Prussian broke into a string of what sounded like cussing, even though it wasn't in English. "I wish Israel had taken the excuse and gone back with those cowards."

"Can you ride?" Odell asked. "This grass is like tinder, and if the wind was to swap, that fire's going to be hard to outrun."

The Prussian merely nodded his head. The fire had run out of the gully and was rapidly spreading as it raced north in a wall of smoke and blazing grass. Even with the strong south wind the flames had steadily neared them on the downwind side of the gully. The air was thick with smoke and ashes. He made it to his feet with Odell's help, and the two of them managed to get him mounted. Odell started to get on behind him, but the Prussian pointed to his trophies on the ground.

"Get my heads for me," the Prussian said.

"No, I don't think I will."

"Get them." The Prussian sidled his horse away, forbidding Odell to swing up behind.

Odell sighed and went over to where the Comanche heads lay in the grass. The Prussian had braided the hair of the two together for a handle, and Odell carried them back and handed them up to him.

"Now go take the head from that Comanche Israel shot off of you." The Prussian offered Odell his sword.

"You get down and fetch it yourself." Odell waited until he saw Prussian was resigned to the fact that he wasn't going to gather another trophy. He handed up his rifle for him to hold while he crawled up on the horse behind him.

"What about Mr. Wilson?" Odell asked.

"I assume he is very dead?"

"He's past helping, but we ought to bury him."

"Herr Odell, we've nothing to dig with. The buzzards and coyotes will tend to him soon enough. We'll tell his family that we buried him."

"Still, I hate to leave him lying like that. He's in kind of a bare spot there, so maybe the fire won't scorch him."

"He's long past caring."

They walked the horse eastward and the Prussian pointed out the two dead Comanche horses. "Herr Odell, you are a horse killer."

"Those bucks didn't give me proper time to aim."

"Oh, I thought you were aiming for the horses."

"No, I guess I put up a pretty poor fight."

The Prussian stopped at the far horse carcass and motioned to the bladder water bag tied to the animal's neck. "We might need that."

Odell slid down and fetched it. The Comanche canteen was made from the bladder of a buffalo with the dried flesh molded around a wooden stopper at the drinking end. He slung the carrying strap over his head and mounted back up behind the Prussian.

"You might think you've fought poorly, but I'd say you did quite well for a boy so green," the Prussian said.

Odell didn't like to be called a boy. "How do you figure that, Karl?"

"Any time you fight Comanches and come out alive, you've done okay."

"I don't feel like a winner."

"By *Gott*, I promise you are, and I'll wager you'll get another crack at those red devils if you stay in Texas long enough. That Comanche that got away might be riding right now to get some help to finish us off."

"I intend to stay after them until I get that Injun that did for Israel."

"That might be a very long ride indeed."

"I don't care how long it takes."

Odell scanned the country around them for signs of Crow. The black horse apparently hadn't died where Odell had left him but was nowhere to be seen. Odell whistled as he'd heard Red Wing do, but there was still no sign of Crow. He regretted the loss of the horse terribly but was glad that the animal might survive his wounds if the fire didn't get him. He continued to whistle while they rode along.

The Prussian altered their course just enough to pass by a clump of mesquite trees. He pulled up beside one of them and hacked a hole in the thorny limbs with his saber, leaving one bare branch about horse height above the ground. He draped the braided handle of the heads over the limb and left them hanging there.

When they were fifty yards away Odell looked back at the heads dangling from the tree. "Why'd you do that?"

"I left them for any Comanche who passes by to see. It

lets them know that Major Karl von Roeder was here, and
that his blade is sharp."

"I don't like it."

"Forgive me, Herr Odell. I am most impolite. Do you
want me to ride back so you can get their scalps?"

"No, just keep on riding. I ain't much for scalps."

The Prussian nodded as if he had heard some sage advice.
"I'm not fond of scalps either. Heads are much, much
better."

"Texas has to be the hardest place on the earth," Odell
said quietly to himself.

The Prussian heard him. "Indeed, Herr Odell, indeed."

L ittle Bull stopped at his camp in the narrow pass through
the hills and watched the two Tejanos heading east. His
left arm throbbed where the Running Boy had shot his shield
with the big gun. The bullet had failed to penetrate the bull
hide, but it had left a deep bruise on his forearm. He had
never expected the boy to be such a fighter.

He knew of the Prussian, as word of the strange talking
man had spread across Comancheria. The Tonkawas called
him Cuts Deep, and the Lipans called him Long Knife Man.
The Mexicans and Tejanos called him the Prussian, and
there was no doubt the man was a brave fighter. Little Bull
had seen him cut down the two Penatekas like they were
helpless children. The Penatekas were soft, but he had to
admit the Prussian wasn't to be taken lightly.

He rose and went to his stolen horses and untied all their
hobbles. He kept one fresh mount and waved his arms at the
rest of them to run them off. He went and untied his milk
cow after they were gone. Alone, he couldn't take the cow
and the horses too. The cow was a greater prize to him, even
though horses were the riches Comanches centered their
whole economy around.

He climbed on his new horse with the cow's lead rope in

his hand and started north with the black wall of smoke looming behind him in the distance. He already had one hundred horses to his name when he had left his band in camp far up in the Antelope Hills. The cow was something he wanted and did not have. His chest burned and his gut churned bitterly. He would stop and milk the cow that evening, and maybe the cream would cool his angry belly.

He passed the time on the trail by keeping an eye on the progress of the prairie fire and thinking of what he would do to the Running Boy and the Prussian. Tejanos were too foolish to fear the Comanche as they should, and he knew there would come a day when he would have another chance at the two. For some reason he wanted the Running Boy's scalp the most.

Chapter 7

Odell lugged a hide bucket of water from the creek to the beehive-shaped grass hut where he and the Prussian had been staying for better than a week. According to his hosts it was squaw's work, but he was getting restless and needed something to do. He hung the bucket on a stob at the doorpost and went to sit down beside the Prussian on a deer-hide rug under the shade of a thatched arbor fronting the hut. The Prussian had his wounded leg propped up on his saddle before him and was running a whetstone up and down the blade of his saber. The stone slid along the metal in long, grating passes that were so evenly spaced as to make a rhythm all their own. Odell's father used to make such a rhythm when he stropped his straight razor before shaving.

The Prussian was looking unusually sour, and Odell kept quiet. The wounded leg had been slow to heal, and even if it did, the hoop-iron arrowhead lodged in it was probably going to give the Prussian a permanent limp. Odell watched the village stir around them and listened to the whetstone running up and down the blade.

They had been lucky to run across the Wichita village at a time when the Prussian was looking like he might not make it. Without rest and shelter, the loss of blood and the fever that racked his body would have killed him long before they made it back to their homes on Massacre Creek. For two weeks the Wichita medicine man had come to visit them daily, bringing the Prussian vile concoctions of bitter broth and smelly poultices. The wounded Prussian finally appeared to be on the mend, but Odell couldn't tell if it was the medicinal applications or the healthy dose of gourd-rattling and chanted incantations meant to run off evil spirits that did the trick.

The medicine man was nowhere to be seen, but the rest of the village was already going about their morning business. The Wichitas seemed friendly enough, but Odell hadn't been quite sure of them when he stumbled across their settlement. His recent experience with Indians had left him more than a little leery.

Like most of the Indians Odell had run across, the men wore breechclouts and moccasins in the summertime and nothing more. The women wore long deerskin dresses, some of them finely decorated with elk teeth and painted designs. They were a short people, and both the men and women wore tattoos on their faces. The men had horizontal lines and dashes running from the corners of their eyes and down their chins. The women had similar lines on their chins and a circle around their mouths. Once he got past their strange looks he found that they were pretty nice folks.

"We were lucky to catch them in their town. They'll be leaving their crops to go out after buffalo before too long. They plant and harvest between spring and fall, and hunt and gather the rest of the year," Odell said.

"You've learned a lot about them for a man that doesn't

speak their language." The Prussian never looked up from his blade.

"Old Star, that medicine man, he speaks a little English, a little Spanish, and a whole lot of stuff I don't understand. But somewhere in the middle of all that I've picked up a thing or two, and even learned a little sign language."

"Don't you go to trusting these little farmers. I don't care how much corn and watermelons they eat, they're still Indians."

"They took us in when we needed it and seem scared of Comanches."

"Everybody is scared of Comanches, but don't think that makes the Wichitas our allies. When the Comanche are in the mood they trade with them, and I've even heard they've fought together before."

"Are you saying we aren't safe here?"

"Herr Odell, I'm saying don't trust any Indian. No white man can understand how they think. The same warrior that gives you food and shelter one day might scalp you the next."

"There's bound to be some good Indians."

The Prussian adjusted his wounded leg to a more comfortable position. "Yes, but as a whole I don't trust them. Among their own kind they can appear to be a loving people who sing and dance and live and die just like we do. But that same Indian you see playing with children or telling jokes around the fire might think anybody outside his tribe is an enemy and maybe even less than human. He'll kill you or torture you and laugh while he's doing it, like a kid poking around in an ant mound."

Odell watched the women and children heading to the fields, laughing and telling stories just like his people would to pass the workday. "I trust this bunch."

"You tend to your scalp, and I'll tend to mine." The Prussian smiled thinly and tested the edge of his saber against the hair on the back of his arm. It shaved like a razor.

"That suits me," Odell said. "I can look out for myself."

The Prussian gave him a sour look. "You sure don't know anything about Indians. Just what did you say you were back in the States?"

Odell shrugged. "My pa was a barber, but he was intending to build a riverboat if he had made it to Texas."

The Prussian shook his head. "No, I want to know what *your* trade is, or what you're considering making *your* living at. This Texas is a place where a man with a little luck and vision might one day make a fortune in land or the right business venture."

The Prussian's talk irritated Odell. Pappy too had always prodded and poked and questioned him about what he intended to do with his life. Pappy Spurling had set great store by a man amounting to something, even if was just his own measure of self-worth. Across three states and one failed homestead after another, he had thrown down his farming tools and picked up his rifle every time some big talker came along and claimed the government needed him to fight Indians or Britishers. Pappy proudly claimed he was just doing his part to help build a country. He busted his back breaking ground for the crops he was sure the fickle weather would one day actually allow him to grow, and for all his trouble all he got was hacked to death by some Comanches.

Odell wasn't sure just what it was his parents had dreamed, but he recalled vague bits and pieces of big ideas and bold hopes that to a young boy sounded as sweet as candy and sure to happen. But in spite of all their praying and hard work and measuring their life by the meager hoard of coins in an old lard can in the cupboard, they ended up broke and then dead on the banks of a muddy river in a place they had never even dreamed of. Who could plan for such?

Odell made no claims on wisdom, but he was sure that anybody who thought they could plot out the course of their life on a calendar was just fooling themselves. Life was just generally unpredictable as hell, and he had learned not to make a habit of thinking past the day at hand. Things were easier that way, and the lumps you took wouldn't come as any more of a surprise than if you had tried to plan for them.

"I get the notion you were a soldier once." Odell sought to change the subject.

"In my former country, all men of any quality are soldiers."

"I once heard that horse soldiers don't keep their swords sharp for fear of cutting their horse on accident."

"Maybe American soldiers don't, but Prussian cavalrymen do, or at least some of us did. A dull saber isn't any better than a club in a fight."

"You were fighting back where you came from?"

"I am a hussar. I have always fought, as did my family before me. My father charged the French emplacements at the Battle of Leipzig with nothing more than a pistol and a saber in his hands. He and his men charged two more times with just their sabers."

"That sounds like some fierce fighting."

The Prussian let out a scoffing hiss of air and shook his head. "The French are not made for war. They are better at sipping wine and bragging about their own art."

"I heard you fought with Houston at San Jacinto."

"I was there."

"I'm going with the Wichitas on their buffalo hunt," Odell said.

"What if you run across some Comanches and these new friends of yours sell you out?"

"It's a chance I'll take."

"By *Gott*, even if they don't get you killed, how do you think you're going to find the Comanches you're looking for when it's hard enough just finding any kind of Comanche?" The Prussian waggled his saber point at Odell for emphasis like a shaking finger.

"I know I wouldn't recognize most of Pappy's killers if

I came face-to-face with them, but I'll never forget one of them. He was the one that killed Mr. Israel, and I'm going to try and find him," Odell said. "I'm going to give it until winter, or maybe spring. I owe Pappy and Israel that much."

"I've my farm waiting for me and I'm going home as soon as I'm well enough," the Prussian said.

"Maybe you think Red Wing's waiting for you?"

The Prussian didn't flinch. "If she'll agree, I will give her the finest plantation in Texas."

Odell tried to tell himself that Red Wing would wait for him to return, but he was doubtful. The thought of the Prussian marrying his girl scared him almost as bad as going out on the plains with the Wichitas. He already felt infinitely alone and he hadn't even left yet.

"I ain't ready yet to quit what I started," he said.

"You're a young fool. Finding one particular Comanche out on these wastes is impossible. Come home with me and be glad you're still alive to make the trip."

Odell shook his head fiercely, as much to shake away any doubt that might be creeping into his mind as to disagree with the Prussian. "I reckon I can spare the time to stay after that Comanche a little longer."

"Looks like you have company, and they're bearing gifts." The Prussian pointed his saber toward the cluster of Wichita men coming their way.

Odell stood and went to the edge of the arbor with one hand shading his eyes against the sun. "Damn, they've found Crow!"

There was a half dozen warriors walking in front of the horse they were leading, but even at a distance Odell would have known the black gelding anywhere. He never expected to see that horse again, and he trotted out to lay hands on the animal while the Wichitas laughed and jabbered their strange talk in his ears.

Crow was gaunt but seemed little worse for the wear. The arrow was gone from his shoulder, and all that remained of the wound was a puckered lump of healing flesh. Odell rubbed Crow's jaw and resisted the urge to hug his neck. He and that horse had come a lot of miles together, and seeing him was like seeing a long-lost friend. Having Crow back was like having a little piece of Red Wing with him again.

Old Star, the medicine man, took hold of Odell's arm and focused his attention away from the horse. His dark eyes twinkled in their wrinkled seams of weathered hide and he smiled and gestured grandly to the horse. After five minutes of talk in three languages, hand signs, and a good bit of pantomiming, Odell understood that Crow had wandered into the edge of the village with the remains of Odell's saddle hanging under his belly. The girth had slipped and loosened and the saddle had probably turned when the horse lay down or rolled in the grass. Not many horses would tolerate being tied to something flopping around under them, and Crow apparently had kicked the saddle to pieces. The Wichitas had rigged a halter with a braided rawhide riata, as there was no sign of Odell's bridle.

"Were you just waiting to show up after you had lost all my gear?" Odell gave Crow one last pat on the neck and led him toward the arbor.

The Prussian was back at sharpening his saber, but he looked up long enough to nod at Crow. "You're lucky to get him back. There are Indians that would ride two weeks to steal a horse like that."

"He's the best horse in Texas."

"No, my Baron can outrun anything I've come across."

Odell eyed the tall Kentucky horse tied to one of the posts supporting the arbor. It was common knowledge on the frontier that the Prussian had won him in a high-stakes poker game with a New Orleans cotton buyer. He was so cautious with the horse that he kept him tied, lest the Wichitas try to steal him.

Odell had been hand grazing and watering the Prussian's thoroughbred ever since they had arrived at the village. The

Kentucky horse was indeed magnificent, but for all his beauty, he looked like only a shell of his former self. Wichita corn and some rest had fleshed his sorrel hide back out a little, but he wasn't fit yet for a hard journey. Crow, despite his wound and nothing to live on but grass, looked much more fit and ready to travel. He might not be as pretty, or as fleet, but he was mustang tough and smart as a whip.

"When you get back home, you tell Red Wing that your horse is better, and see what she has to say," Odell said.

"She's as silly over that black Indian pony as you are and thinks the sun rises and sets under his tail."

"I think he can smell Indians. He warned me those Comanches were fixing to attack me."

The Prussian cocked one eyebrow. "How come he isn't doing anything now? There are Indians all around him and he doesn't seem bothered."

"Maybe he knows the difference between Comanches and Wichitas."

"I guess you're going to tell me next that he can talk."

"He just ain't learned yet."

The Prussian sheathed his saber and sat up a little straighter where he could see past Odell to the edge of the village and the prairie beyond. "By *Gott*, Herr Odell, that's what I love about this Texas. There's nothing wrong with a country where men brag most on their horses and guns."

The Wichitas were leaving camp in a long, shambling line. The buffalo were returning south in numbers, and the Wichita grass houses were being exchanged for hide tepees carried on travois behind their ponies. The crops were harvested and put away, and the whole village laughed and shouted, excited to be leaving for the fall hunt.

Odell checked his gear one last time and hung his Bishop rifle from the horn of the saddle he'd traded one of the Wichitas out of. None of the tribe rode saddles except for a few of the squaws riding Indian-made, high-backed wooden rigs that looked more like packsaddle trees. He was afraid to ask where they had gotten a Texas-style rig, but he was glad to have it. His water bag was full and Crow was ready to travel, but he didn't mount yet. The Prussian had already climbed on his Kentucky horse and was watching the village leave. Odell wasn't especially fond of the man, but he still found it hard to part with him.

"You'd best be careful going home. That leg of yours ain't right yet," Odell said with his back to the Prussian.

"I think I'll be all right. I haven't forgotten the way back."

"Well, you'd better travel by night. A man alone is easy pickings for any Indian laying for him." Odell swung into his saddle. He felt a little foolish giving the Prussian advice for traveling through hostile country. The truth was, he pitied any savage that had the misfortune to tie into that mean-ass foreigner.

The Prussian rode up alongside him and looked long into his face. "Herr Odell, you are the one who should be careful. Many a man has found his grave out here, with nobody the wiser or even to know where his body rots."

Odell lifted his rifle and laid it across his thighs. "I'll be back home come winter, or maybe spring. Don't you forget that, and you be sure and tell Red Wing just what I said."

The Prussian gave him a thin smile. "I think you'll die out here and I'll have Red Wing all to myself."

"Don't get your hopes up too high, 'cause I'll be back on Massacre Creek before planting time."

"So long, Herr Odell." The Prussian turned his horse and started southeast.

Odell watched him for a long time, but the Prussian didn't look back. When the man was out of sight, he kicked Crow forward after the Wichitas. What might have well been the only white man for hundreds of miles wasn't gone for more than a few minutes, and Odell already felt lonely. He thought about just what a predicament he was putting himself into and wished he could have talked the Prussian into going with him. That sword would come in handy if he caught up with those Comanches.

He loped along in the dusty wake of the village on the move and studied the western horizon with a little bit of dread and an equal measure of hunger to see what lay out there. For all he knew he might already be as good as dead, but he couldn't bring himself to quit, no matter what was ahead of him. The stubborn streak that ran down the center of him wanted vengeance, but his heart wanted to turn around and race Crow back to the girl he'd left behind. He kept telling himself that she would be waiting for him when he finally made it home. He owed his Pappy a little more effort, and the hurt in him needed more miles to spend itself. Odell should have paid heed to his own advice and reminded himself that life never tolerates too much planning, especially in a place called Texas.

Chapter 8

The breeze through the open window shutters was cool but not uncomfortable. The winter had been a long, cold one, but spring was finally at hand. Honeybees buzzed among the tiny wildflower blooms, the trees were budding and bursting, and the pollen dust danced thickly in the sunlight before the window. It seemed as if the whole world had decided to turn green at the same moment, and it was enough to make the birds sing.

Red Wing sat at her piano and tried to focus her attention away from the open window and on her music. The complexity and richness of the sounds possible from the instrument never ceased to amaze her, and she thought it the greatest gift her mother had ever given her. There seemed to be notes and melodies for whatever moods or emotions might possess her, and her nimble fingers and natural talent involuntarily pulled songs from the piano as magically as mist rising from the ground on a foggy morning. At such times her eyes became blind to the sheet music before her, and she was lost in the ringing lift of music that poured from somewhere within her. There had been no such music in her life among the Comanche camps. She had been only a child in that former life that became more vague by the year, but what little she could remember had been harsh and without music.

But her heart was not in the music on that beautiful spring morning. The notes she played sounded flat and off-key to her, no matter how hard she tried, and she couldn't seem to shake the melancholy from her soul. She shivered beneath her shawl despite the sunny morning. It was as if the winter wouldn't leave her bones. It was going to take a lot of time and sunshine to warm her again.

Her fingers paused over the piano keys as she spotted the travelers coming along the creek. She rose from her stool and walked out the front door to stand with her mother at the edge of the porch. She placed an arm around the shorter woman's waist and pulled her to her side. Her mother leaned into her and sighed but kept her gaze on the party of men riding to the house. Red Wing studied the parched, hollow cheeks and the deep lines etched at the corners of Mrs. Ida's dry blue eyes. It was plain to all that she had once been a lovely woman, but time and the sun had not been kind to her and she looked far older than she really was. The news of her husband's death that the Prussian had brought home the previous fall seemed to have aged her ten more years in the span of the winter.

Bud, Red Wing's oldest brother, had spotted the riders, and had left his plow mule in the field he was working to come to the house. Mike, the youngest Wilson boy, followed closely on his heels, his bare feet padding through the fresh-turned furrows of earth. When they reached the porch, Red Wing handed Bud his rifle, and he turned to wait the riders' arrival with a cautious look upon his face.

Red Wing felt a little sick to her stomach for no good reason at the sight of the nine riders, and it wasn't even the fact that most of them were Indians. She knew more about

Indians than most of her family, and at a glance she recognized three of them for tame Delawares dressed in white men's clothes, and another for a Waco by the cut of his buckskins. A small sliver of her was still Comanche, and she had no fear of them. Her ancestors had outfought and out-traded them for better than a century. Three others in the party were white strangers to her, but it was Colonel Moore and the wild Indian beside him that caused her fear. She knew them both, and instinctively, she felt something awful about to descend upon her, just like she did when the clouds turned black and thunder sounded in the distance. Those two men had done her a favor once, but their arrival still felt like a bad omen.

"Hello, Mrs. Ida," the tall man in the lead said through his long whiskers. His horse was white as his beard and he pulled him to a stop just in front of where Bud stood off the edge of the porch.

"Hello, Colonel." Mrs. Ida's voice sounded as scared as Red Wing's pounding heart.

"I heard the bad news in Austin, and I'm sorry about your man. He was a good'un," Colonel Moore said.

"Yes, he was." Mrs. Ida's eyes darted back and forth between the colonel and the Indian beside him. "What brings you and that Indian to these parts?"

Red Wing knew the warrior at Colonel Moore's side by more than name, as did many in the Republic of Texas. He was Hashukana, Can't Kill Him, to the red man, and the whites knew him simply as Placido. He was a Tonkawa warrior chief of great renown, and many a Texan fighter's right-hand man in scraps with the Comanche. Placido had fought with the likes of Old Paint Caldwell and Colonel Burleson. Most Texas Indians ran to the short side, but Placido was taller than almost anybody Red Wing knew, except for Odell. The thought of her sweetheart made her even sadder.

Red Wing had to make herself stand her ground when

all that she really wanted to do was to flee back inside the house. The sight of Placido made her hackles rise for no good reason, other than somewhere in her childhood she had been trained to hate the Tonkawas. Despite the fact that it had been the colonel and Placido who had cared for her so tenderly while bringing her to her new home years earlier, she couldn't help the revolt she felt at the sight of an ancient Comanche enemy—wolf people and man-eaters, never to be trusted.

"Hi, Bird Woman," Placido grunted and grinned at Red Wing's mother.

"Hi yourself," Mrs. Ida said with no love in her voice.

While a woman who constantly complained about the uncivilized nature of the frontier, Mrs. Ida Wilson was a salty sort herself, despite all the ladylike manners she preached to Red Wing. She could quote Shakespeare lines and John Locke's philosophy from memory, spit Bible verses out as if she had written the book herself, and tell you the thousand and one things a proper lady should or shouldn't do with effortless abandon. She knew how to hold a teacup properly and was proud of her genteel upbringing in South Carolina, but the frontier had long since affected her in ways she would never recognize nor admit. She had become a settler's woman over the years, and her tongue was as sharp as a skinning knife. The friendly Indians had aptly come to call her Bird Woman for her talkative ways and scolding chatter.

"Who else have you got with you?" Mrs. Ida asked Colonel Moore.

Colonel Moore ignored the other Indians who had dismounted behind him and were tying their horses to the corral fence. He motioned the three white men with him forward. "These men with me are here on Sam Houston's orders. He's given them a mission that he thinks is important."

"That's not much of a recommendation, even if Sam was sober."

The colonel let that remark slide, although he was fond

of the young republic's president. Old Sam was the hero of the Battle of San Jacinto and a hell of a Mexican fighter, but when in his cups he could be a little unpredictable about making governmental decisions. He had everybody west of the Brazos mad over his moving the government from Austin to Houston. The republic was flat broke and besieged on all sides by Mexican armies and hostile Indians, and there was a lot of talk going around about Texas giving up its independence and joining the United States. Drunk or sober, Sam Houston had his own plans about seeing Texas through difficult times, and he didn't necessarily care who he made mad implementing his wily schemes.

"He was sober as Sunday the last time I saw him," Colonel Moore said.

"Hello, Mrs. Wilson. May I introduce myself?" The youngest of the three white strangers doffed his straw planter's hat in a sweeping wave. The rows of polished brass buttons on his blue military jacket shone in the sun like crystal.

Mrs. Ida grunted and huffed, but was obviously pleased with the pompous show of chivalry and grand manners. "That's a silly thing to ask."

"I'm Will Anderson, Commissioner of Indian Affairs." He put his hat back on his head, straightened his jacket, and touched up one corner of his well-groomed mustache. He was young and obviously very considerate of his appearance.

"That must keep you awful busy. I guess these other two fellows are colonels or commissioners too?" Mrs. Ida pointed to the men lingering slightly behind and to the right of Anderson. She had lived long enough in Texas, and the South in general, not to be surprised at so many titles.

"No, ma'am, I'm just plain Tom Torrey, Indian Agent." A small man in thick-lensed, wire-rimmed glasses and a stovepipe hat held up one nervous hand to them as manner of identifying himself. He had a bookish look about him and appeared out of place and worried to be sitting on a horse, as if he feared he might fall off at any moment.

"What about you?" Mrs. Wilson focused on the fourth man.

"H. P. Jones, at your service." He too doffed his hat, but not in such a dramatic a manner as had Colonel Anderson. He was a stout, portly man with a thin goatee and mustache below his round, flushed cheeks. He wore a buckskin jacket with military patches sewn onto the shoulders and a red sash girthed his waist and held in his prominent belly.

"I guess you're a general and are running this errand Sam has you all on?"

"No, he's just a militia captain and along for the show," Colonel Moore said. Red Wing thought he seemed awfully impatient with all the small talk.

"Well, Sam must really have you doing something he thinks is important to have sent so many of you on this journey," Mrs. Ida said.

"President Houston considers their mission very important," Colonel Moore said.

"What about you? Are you bossing this deal?"

"No, I was just to guide them here, and then I'll go back home." When he received no answer from her, he frowned and rubbed painfully at his lower back as if he'd been in the saddle for a long time. "Mind if we get down and have a talk with you?"

"I thought talking is what we'd been doing."

"We've important matters to discuss with you, and a cool sip of water and a chair would be welcome," Commissioner Anderson said.

"Well, get down, but I don't know how I'm going to keep all of you straight in my head. The man in the funny hat I can remember, but there's too many of you other important types."

"Never mind me. I need to go talk to our guides and interpreters." H. P. Jones seemed glad to have a reason to excuse himself. He rode over to where the Delawares and the Waco squatted in the shade of a live oak beside the corral.

Colonel Moore, the commissioner, and the man in the stovepipe hat dismounted and came up on the porch. Mrs. Ida took a seat in a wicker-bottomed chair and offered the remaining two to her visitors. Anderson and Moore took the chairs and the man in the glasses and tall hat sat on the edge of the porch. Placido stayed on his horse, his face bland and as inscrutable as ice. Red Wing was sure that if he smiled his face would break into pieces. He seemed oblivious to their conversation, but she thought she detected a slight twinkle in his eyes when he glanced at her.

She turned away from him and stood behind her mother with both her hands on the back of the chair. She realized that the newcomers were all looking at her, and the look on Colonel Moore's face made her even more uncomfortable than the Tonkawa had. She fought down the urge to run once more.

"Why, Red Wing, I had no idea just how much you've grown and how beautiful you've become," Colonel Moore said.

Red Winged tried to smile. "Thank you."

"Quite beautiful," Commissioner Anderson muttered like the observation bothered him.

"Just what have you come for? From the sound of it, I'd say it has to do with Injuns," Bud Wilson said as he leaned up against a porch post with his rifle cradled in the bend of his elbow.

Colonel Moore looked down at the oak boards beneath his feet for a moment and then passed a look to Commissioner Anderson. He rose and walked over to the water barrel at the end of the porch and took up the dipper there. He stood quietly with his back to them and the dipper dripping and poised halfway to his mouth.

Commissioner Anderson cleared his throat and looked uncomfortably at Red Wing before saying to Mrs. Ida, "I'd think it best if we spoke in private."

"Commissioner . . ." Mrs. Ida started.

"Call me Will. It will save you some confusion with so many men of rank present."

"What have you to say that my daughter should not hear? I assure you that she's no wilting lily and is quite levelheaded and capable of listening to men's talk without fainting or becoming confused by any complex revelations you seem to feel you possess," she snapped.

Commissioner Anderson winced. "I assure you that isn't the case. Perhaps you should hear me out and then maybe you can relate what I have to say to her yourself."

Mrs. Ida locked eyes with him for a long moment in a test of wills and then turned to Red Wing. "Go for a walk, girl, and let me hear this silly man out."

Red Wing started to protest, but the fear and premonition that was steadily growing in her took the out that was offered. She passed a glance to Bud, and he gave her a slight nod as if to say that he would listen for her. She gathered her skirt and left the porch with her chin a little higher than normal. She wasn't about to let them see her concern, and she was glad the folds of her dress hid her shaking hands as she walked away.

She passed by the corral and although she didn't look their way, she could feel the eyes of the men on her. The Delawares in their white shirts and homespun pants looked at her the same as the wild Waco with the tattoos on his face and one side of his hair shaved close and the other hanging long in a braid. Captain Jones had taken a seat against the wall of the barn. She nodded at him, but he had already tipped his hat down over his eyes for a nap. Once she reached the creek, she quickened her pace and circled around back of the house. She stopped and began picking flowers fifty yards away, but she could plainly hear bits and pieces of the conversation on the porch.

"If you want to help with the Comanche problem, why don't you bring soldiers and kill all of them you can? You can't make peace with them; they don't even understand the word." Her mother's voice rose loudly and Red Wing wondered what she had missed hearing that had the woman so stirred up.

She could hear Anderson speaking but couldn't make out all of his words. He was talking about some Peace Commission out west, but that was all she could gather at a distance.

"Lord, no! Bud, give me your gun!" Mrs. Ida cried.

There was more hushed conversation, but that only led to Mrs. Ida bawling and sobbing and the sound of a scuffle on the porch. Red Wing started back to the house.

"Not my baby!" her mother cried again, and to Red Wing she sounded like she was dying.

Before Red Wing had taken more than a few steps Placido rode around the house to her. His face was as unreadable as it had been earlier, and even the twinkle in his eye was gone. She thought maybe she had just imagined it earlier.

"Come with me." He sounded as if he thought she might flee.

It had been almost five years, but that day so long ago came back to her as more than a memory. In fact, she felt as if she was reliving the moment when Colonel Moore's men had charged into her camp yelling and firing and had taken her away from all she knew. Truly, she did want to run like a little rabbit in the grass, because she felt like a captive once again.

"What do you want with me?" she managed to ask.

Placido glanced briefly over his shoulder at the house as if weighing what he should or shouldn't say. "You're coming with us."

Red Wing wondered if she stood a chance of outrunning his horse the short distance to the timber along the creek. She wished her Odie had come home like he had promised.

Chapter 9

"I hear what you're saying, and I don't like it any more than you do." Commissioner Anderson dabbed at the fresh cut over his right eye with his handkerchief. "But for all that you've said, she's still a Comanche, and there is no denying that."

"She's my daughter, and has been for nigh onto five years," Mrs. Ida said. She was still crying, but she forced the words out between gasps and sobs.

"It's Houston's orders, and as the commissioner assigned to the Comanche, I have no choice but to obey them."

Captain Jones and Colonel Moore had Bud Wilson disarmed and pinned against the wall. He wasn't putting up a fight at the moment, but it was apparent that he'd tried to whip the commissioner. He was panting from his scuffle with the men and glaring hotly at the two who stood between him and Red Wing, who had come up to the edge of the porch. There was no blood relation between her and him, but it had been a long time since he had treated her like anything but his true sister. Even little Mike was hovering around with a stick in his hands ready to fight for her.

"If you take her back to those savages, it will be over my dead body," Mrs. Ida said.

The commissioner sighed and rolled his hat brim around in his hands while he thought. "We're taking her, but maybe the Comanches won't even want her back, or won't be willing to trade hostages for her. If so, I think we can manage to bring her back to you."

Mrs. Ida steadied herself and lashed out at Colonel Moore. "You're word isn't worth spit. You look me in the eye and tell me you didn't give this girl to me."

The colonel didn't meet her eyes; he couldn't. He'd fought Mexicans and Indians more times than he cared to count, but he didn't have the stomach to face her anguish or deny the truth of what she said. He cussed Sam Houston under his breath. The president thought you could deal with Comanches like civilized people when everyone in Texas knew that peace with them was a joke. Former president Lamar had been an ass, but at least he had understood that. The only way was to kill them all, or just outlast them, and the colonel had a sneaking suspicion it would be the latter of the two choices that eventually worked. Comanches were damned hard to run down, and harder yet to kill in a fight.

He watched Placido standing guard over Red Wing at the far end of the porch. She had changed much, but the colonel couldn't quite shake the vision of her as a tadpole of a little girl with a dirty face and chopped-off hair, dressed in a tow sack of a deerskin dress. He remembered how he'd found her standing in the middle of the Comanche village among the dead bodies of her people. She'd looked up at him on his horse without a tear in her eye. After the long day's fighting was over he'd taken her up on his horse and carried her in front of him for the first few days, while the rest of his captives walked before his volunteer troops.

Red Wing too was reliving that moment over and over

again. Her capture from the Comanche had been more violent, but the thought of being carted off again was even harder for her than it had been on that day in her village. She had nothing to lose back then, an orphan even before Colonel Moore killed over fifty of the camp that had been her home at the time. The only thing similar for her about the moment was the numbness of mind and spirit that came over her when she heard what Commissioner Anderson intended to do.

She went into the cabin and gathered a few personal belongings from the house and stuffed them into a valise while the Tonkawa watched over her. She knew it was foolish, but she had a faint hope that some miracle would happen and keep her from having to go with the expedition. Such things only happened in the books she had read, and the only miracle she had ever known was the family she was about to be dragged away from.

"There's no sense fighting us. Red Wing is a Comanche, and as a measure of our goodwill, Houston wants us to offer her back to them in hopes of having peace with all of the Comanches that we can get to come into Fort Bird and talk with us. He also hopes that they'll be moved by such a gift and offer us white captives in exchange," the commissioner said.

"She's no more a Comanche now than you or I. Did you know that her father and mother were both dead long before Colonel Moore captured her? Did you know she can hardly even speak a word of Comanche anymore?" Mrs. Ida shook her finger under his nose. "You tell me, would you take a white woman and offer her to the Comanche even if it meant peace for all times? What if she was your daughter or sister?"

"Mrs. Wilson, you know that General Woll's army sacked San Antonio again last year. The word is that the Mexicans are forming up again and sending ambassadors out to make agreements with the Comanche to aid them. President

Houston believes that peace with the savages may be all that saves Texas from invasion."

"You don't need my daughter to bargain with the Comanche. It sounds like the Mexicans are doing fine without giving away their women," Mrs. Ida snapped.

"I'm truly sorry, but I have my orders and will follow them as they are." Commissioner Anderson got up from his chair and put his hat back on.

"Like hell you will." Mrs. Ida produced a single-shot pistol from the folds of her dress in the wink of an eye. "I didn't love and raise that girl all this time to lose her to the likes of you, Colonel, Commissioner, two-bit chicken thief, or whatever you call yourself."

The hammer on that pistol was eared back and she was ready to shoot. The commissioner made a move to jerk the gun from her hand, and it would have proven a fatal tactic if it had not been for Placido bounding from the door and knocking off her aim with his long arm. As it was, the pistol sent a ball through the bookkeeper's hat. The little man pushed his glasses up on his freckled nose and then jerked off his lid to study the hole in the crown. He measured the distance between where the bullet had entered and the silk band, as if to gauge how close the woman had come to putting the bullet in his head.

"I daresay, she almost killed me," he said, and he had gone white around the gills.

"Agent Torrey, you'd best get on your horse," Colonel Moore said.

The squeamish Indian agent looked at a loss for words but did as he was told. Nothing he had known in Baltimore had prepared him for what he'd seen in just a few years in Texas. There were no women where he came from to shoot hats off your head, or the need to trade civilized women to savages for goodwill. He found himself wishing he'd married that fat shoemaker's daughter next door and stayed back in Maryland to raise fat little kids and sew on boot soles, happy in the ignorance of any place such as Texas even existing.

The Indians with the party had mounted and ridden up to the porch. They were well-armed and looked determined. Mrs. Ida didn't care if there had been fifty of them; she continued to wrestle with Placido over her gun. The Tonk finally let her have the gun back, as it was empty and he thought it harmless enough. As soon as he let go she reared back with it like it was a tomahawk and swung it viciously at him. He ducked easily, but she did manage to hit Torrey in the back of the head just as he was stepping off the porch to go to his horse. He landed in the dust with all the grace of a sack of corn.

"Ho there, Agent Torrey, are you all right?" one of the Delawares asked.

It took Torrey a minute to find his glasses in the grass, but he finally swayed to his feet. Even after he had his spectacles back on, he had trouble making out anything. His head swam and he was almost too dizzy to walk. He somehow managed to reach his horse, although he nearly fell off the other side when he swung into the saddle. He teetered precariously until he finally righted himself. The Delawares laughed at him.

He supposed he might have almost fallen off the horse merely because he was too dizzy to properly mount, but he had no faith in his horsemanship even under good conditions. Horses vexed him, especially broncy, snorty Texas ponies, and they were almost as bothersome as women with weapons and Indians who mocked him. His head throbbed already, and he could hardly wait for whatever else the day had in store for him. He was sure it would be highly uncomfortable and humiliating. For the life of him he couldn't even remember just how he'd ended up as one of Houston's Indian agents. He chalked it up to bad luck and a serious lack of judgment on his part.

The commissioner took the pistol away from Mrs. Ida

and fended off an assault of scratching and clawing until she finally sank weakly back into her chair. He tried one last time to talk with her, but her chin dropped to her chest and she cried quietly.

"My baby, my baby. Bud, get your gun back and shoot them. Don't let them take your sister. It'll kill me for sure," she said softly.

Bud prepared himself to tackle the entire party, but Red Wing's voice stopped him.

"It's all right, Bud. There's nothing we can do. Make sure Mama's okay, and then go and get Karl once we're gone. He'll know what to do," she said.

Bud studied her carefully. He wanted to fight, but she was right. There was no way he was going to whip the entire party. The best thing to do was for him to gather a party of neighbors and run the Peace Commission down and take her back. He took a deep breath to settle himself. Red Wing always made perfect sense. He'd known for a long time that she was the smartest one in the family, and maybe the bravest.

"Karl won't let them get too far off with you. Just you wait and see," he said.

The commissioner looked a question at Colonel Moore.

"You keep that Prussian out of this. There's no need to get him stirred up. Houston wouldn't like his representatives being harassed by foreigners," Colonel Moore said. He knew the Prussian well, and was sure that if that German had an interest in Red Wing that Commissioner Anderson was going to have his hands full. He was glad he was leaving the expedition as soon as they got away from the Wilsons' farm.

Red Wing hugged Bud and wiped the tears from Mike's eyes before hugging him too. "Don't cry, little brother, or you'll make me cry too."

Placido tied her valise on the saddle of the horse they had for her and stood back while she mounted. Red Wing looked at her mother, hoping to say good-bye, but Mrs.

Wilson wouldn't or couldn't lift her head from her chest. She sagged limply in her chair, and the only sign of life in her was the subtle quiver of her shoulders and an occasional sob.

"Good-bye, Mama. I love you." Red Wing hoped her mother was all right. She feared they had broken her emotionally, if not physically.

"Mind that commissioner. He has eyes for you, and that won't hurt your cause," Mrs. Ida croaked in a ragged whisper when Red Wing rode close to the porch.

Red Wing looked quickly to see if the others had heard her mother. None of the men acted as if they had heard the whispered advice from a woman crazed by grief and rambling incoherently. Before long, the entire party was mounted and leaving. Red Wing watched her home disappear behind her as the trail west took her away from all she had come to know.

"Buckle down, girl. I won't let the Comanches have you if it looks like it will be bad for you," Commissioner Anderson said beside her.

She started to reply angrily but cut herself off short. She remembered her mother's last words and tried to keep from crying. She steeled herself and gave the commissioner a smile she didn't feel. "I'm sure you'll look out for me, and I feel better knowing it."

She wanted to spit out the bad taste in her mouth as soon as she said it, but her mother was wise. It might pay to use whatever weapons she had at hand, and young as Red Wing was, she already knew men liked to look at her. That knowledge scared her and intrigued her. She couldn't muscle her way past the men around her, but she might outfox them with "feminine wiles." She wasn't sure what her mother always meant by the term, or if she even possessed such things.

She felt defeated but knew that would pass with time. Stubborn defiance was steadily gaining a hold within her, and she already felt better for it. Her chances of escape were slim, but she had to try. She was tougher and cooler-headed than any of them could have ever guessed. She had once been Comanche, and that old training wasn't entirely forgotten. She was alone in the world once more, but patience could be the price of survival. She would have to wait until an opportunity for freedom came along.

Chapter 10

Bud Wilson unhitched from the plow and rode just as fast as his poor mule could go all the way to the Prussian's farm. A crew of men busy building a new house watched him come down the little creek valley with cautious looks. Every man of them set aside their tools and went to stand beside their guns, at least those that had them. A fast-approaching rider in that neck of the woods was never a good sign and often meant danger was at hand.

Bud pulled up before the framed beginnings of the house that stood like a skeleton in the clearing with its bare, white lumber looking more like bones than wood. The Prussian stood at a long table set up in the yard, poring over a set of building plans with a square and a pen. He straightened the silk sash around his waist and adjusted his saber before coming up to greet Bud.

"Herr Bud, you've come fast and look tired. If I didn't know you only live four miles from me I'd say you'd come all the way from Austin."

Bud felt a little silly when he realized he was indeed breathing hard, as if he'd run the distance himself and not been carried by his mule. He tried to calm himself and managed to finally blurt something out. "They've run off with Red Wing and are going to give her to the Comanches."

The Prussian studied the young man while he absorbed the news. Bud gathered his breath and a jumbled, confusing version of the day's events at the Wilsons' farm poured out of him in one quick rush. The Prussian held up a palm to slow him down and invited him to dismount and take a seat under the shade trees surrounding the house they were building.

"This will steady you some." The Prussian poured a tin cup full of whiskey from a jug and offered it to Bud. It was well known among the settlers on the upper Colorado that the Prussian's stills turned out especially good sipping liquor.

"I ain't a drinking man." Bud was just barely sixteen, and the fact was, he had never been offered any.

"Go ahead and drink it. It'll take the edge off your day, and then maybe you can slow down and tell me just what happened."

Bud tossed down the liquor in one gulp and took the chair the Prussian offered him. His host remained standing, and despite all his calm talk, it was plain that he was impatient to hear what Bud had to say. The whiskey burned Bud's throat to the point of almost bringing tears to his eyes, and it was a moment before he could give another go at telling his story.

The Prussian listened quietly until Bud had told him of the Peace Commission taking Red Wing from Mrs. Wilson. Bud had expected him to react powerfully, but the Prussian went back to his table and traced a finger over the blueprint pinned down on the tabletop with small creek stones at each corner. He studied the house framing as if he was seeing the construction finished in his mind, and then surveyed his hired men standing around doing nothing but staring at him.

"You've four men here, and with you and me that should be enough to run the Peace Commission down and take her back," Bud said.

"Yes, I have four men here, but they're carpenters and farmers and not fighters," the Prussian said.

"You mean to tell me you're just going to let them take her? I thought the congress appointed you some kind of militia officer or something. She sent me here, counting on you." Bud had always looked up to the Prussian and was more than a little shocked at the man's complacency. He took new measure of him and wondered if it had only been the sword that had impressed him. Rich foreigners with fine manners, gold money, and a fancy horse were certainly inspiring to a frontier boy.

"No, I mean nothing of the sort." The Prussian pointed to the white framing of the house being erected. "I'm building this for Red Wing, and as soon as it was finished I was going to ride over to your home and ask her to marry me again."

"Well, you ain't going to marry her if they trade her off to the Comanches." Bud could see no need to dawdle around talking while the men who'd taken his sister got farther away by the minute.

"Rest assured, I will bring her back." The Prussian waved his laborers back to work. "You men know what to do, and I expect my house to be finished by the time I get back. And I expect it to be built according to my plans."

Bud thought the big house the Prussian was building was a little silly. Nobody on the frontier built frame houses, even if they did own a sawmill. And besides, there was already a good log cabin on the farm that was bigger than the one the entire Wilson family lived in. There was a round-topped barn with a loft and a nice set of split-rail lots, a large corn crib, cotton press, and wagon shed on the place. In Bud's

opinion, such hard work and money as the new house required would have been better spent clearing brush and
breaking new farm ground. Corn would feed you and cotton
would make you wealthy, but a big, fancy house was nothing
but showing off to the neighbors or his sister.

"Let's get going. Maybe we can pick up more men as we
go," Bud said as he started for his mule.

"You go back to your mother and see that she's all right.
With your father gone, you're all she has to take care of her."

"I ain't going back home. I'm riding with you."

"By *Gott*, that old plow mule of yours wouldn't make it
a day on a hard ride." The Prussian could already tell he
might have to tie the boy up to keep him from going. "If you
want to help, you'll stay and protect your mother so I can
go after Red Wing without worrying she won't have anyone
to give her away in marriage when I get back."

"You can't talk me out of going with you." Bud jumped
to his feet and stuck out his jaw.

"Oh, well, you're a man grown." The Prussian shrugged
and quit the argument as quickly as it had begun.

He went to his cabin and disappeared inside for a long
while. He finally came out balancing a roll of blankets
bound inside an oilskin groundsheet, an odd-shaped, small
box on one arm, and a stubby carbine in his other hand. One
of the carpenters brought up the Kentucky horse, and the
Prussian tied his bedroll and the box behind the saddle and
hung the carbine by its sling from the saddle horn. The
ancient, decrepit Mexican woman who served as his cook
followed behind him with a thin wooden chest, and he
opened it while she held it in her outstretched hands and
pulled out a matched pair of flintlock pistols. He checked
the priming on both pans before attaching the pistols to
lanyards tied to his belt, and then stuffed them into the
holsters on each hip at a cross draw.

"Herr Bud, can you go inside and get my saddlebags?
They're on my bed."

Bud leaned his rifle against the worktable and did as he was asked. He came back out of the house just in time to see the Prussian take up the rifle he had left behind and lay it across the mule's rump. He pulled the trigger on Bud's gun and the exhaust from the muzzle burned the mule enough to cause him to leave in a crazed runaway.

"What'd you do that for?" The mule had always been a little harebrained, and Bud was surprised more by the Prussian's act than he was to see the animal fleeing wildly over the hill toward home.

"It's a short walk home for you, and I am sure you will find your mount waiting there."

The Prussian took the saddlebags from Bud and handed him the empty rifle in exchange. He tied the saddlebags behind his cantle and mounted without so much as a word of apology. By the time Bud had thought about what had just happened long enough to get angry, the Prussian was already loping away and out of hearing distance of any complaints. Bud knew he should have at least returned the favor and ran off the Prussian's horse, but it was already too late. He was disappointed by his own inaction and being left standing there like a fool. If he had been given more time to think, he might have made a better account of himself, but Bud had never been the brightest of the Wilson children. He wished Red Wing had been there to help him figure things out. As it was, the only thing left for him to do was to go after his mule.

The Prussian felt bad for treating the boy so, but he knew it was better than getting him killed somewhere out on the trail. He was going to have to ride fast if he was to gather the help he needed and then catch up to the Peace Commission. He had no time to babysit young boys with poor rifles and slow mules.

He knew the expedition had taken Red Wing up the Colorado, but he rode southwest instead. He hated to abandon the fresh tracks they were sure to leave, but he was outnumbered and hoped to remedy that by traveling out of his way to get some help. He could have gone into Austin, or downriver to Bastrop looking for men to aid him, but he had no use for cautious family men or drunken brawlers loafing in taverns— not for what he intended.

If Colonel Moore and Placido weren't going with Commissioner Anderson, then his guess was that they would be heading for the headwaters of the San Marcos. Placido often left his wife there while he went off to fight with various ranging companies. Colonel Moore might have ridden there with him, but the Prussian blamed Moore too much for Red Wing's predicament to want his help. To his way of thinking, much of Colonel Moore's reputation as an Indian fighter was ill deserved anyway. However, Placido was known to be a fine tracker and killer of Comanches. The Indian might know the route the Peace Commission intended to travel, and maybe he could round up some more Tonks to help fill out the war party the Prussian hoped to gather.

Against his better judgment, he did stop at several homesteads far to the south to try to stir up some settler men with a little Indian fighting experience to ride with him. None of them had been neighbors of the Wilsons, and they didn't seem to care about a captive Comanche girl being taken back to her murderous tribe enough to leave their work and families. He didn't even mention the fact that the Comanches had killed other settlers and had stolen livestock, and left the farmers to their corn and barefoot children.

By nightfall he was in a foul mood from the long ride and cussing everything in general. Although more than a little put out with some of his fellow Texans' apathy and prejudice, he was no less determined to free Red Wing from her captors. Texas was a paradise to his way of thinking, but the one thing it lacked was women, especially women beautiful enough for a man who liked the best of everything.

He wished he had a regiment of Prussian hussars to ride

with him, because he was sure no force in Texas was strong enough to stand up to his fellow countrymen in arms, even Comanches. The hussars were the finest light cavalry on the face of the earth. The fact that he had been forced to flee the place of his birth due to political difficulties didn't diminish his pride and assurance of Prussian superiority over all makes of men. His homeland might suffer under foolish tyrants, but there was nothing wrong with the men bred there. Where other soldiers might falter, a Prussian never did.

The Prussian was a hot-blooded and violent man at heart, and the illegitimate son of an important baron had been no match for him with a saber. He had killed the slanderous dandy in a duel, and rather than waiting to be executed or locked up in prison, he had fled the country with his extended family aboard a chartered English ship. Texas at the time was nothing but a vague spot on a map to them, but it promised to be a place where stubborn, free-thinking men could live their lives without interference. To the Prussian's surprise, Texas had proven more than he had dreamed. It wasn't long before he began to consider killing the baron's bastard as the greatest stroke of fortune in his life. Granted, Texas was a primitive place, but a tough, smart man with a little ready gold and the ability to lead men might one day make a fortune there.

It was as if Texas was made for him, and the bloody attributes that had almost landed him in a Prussian prison served him well in his new home. The best thing about the frontier was that a man could always find a fight, or it would find him. Wild, violent men in Texas were as common as flies, and their deeds often led them to rank and position, rather than jail. Adventurous rogues seemed drawn to the land like moths to a flame, and the Prussian was a bigger rogue than any of them.

He considered Sam Houston as no fool, and surely the old general had picked competent men to man his expedition to the Comanches. It would be no easy task taking Red Wing away from them. The Prussian knew defying the president of the republic was liable to cause him problems, but he wasn't the type to be thwarted in what he set out to do. Life could be like playing high-stakes poker, and a man sometimes had to take his chances in the game. Red Wing was a prize worth gambling for, and just to sweeten the pot, his journey chasing after the Peace Commission was likely to be long and land him in the middle of Comanche country.

Thinking of Comanches excited him, and a new plan began to form in his mind. He had no doubts that he could rescue Red Wing, but why not kill two birds with one stone? All he needed was a good band of fighters to help him. A man who could successfully lead a battle against a large number of Comanches might go all the way to the presidency of Texas. President Houston had made some very unpopular decisions of late, and there was no way he was going to be reelected.

What the Prussian would have admitted, had anybody been there to ask him, was the fact that the promise of another bloody fight with the Comanche excited him more than the woman or his position in Texas political affairs. He would take his prizes as they came to him, but war trumped all pleasures.

Thinking of Red Wing and glory made him push the Kentucky horse a little faster down the trail to San Antonio, and his hand went inadvertently to his saber handle. He intended to one day be the king of Texas, and as such, he would need a queen—Sam Houston, Comanches, or anyone else who got in his way be damned.

Chapter 11

*

Odell gathered his buffalo robe tighter about his throat and shivered in the breeze. A good squaw would have done a better job, but he'd tried to tan the hide himself and it was stiff and almost unmanageable. His hand cramped from holding the hard, dried edges of the ill-cured robe tight enough to keep the cold from leaking in. A late spring norther had blown a short-lived snowstorm down on the plains and had almost frozen him. But that was nothing unusual. It seemed the country had been trying to kill him ever since he left his home to chase Comanches.

When the April storm had struck in the night he'd been unable to light a fire, so he saddled Crow and just let the wind carry them along, hoping that by keeping moving they wouldn't freeze to death. Although the blizzard had barely lasted until daylight, that was more than enough time to drive him far enough south on the plains that he didn't have a clue where he was at. But that was nothing new either. Since leaving the Wichitas he had grown used to not knowing his exact location on a map, even if there had been proper maps of the country he rode. He had decided that half the battle was just getting used to being lost, and he was content to simply wander. If he could find his way to the nearest water in time to save himself, then he considered it a good day. The plains he rode were flat and almost without landmarks, and he had come to think that feeling lost went with the territory, at least for a white man.

The sun was leaking white light through cracks in the gray clouds and the wind had shifted again to blow from the south. That was the thing about the plains—it could be spring one moment and winter the next. He could already feel it warming up and hoped it would be spring again by the late afternoon.

Despite the fact that the storm was over, he couldn't quit shivering or seem to warm himself. Most of the ground was free from snow, as the wind had swept it into powdery white lines that ran in long, wavy rows across the prairie. What he needed was a fire, but he wasn't sure his cold-stiffened fingers would function well enough to gather some buffalo chips, much less strike an accurate spark from his flint and steel.

Just when he'd given up hope of warmth and had decided to angle east to the caprock that edged the Llano Estacado somewhere in the distance, he spotted a campfire burning brightly through the early morning light. It seemed very near, but his eyes often fooled him on such an expanse of nothing, and the fire turned out to be almost three miles away.

Odell had nearly gotten himself killed by various follies during his fall and winter upon the plains, but he had learned to approach campfires cautiously. Most of those he ran across out on the buffalo grass were liable to be his enemies. He did cut a wide quarter circle around the flickering orange eye before him, but he was pretty sure that whoever was stopped there wouldn't be Indians, or at least not very many of them. Most Indians had better sense than to be caught out in the open during a blizzard without at least the shelter of a tepee. Although spring was at hand, most of the Comanche were still huddled up in their winter camps in the canyons north along the Canadian and Red, or east along the edge of the high walls of the escarpment that fronted the headwaters of the Brazos and Red Rivers.

What Odell found beside the fire was a single little man with his feet propped up on a rock to warm them before the flames. Well, that wasn't entirely true, as the man had no feet or much above that either, and it was merely the scarred stumps of his legs shorn off just above the knees that must have needed warming. The only other occupant of the camp, if it could be called that, was a skinny burro that stood three-legged with its side practically in the small fire. It appeared to be asleep, and must have been cold, because Odell was sure that the hair on its ribs was getting singed.

"Mind if I use your fire? I have a little buffalo meat to share." Odell pulled up at a polite distance.

The little man beside the fire didn't answer and seemed content to study the stumps of his short legs stretched out before him. Odell assumed that the Mexican might have been asleep like the little donkey, or else he didn't speak English. He stepped down from his saddle anyway and loosened Crow's cinch. After rummaging around in his saddlebags he drug out the dry buffalo tongue he'd been carrying there for the better part of two days. He carried it over to the fire.

The Mexican was awake, and the sight of the buffalo tongue seemed to interest him more than Odell's arrival had.

"You *habla* English?" Odell asked.

"*Sí*, I speak a little," the Mexican said through his broken and rotten teeth.

"You look like you're having maybe a harder time than me and could use a little something to eat."

Odell thought the Mexican was a poor sight indeed, and

it was not just the fact that the man was a cripple that gave
him that impression. The Mexican was obviously shoeless,
but he was also hatless. His long black hair hung over most
of his shriveled face, and it was so interwoven and tangled
with grass and prairie debris that it might not have even been
hair at all. It reminded Odell of the mat of wooly tangles
covering the shoulders, neck, and head on a buffalo in winter
prime.

The Mexican's woven wool scrape was soiled and torn
and unraveled to what had to have been half its former size.
Beneath that, the man wore a rotting sheepskin vest, wool
side out, that smelled just like it looked, and a pair of thin
cotton pants that might have once been white a hundred
years before. Odell was cold even beneath his heavy buffalo
robe, but the little Mexican didn't have so much as a single
goose bump showing on the portions of his bare shoulders
that were visible before his arms disappeared under the
cover of the serape.

"Do you have a pot to boil this tongue in?" Odell asked
as he hunkered down before the fire between the Mexican
and the burro.

The Mexican shook his head somberly, and one of his
skinny arms withdrew from the serape to wave dramatically
around him at his lack of possessions. Odell saw nothing
that the man might own other than the burro, who had finally
awakened long enough to swap the hind foot he was resting
on before closing his eyes again.

"I reckon I can just cook this tongue over the fire," Odell
said. The Wichitas he'd lived with had considered the tongue
a prime cut of meat, as did many a frontiersman. But Odell
had no squaws to chew on the tongue and tenderize it, nor
a pot to boil it in long enough to soften the dense muscle.

A little trickle of drool leaked out of one corner of the
Mexican's mouth while Odell skinned the tongue with his
butcher knife. He crosscut it into thin slices, going against
the grain of the muscle. There were no sticks available to

roast the meat on, so he laid it out on the ground while he went to fetch the ramrod from his rifle hanging on his saddle. By the time he got back to the fire the Mexican was already chewing on a raw chunk of the tongue. He seemed extremely happy with the taste of it from the rapturous look on his face.

"I take it you ain't picky about your cooking," Odell said while he poked holes in a couple of pieces of the tongue and slid the brass end of his ramrod through them.

"I haven't eaten in four days, maybe five," the Mexican managed to say while he gummed around on the tough meat. *"Cuántas días? Cinco?"* Odell thought the Mexican dangerously skinny, but five days without food seemed a little unbelievable for a man still alive, even a walking skeleton with most of his legs missing.

"I ate a scorpion and a little green beetle I found while crawling to my donkey yesterday, or maybe it was the day before." The Mexican seemed a little bothered by the measuring of time.

"I admit provisions are scarce in these parts, but I take it you aren't much of a hunter."

"I have no gun, and as you can see, I'm not swift enough to run down a buffalo or an antelope. I don't even have teeth enough to hang on if I were to catch one." The Mexican had managed to swallow his raw meat and was looking longingly at the remaining tongue at Odell's feet. Odell pitched him the pieces one at a time, and the Mexican caught them one-handed. Before Odell could offer him the use of his ramrod to cook them with, the man stuck another raw chunk in his mouth with the utmost pleasure.

"I sometimes find a dead carcass, but I can't always whip the wolves off of it," the Mexican added.

"These plains are a hell of a place for a man in your condition," Odell said. "What brings you out here?"

The little Mexican considered the question for a long time while he worried his meal around under the jaw teeth in one cheek. "I gather honey and sell it to the traders in Santa Fe."

Odell looked at the empty prairie surrounding them and thought the man was as crazy as he looked. There wasn't a tree anywhere for miles, and not even a single flower blooming amidst the dry grass. "I don't know where you'd find honey out here. Bees are bound to be as rare as water."

The Mexican started to laugh but seemed to run out of energy before he could. "Oh, no, I did my hunting in the mountains west of the Pecos. There are lots of beehives in the rocks there."

"Well, what brought you out on this godforsaken flat?"

The Mexican did laugh at that. "God is here too."

Odell looked around them again. "I'd say he ain't. If he was, he'd be real easy to spot."

"He is here, it's just a matter of knowing where to look, like spotting a single bee flying to or from the hive. A man can get caught up looking at all the nothing and miss what is right before him and all around him."

"Well, I'd say that's a funny way for a God to operate."

"The greatest mystery is why He even bothers with us at all." The Mexican crossed himself three times and muttered something to the Virgin Mary in Spanish.

"You ain't said how you ended up out here if you're a bee hunter."

"The bees disappeared above the Pecos, and I had a dream there was a canyon of honey to the east."

"You came across the plains in your shape because you had a dream?" Odell held his meat over the fire and tried to keep from scorching it.

"Dreams are not to be taken lightly. Sometimes I'm not sure if this is the dream, and the lives we live in our sleep are the reality."

"You must be a man of great faith to venture out here with nothing but a donkey and two little stubs for legs,"

Odell said. "Why, you don't even have anything to carry water in. How'd you make it this far?"

"I crawl to my burro every morning and then ride until I fall asleep. Sometimes he carries me while I dream, and sometimes I fall off and that is where we camp." The Mexican was already sticking another piece of buffalo tongue in his mouth. He started off again in Spanish, but saw the confusion on Odell's face and swapped back to his broken English. "*Gracias a Dios y sangre de Cristo*, he leads me to water when I need it. I drank yesterday evening from a buffalo wallow that still held a little water from the last rain."

Odell took his own breakfast from the fire and set it aside to cool. He himself had once tried following a herd of buffalo to some kind of water, but the stagnant, bug-ridden mudhole he found made him sick and worse off than he'd been before he discovered it.

"God provides if we have but a little faith," the Mexican said.

"He doesn't seem to be too generous with you," Odell pointed to the terrible scars where the Mexican's knees had once been. "What happened to your legs?"

"Iron Shirt broke my ankles and then gave me a knife to cut off my feet."

"Iron Shirt?"

"He's a medicine chief. I've been long on the Llano, but he's the meanest Comanche I've run across. I once had some sheep and a woman at Bent's Fort on the Arkansas, but Iron Shirt carried them away. I once hunted buffalo with the men of my village, but he killed many of us, stole my horse, and took my weapons. And when I decided to gather honey he caught me and roped me by the feet and drug me out on the Llano to die."

Odell tried to take a bite of the meat on his ramrod but it was too tough, and he had to stuff a whole piece in his mouth. His jaws were strong and his teeth in far better shape than the Mexican's, but they were no match for the tough tongue. The juice was at least satisfying, and he spat out the piece for a new one once he'd worked it dry.

"I thought you said Iron Shirt gave you a knife so you could cut your feet off. How come he didn't just do it himself?"

The Mexican laughed in a way that was a little disturbing. "He and his warriors sat around and watched to see if I could cut my feet off myself. They were already rotting before he gave me the knife and I would die if I didn't do it. It was more fun for Iron Shirt to wait and see if I would suffer more to live as a cripple than to torture me anymore himself. Comanches have strange senses of humor."

"So you cut your own legs off?"

"I did. My calves had already started turning black by the time I found my courage, and I wanted to make sure I cut high enough to get above the poison. After that, I stuck my stumps in a fire to stop the bleeding. I screamed until I lost my voice for many days."

"Well, I ain't no lover of Comanches, but I'd say you've got a grudge to top mine."

"Iron Shirt was impressed by the fact that I would cut my own legs off and then live through it. He didn't expect my medicine to be so strong, and he assumed I would lay there until I rotted and died or bled to death."

"Yeah, he sounds like a swell fellow."

"He brought me this burro and a bag of water the next day."

"I reckon he thought he was just torturing you more," Odell said.

"There is no knowing what a Comanche is thinking. I once thought I knew them, but I was a fool."

"They sure played a dirty trick on you."

"It was my own fault. I was vain and full of too much pride to think I belonged on the Llano. It asks a price of every man." The Mexican crossed himself again.

Odell hadn't slept at all the night before, and the warm meat juice in his belly was causing his eyes to droop. He wrapped his robe tight about him and lay down on his side in a faint patch of sunlight near the fire. He was asleep almost as soon as his shoulder touched the ground.

A noise woke him hours later. It was the sound of something dragging on the ground. He sat up groggily and it took him a moment to locate the sound. It was the Mexican crawling on his belly to where his donkey had grazed away from the fire.

"Hold on there, and I'll give you some help," Odell called out.

The Mexican just kept crawling. The burro was fifty yards off and grazing farther away. The sun was shining like the blizzard had never even been, and Odell tied his buffalo robe behind his saddle and checked his gear. He gave Crow half of the remaining water in his buffalo bladder canteen, pouring it in the crown of his hat for the gelding to drink. When Crow had finished, Odell squeezed the wet felt in his fist above his upturned face and let a few drops of liquid trickle into his mouth. He took one swig from the water bag and mounted and went to help the Mexican catch his burro.

He rode alongside the burro and caught hold of the hemp hackamore and lead the little animal was wearing. He led the gaunt long-ear to where the Mexican bee hunter was crawling through the short grass. He dismounted and brought the burro close to its crippled owner.

"Here, let me help you. You'd be in some shape if you let this old jackass get too far away."

The Mexican never looked up at him and shook his head vigorously while he continued to crawl. "No, I don't travel anywhere fast, but I eventually get where I'm going."

"I could just pick you right up and set you on him," Odell offered. It made him highly uncomfortable to see a man crawl like that. The bee hunter wiggled his torso like a snake and his arms pulled him along in a fashion that reminded Odell of an insect—as if the Mexican were no man at all, rather some new kind of animal alien to the world as it should be.

"No, this may be my penance and I wouldn't want to prolong it by taking your help." The Mexican had reached the burro and pulled himself up to a sitting position by its tail. He was breathing raggedly, but there was a smile on his face. "We all must crawl at some point in our lives. If we are lucky, we start out that way, but some come to such an end."

Odell went to his horse and retrieved the buffalo robe. He spread it across the burro's back. "Here, take that. It will give you some padding and keep you warm at night."

"*Gracias*, senor, but how will you keep warm?"

"I'm headed south, and besides, I think spring is here and I'll have plenty of time to kill me another one before next winter."

Both of them gave the empty distance an unsure look, bonded for a brief instant by the uncertainty that was the Staked Plains.

"Senor, you never said what brings you out onto the Llano."

"A Comanche tortured my pappy to death and scalped a neighbor of mine. He stole all our stock, burned our house, and killed my dog." Odell was getting to where the thought of that night wasn't as bad as it had been, but any mention of it still brought the pain back. "He wasn't much of a dog, and I guess they just killed him for pure meanness."

"That sounds like Iron Shirt."

"He was a little Comanche with big muscles and not much older than me."

"I don't know him. Iron Shirt wears Spanish chain mail and is an older man."

"Then he ain't who I've been after."

"I've heard about a small warrior they call Little Bull. He's supposed to be a great horse thief and war leader. Maybe that's the man who raided you. He is said to live far to the northeast along the Canadian. Maybe you can find him there."

"I'm about hunted out, and there ain't enough black powder left in my horn to blow the hat off of my head. I think I'll go back home and see if my girl will marry me." Odell didn't mention how tired he was. What he needed more than anything was rest away from all the worries of trying to keep himself alive in a land that didn't seem to want his company.

"See, the Llano has already given you wisdom. Go back to your home and marry your *novia*," the Mexican said.

"You wouldn't happen to know the quickest or best way to Austin would you?" Odell could only guess that the town lay somewhere to the southeast, or maybe it was just due east.

"No, I've never been there." The Mexican looked perplexed for the first time.

"Maybe you could just point me to the Colorado River."

"There is a supposed to be a big spring a day's ride to the east of here. It's in a little canyon just off of a big draw, and the Comanches use it enough that you ought to find it if you're careful. Angle southeast from there and in another day or maybe more you should come to the San Saba somewhere close to the old presidio," The Mexican offered a little tentatively.

"Thanks."

"Don't thank me. Thank God if you get there. I've never been east of the Llano, and what I tell you is only rumor. Your journey may be far from over."

"Well, that's more than I've had to go on since I left Old Star and those Wichitas last winter," Odell said.

The Mexican gave the burro's tail a couple of quick jerks, and to Odell's surprise, the little animal lay down docilely. The bee hunter crawled on his back and chucked until the burro rose back to its feet.

"Now that's a neat trick. How long did it take you to teach him that?"

The Mexican seemed a little perturbed at another question that regarded the consideration of time. "Maybe two years, maybe more."

"How'd you get on before that?"

"It wasn't easy."

"Well, I guess I'd better be riding," Odell said.

"Vaya con Dios, caballero."

Odell reined away, but pulled up short. "I didn't even catch your name. I'm Odell Spurling."

"I just saw a bee. *Andale*, burro." The Mexican swatted the burro's rump with his hand and rode off in a trot with his eyes madly searching the horizon to the east.

Odell followed along, as the bee hunter was going in the direction he needed to travel. They trotted a distance of two or three miles in an arrow straight line, until the Mexican suddenly turned and came back in the opposite direction. He passed by Odell as if he weren't there, blind to anything but the bee he thought he'd seen and the fevered vision that had led him out onto the Llano Estacado.

"Where are you going old man? Your canyon of honey is supposed to be to the east."

The Mexican didn't answer him. Odell thought about going back and leading the Mexican to water, but something told him that wasn't the thing to do. The Llano was a crazy, endless place, but he couldn't think of anywhere else the mad bee hunter might belong.

The two men traveled in opposite directions until they were diverging and vanishing specks on the plain who might not have ever even met. The only sign of their passing was the dust that rose under their animals' feet, but even that was short-lived and soon gone under the expanse of sky.

Odell finally quit looking behind him and cast his gaze homeward, or at least in the direction where he thought home might lie. He was whisper-thin and weather-cured, with the scraggly beginning of a man's beard hanging from his chin and the faint hint of coyote wisdom showing in his eyes. The hurt and turmoil within him had all but been boiled, frozen, and starved away by the wild country like the slow erosion of soft, red sandstone exposed to the elements. Lost as he was, something told him he was riding toward Red Wing, and he kicked Crow up to a lope with the sweet south wind cutting across his right cheek.

Chapter 12

Three days of monotonous travel had only deepened Red Wing's depression. The Peace Commission rode hard from sunup to sundown, and every mile they put behind them brought her that much closer to no longer being who she had become, to losing all that she had come to cherish. Every time she turned to look back behind her, a little bit of hope floated away from her like the faint smoke from coals banked beneath ashes. She hated the fear and cowardice that turned her cold and numb on the inside and made her feel like the wretched little squaw in a filthy rag of a dress she had been so many years before.

She passed the miles and days trying to remind herself that she was more than the color of her skin or the wild blood that ran in her veins. She wavered between angst and anger, between the urge to cry and the desire to scream at her captors. Memories of earlier pain and loss made her fearful of what was to come, but they also stiffened her resolve with the knowledge that she had already seen much of the ugliness life contained and was a survivor in spite of that. At those times she straightened her dress, pinned her hair back in place, and tried to sit a little straighter in her side-saddle. She gave her captors cold, haughty looks, and her eyes dared them to deny that she was anything but a lady.

The party was scattered in a single-file line with the Delawares scouting their front and flanks and the Waco chief guarding their rear. Commissioner Anderson usually rode at the head of the column, but he drifted back down the line to ride beside her. She observed how he knocked some of the dust from his jacket and ran his fingers through his hair beneath his lifted hat before coming her way. She knew he would soon make some attempt at polite conversation or ask about her comfort, as if the charade would convince her that he had her welfare at heart and that her situation was nowhere near as bad as it appeared to be. She wanted nothing more than to slap the smile from his face.

"We should reach the Waco village just before dark. Old Chief Squash back there has assured me he can provide us with warriors to guide and protect our party out on the plains," Commissioner Anderson said merrily.

"You're a fool if you think a handful of Wacos can protect you from the Comanche, much less that fat old chief." Red Wing stared straight ahead, but pointed her hand to the west. "Out there is Comancheria, not Waco land."

The smile on his face disappeared quickly, and it was plain that he didn't like to appear a fool to anyone. His free hand once again tugged at the front of his fancy jacket, and his back straightened even more in the saddle, as if braced by a steel rod. Red Wing remembered what her brother Bud had always said about such folks. She watched the commissioner out of the corner of her eye and thought that he did indeed look like he had a cob up his butt. She stifled a giggle with the back of her hand, not quite managing to keep it quiet.

"Do you find enjoyment in mocking me?" He too was now staring straight ahead.

"Commissioner, I've had no enjoyment whatsoever since I first laid eyes on you."

"Call me Will, please." He turned to look at her with his sharp blue eyes.

He was a handsome man. In fact, he was about the prettiest man she could ever recall seeing. He cut quite a figure sitting on his fine gray horse with his fancy coat and broad hat. But something about the brushed and polished look of him made her even madder, as if the spectacle of such a man in such a country teased and taunted her terrible predicament by his very existence.

"I could call you Will, but the good men of Texas will name you a low-down kidnapper and Comanchero when they learn of what you're doing."

"You can hate me if you want to, but it won't help you. If you'll keep your cool and cooperate with me, maybe we both can get out of this situation no worse for the wear." It was clear to her that he was fighting to maintain his calm.

"You want to trade me to the Comanches, and yet you ask me to be happy about it? What a scoundrel you are."

He took in the high lift of her little chin and the tight line of her full lips. Her hair was so thick and black that he couldn't help wanting to reach out and run his fingers through it. She reminded him more of some of the Mexican girls he'd danced with at the bailes and fiestas than a Comanche squaw. He wondered if President Houston had any idea of just what kind of girl he wanted traded to the Comanches.

But then again, his own ambitions had landed him in more than one difficult situation. One of his greatest regrets was that he had been born too late to fight against Santa Anna's forces in the War for Independence. It was a shame, because killing Mexicans was a surefire way to gain political office. Texans liked to vote for heroes, and the sad fact was that he was far too young to compete with the glut of veterans and old colonists that controlled the republic's destiny.

Family connections had once promised to open certain doors for him, but somebody always seemed to be a little better connected when it really mattered. At the ripe old age of twenty-five, a touch of wisdom and of introspection finally took hold of him in a roadside tavern on the way to San Antonio. The truth hurt, but he saw himself clearly for what he was—a penniless but educated adventurer with few prospects and not the price of a drink in his pockets. Big ideas had never materialized themselves into anything other than just ideas. His family had written him off, and all his business schemes and pandering to those in power had failed him in the end.

Just when it seemed his reckless life choices had ruined all his hopes of ever gaining the position and status he desired, a bone had been thrown his way in his appointment as a commissioner to the Comanche. President Houston had his enemies, but he had offered a promising young hellion a last chance at gaining the political station and status he sought. There were far better Indian fighters than Will Anderson, but anybody who knew the young man would tell you that he was smart as a whip. The republic's new Indian specialist had listened intently to Houston's plans for a peace expedition to the Comanche. He was a keen study of frontier gambling dens, and as such, he quickly surmised that while the odds were long against him, the prize was great indeed. The man who could put an end to the Comanches' raiding and pillaging of the frontier could go far in Texas.

He continued to study Red Wing's profile while he ran through a long checklist of his earlier failures. Begrudgingly, he had to admit that, thus far, the only thing Will Anderson was known for in Texas was a penchant for the ladies and a rare ability as a duelist. Both of those skills, in a roundabout way, had landed him on what he thought was a foolish trek westward to locate some Comanches who probably had no desire to talk peace with the hated Texans.

However, he refused to consider failure. There was no place for that in any of his plans.

"I've found that nothing ever turns out quite as bad as we expect," he said.

"I've found that they often turn out worse than we can even imagine." There wasn't a hint of remorse or complaint in her voice, and her gaze was steady and unblinking.

It wasn't the first time he had tried speaking with her to break the monotony of the trail, but he was having no better luck than usual. And that was a shame. She was really quite beautiful, and he would far rather pass the time of day with her than with the men of his expedition. Agent Torrey was a man lost and too overwhelmed with the wilderness to provide decent conversation. Captain Jones was as ambitious as he was and was cagey around his competition. The Delawares might have dressed like white men, but the mercenary gleam in their eyes made him sleep with a pistol in his hand. Chief Squash, the Waco, was talkative for an Indian, but the crafty wrinkles at the corners of his dark eyes and the overly zealous, fawning smile he had ready at a second's notice made him more of a nuisance than a companion.

Red Wing was well aware of the way the commissioner was staring at her. She reminded herself of her mother's words, and tried to temper her actions toward the man. "It isn't too late to turn around and take me back home."

He smiled, but it was easily apparent that it was just for show. "Well, that's the most civil thing you've said to me today."

"If you're worried about defying Houston, you can just turn away and act like you don't see me riding off."

The same tolerant smile was still on his face, but he was shaking his head solemnly. "I wouldn't have agreed to this if I'd known you first, but it's too late to back out now. Peace with the Comanche will save a lot of lives, and maybe all of Texas is at stake if the Mexicans are trying to get the

Comanche to ride against us while they attack from the south. President Houston trusted me to see this mission through. I gave him my word, and always finish what I start."

"Maybe breaking your word would be wrong, but so is taking me against my will. Where is the honor in that?" She was sure her words would have no impact on him, but she had to try.

"I wish life were as simple as that. I wouldn't expect a woman to understand, but I'll trust to duty to see me through." As he had for days since laying eyes on Red Wing, he reminded himself that he was only giving a girl back to a life she was born into, and that it was for the good of the republic that she went back to her people. There was little sacrifice in that. For all her talk and trappings, she was still an Indian.

Her anger grew until it almost broke through the cool outer shell she was fighting to keep up. It wasn't just his spit-and-polish vanity or his righteous excuses that drove her crazy. It was the way he looked at her, as if she were nothing more than a prize to be had and traded away on a whim. She had known that life with the Comanche. There were warriors among the bands who loved their wives and spoiled them, but as a whole, women were just another commodity to be bartered for or stolen. Wealth was measured by the number of wives a man could support, or the size of his horse herd and the bounty of his lodge. There had never been a time among the tribe that she was sure that the horses weren't rated higher than the squaws.

She cherished her new life as a member of the Wilson family, but that was one thing that hadn't changed among the whites. Since she had come into womanhood, supposedly civilized men had begun to look at her with hunger. It wasn't love that she felt in their stares but instead the desire to possess. She had a mind and a soul but wondered if any man would ever want them.

"Sometimes you remind me more of a Mexican senorita than a Comanche," he said.

"My mother was Mexican." She said it without thinking and immediately regretted sharing that with him, as if such information might lead him to assume he was her confidant.

"I've never been in a Comanche camp, but I've heard that there are a lot of Mexican captives."

"White, Mexican, it doesn't matter if they get you young enough. A Comanche can be made out of just about any kind of human on this earth."

"So, you're half Mexican, half Comanche?"

"I'm Red Wing Wilson, a settler's daughter you're taking away from her family."

"But your real father was a Comanche?"

She hated that she had gotten herself cornered into such a conversation. "Yes, he was a Comanche, and a noted war leader and hunter."

"I guess he stole your Mexican mama?"

"No, he traded three horses for her from a warrior called Dog." She tried to stem the tide of memories coming to her. She had sworn that she would never let any of her captors see her cry.

"Was it her that made you want to get away from the Comanches?"

"No, she loved her husband very much."

"Well, I thought maybe that explained why you don't want to go back."

"Do you mean that I'm more Mexican than Comanche?"

"Maybe your mama raised you to think that way."

"If I'm Mexican, then you have no right to give me to the Comanches."

The conversation wasn't going to the commissioner's liking, and he couldn't hide his frustration. He liked his women laughing or even slightly drunk, and not at all so smart or argumentative. "Colonel Moore captured you from the Comanches, and that's who I'm taking you back to."

"If he had found a white captive in the camp, would you take her back?" she asked. "I'll ride back home on my own, and you just tell Houston he was mistaken. Tell him that I was a Mexican captive instead of a Comanche."

He at least paused to consider things, if only to form another excuse. "No, that wouldn't work."

"You mean that it wouldn't matter if I was truly a Mexican? Just another shade of brown in your world, right?"

"President Houston says you're a Comanche, Colonel Moore says the same, and so does a lot of Texas. I guess that makes you a Comanche." He felt like cussing, but a gentlemanlike approach had always gotten him farther with the opposite sex.

It was plain to her that he was looking for a way to have his cake and eat it too. "If you think I find the company of a woman stealer and slave trader enjoyable, you are sadly mistaken. I would suggest you ride elsewhere and leave me to my misery. A good man would reconsider his actions and find reason to protect me and see me free. Perhaps such a man will come along and see justice done to a woman in need."

He clenched his jaw and his brow drew down over angry eyes, but he showed no willingness to leave her side. Before the conversation could go farther she spurred her horse ahead. She pulled up alongside Agent Torrey and smiled at him. The shy man gave her a bewildered look while he shoved his glasses back to a proper position on his nose. Even though he managed only a stuttered greeting, she laughed loudly and laid a light hand briefly on his shoulder. All the while she kept a watch on the commissioner out of the corner of her eye.

From the fierce scowl on his face she was sure he was taking it all in. Agent Torrey was still stuttering, but she laughed again anyway, as if he was the most charming man in the world, instead of the most awkward, bookish human she had ever met, too shy to even look her way after three days of travel.

Commissioner Anderson jabbed his horse too hard with his spurs, and the animal wrung its tail and kicked up behind as they loped back toward the front of the line.

"Agent Torrey, keep an eye on her and see that she doesn't try and run away again," he snapped at them in passing.

Before Red Wing could survey the position of the outriders to see if there was a chance to run, Chief Acequosh, or Squash as the white men in the party called him, also came loping by. He grinned at them and pointed up the trail. Red Wing studied the distance until she made out what he was trying to show them.

"Miss Wilson, you look like somebody just stepped on your grave," Agent Torrey finally managed to say.

He hadn't yet seen the smoke from the Waco village rising up from the river bottom ahead of them. Only minutes separated Red Wing from being under the watchful eyes of even more guards, and her chances of escaping would grow even slimmer. In a panic, she whirled her horse and cracked him across the hip with the tail of her reins. Agent Torrey's mount almost unseated him when it tried to follow hers. He righted himself in the saddle and watched her fleeing down the trail with the long braid of her hair bouncing against her back. The Delawares had spotted her, and they were whooping wildly and racing to head her off.

Red Wing urged her horse to all the speed it was worth and judged the narrowing funnel of the Delawares closing in on both sides of her. There was a slim chance of getting through before their converging lines intersected before her, but she had little hope of success. She had tried flight twice in the preceding days, and the Delawares had caught her every time.

Chapter 13

By the time Odell finally reached Sulphur Draw, he had been a day without water, and two days without anything to eat. To make matters worse, it didn't look like he was going to get any relief. Smoke was rising from the little side canyon where the Mexican bee hunter had told him the big spring was located, and several tepees were visible along the trickling stream at its mouth. Considering how scarce water was in those parts, Odell wasn't at all surprised that the place had so much company. He just wished the neighbors were a little friendlier.

Although Comanches had beaten him to the spring, he still had hopes of getting a drink. He was far away, but the thin line of a larger creek channel was clearly visible running down the huge draw. He had no idea whether it was good water, or if it had anything in it at all. Still, he couldn't help but imagine it running bank to bank with cool, clear water.

His first thought was to circle wide until he was far

enough downstream to be safe, but a long study and a brief
scout only served to inform him that the creek was bone
dry. Furthermore, it seemed that the spring-fed stream that
ran out of the side draw and through the middle of the Comanche camp seemed to soak into the ground before it went
much farther. Sulphur Draw was miles wide and treeless,
and it was plain that he wasn't going to get a drink that afternoon unless he was willing to trade his scalp for water.
The Mexican had told him it was over a day's ride on to the
San Saba, and neither he nor Crow were going to make it
that far without quenching their thirst.

He decided to hole up high on the opposite side of the
draw from the Indian camp and wait. Once night came, he
and Crow would slip down to water right under the Comanches' noses. There was even a chance that the camp might
move on during the afternoon and leave the oasis to him.
But he had little hope of that and settled temporarily for the
shade of a large rock. The Mexican had sworn that the big
spring was crystal clear and fourteen feet deep, and Odell
daydreamed of splashing and swimming in water so cold
that it put goose bumps on his skin.

Odell napped throughout the afternoon, and by dark his
tongue had begun to swell and his head was too foggy to
think straight. The glow of the campfires below told him
that the Comanches hadn't left. He saddled Crow and started
down to the floor of the draw. He stopped often to listen and
to consider his best approach. He was too thirsty to turn
back, but the hair on the back of his neck stood up every
time he heard something go bump in the night.

Not many months before, he might not have been so
worried about sneaking a drink in the night, but he had
grown more cautious where Comanches were concerned.
Despite all his plans for vengeance, he had failed to even
begin the war against them that he had once hatched in his
heart. In fact, he had found that a man alone could get himself killed in a hurry prowling around their country, much

less near their camps. A bad attitude and a little foolish courage meant little when you were vastly outnumbered and totally lost half the time.

Despite his travels, he had seen Comanches only twice since leaving the Prussian the fall before. The first time came when a small bunch of decrepit old men and a handful of squaws had come into the Wichita hunting camp to trade. They were a pitiful, starving lot who seemed to have come on hard times. Apparently their headman had gotten himself and his relatives kicked out of his former band over some gambling feud. Odell could find none of his recent hatred for Comanches when he looked at them.

His last encounter with the Comanches was after he had left the Wichitas to wander the Llano. He had topped a swell of land and stumbled right into a Comanche camp. There must have been at least forty lodges there, and he was almost in the middle of them before he knew it. By the time he recognized his predicament, the squaws going about their chores and the children on horse guard were already yelling warnings. Several braves returning from a hunt had closed off retreat behind him. There was nothing left to do but stick the spurs to Crow and ride right through the Comanche camp. He was there and gone before the highly surprised Comanches even had a chance to get a good look at the crazy white man on the fast black horse.

The predicament Odell was in at the moment felt like running that gauntlet all over again. A large herd of horses was scattered out some two hundred yards from the Comanche camp, and that meant there were guards about. His pappy used to tell him that sometimes you had to sink or swim, and he had come too far to back out. The moon was just a sliver in the sky, and he dismounted and led Crow among the herd, staying close to the horse's side. He stopped and started intermittently, hoping any sleepy guard would mistake Crow for just another grazing horse.

The night was dark, and he moved toward the camp more

by feel than anything else. He tried to picture just how far from the camp he had seen the Comanche horses watering during the afternoon before. He could see the Comanches' fires glowing through the hides of the nearest tepees, and he had no wish to get any closer to them than he had to. As it was, he was barely sixty yards from the edge of the camp when he almost stepped into the shallow creek before he saw it. He knelt beside Crow and lifted a handful of water to his lips. His nerves were wound tight, and the drops that escaped from his cupped palm sounded incredibly loud to him in the stillness.

He drank slowly and long, enjoying the cool water coursing through his body. When neither he nor Crow could hold another drop, he filled his water bag and started back the way he had come. He heard someone cough nearby, and his return trip seemed to take even longer than the eternity he had spent making his way to the water.

Once he was high above the draw, he climbed back in the saddle and started southeast. The safest thing for him to do was to ride by night until he was far away from the Comanches. The stars were bright overhead, but he knew nothing of navigating by the heavens. The San Saba River lay somewhere to the southeast, and he hoped he couldn't miss it. He looped his reins around his saddle horn and trusted Crow to keep them pointed in the general direction they needed to go. The water had saved him, but now that he was not dying of thirst he realized just how hungry he was. He dozed off and on in the saddle and dreamed of fried venison dipped in honey and glass after glass of cold buttermilk.

Come daylight he was twenty miles beyond the Comanche camp. His hunger was so great that it became all he could think about. The sight of a herd of antelope grazing his way excited him greatly, and he dismounted and took a stand behind a yucca bush to see if they might pass within rifle range of him. The buck must have spotted him, for he circled his little harem around Odell until he was straight downwind. Odell had only two more bullets left and barely enough powder to put behind them. There was nothing left to replace the last charge in his shotgun barrel. He debated on risking a long-range shot. Any Comanches around were sure to hear it, and he wasn't going to put up much of a defense with so little ammunition as was left to him. Just as he made up his mind to try a shot anyway, the entire bunch winded him and ran off with their white bottoms flashing and bounding away at a speed that made even Crow look slow.

Odell mounted up, and by afternoon he felt so light and hollow he feared he might blow away. The day was hot and the whole country seemed like a sweaty dream. He prayed for a buffalo, or anything that resembled good red meat. He must have gotten lost in his fancies of bountiful game prancing all around him, for he found that Crow had stopped in the middle of a wide-open plain with little of anything that could be considered a landmark. Even the high, flat-topped mountain that he had kept behind his right shoulder all morning had vanished in the distance. Odell had no clue whether he had stopped the horse, or if Crow had decided to take a break of his own accord. He studied the horizon all around him and wasn't even sure they were still headed east.

Some movement at the corner of his eye caught his attention, and before he could see what it was, something else moved right in front of him. He rubbed his eyes and stared at the little critters sitting on their haunches and staring back at him. They were about the size of a cottontail rabbit and looked something like a fat-bodied squirrel without the bushy tail.

He finally got his brain wrapped around the fact that he was looking at a huge prairie dog colony. He hadn't heard of anyone eating prairie dogs, but looking at them right then, he was quite sure they were the tastiest morsels on the face of the earth. He caught himself dreaming again and got down off his horse.

The little varmints sat by the mounds of earth around their burrows and craned their necks to study him and twitched their stubby tails. He hated to use up his last shotgun load, but the more he thought about what a prairie dog might taste like, the more practical it seemed. The trouble was getting into range before they ducked into their holes.

He slipped toward one bunch of them after another with Crow following loyally behind. Every time he was almost close enough to shoot, they disappeared into their dens. They waited until he had gone on in pursuit of their more distant neighbors and popped right back out behind him. They gave out shrill little whistles to warn each other, and he soon realized that he had been led along a giant circle through the dog town. It was if they were playing with him. He needed food in a most dire, primal sort of way, but the hunt was becoming a matter of honor. A strong dislike of prairie dogs began to build within him.

A particularly bold little rascal kept popping up some seventy yards away from him, and Odell tried a new tactic. If he stared directly at the animal, it would dive back into its hole, but if he kept sideways to it and didn't make eye contact, it didn't seem so nervous. Odell avoided looking that way and ambled along as if he were focused on something else. He chose a course that would take him near the prairie dog, without appearing to be stalking it. He was only forty yards away when he whirled and fired the shotgun. All he saw was a flash of brown fur as it disappeared in an explosion of dirt.

Odell shouted his victory and ran to the hole. When he arrived he saw only chewed earth, and no carcass. He fell to his knees and cocked his eye right over burrow opening. He remained on hands and knees, swapping eyes occasionally, but continuing to stare down the hole. He finally looked up and noticed a prairie dog sitting on a mound straight out in front of him. Starvation messed with his mind, and he wasn't at his rational best. As a result, he was sure it was the very same one who had dodged his shot.

"You think you're smart, don't you? Well, you have to get up mighty early in the morning to fool Odell Spurling."

Little white caliche rocks littered the ground, and he gathered one up. He threw it as hard as he could, but the prairie dog ducked into its hole. It quickly dawned on him that his aim and his velocity were no match for their reflexes or their sharp eyes.

He wondered how bad his big-bore rifle would tear up one of them while he waited for the dog to pop back up and laugh at him. He thought about how many times he had passed through prairie dog towns, and taken them for granted. Never had he imagined what devious little creatures they really were. Right then he promised himself that as soon as he got back to civilization he would purchase a couple of kegs of black powder and come back. Imagining the explosion and hundreds of prairie dogs blown from their holes soothed his wounded pride.

One of the enemy popped up in front of him. He watched the little whiskered nose curl up in a sneer as it rose up as high as it could on its haunches. He reared back to let fly with another rock, but the prairie dog disappeared in a flash. Odell drew his knife and charged toward the hole bellowing like a mad bull. It wasn't just food he wanted, it was a reckoning.

He stabbed wildly down the hole with the knife. When he realized the little genius had evaded him, he began to attack the burrow itself. He dug with the ferocity of a badger, and great spurts of dirt flew out between his legs and behind him. When he had worked down a foot, and widened the hole sufficiently enough to get one shoulder in, he stopped to listen. His keen hearing detected a faint sound.

"Now we'll see who has the last laugh." Odell was already laughing very oddly.

He dug more, and the sound grew louder and nearer. He plunged his arm into the burrow all the way up to his shoulder and his fingers groped blindly to find the prairie dog's hide. Something bit his hand, and he angrily shoved farther into the hole. His fingers wrapped around a victim, and he had drug it halfway out before it dawned on him that it was no prairie dog in his grasp. A shiver ran down his spine and he let go and scrambled back from the hole. Instead of fur he had felt scaly hide.

The rough treatment put the four-foot rattlesnake in a foul mood. It coiled at the mouth of the burrow and rattled its tail in fierce indignation. Odell raked the diamondback along the ground with his rifle until he could stomp its head. He decapitated it with his knife and flopped down beside it to examine his wound.

Two fang holes punctured the web of his right thumb, and he wondered if he was going to die. He remembered that one of his neighbor girls back in Georgia had died from a rattlesnake bite while picking huckleberries. Such thoughts weren't good for his morale. He reminded himself that the girl had been bitten on the neck by a seven-foot snake with a head bigger than a grown man's fist, and not just any run-of-the-mill, little prairie rattler.

Somewhere in the back of his mind he recalled hearing that the flesh of a serpent was supposed to be able to draw out venom. He quickly skinned and gutted it, and cut a cross section of the pale white meat. He held the snake meat poultice to his wound while he scowled at the prairie dog only a few yards away. The rodent seemed especially proud of itself and amused by the clumsy human's antics. Odell waved his good hand to scare it off, but the animal just sat there and stared.

"Dumb prairie dogs," Odell muttered.

He went and gathered enough dead yucca stalks to build a fire. He soon had a tiny blaze going, and meat roasting over it. He had no way of knowing if the snake's flesh would draw the poison from his body, but his stomach could well make use of some nourishment. Never would he have pictured himself eating such a thing, but after the first bite he decided that prairie dog would surely be poor doings compared to rattlesnake.

He finished off almost half of the snake and lay down beside the fire with a fresh piece of it held against his hand. He thought the pain had gotten better but decided it wouldn't hurt to rest a little. He felt the prairie dogs' beady little eyes on him, but he was too tired to worry about what evil plans they were hatching.

The stirring of Crow grazing around him and the hot sun scalding his face woke him after a long nap. His hand was swollen to twice its normal size and turning black. He was as thirsty as he'd been the day before, and he went to Crow and took down his water bag. He guzzled greedily and then poured some in his hat for the horse.

While Crow drank, Odell leaned against his saddle. He felt even sicker than he had before he fell asleep, and his whole right arm ached terribly. He tried to recall all the things he knew about snakebites and hoped he wouldn't lose his arm. There were dark streaks running up from his wrist, and he wondered if he would have to watch the poison spread through him one limb at a time.

The threat to his appendages brought the crazy Mexican to mind, and the image of spending the rest of his life limbless and worming around in the dust wasn't a pretty one. He had just about convinced himself that he was doomed to die a most heinous death when he looked across his saddle and saw a dozen Comanche warriors coming across the flat barely two hundred yards away. He looked to his little pile of ashes and knew that his smoke had called them to him.

Death by venom was much preferred to what the Comanches could dish out. He grabbed up his gun and the snakeskin and hit the saddle. He slapped Crow across the hip with the snake hide, and they lit out of there hell-bent for leather and barely three jumps ahead of the Comanches yipping and yelling at their heels. Crow must have been just as leery of Indians and rattlesnakes as his rider was, for he was motivated to a speed even Odell hadn't guessed he possessed.

It was a pretty close race for a mile, and Odell was praying Crow didn't trip or falter. His only chance lay in outrunning his pursuers, and Crow didn't disappoint him. Odell continued to whip him with the snakeskin, and after another bit the Comanches had fallen back to a more proper distance. Odell slowed Crow to a lope and then to a trot. He looked behind him and saw that the Comanches had pulled up, their horses used up after such a long sprint. Odell stopped Crow and slid off of him. The horse seemed to be breathing fine, but for the first time Odell really recognized just how thin and used he looked.

"Partner, you are starting to look like I feel," Odell said.

Crow shook the lather from his sides and tried to rub his sweaty bridle off on Odell's chest. Odell led the horse on, keeping an eye on their back trail, lest they have to run again. He intended to walk and rest Crow for a while, but he wasn't sure how long his own legs would hold up. He felt like death warmed over and hoped it wasn't far to the San Saba.

He thought they might make it if his hand didn't rot off, or if they didn't run out of water or rattlesnakes before they got there. Men who knew better might have called him a damned fool for such optimism, but he was sure that a little luck and a fast horse could see a man through some awful hard times.

And the Comanches had already begun to speak of him around their campfires at night. Word of the Running Boy who wandered the prairie alone spread from camp to camp and band to band throughout Comancheria. Many young warriors dreamed of taking the scalp of the young white giant who shot the big gun, used a rattlesnake for a quirt, and rode a horse as black as a thundercloud and as fast as the wind.

Chapter 14

The Waco escort Chief Squash had promised wasn't to be. Instead of a healthy bunch of warriors that would follow his lead, what the Peace Commission found was a village with half its population taken sick with a fever. Squash's wife hadn't eaten in two days, and lay in a sweaty state of delirium. The demons that ailed her were too strong for the healers, and Squash appealed to Commissioner Anderson to see if his white man's medicine could save her and the rest of the sick.

"I would just ride on. Indians are notional and superstitious folks. None of us are doctors and whatever illness has taken a hold of this camp looks to be bad." Captain Jones surveyed the village cautiously and wouldn't even dismount.

"Are you sure it ain't the pox?" Jim, the leader of the Delaware scouts, asked. He was the only one of his trio of tribesmen who would even ride in. The other two sat their horses at the edge of the village, having a somber discussion.

Red Wing could understand Jim's fear, because he was called Jim Pockmark. The pitted scars on his face let it be known that he had already suffered from the disease and lived to tell about it, as had Red Wing herself. No Indian survivor, or white for that matter, ever lost their fear of the killer that wiped out entire villages.

"It isn't smallpox." Agent Torrey followed Squash out of the lodge. He shoved his glasses back up his nose and looked up at the party still on their horses before the door. "She has a bad fever and nausea, but no lesions."

"It ain't the typhoid or cholera, is it?" Captain Jones asked.

"I don't think so."

Commissioner Anderson looked to Chief Squash. "Is it the same with all the rest of the sick ones?"

Squash merely nodded, his sly old eyes all but pleading.

"How long have they been sick?"

"Three days," Squash said.

"I'm telling you, don't get mixed up in this," Captain Jones said quietly.

Commissioner Anderson considered his predicament with a frown. "We need Squash's help, and we need the food he can supply us with."

Captain Jones looked to the corn, watermelon, and squash plants growing in the river bottom field just outside the village. "It's too early yet for them to supply us. The first of their crops won't be producing for another month."

"Jim and his Delawares may squawk about Squash being our Indian ambassador on this expedition, but he's the only one that has had any contact with the Comanche and can speak their language. You know as well as I do that the Comanche would just as soon kill a Delaware as a white man. Our mission would be in serious jeopardy without Squash."

Captain Jones studied the fat chief disapprovingly.

Squash was notoriously crafty, despite a reputation for being helpful. He had lived in peace with the Texans for years, but his motivations were always driven by what he could get in exchange for his goodwill, whether it was material goods or simply aid in the defeat of his tribe's traditional enemies. His guttural English was plenty good for him to understand everything they were saying.

"I don't trust him one bit," the captain whispered.

"Neither do I, but he's our ticket to meeting peacefully with the Comanche."

"We don't have time to dally here while you try and heal this village."

"We have all summer to get as many Comanches as possible to Fort Bird. Unforeseen delays and difficulties are bound to happen."

"I still say we ride on."

Commissioner Anderson ignored the captain and dismounted. "Agent Torrey, it is said you have some medical experience."

"I came to Texas overland with a doctor, but I wouldn't say what little I learned gave me any skill to speak of." Torrey looked extremely uncomfortable with where the conversation was leading, but then again, he generally looked uncomfortable.

"Nevertheless, you were given charge of outfitting us with the necessary medical supplies for our journey," the commissioner said.

"We have little in our kit beyond bandage material, a bottle of laudanum, some herbal concoctions, and two quarts of whiskey."

"Fetch the kit, and let's get to work."

"I wouldn't even know where to begin. How can we doctor them without even knowing what they're sick with?"

"Let's just give it our best, and make a show of wanting to help."

Agent Torrey wanted to stand his ground and refuse, but

Commissioner Anderson intimidated him far more than pretending to be a doctor. He wasn't an assertive man, and his whole life had consisted of taking orders that led him to do things he would rather not. He wasn't even sure how he had ended up being chosen to go along with the expedition. It was readily apparent to him that such confident men as the commissioner seemed to look for adventure as a matter of everyday occurrence.

"Forget whatever you're thinking about and get the medicines. The whole village is staring at us." The commissioner's voice was gentle, yet commanding.

Torrey started for the packhorses. The commissioner's reminder made him all too aware of the crowd of Wacos surrounding them. Normally, a friendly arrival in an Indian camp was a noisy, happy affair, but the worried Wacos stood somberly with their dark eyes boring into him. Too many people's attention on him all at once always left him feeling like he was too small for his clothes and awkward to the point that he wasn't even inside his own body. At least walking to retrieve the medicine bag alleviated some of that shrinking, disjointed feeling.

Once he returned with the medical kit, Chief Squash led him and the commissioner into the lodge. Captain Jones with Jim Pockmark and the Delawares went off to tend the horses. Agent Torrey was surprised that Red Wing followed them inside. Her face was unreadable but calm, and somehow that soothed his shaky nerves.

The circular lodge was large with sleeping platforms spaced along the curve of the wall surrounding the center support posts and fire pit. The grass roof had a hole at its peak to vent smoke, and the only light within was a spear of sunlight that pierced down through it to ricochet in a small circle in the center of the room. The beds along the wall were partitioned for privacy, but the hide curtains were pulled back where Squash's wife lay attended to by a small group of female family members.

Both white men were a little surprised at Squash's demeanor. He exchanged a few quiet words with the eldest of the squaws before taking a seat next to the cold ashes of the fire pit. The commissioner and his group stood unsure while the squaws seemed to debate whether they should give way to the strangers or not.

"Wacos are like the Wichitas and Keechis. Women head the family," Red Wing said.

"Ah, they are matriarchal," Agent Torrey said.

"Matri-what?" The commissioner frowned.

"Family descent is through the mother rather than the father. I would assume that the lodges are family units ruled by an extended group of sisters and their female offspring. When a man marries, he goes to live among his wife's people."

"I thought what you said the first time sounded bad," the commissioner muttered. "That just goes to show how backward Indians can be."

"Comanches would never give their women such power." Red Wing was more than a little surprised at the hint of scorn in her own voice.

"If these women don't want to move, we may have some problem wading through them. That old crone with the soup bowl looks plumb mean. As well armed as we are I'd say it's about a standoff." The commissioner tried to keep smiling at the squaws even while he spoke.

The ancient matriarch said something loudly in her native tongue and pointed one bony finger at Agent Torrey, who had the bad luck to be standing slightly forward of the others. The old woman's flat, bare breasts swayed against her potbelly as she waggled her finger's aim back and forth from him to the sky. His pale face blushed red at the sight of the ponderously flapping remnants of what had once been the source of his greatest interest in the female anatomy. From his first arrival at the village he had been bashfully ducking his eyes and avoiding the ripe offerings of half-naked womanhood evident everywhere, but somehow he couldn't look away from sagging teats of a toothless crone scolding him without concern for the discomfort her lack of dress was causing him.

Squash said something loudly, and the old squaw glared at his back and grunted. She gave Agent Torrey's medicine bag a disdainful look and stepped aside. The younger women moved back to give him some room, but he still felt too crowded to move. The commissioner's hand on the small of his back nudged him forward.

"I don't have a clue what to do for her," he said.

"Just act like you care. Do a little hocus pocus and give her something." The commissioner was standing behind Agent Torrey and looking at the sick woman over his shoulder.

Agent Torrey couldn't tell whether the patient was conscious or not. Her eyes were closed and her breathing was so shallow he couldn't see the rise or fall of her chest beneath the robes she was covered in. Her forehead was hot to his touch, and his shaking hand came away wet. Gently, he pulled back her covering and the soured smell of sweat and sickness almost made him gag. Nobody around him seemed to notice that she was naked, and he forced himself to gently probe her abdomen. A faint moan issued from her lips, and she grimaced and tossed wildly when he pressed harder.

"What do you think?" the Commissioner asked impatiently.

"I think she's sick and dying." Agent Torrey lifted his ridiculous hat to wipe the sweat from his bald little head.

"Well, give her something."

"I could kill her just as easy as I could heal her." The press of bodies around Agent Torrey had him feeling jittery and sick himself. He sat on the edge of the bed and took a few deep breaths to steady himself.

Red Wing took a seat at the patient's head and began to

bathe the woman's face with a wet rag from the pot of water the squaws had been using. She smiled at him and looked to the crowd around them. "Perhaps Agent Tom could work better if we could give him more room."

Squash and the squaws had a short, contentious discussion. The result was that the women didn't leave, but they did move back several steps and made a halfhearted attempt to appear busy with other things.

"Has she been vomiting or had any loose bowels?" Agent Torrey tried to sound more assured than he felt.

The commissioner repeated the question to Squash, and the chief replied with a negative shake of his head.

Agent Torrey opened his bag and stared dubiously at the contents within. The leather satchel had been the property of a drunken doctor who had fallen from his buggy in a state of intoxication and had his head run over by the rear wheel. His wife had been willing to sell her deceased husband's tools of the trade on credit to the Peace Commission, even when many were beginning to scoff at the notion that the Republic of Texas ever paid its bills. Agent Torrey had been glad to check off another item on the expedition's purchase list of supplies, but he didn't have a clue what most of the various compartments in the medical bag contained.

He took out a few tiny jars and paper packets and stared at them dumbly while he stalled for time. Of all his choices, only a pint bottle labeled "Croup Tonic" showed any promise. People called any cough or winter illness "the croup." While he had seen no signs of coughing or raspy lungs, he was almost sure that such a generic term was bound to encompass what ailed Squash's wife. Spring rains and damp conditions could give anyone a cold. Very few people except children died of the croup, and surely the medicine required for such a simple illness couldn't do any harm.

He considered himself a well-read man and abhorred most all kinds of ignorance. He had never claimed to be a doctor, and he was unable to make a random guess when

lives were at stake. Just when he was about to give up hope
and flee from the lodge a gleaming chunk of red in a paper
sack at the bottom of the bag caught his eye. He immediately
snatched it up and touched it to his tongue. A wry smile
showed faintly on his face and he quickly slipped the large
pill between his patient's lips. She struggled for a moment
to spit it out, but Red Wing cupped her hand gently over the
woman's mouth and held it there until she ceased to fight.

As if gaining courage by his choice, Agent Torrey un-
corked the croup tonic. He squeezed the sick woman's
cheeks until her lips puckered open in a little circle, and
poured a slug of the medicine into her mouth. Most of it
leaked out over her chin, but she didn't choke. Displeased
with the dosage, he repeated his actions. He spilled less the
second time and upon inspection found that she had swallowed the pill with the tonic.

He buckled the leather bag shut and looked up to the
commissioner. "I understand that she hasn't drunk for two
days. Make it plain to Squash that she must have fluids or
she will surely die. Broth and all the water she can be made
to take would be best."

"Squash does speak English."

Agent Torrey looked timidly at the chief through the haze
of his sweat- and grease-smeared lenses. He was sure that
the biggest joke in the entire world was the fact that he had
been appointed an Indian agent. Until coming to Texas he
had never laid eyes on a wild Indian. His only qualifications
were his reading of several journals by American naturalists.
Upon his arrival in Houston he had attempted to sketch the
natives he had met, and the president must have been highly
impressed with his clerk's renderings—as if simple sketches
implied some knowledge of his subjects.

He was sure he was by no means qualified to speak with
any Indian, much less a chief. "I think I need some fresh air."

They all watched as he took up his bag and sidled his
way through them and out the door. Red Wing handed care

of the patient back over to her family and followed him while the commissioner relayed Agent Torrey's instructions to Chief Squash.

When Agent Torrey burst out the door the first person he saw was Captain Jones squatted in the shade of a nearby arbor. He had his rifle across his knees and was watching the crowd of Wacos with no love at all. The Delawares were nowhere in sight.

"Don't quit now, Doctor. There are more patients to attend to," the commissioner said before Agent Torrey could take a seat.

Agent Torrey looked at his superior with horror but obediently followed him to the next lodge. More determined in his actions, he dispensed with the tonic all together. Twenty house calls later and his sack of red pills was all but empty.

The Wacos offered the party the use of an arbor with a raised floor for the night, but they refused and set up camp just outside the village. Spending the night in a village with sickness running rampant made them afraid of hospitality. The Delawares had killed a yearling deer and the group gathered around the fire and made quick work of the venison.

Agent Torrey found it amazing just how much food active men on almost a straight meat diet could consume. Normally, he could have eaten more than his share, but weariness and frazzled nerves had ruined his appetite. He dragged his saddle to the downwind side of the fire, hoping the smoke would keep the mosquitoes off of him. It was too sultry to need a blanket, and he simply flopped down with the saddle for a pillow. He stared sleepily between his outstretched feet at the flickering flames.

"Well, Agent Tom, did you cure them or kill them?" Captain Jones asked from across the fire.

"I don't know."

"What was that pill you were giving them? Some chewed

it up before they swallowed it, and seemed to even like it. I'd swear it looked like hard candy," the commissioner said.

Agent Torrey managed to laugh. "That's what it was, just plain old red candy."

Commissioner Anderson tried to glare a hole through him. "Just what good is that supposed to do them?"

Agent Torrey was too tired to cringe. His eyelids were impossibly heavy and he gladly closed them and forgot about the commissioner's accusing stare.

"Well, one thing's for certain. He isn't going to kill them with candy." The commissioner pitched the dregs of his coffee cup in the fire.

"No, but them dying of their own accord might be just as bad as if he killed them. The Wacos aren't going to know the difference," Captain Jones said.

The commissioner scowled at him and turned from the fire. He liked being in command when everyone wasn't giving him bad reports or discomforting observations. While he thought about their predicament, it dawned on him that something didn't seem right. He whirled back to the fire.

"Where's Red Wing? We've let her run off again!"

Red Wing hadn't run, at least not yet. She stood at the picket line beyond the fire and stroked the muzzle of her horse. She could hear the captain plainly, and her mind raced to determine if the night still offered her any chance of escape. Had she known the men were so tired and distracted she would have already been gone. Now the Delawares were probably slipping through the darkness searching for her.

The commissioner may have been proud of his tame scouts, but the way they looked at her sometimes made her skin crawl, especially Jim Pockmark. Thinking of his hungry, predatory eyes and the constant sneer on his face made her hand reach for the little antler-handled knife in the pocket of her dress. She had stolen it from one of the Waco lodges, and she turned the weapon in her hand slowly. It was a puny thing, more fit for cutting up supper than killing a man, but anything that might give her a fighting chance felt good with the Delawares prowling around.

She heard running footsteps to each side of her and made a beeline for the fire shining through the trees. She slipped the knife back into her pocket and smiled as she stepped into the firelight, as if she'd only left for an evening stroll.

Chapter 15

The Prussian stopped his horse in an oak thicket atop a little mountain and scanned the ground between him and the river for sign of his Tonkawa scouts. After a long look, he finally made out Placido loping back to him with three of his warriors, dodging and weaving through the sparse brush on the little stretch of prairie. From the Tonk chief's demeanor, all seemed well with the trail ahead, but the Prussian paused before starting down the slope. He studied the men to either side of him with pleasure.

The Tonks under Chief Placido had been at the headsprings of the San Marcos River just as he had hoped, and thirty-two of them had been more than willing to ride against their ancient enemy, the Comanche. The Prussian was a well-known fighter, even if a strange and not particularly likeable man. Any company under his leadership was bound to mean there would be victory spoils.

What hadn't been certain was his ability to locate and entice the kind of Texan fighters necessary to fill out his war party. A land where the threat of Indian attack was more certain than the weather was bound to produce men skilled in the ways of frontier warfare—survivors of a brutal testing ground where the weak were sifted like chaff on the wind. The problem was that such men were fiercely independent and notional to say the least. Any number of them could be counted on to ride to avenge an Indian raid, but the trick had been to get a suitable number of them to buck the will of Sam Houston and to convince them that he could locate a Comanche camp without being ambushed first.

However, two things played well in the Prussian's favor. Houston's pet theories on peaceful relations with the tribes weren't very popular with most Texans, and the Prussian let it be known that he intended to follow in the Peace Commission's wake and let them lead him to the Comanche. The fact that the Wilsons were well-known and loved members of Stephen F. Austin's original colonists, or the Old Three Hundred, didn't hurt. No matter that Red Wing was Comanche herself, the audacity of Houston taking the Wilsons' adopted daughter didn't play well with the kind of men brave enough to do something about it.

The news that he was mounting an attack on the Comanche and going to get the Wilsons' daughter back ran like wildfire along the frontier grapevine. The Prussian had spread the word as he traveled, and volunteers trickled in one at a time, and sometimes in bunches of twos and threes. They were all grim-faced men with good horses and well-cared-for weapons. They were the kind that needed little encouragement to fight and that died hard. Many of them had chased Indians for the government when it wasn't too broke to pay such ranging companies. They had no official sanction for the Prussian's expedition beyond his militia appointment, but then again many of them had been going out after the Comanche long before Texas was even a republic. By the time the Prussian struck the Colorado where it bent to the west, he had twenty-five of Texas's finest at his side, plus Placido's Tonks.

He looked to his right and the first man he saw was Hatchet Murphy. A Comanche war club had twisted and crushed his right cheekbone, and left the eye on that side of his face a sightless, weeping, white orb. He had once been a blacksmith, and besides the shotgun he carried like it was an extra limb, there was a blood-rusted, custom war hatchet stuffed in his belt. His wife and children had died at Victoria in the Great Comanche Raid of 1840, and it had driven him more than a little crazy. He had left his trade and disappeared for two years before anybody saw him again. When they did, he had five tanned Comanche scalps and twice that many ears hanging off one of his latigo saddle strings.

And then there was Manuel Ortega. He wasn't big as a minute, but the little Mexican was hell on wheels in a scrap with a gun or a knife and he was an equal match on horseback for any Comanche ever born. He had spent three years of his boyhood as a Comanche captive, and that time hadn't improved his opinion of those he called "*los diablos de Tejas.*"

To the Prussian's left was Kentucky Bob Harris, hero of San Jacinto, and survivor of the Santa Fe Expedition. He was possibly the best rifle shot in Texas, and to those present that meant the world. The veterans of the Cherokee War had watched him kill two Cherokee warriors with his fancy squirrel rifle at distances that seemed impossible. Kentucky Bob never went anywhere without his brother, Dub. Dub wasn't as fine a marksman, but he was an uncommonly strong, mean bastard. Anybody who could pick two Mexican soldiers up over his head and throw them back among their own, as he had during the fight with General Cos at San Antonio, was a good man to have in a fight.

And just beyond the Harris brothers was the one man besides Placido that the Prussian was most glad to see. There was no guessing just how old Son Ballard really was. He had been traipsing around Texas when there wasn't anything there but mustangs and mesquite beans. He looked to be a hundred, but he could travel all day either on horseback or afoot without complaint. When foul weather and hardship turned most men back, old Son was still grinning and laughing. He knew Texas as few men did, and nobody who called him friend was ever surprised if he showed up anywhere from the Rio Grande to the Red, from the Sabine to the Pecos. He was a wanderer to say the least. Son swore he could smell Comanches, and that the hair on the back of his neck stood out and warned him when an attack was imminent. Maybe that was true, because after all his years traipsing the distances alone, he still had a full head of hair, and nothing more than a faraway look and a weathered countenance to ever prove where he had been.

The other twenty white men that rounded out the Prussian's volunteer ranging company were all of the same sort. The Comanche had pretty much pillaged and plundered at will as long as there had been Texans around to kill, and it was high time the hostiles got a dose of their own medicine. If President Houston's Peace Commission worked, it was going to gather a large number of the Comanches together for them to attack. Old Sam might have good intentions, but he never had understood that the only good Comanche was a dead one.

The Prussian started them down off the mountain, a tiny army of good men, if a touch hardened by the times, filibusters and self-motivated mercenaries every one, loyal to nothing but their families, friends, and their own ideas of justice. No drums or regimental flags proclaimed their march, and few would remember their daring if they didn't return. Earlier failures had taught these men that the only way to whip Comanches was to copy many of their tactics, and that meant traveling fast and light, and striking hard when they got there. There were no supply-laden pack trains to slow them, and every man carried his own larder in his saddlebags, mostly relying on nothing more than a little salt and coffee and whatever they could procure during their travels to feed them in the coming days or weeks. If game was scarce, they went hungry; if water couldn't be located, they died.

Grown men and weapons were heavy enough, and there was no grain for their horses to further weigh them down. The individual mounts were the best each man could procure, speed at a premium and endurance a must. Their war-horses had to be as tough as the Comanche ponies and able to live off nothing but whatever grazing was at hand after a hard day's travel. A man afoot in the country where they were going was as good as dead, and he had better choose his mount wisely.

While their weapons were different from the Comanches', the men following the Prussian were savages of a sort themselves. No town-tamed citizen of more civilized parts could view them and not wonder what barbaric horde they belonged to. They brought the blood feud with them from places like Tennessee, Arkansas, Louisiana, and Alabama. They migrated from mountains and backwoods bayous already hacked into submission by blood, sweat, and ax. Some of them came to Texas to avoid debts, others to avoid being hung, and some because the lands they left had already grown too tame and stagnant for such free-thinking men. The Comanche were their sworn enemy, gave no quarter, and had no understanding of mercy. Neither did the Texan fighter, and he would keep at the Comanche until one of them was wiped off the face of the earth.

They rode hard for two days, and when nearing the old presidio forty miles along the San Saba River, the entire party pulled up to study the lone figure waving at them from the rock ruins. The Tonk scouts were already cautiously flanking the man on the north bank, but most of the party didn't need their guides to tell them what their own eyesight already had. It was a white man yonder, and he looked to have come a long way and played hell getting back from wherever he had been.

Chapter 16

Odell sat on a tumbled section of stone wall and studied his visitors around the campfire. The sight of them made him uneasy, and it wasn't just the fact that he had been long away from his own kind. He had been looking forward to talking with the first Texan he met on the trail, but never had imagined running across the likes of this war party. At first he had hidden in the ruins of the presidio, alarmed by the sight of the Indian scouts riding in advance of the procession. Time in the wilds had made him cautious, and even after spying the white men he took long to come out of hiding.

"Herr Odell, I didn't expect to see you again. You are strong to survive so long alone out there." The Prussian pointed to the west with the curved stem of his pipe.

The sight of that pipe made Odell think of his pappy. He poked at the campfire with a mesquite root while he tried to shut out such thoughts. "I don't know that I ever expected to see you again either."

"What happened to your hand?" the Prussian asked.

"My supper bit me." Odell studied his still discolored, but healing snakebite. Three days of rest, and the venison from a whitetail doe who had wandered too close to the ruins had gone a long ways toward nursing him back to health.

"You've come far and must have seen many things that few men have," the Prussian said.

"Huh?" Odell answered absentmindedly. He was acutely aware of the men around the fire quietly and expectantly staring at him.

It came as a shock to him to remember that it had been nearly a year since he left the settlements. How could he put to words how he had lived for the past long months—the heat and cold, the eternity of stars glittering in the night's blackness, the endless nothing all the way to the horizon that was as much an origin as it was a destination? He thought of running buffalo with the Wichitas, of the shrill cries of the hunters coming out of the dust, and the drum of thousands of hooves thumping the ground. He closed his eyes to the hot glare of the fire and he could see again the long procession of the village on the move with chattering children and barking dogs weaving in and out of the line of march. They were a laughing people, migrating to the rhythm and surge of their horses' strides, called into the distance as if by some primordial memory and urge that even a white man such as he could feel. How could he explain to them just what it felt like to leave all civilized concerns behind and live like the life between sunup and sundown was all that mattered?

"I've seen some things," Odell said quietly.

"Did you ever find that Comanche, or any Comanche?" the Prussian asked.

Odell didn't want to admit how fruitless his wanderings had been after all his bold predictions of vengeance. His so-called knack for survival had less to do with his courage or skill and more to do with Crow being able to run almost any old Comanche pony into the ground. "I've cut their sign a time or two."

"I intend to find the Comanches, and a large village of them if possible." The Prussian's eyes were unblinking as a snake's. "We've come to fight, and we have the men and the numbers to do it."

Odell wasn't about to tell the men around him that he thought looking for Comanches in large numbers was like going bear hunting with a switch. The Prussian's Texans looked formidable, but having seen the Comanches up close and personal, he wouldn't guarantee whipping them even when the numbers on both sides might be even. And he had no hope of outnumbering them. He had seen signs of a lot of Comanches on the plains.

"I'm no tracker, but I think the Comanches are already riding the war trail. I came across a camp two days west of here, and all the tracks away from it were pointed south to Mexico," Odell said.

The Prussian considered what he had just heard. He knew as well as many in his company did, that it was hard to find Comanches in any numbers, except when you didn't need to find them. The springtime would have the bands broken up into small hunting groups, but he was counting on the Peace Commission to gather the enemy for him. The best way to fight Comanches was to attack them in their camps. The confusion of a swift surprise attack had far more chance of success than a set battle where the enemy had time to organize.

"If we don't strike the Peace Commission's trail to the north by the time we reach the Concho, I intend to ride for the Red." The Prussian looked around him at the faces of the men gathered around the fire. "Herr Ballard, what do you think?"

Son Ballard stretched a buckskinned leg to the fire and the craggy lines of his face deepened into a grimace of aching, old joints. "That country between good water on the Brazos and the Red is a hard stretch of ground if you don't bear to the east. If we ain't half starved and afoot by the time we make the Red, the country between there and the Arkansas is pretty easy traveling."

"You think we might have to go so far?" the Prussian asked.

"We might. The Comanches will be following the buffalo north. The Peace Commission is going to have to hunt them down just like us, and the Comanches ain't waiting around for anybody when there's meat to be put up after a long winter. From what you say, I guess Chief Squash will take them up the Brazos past his village and on to the northwest of Fort Bird on the Trinity. It figures that they'll head for the Canadian if they have any sense. The water's better along that route, and they have a better chance of getting the northern bands to come to a meeting at the fort. They've had fewer run-ins with us Texans over the years."

"Then we ride north by northwest until we find them." The Prussian pitched a piece of salty, hard bacon rind into the fire and all were silent while it hissed and sizzled on the coals.

"Where we're going you'd better save even your rind. It might not be so long until we'll all be chewing on our saddles," Son said.

"What's this Peace Commission y'all are talking about?" Odell asked.

The Prussian stared at him with his brow lowered, as if the question angered him. "President Houston has assigned them to trade Red Wing back to the Comanches."

Odell fought not to stutter or stammer. "What?"

"They're a damned party of Injun agents and they've kidnapped that girl," Son Ballard said.

"I don't just intend to kill Comanches. Red Wing and the Peace Commission is what brought us out here," the Prussian said.

There were a million questions running through Odell's mind. "What chance do we have of heading this Peace Commission off?"

"If we catch up to them, we will convince them or bluff them into setting Red Wing free. They aren't likely to give her up to us without a fight, and Sam Houston isn't a man to make an enemy of. Will Anderson may be the spoiled son of a Galveston schooner captain, but he has a reputation as a fighter. Killing him or his men is a quick way of becoming an outlaw," the Prussian said.

"I thought you were riding to rescue her," Odell said quickly. The thought of Red Wing in danger and lost to him churned his guts and made his heart pound. He didn't care who he had to fight, Texans or Comanches either one. He was going after her, and anybody foolish enough to stand in his way could take the medicine they had coming.

"Herr Odell, I am going to get her back, but we have to play this carefully. If they won't give her up, our best bet may be to join their party. If we can attack the Comanche at just the right moment, we can put an end to Houston's crazy peace talks. Without anybody to trade with, Commissioner Anderson will have to give Red Wing back to me."

"To you?" Odell didn't like the blunt hint in what the Prussian said.

The Prussian sighed as if he had news that he would rather not deliver, and then lied, "Herr Odell, Red Wing and I planned to be married this spring."

The news hit Odell like a punch in the stomach. "I don't believe that. She as much as told me she was my girl before I went after those Comanches."

"Maybe. I'll call no man a liar without good cause or a willingness to defend my word as a gentleman." The Prussian paused to let that soak in with Odell. "You were gone a long time, and we all assumed you were dead. I asked her and she said yes."

Odell's hands gripped the mesquite root until his

knuckles turned white. The Prussian was within easy reach and he wanted nothing more than to knock the smug look off of his face. He tried to calm himself enough that his words wouldn't come out shaky.

"No offense, but I'll hear it from her myself. If what you say is true, it doesn't mean she can't change her mind."

"I take it that you are riding with us?"

"You can bet your sword I am. I don't intend to lose Red Wing to you or anybody else."

The Prussian smiled coldly. "We shall see, won't we?"

"I reckon." Odell kept his eyes on the Prussian's sword and the pistols at his waist. He wasn't fool enough to believe that smile meant anything funny.

The two of them stared across the fire at each other like buffalo bulls taking a breather between butting heads. Odell wasn't about to blink first or seem unwilling to take things as far as the Prussian wanted them to go.

"There's nobody following us." A giant Indian with a rifle cradled in one elbow stepped into the firelight to stand beside the Prussian.

Odell had never seen an Indian so big, and he wasn't sure what to make of him. There was a look about the Indian that reminded him of the Comanches. The savage face was covered in small scars and the statuesque nose and jaw bespoke a fierceness and a wild restlessness that put Odell instantly on guard.

"I feel it in my bones that Comanches are following us, and yet your scouts have found nothing." The Prussian seemed as comfortable with the big Indian towering over him as he would be swapping stories with family.

"Nothing but old tracks." The Indian's English was good but short and clipped. Despite his appearance, he seemed at ease and familiar with the company of whites.

"Comanches?" the Prussian asked.

"Yes, and others too. Many tribes are out after the buffalo."

Odell still couldn't get over the presence of the massive Indian.

The Prussian must have noticed, because he jerked a thumb at the man beside him. "I see you haven't met the famed Placido, Tonkawa chief, terror of the Comanches, and the finest ally a Texan ever had."

"No, I never."

"Placido, meet Herr Odell Spurling. By *Gott*, the two of you are pair big enough to pull a wagon."

The Tonkawa acted as if he noticed Odell for the first time. His face was unreadable, but there was a devilish twinkle in his eyes. "How, Odell. Not many white men can make it to the Llano and back alone."

Odell merely nodded, not quite knowing what he was agreeing with.

"Herr Odell, I'm sure the men will donate enough powder and lead to rearm you. We ride at daylight and I swear by King Frederick's hairy ass that we'll keep on riding until we find Red Wing and have given the Comanches a fight." The Prussian turned away and walked off into the night.

Odell was left staring at where the Prussian had been. He kicked the coals at the edge of the fire angrily and brooded over his concerns. Son Ballard chuckled and a couple of the men joined in.

"What are you laughing at, old man?" Odell snapped.

Son's pale blue eyes, made paler and watery by years under the prairie sun, seemed to look right through him. "If the Comanches don't kill you, the Prussian is liable to."

"Me and him have ridden together before. We've got no grudges that would require a killing."

Son laughed softly again. "Karl doesn't need much reason to cut a man wide and deep. From what I just heard, you and him want the same woman, and that's been reason enough for more than one bloodletting."

"I reckon we'll have the Comanches to keep us busy," Odell said.

"If you cross that German, you'd better keep an eye on that pig sticker he carries. Old Bob Carney complained about his run of cards and the Prussian's dealing one night. Bob was drunk and slow and got himself opened up from his gizzard to his pecker." Hatchet Murphy leaned into the flames and leered at Odell with his one good eye.

Odell didn't tell any of them that he had seen what the Prussian could do with his saber. "I'll do my share of fighting when you need me, but I ain't looking for trouble."

"Nobody goes looking for the Prussian. They must raise 'em mean where he comes from," Son said.

Odell pitched his poker in the fire. He was sick of hearing how tough the Prussian was, and hoped his silence would turn the conversation elsewhere. He reached to his belt and pulled out a massive sheath knife and studied it by the firelight.

"What's that you've got?" Son Ballard asked with a hint of something more than just natural curiosity.

Odell held the knife a little farther out into the light. The once rusty blade showed brightly where he had been polishing it with handfuls of sand. "I found it not far from here."

"Would you mind if I look at it?" Son reached out for the knife, and Odell noticed that a couple of the other men were looking on with equal interest.

Odell passed the knife across the fire to the plainsman. He couldn't explain it, but he felt a jealous pang at seeing the knife in someone else's hands. There was something about the knife that that he liked, something special.

"Where'd you say you found this?" Son turned the knife in his hands and studied it as if it were the intricate workings of a watch.

"I found it at the foot of a runt oak in a thicket," Odell said.

Son turned to look at Hatchet Murphy who had ceased sharpening his hatchet with an Arkansas stone to stare at the knife. "Murph, it couldn't be, could it?"

Hatchet Murphy took the knife for a while, and then passed it on to the man beside him. "I was in San Antonio when Colonel Jim came back from these parts. He said he'd lost his knife and thought maybe he'd left it lying on the ground at one of their camps."

Odell didn't have a clue what they were talking about. It was just a big blade the length of his forearm with a wide brass hilt. The handle was so brittle and dry-cracked when he found it that it broke when he accidentally dropped it. He had taken a wet strip of rawhide and wound it around the broken grip to hold it in place.

"There's no way that's the knife," Manuel Ortega said in his strongly accented English. "I always heard the handle was mounted with silver."

"To hell it ain't," Hatchet Murphy said. "I rode with Colonel Jim, and I've seen that knife many a time. He had a fancy one that he wore when he wanted to show off at some fiesta, but his original knife was as plain as a spinster's dress."

Son Ballard pointed to the knife in the little Mexican's slender hands. "Feel that balance. There hasn't been another one made to match its like since."

Odell held out his hand for the knife, and when he got it back, he hefted it in his palm. Now that he thought about it, the knife did have a wonderful feel for being so big, like it was a natural extension of his arm. "What are y'all talking about?"

"I'll trade you a pound of powder and a half bar of lead for that rusty blade," Son said.

Odell needed makings for his rifle, and he hated to have to arm himself by the charity of strangers. He studied the big knife but couldn't bring himself to part with it, no matter how badly he would be beating the older man in such a trade. "Why would you give so much for this old Bowie?"

"That isn't just any Bowie. That's *the* Bowie," Son said.

It was slowly dawning on Odell just what Son meant. He thought for a minute and then shoved the knife protectively back in the sheath he had made for it. "Do you mean to tell me . . . ?"

"That's what I mean. That knife isn't any old cheap, Sheffield-made Bowie," Son said. "That was Jim Bowie's original sticker."

Odell had been in Texas more than long enough to hear all about Jim Bowie, the famous knife fighter, and one of the martyred heroes of the Alamo. Even the folks back in Georgia were telling stories of Bowie and his brothers when Odell was just a boy.

"When Murph saw Colonel Jim in San Antonio, he and his brother Rezin Bowie were just back from hunting the San Saba Mines. They never found the silver they were looking for, and all they got for their troubles was a big fight with about a hundred Tehuacana and Waco Injuns," Son said.

"That fight took place somewhere right close to this old fort," Hatchet Murphy threw in. "And Colonel Jim's boys took cover in a thicket."

"Bowie's name is carved into the rock wall of that gate." Manuel Ortega pointed into the dark in the direction of the arched gateway leading into the ruins of the presidio.

"I reckon I'll have to keep it," Odell said to Son, "but thanks for the offer."

Son nodded as if he was almost pleased with Odell's decision. "I don't blame you."

"They say the steel in that knife is as hard as a whore's heart and tempered in hellfire by the greatest blacksmith that ever lived." Hatchet Murphy pitched his whetstone to Odell. "Such a weapon dull is sacrilege, so you sharpen that old gut knife up until it has an edge as fine as a frog's hair."

Odell pulled the knife back out and began to try and put an edge back on it. It was too long to pass across the stone without cutting his hand, so he worked the stone along the blade like he had seen the Prussian do when sharpening his sword. The swish of the softer stone passing along such hard steel was sweet, and he understood why the Prussian enjoyed the sound so much.

"That cutter has taken the life of some pretty brave men. Do you think you're as tough as Jim Bowie was?" Dub Harris didn't try to hide his jealousy. He had a bully's eyes and fists the size of feet, with every knuckle scarred or knocked down.

"I can't ride alligators or kill ten Mexican soldiers from my death bed, but I aim to keep this knife just the same." Odell put the knife away again.

"With a knife like that the kid might be a match for the Prussian and his sword," Son said.

"Well, he has the gun for it too." Hatchet Murphy cackled like a setting hen. "That cannon must weigh twenty pounds or more."

Odell picked up his rifle proudly. "My pappy traded a Pennsylvania Dutchman out of this gun on his way to Texas. That fellow had it custom built to fight Injuns and shoot the buffalos he'd heard about in Texas, but he took sick coming down the Mississippi before he even made it past Natchez."

"I don't care if it does have two shots, I'd hate to carry it." Dub Harris sounded like he still wouldn't mind picking a fight with Odell.

"It ain't too heavy for me." Odell met the brawler's stare and unconsciously puffed his broad chest out against his buckskin shirt. "I'd say it's just about right for a man with some size to him."

Dub Harris was a big man in a little package. He was as wide as he was long, and liked nothing more than whipping men noticeably taller than he was. He clenched his big fists and jutted forward his bulldog jaw.

Son Ballard knew what a troublemaker Dub could be and moved quickly to change the subject. "With that monster gun and Bowie's knife, old Major Karl out yonder had better keep a sharp eye on this kid."

Odell had heard enough talk of trouble between him and the Prussian, and he rose and stalked away. He didn't know why the men were trying to get his goat, but he wasn't going to let them have any more fun at his expense. He threaded his way through the mix of men gathered around several fires and made his way near the river. The cool night air helped to steady him. He walked and mulled over everything he had come to learn.

He couldn't believe that Red Wing would marry another after what he thought she had hinted at when he last saw her. Perhaps he was a fool to have read too much into what she had said and what he felt from her. Bitterly, he had to admit that the Prussian had far more to offer as a husband. The man had money and was building a plantation that showed promise. Odell could think of nothing he had to give Red Wing.

The thought of losing her to either the Comanches or the Prussian was almost as hard a lick to take as the death of his pappy. Even if she was to marry the Prussian, Odell couldn't abandon her. He didn't care if she was really Comanche, Mexican, or black as a well digger's ass. She was his closest friend and the most beautiful thing he held dear, and he would see to it that she was freed or die trying.

He wandered to where the horses were corralled within the broken walls of the old fort. He petted Crow some while he talked to him about what he had learned and what it was he had to do. The horse didn't answer, but Odell knew that all those men back there had nothing to ride that would keep up with Red Wing's good black gelding. The Prussian might intend to fight Comanches and risk losing Red Wing, but Odell had different plans. Given the chance, he would steal her away from the Peace Commission and the Prussian and his men could play hell catching him on Crow.

His bedding was within the round stone tower at the northwest corner of the presidio, and he wound his way through the rubble toward an arched doorway. A shadow rose out of the night and Odell almost brought his rifle up.

Placido's voice sounded out of the darkness. "Don't let those men bother you. They are warriors, and when there is no fighting such men must talk of fighting."

It bothered Odell that the Tonk had snuck up on him. "They seem like they want to make trouble."

"No, they just want what the world wants—to know if you are brave. Those men want to know if you bleed well, if you are a warrior."

"I don't have anything to prove."

"Ah, but you do. When we meet the Comanche, you will have to prove to them that you are willing to die to kill them. When you suffer on the trail, you will have to prove that you can last. Cuts Deep wants the woman, and you will have to prove that you are more worthy than him."

"Come trouble, I'll be ready to scrap with whoever I have to."

Placido shifted in the night and his moccasins scratched on stone. "The priests once built a mission near here to teach the Apache about their god who hangs on a cross. They were fools and thought the Apache wanted this. What the Apache wanted was someone to fight the Comanche. Soldiers had to come to protect the priests and they built this rock fort in the time of my grandfather."

"Mexicans?"

"No, Spaniards in steel hats with slow-shooting guns and long lances like the Comanche. They were warriors who thought they had nothing to prove to the world, but then the Comanche and many more tribes came to give them battle. The Spaniards died and there is nothing left of their fort but these walls."

"I've fought the Comanche and ridden their country alone."

"Good. The Comanche are proud like the Spaniards were, and the only thing they understand is death. We will have a heap big fight soon, and the world can see how brave we are."

The Tonk disappeared as quietly and quickly as he had appeared. Odell tried to follow the warrior's movement or detect a hint of sound, but he couldn't. He went inside the tower and lay down with his rifle clutched to his chest. He fell asleep thinking of the strange chief's words and wondered if he could bleed well enough to save the woman he loved.

Chapter 17

Little Bull rode his horse to the top of the little mountain where he could look down on the Comanche camp below. Gray light was just showing where the sandy swath of the riverbed disappeared into the eastern sky. He sat in contented silence and studied the immense country that surrounded him until the pewter world was set afire by the slow climb of the morning sun. There was a brief sense of peace and perfection at the beginning of the day that he could never seem to keep within him. Many of the Kotsoteka warriors believed in personal medicines and spirits to guide them and give them power, but he had never felt a force outside or within him as strong as the land. For a Comanche, all that the eye could take in, and for many horses farther, was Comancheria. There was power in pride.

The only thing disturbing his peace that morning was the dull ache in his stomach and the bile that rose up in his throat and burned his chest. Even on his best days the discomfort was always there, and that morning was a little worse than normal. The milk cow he had hoped would cure him had turned out to be a silly idea, and the long hard winter had proved too much for her. She had lost weight rapidly after the first snow, and quickly ceased to give milk He had come out of his lodge one morning to find his prize dead and frozen. Apparently, she was no hardier than the Tejano farmers he had taken her from, and he felt a fool to have gone through so much trouble to get an animal he knew nothing about taking care of. If he had it to do over, he would have captured a white woman to tend to the cow.

The smoke from the lodges hung lazy and heavy in the air as he came down off the hill. A dog yelped where somebody kicked it out of their doorway, and quiet greetings were passed by the women going about their morning's chores. He made a slow tour through the horse herd and noticed that his favorite buffalo runner seemed injured. He shook out a loop in the braided rawhide riata he carried and roped the gray gelding as expertly as any Mexican vaquero. Once the loop was settled over his head, the horse limped to him docilely.

Little Bull dismounted and lifted the gray's left forefoot. There was no swelling of the leg, but when he pressed firmly on the sole of the hoof with his thumb the horse flinched with pain and almost jerked away. He could see where fluid was seeping out around the spot where he had pressed, and he touched his thumb there again and then passed it under his nose. It smelled like rotten death.

He remounted and led the gray in the direction of his tepee. Halfway there a group of boys playing stopped him. Dressed in nothing but moccasins and breechclouts, their slim brown bodies flashed among the willows along the river. They were having a rowdy game of chase, and the smallest of them was proving to be the fastest. Try as they might, none of the bigger and older boys could run the wiry seven-year-old down. He leapt and dodged through the thicket like a deer, and Little Bull's heart warmed with pride at the sight.

The small boy was deeply involved in the game, but he finally saw Little Bull sitting his horse nearby and veered his course toward him. Comanche children grew up with horses, and the boy had the good sense to slow his approach, lest he spook the mounts. He smiled up at his father and danced slowly from one foot to another, as if unable to contain the happy energy that made him want to run and play before the sun was even good and up.

Little Bull studied his son's round little face staring up at him. Comanches tended to run toward the short side, but the boy was small even for his age. Pony Heart might be little, but he was already showing signs of being brave and smart. Little Bull was very short himself, even for a Comanche, and knew that being a warrior had little to do with physical might and more to do with cunning.

"Come with me. We need to work on Badger's hoof," Little Bull said.

The boy cast a longing look over his shoulder to where the other boys had started to chase a new victim, but he didn't hesitate long. He took hold of the hand his father held out to him and let him swing him onto the back of the gray. He tried to hide his desire to stay and play.

"There will be plenty of time for your friends later. A warrior must learn to take care of his horses, even little Pony Heart," Little Bull said more sternly than he intended to.

The boy's education was important, but Little Bull wasn't at all disappointed that at such a young age Pony Heart would rather play games. He was proud of how the people of the camp loved the boy, and how easily he made friends. Little Bull's two wives spoiled his only child, but he had to admit that he was just as guilty. The love for his son almost filled the spot in his soul that had all but been emptied so long ago.

Fate had been kind, and his son didn't know what it was like to be a shunned orphan moving constantly from one lodge to another, from one band to another, seeking food and shelter from anybody that would have him until he was big enough to fend for himself. Little Bull knew all too well how harsh life could be. His family taken from him and his friends few, he had grown up the butt of every childish joke and a whipping post for boys his age with the social network to protect them.

His boyhood had been hard, but somehow he had scrapped and clawed his way to a place among the Kotsoteka band. At thirteen, he had left the village alone and returned two weeks later with a small herd of horses and two Apache scalps. None of the people could recall a warrior so young raiding alone. In the years to come he went against Tonkawa, Osage, Ute, and Mexican. His horse herd grew and his lodge was always full of meat. He never forgot those who befriended him, or those who had once insisted that he was less than a real Comanche because of the tainted blood in his veins. He was only twenty-three, but many believed there was no warrior among all the Comanche who could stand his equal in a hunt or a fight, even the great Iron Shirt. The people might have laughed at the poor half-breed boy with no family or band to protect him, but not the man, Little Bull. His friends were still few, but those willing to follow his leadership on raids were many.

Buffalo Butt, the fattest of his wives, was preparing his breakfast over a fire built outside their tepee and she looked up from her cooking long enough to smile and motion them to get down and eat. She seemed to always read his mind, and this breakfast was no different. She knew he was long tired of eating buffalo meat and had broiled four big blue quail. He and the boy dismounted while she went to fetch his wicker backrest from the tepee. Buffalo Butt was his first wife and Pony Heart's mother. Some said the five good horses he'd given her father for her were too much to pay for such a homely woman, but he had never regretted it. Her heart was as big as the outside of her, and she was a loving wife, if a bit strong willed.

Speckled Tail should have been helping with the morning's chores, but as usual, she had managed to be elsewhere
when there was work to be done. The Kiowa thought she
was beautiful enough to do as little as she wanted to and
that he would forgive her laziness. Thus, she spent far less
time tending to his lodge than she should. She was nowhere to be seen at breakfast, but Little Bull assumed she
was in the tepee preening and admiring herself before the
mirror he'd given her. She was very vain. He'd sworn to dash
the looking glass to pieces many times, but could never
bring himself to do it. Buffalo Butt kept him well enough
fed and clothed by herself, and it wasn't as if Speckled Tail
didn't have her own qualities. She was always waiting for
him under his blankets and seemed to thoroughly enjoy
what, in Little Bull's experience, most women merely tolerated. He knew he should send her back to the Kiowas, but
rutting with Speckled Tail always made him forget how lazy
she was.

The three of them were almost finished with their breakfast when Speckled Tail finally appeared in the door. She
tried to ignore the scowl Buffalo Butt gave her but walked
a noticeably wide arc around the other woman as she made
her way to the fire. Little Bull could tell Buffalo Butt was
considering taking a stick to the slim little squaw, but she
seemed to decide against it and merely stuck to her glare.

Speckled Tail stretched her arms high above her head
and yawned like a cat just waking from its nap. The elk-tooth
Wichita dress she wore clung to her lithe body, and even
through the deerskin he could see that her nipples were hard.
Contrary to Comanche custom, she wore her hair in the
Kiowa style. It was almost as long as Little Bull's, and he
watched as she fondled and twisted it into a thick rope above
her ear. He thought about taking her back to bed right then,
but the look Buffalo Butt was giving him changed his mind.
He tried his best to focus on the quail and smiled and rubbed
his belly so that she could see how much he loved her too.

Her sour look didn't change, and the idea of taking both of them back into the tepee was fleeting.

Speckled Tail brushed a hand lightly across the back of his neck and smiled coyly at Buffalo Butt, who merely mumbled something to herself. The two of them had been at odds since the moment Little Bull had brought Speckled Tail back from a visit to the Kiowas early that spring. He had hoped that time would bond them, but it was plain that Buffalo Butt still had no wish to share her man or her lodge with a vain Kiowa girl.

"It's about time you got up," Buffalo Butt said. "Our husband would never have breakfast if it was left to you."

Speckled Tail continued to smile and tickle the back of Little Bull's neck with her fingers. "Why doesn't it surprise me that you would get up so early for food?"

Buffalo Butt mumbled something again, and Speckled Tail reached out for the last remaining quail on the spit with her free hand. Before she could lay claim to it, Buffalo Butt snatched it away and pitched it to the nursing yellow cur and her litter of puppies waiting for scraps at a hungry, yet safe distance from their masters. The quail was gone in a split second of growling and snapping, and Speckled Tail was left with nothing but the pout on her lips.

Buffalo Butt did a passable job of appearing regretful. "I'm sorry. Did you want that? Our husband said it was for the bitch, and I must have been mistaken as to which one he meant."

"You fat pile of guts." Speckled Tail's knife was suddenly out and pointed at Buffalo Butt.

"You Kiowa slut!" Buffalo Butt must have changed her mind about the stick, because she raised it over her head clutched in both her stubby fists. She swung it in a mighty downward stroke that would have killed Speckled Tail had she not been quick to dodge.

Speckled Tail's defiance was all bluff, and she broke and ran so quickly that she dropped her knife. The two of them raced away with Buffalo Butt's stick swishing the air around the Kiowa's head. Most of the blows missed, but Speckled Tail squealed like a little girl with each swing of the stick.

The fight got the large pack of camp dogs stirred up and they too joined the chase, barking and yapping behind the two women. The dogs were long since wise to the wrath of Buffalo Butt's stick, but Speckled Tail's shrieking was more excitement than they could bear. One of the mongrels latched his teeth onto the seat of Speckled Tail's dress and held on for dear life. Normally, Speckled Tail would have been far too fleet of foot for Buffalo Butt to catch, but the added encumbrance of a growling, shaking dog dragging from her skinny rear made the footrace just about an even match. The entire camp laughed and cheered Buffalo Butt on as the two of them passed by.

Little Bull noticed that Pony Heart looked concerned. "Don't worry, Buffalo Butt is already breathing too hard to catch her."

"But what if she does? Mother will kill her with that stick."

Little Bull pitched the last of the bird bones aside and wiped his greasy fingers on his bare thighs while he considered the possible outcomes of the fight. "No, they've fought before, and Buffalo Butt hasn't killed her yet. If she can catch her, I imagine she'll just give her a good whipping and then Speckled Tail will do a little work for the next few days to get back on her good side."

As if to prove his point, Buffalo Butt came parading back through the camp with her stick propped over one shoulder and a triumphant smile on her face. Most of the camp had followed along to watch the fight, and from the fact that they were still laughing Little Bull was sure that Speckled Tail was still alive.

"If that slut keeps messing with me she won't look so pretty for you, because I'm going to stomp moccasin tracks in her skinny ass." Buffalo Butt stopped in the door of their tepee with one hand on her rounded hip and the stick waving at him in the other.

"Calm down, woman. Speckled Tail will eventually come around, and then you won't have to work so hard. You just have to give it some time and try to remember that we can't always get our way." Little Bull thought it was high time he put an end to all the feminine catfighting and to remind her who was the master of the lodge.

"I'll remember that the next time that Kiowa has a headache and you come rubbing up against this fat old butt in the night with your stinger hard." She tossed her stick aside and disappeared into the tepee with a huff, slamming the hide door shut behind her.

Little Bull looked to the boy sheepishly. "Well, I'd say that went well."

"Father, when I'm a man I think I will have only one wife," Pony Heart said seriously.

Little Bull tried to keep a straight face and clapped the boy on the back. "You are wise beyond your years. Let's leave the women to their warpath and see if we can fix Badger's hoof."

Pony Heart held Badger's rope while his father picked up the lame foot. The boy hoped that some day he would have a buffalo runner as good as the gray. Once Little Bull had been offered fifty horses for Badger, but refused. Like the ill-tempered, masked burrower of the plains that was his namesake, Badger was gritty and tough. While there were swifter runners, Badger never seemed to tire or want to quit, and he had never fallen, even at a dead run over the roughest ground. Once brought alongside a running buffalo he would guide himself in for a close thrust from his rider's lance or a shot from his bow. He would pin his little ears back and willingly rub shoulder to shoulder with a half-ton animal that could gore him to death with one swipe of his curved black horns.

"Come see." Little Bull held the horse's hoof between

his knees and waited for the boy to walk around for a better view.

"What's the matter with his hoof?"

"See the little spot where the sole is soft and wet?"

"Yes."

"He has bruised it on a rock or something, and it's rotting from the inside. We need to cut a hole to let the poison drain out."

"Will he heal?" Pony Heart was genuinely troubled by the thought that Badger might be forever crippled. He had always envisioned his first hunt on the back of the gray.

Little Bull took his knife's point and carefully drilled into the sole of the hoof. He only had to dig a little ways before serum and stinking pus ran from the hole. The abscess was deep, and he widened the drain before setting the foot down.

"I think he'll be fine before long. We'll pack the sole of his hoof with your mother's good poultice for the next few days," Little Bull said.

Buffalo Butt had already gotten over her mad enough to bring them a moist pack of clay and various herbs known only to her, and they tied it in place with a soft strip of deer hide. Little Bull led the horse to a picket rope near the tepee and staked him out where he could graze but still be close to hand.

"I think he is walking better already," Pony Heart said.

"Yes, I believe you're right. He'll be ready to run buffalo again before too long."

Pony Heart looked at his father adoringly. "When will I know all the things you know?"

Little Bull laughed and jumped on his black warhorse, then swung his son up behind him. "You will be a man soon, but ride with me today just as my son."

Pony Heart had been riding his own horse since he was three, and he knew his friends would tease him when they saw him riding double behind his father. He started to ask to retrieve his own horse but thought better of it. He hugged close and smiled around his father's broad back as they passed through the camp. His friends could think what they wanted. None of them had a father like Little Bull.

They wove through the cluster of tepees scattered along the shallow river until they reached the far edge of camp. Two elderly squaws were beating a young white woman with switches and shouting at her. The slave had dropped the water buckets she had been carrying and was cowered on the ground with her knees drawn up and her arms protecting her head. Bloody welts already crisscrossed her back and legs, and she whimpered pitifully.

Little Bull didn't stop, but Pony Heart studied the filthy, half-naked white girl in passing. "Why must they beat her so? Can't they see she won't get up?"

Little Bull cast a bland glance back behind him at the captive girl lying in the trail while they splashed across the river. "Have no pity for the Tejano slave. She is less than nothing."

"But you told me there is no pride in killing a weak enemy."

Little Bull pulled up his horse halfway up the side of the mountain where he had sat earlier that morning. He sighed and reminded himself to be patient with his son. "Yes, but I did not say there was no pleasure in it. Revenge is big medicine, and it is good for our people to see our enemies captive and crying out in pain like babies. A people who hate strongly will fight strongly. It has always been our way."

Pony Heart wrinkled his brow. "What if the warrior who captured her takes her as his wife?"

"Some captive wives become Comanche, others just bear children until they can be ransomed. You already know these things and are talking yourself in circles."

"But even if she becomes Comanche, her white body will still be the same."

"But her heart will not be. At least for now, that one is

still a slave and her masters can do what they will with her. She will be beaten until she sees that we are superior to all men. If she is strong, maybe she will live to raise more Comanche; if she is weak, she will die."

He swept his hand before him, tracing the arc of the horizon around them. "All that you see is ours. None of our enemies have yet stood long before us. The corn growers cower in their villages because we let them so that we will have trade for our horses. The Lipan and the Tonkawa have fled east before our fury, and the Mexicans are weak and only know how to die."

"I understand these things you say, but why do you hate the Tejanos so much? All of the Kotsoteka speak of your hatred and how you will ride far to raid them even when other enemies are closer." The boy hoped his face looked as fierce as his father's.

Little Bull swung his left leg over his horse's neck and dropped to the ground. He took hold of Pony Heart's leg with one hand and looked up into his eyes with an anger simmering there that scared the boy. "You remember this always. The Tejanos are different. They are still learning this land, but most of them fight and die well. And they have one thing that can't be tolerated or forgiven. To do so will be the end of us."

His father's grip was digging painfully into his leg and Pony Boy bit his lip and tried to think. "What thing is that?"

"Pride."

"Pride?"

"Our pride is our strength. As long as we are fearless we are proud, and as long as we are proud we will be fearless and hold these plains forever. But the Tejanos have a strange pride too, and there is no room for two such people." Little Bull softened his grip, embarrassed that he was so caught up in the passion of the truth that he hadn't noticed he was hurting the boy.

"The Lipans and the Tonkawas have made peace with

the Tejanos." Pony Heart's voice was a whisper, and he felt that perhaps he had caused his father's anger.

"Without fighting there is no life for us, no warriors, no Kotsoteka, no Comanche. We would grow weak and die. We would become like the Tonkawas and the Apaches who the Tejanos have conquered with this word 'peace.' What is peace? I say there can be no such thing between true enemies."

"My enemies." Pony Heart's little chin lifted defiantly.

"They are the worst of our enemies. In your time you shall see the truth of this. There is no room here for both, and one of us must die," Little Bull said. "We are the People and the pale-faced Tejano thinks he is the people. That is his pride too. He cries that the Comanche break their word when the old chiefs bluster of peace, but the Tejano breaks his word too when it suits him. My father, your grandfather, went to one such gathering at the old Mexican village on the River of the Bells, and the Tejanos tried to take him prisoner after promising peace."

"He shouldn't have trusted the Tejanos." Pony Heart felt his own anger rising up in him.

"You are right to never trust them, no more than they should trust us. They claimed your grandfather had agreed to bring in all the Tejano women and children held captive by the Comanche. He tried to tell them that he had brought in all that he had, and that he had no control over the other bands. They claimed he was holding prisoners back to bargain for more of their goods later, and they killed him."

"They killed him?"

"They were going to make him their captive, and that is death enough for a Comanche warrior. He fought them with his knife until they shot him many times with their guns."

"I will fight the Tejanos."

"I know you will. You have the heart to be a great warrior and killer of our enemies. So, feel no mercy for that pale girl being beaten with switches, or for the scalps you see hanging in our lodge. Slay the Tejanos where you can find them until there are no more of them left to die. Steal their horses and their women and children until you are rich and well satisfied."

"I promise, Father, I will."

Little Bull jumped up behind Pony Heart this time and started them down off the mountain. He hugged the boy tight to his chest and told him of all the Comanches who had died at the Tejanos' hands, of the sicknesses the white men brought, and the treachery of their lies and promises. He told the boy of mighty Comanche warriors of old and of their great deeds in battle against all comers, and how the people had ridden from the north long before to conquer many tribes and come to rule over Comancheria. He recited the names of their enemies by rote and then Pony Heart repeated them to himself silently.

"Remember that the bull of the herd always has the most to lose and has to fight to keep what is his. We are the bull and our enemies are many. The Tejanos killed my family until there was once only me. Now I have a strong son and I will fight them for you as long as I can, but one day it will be your glory."

"Will it take so long?"

Little Bull scanned the horizon to the east. "I don't know their numbers or the land where they come from. The Comanche have killed many Tejanos, but there are always more. My heart tells me there will still be plenty for you to kill when you come of age."

"One day I will ride with you against the Tejanos," Pony Heart said.

"You will, but that is for another day. For now, let's ride down and see how badly Speckled Tail is beaten." Little Bull ruffled the boy's hair and grinned.

When they crossed the river the white captive girl was still lying there, but the old women had finally walked off and left her. Pony Heart looked down at her angrily and spat on her bloodied back as they passed. "Enemy."

"Never forget that, and who you are. Without enemies there can be no Comanche," Little Bull said.

"I promise I will never forget." Pony Heart hugged his father's forearm to him and began again to say the list of his enemies over and over to himself.

Chapter 18

The moon was so bright and low in the sky that it almost felt as if Odell could ride his horse right up and touch it. It was as if it was no moon at all, but rather something unreal hovering in the dark night. He had slipped away from his second camp with the Prussian's war party to ride out upon the expanse—looking for something and finding another thing altogether. He sat Crow in silence and felt small upon the face of the earth. The white light lay gently on the land and the silhouettes of brush, cacti, grass, and the dry waste of the plain were lit in soft, glowing black—all somehow made alien and magical under the illumination of the strange moon. He had only intended to be alone with his thoughts and not to ride into a different world.

Trouble rode Odell's soul with sharp spurs, and the nights could be especially bad. Often, when sleep wouldn't come and doubts and frustrations crept in on him, he went out alone to do nothing more than sit his horse in the dark. The quiet and the emptiness surrounding him calmed him like a lullaby, and his thoughts came clearer.

The wind had lost the day's heat, and it touched his face like a cool kiss. Crow was still beneath him and the weight of his rifle lay heavy across his thighs. The months on the trail had left him wild and unkempt, and hard living and loss had left his heart equally ragged. He removed his broad hat and bowed his head and ran a hand up his forehead and back through the tangled mop of his hair. He did so more out of weariness than anything else, but anyone watching would have thought him some pagan bowing before the white orb of the heavens. But truly, there was something in the wide land of his wanderings that spoke to him.

Red Wing was somewhere out there, and his eyes inadvertently made a search of the distances for the glow of a fire, as he did almost every night, but there was nothing to make him feel any closer to her. He wondered if she too saw the big moon, and he swore for the thousandth time he wouldn't quit. He had lost everything dear to him but her, and no matter how long and how far he had to ride, he was going to find her.

He was lost in his thoughts and the buffalo came very near to him on the upwind side before he even knew they were there. It wasn't a large herd, just stragglers from the massive yearly migration north. They passed before him single-file like phantoms. Their humped shadows, bovine grunts, and the brush of their hooves in the grass were all that connected them to the earth. Although the herd was just an old bull and a half dozen cows and calves, he swore that he could feel the heat off of them and smell the musky earth matted into their wooly heads.

The wind must have shifted or they finally noticed him for what he was, for the ghosts lifted their tails and stampeded straight into the moon. Their dust floated up in the moonlight like a thin black veil on the backlit skyline, and he waited to breathe until the dull throb of hooves was gone to his ears and vibrated no more in his heart. Somewhere in the way off, coyotes yipped and yapped until a lone wolf answered them with a long, low wail. And then there was silence once again except for the occasional creak of his saddle when Crow shifted beneath him.

He sat long before the moon until the bawdy laughter of the Texans and the raspy voice of Son Ballard lifted from the camp. Sound carried well in the night, but Odell only half paid attention to the goings-on at the campfire far behind him. He didn't have to catch every word to know what kind of stories Son and the other men were telling. It would be tales of brave men come to hard ends and violent deaths, of bitter fights with Indians and weather, of bad horses too wild to tame, and of abandoned homesteads and starved-out pilgrims too soft for Texas. Like all good frontier sorts, the Prussian's party scoffed at destiny and consequences and the fickle twists of fate that could take your life just as quickly as it brought you fortune. Laughing at what could kill you didn't make you stronger, but it passed the time and made such men bolder by the telling.

Odell was in no mood for storytelling. Somewhere out in the black, Red Wing was waiting. He turned Crow around and started at a slow walk back to camp. Just beyond the edge of the firelight he spied the shadow of a man afoot.

"You should be careful about wandering so far from camp in Indian country, Herr Odell. I would've thought you'd learned that by now," the Prussian said. "You know that is a Comanche moon."

"I didn't see any Indians about." Odell stopped Crow beside the Prussian's shoulder.

"What did you see?"

Odell waited long to answer. "I don't know just what I saw. I don't think I've the words for it."

The Prussian dragged hard on his pipe until the red glow

of it faded and died. "Just the same, a man could get himself killed wandering around in the dark."

Odell waited again to answer. He could just make out the Prussian banging his pipe against his palm and dumping his tobacco ashes out.

"You should be careful yourself, Karl. A man can start a fire if he isn't careful." Odell rode on into camp and didn't hear the Prussian's answer, if there was one. He went to sleep on the ground with Crow's hackamore rope in his hand and the black horse standing over him like a sentinel.

Chapter 19

Much to Agent Torrey's relief, none of the Wacos died from his treatments, but Squash's wife was still weak and the chief refused to leave her behind to go wandering after Comanches. As a result, the escort Squash had promised the Peace Commission never materialized. After two days in the Waco village the expedition rode off up the Brazos River without reinforcement and minus their Comanche translator.

Five days northwestward they reached the western edge of the Cross Timbers and rode out into more open country. For some reason game was scarce and the expedition was soon living off nothing but mush and hard cakes made from coarse-ground Waco corn. Hungry bellies led to bad tempers, and when they reached the Wichita River, Commissioner Anderson argued with the Delawares that it was the Red. Insults were exchanged and for a while it looked like the scouts would quit and ride away. All the men soon became silent and brooding, the corn ran out, and the stringy jackrabbit and screech owl stew Agent Torrey managed to procure for the supper pot did little to lift their spirits, or alleviate the hunger that threatened to put an end to the Peace Commission before it even got good and started.

Twice the Delawares reported that they had come across the tracks of Comanche hunting camps on the move, but the sign was at least a week old. To make matters worse, a spring storm front blew in on them, and they huddled miserable and wet for two days on the south bank of the Red. Their last night on the river, thunder and lightning preceded an enormous roaring wind. The little canvas tent Commissioner Anderson had provided for Red Wing blew away, and she had to join the men under the limbs of a huge elm tree with her saddle held overhead to fend off the falling hailstones, some of them as big as silver dollars. They woke up to find their horses stampeded and a mile-long swath of nearby bottom timber felled by a small tornado that seemed to have just skipped over them.

The Delawares went out and rounded up the horses, but the two pack mules weren't to be found. There had been no food for the contrary animals to carry for days, but the entire party still considered it a great loss. The trade trinkets intended for the Comanches could be divided among each rider, but the mules themselves couldn't be replaced. Only the night before the tornado had hit they had all agreed to butcher one of the long-ears for breakfast. Captain Jones had assured them that the Apaches in New Mexico loved such meat, and that the mules would be more than enough sustenance to see them through two more weeks of travel.

When they were still back in the settlements, all of them but the Delawares would have curled their lips at the mention of eating mules, but none of them had ever gone so many days without a true meal either. Needless to say, the disappearance of the mules almost broke their spirits. Captain Jones seemed to dwell on their loss the most. A day later he was still telling the dream he had where the mules had been blown to New Mexico and the Apaches had eaten them lightly sautéed in a bath of pork fat with green onions. Everyone was in a foul mood, so it wasn't safe for any of them to mention to him that it was common knowledge that the tornados in Texas didn't move west, nor did a savage tribe probably express such delightful culinary skills. Normally, Captain Jones was smart enough to know that himself, but he was a portly man and perhaps valued regular meals even more than the rest of the party.

By the time the expedition reached the Washita, the question on everyone's mind wasn't whether they could survive to find the Comanche, but if they could keep from starving long enough to make it back to Austin. Commissioner Anderson continually attempted to fortify their will with speeches of duty and heroic endurance, but even he was showing the effects of hardship. His fancy clothes were soiled and torn and he had long since ceased to find a reason to shave every morning. He sat each night with his raw red eyes staring into the fire, and his sunken cheeks made gaunter by the clench of his grizzled jaws. He was a stubborn man, but it was plain to all that he was just about ready to quit.

On the afternoon when the commissioner had finally decided to give up their mission, Jim Pockmark rode into camp and asked for help hauling in the meat from a buffalo he had killed. The formerly weakened and sluggish men moved with the electricity of a pack of wolves, and soon breakfast was cooking over the fire. The Delawares had immediately satisfied some of their hunger with raw liver, but the Texans were a little more squeamish, and waiting for the meat to cook was slow torture.

Captain Jones was the first to reach for a portion, and he cut himself a large chunk of backstrap and tore at it with his teeth. He swiped at the bloody juice burning his chin, but his eyes almost rolled back in his head with pleasure as he worked the hot bite around in his mouth. Soon, the rest of them were clutching pieces of half-raw meat. The buffalo had been a lone old bull, and even the tenderest portions were so tough they were nearly impossible to chew. A calf or a young cow would have been much preferred, but none of them were complaining. They tugged at the meat with their teeth, using their knives close to their mouths to cut a portion free.

"I don't think I've ever tasted anything so good," Agent Torrey smacked.

"Even poor bull meat is good when you haven't had any meat in nigh on a week," the commissioner said.

Red Wing ate slowly, savoring the flavor and letting the food warm her stomach. She had starved before, and remained silent while the men celebrated breaking their fast. There had been times among the Comanche camps when the store of meat didn't last the winter, or stretches where enough game couldn't be found. All the creatures of the wild knew the pains of hunger.

"I mind the time when me and Captain Jack were surveying up the Guadalupe," Captain Jones said around a tough mouthful of bull meat. "Our powder got wet crossing high water, and we couldn't shoot any meat. We rode two days back to San Antonio with nothing to eat but a couple of rattlesnakes we caught sunning."

"Rattlesnake isn't bad if you know how to cook it," Red Wing said quietly.

Captain Jones gave her a skeptical look as if he thought it out of place for a woman to barge in and one-up his manly tale. "So, you've ate those slithery old coontails?"

"There are worse things to eat," she said.

The men began to swap rattler stories, but Red Wing barely heard them. The food in her belly was making her sleepy, and she stared dreamily into the fire while her mind wandered back to her memories of the Comanche village on the move. She remembered the young boys scattered out and beating the brush for small game. They shouted and laughed when they cornered a snake or a rabbit, dispatching it with their little bows and racing back to the caravan proudly displaying their kill. All of the adults would laugh and praise the small warriors so determined to learn the ways of the hunt. Food was always something to rejoice about, and the children were the future of the people.

"What say you, Commissioner? Do we push on as we are, or try and double back to the Red to resupply? Abel's Trading Post can't be more than a three-day ride downriver, and we might even luck out and run across a few Comanches trading at the store," Captain Jones said. "It might be that we could get one of them to lead us to his village and translate for us."

"I think the game is stirring better the way we're headed, and Jim Pockmark speaks a little Comanche," the commissioner said. It was plain from the look on his face that he had already been contemplating detouring to Abel's but had disregarded that option.

"Jim might know a few words, but he doesn't speak their language. Comanche is the trade lingo out here, and most of the Indians in this country know a little. But that's a far cry from speaking Comanche, and I don't intend to get killed because somebody translates something wrong," Captain Jones said.

Jim Pockmark nodded. "Nobody speaks Comanche but Comanche. They are hard to understand, and want to fight all the time."

"We'll push on for another day or so and see if we can keep ourselves fed. Jim says we'll reach the Canadian tomorrow," the commissioner said.

"What about you, Agent Torrey? What do you have to say about all of this?" the captain asked.

Agent Torrey was already wrapped in his wool blanket and sound asleep. The long day's ride and a full belly had him snoring softly.

"That's the way it's going to be, Captain. I'll remind you

that you volunteered to accompany this expedition under my command," the commissioner said coolly.

Captain Jones didn't grumble, but it was plain that he didn't like being reminded of his position in the party. Red Wing had long since come to believe that the captain felt it was he who should have been in charge and not young Will Anderson. From the beginning of their journey, he had made a big deal of his service carrying the mail from Austin to San Antonio, and told numerous hair-raising tales of Indian encounters. He was quick to point out the fact that he had led a militia force to head off the Comanches after the Great Raid and the sacking of Victoria and Linneville, no matter that it was common knowledge that he and his company had missed the hostiles by twenty miles and never even made it to the fight at Plum Creek. However much his Indian fighting résumé may have been exaggerated, he obviously felt it superior to that of the stuffy, vain youth President Houston had appointed to lead the expedition.

"Maybe you ought to lead this party, Captain. It sounds as if your plan is the much safer and more practical course," Red Wing said. Anything that delayed their journey was a moral victory for her.

The captain puffed himself up and started to expound upon his merits, but noticed the commissioner glaring at him across the fire. He quickly deflated his expanded girth and shook his head as if saddened by her doubt of the commissioner's leadership.

"It's only natural that you should give such credence to my suggestions, considering my years on the frontier and military experience, but the president sets great store by Will. It's his mission to command, and I can but offer my counsel when needed," he said quietly.

The commissioner stared long at the captain, and then quickly rose and marched from the fire. The captain watched him disappear into the dark, and then jerked his attention back to Red Wing.

"Girl, don't you try to get me crossways with him," he hissed.

"Why, Captain, I am trying no such thing. Forgive me if I would feel much more comfortable with a man such as you leading us," she said in her most demure tone.

"Maybe, but I have no intention of ending up in a pistol match with him because he got his feathers ruffled. My brother served under Will's daddy for two years aboard ship, and I know just how fine-edged that family's sense of honor is," the captain said.

"Seriously, Captain, I doubt the commissioner is going to want to shoot you over questioning his decision making."

The captain looked to where the commissioner had disappeared, and then leaned close to the fire. "Will Anderson may seem like a perfect young gentleman, but don't let his fancy ways and that twenty-dollar smile fool you. The word down on the Gulf has it that he shot his coonass sweetheart's brother in New Orleans, and I know for a fact that he killed a navy officer in a pistol duel on a sandbar at Padre Island. Some say a prominent family paid him to pick a fight with that navy gent."

Red Wing weighed what she had just heard against her impressions of the commissioner. "Surely, the rumors are exaggerated. I would be the first to claim that he is a complete scoundrel, but he does not seem like a murderer."

"You think what you want, but don't try to put me at odds with him. Those fancy pistols tucked in his sash ain't just for show."

"I told you I was trying no such thing."

"I wasn't born yesterday. You're a little squaw trying to play with men, and it'll get you in trouble. Why don't you just keep quiet and hope Will can't find the Comanches he's looking for? Then maybe you can go back and play like you're a white girl again."

Up to that point Captain Jones hadn't said much to her during their long travels, but his prejudice came as no shock.

The mocking scowl on his face every time he looked her way had never been hard to read. "Pardon me if I'm not bothered by your insults."

The captain rose to his feet. "Will can fawn around you playing games like you're some real lady, but I'm too old for anything but the truth. And the truth is, you can dress up a pig and teach it to talk, but it's still a pig. For all your pretty dresses and fancy talk, you're still a dirty redskin."

"Does the color of my skin bother you so much?"

"I think you ain't dangerous no more, but even at the best, you're no more than a tame Injun like old Jim Pockmark over there and his buddies. If giving you back to the Comanches that raised you will get them to quit raiding for a while, then I'm all for it." Captain Jones started off in the direction the commissioner had gone.

"You hate me, don't you?" Red Wing asked.

The captain didn't turn around, but he stopped at the edge of the firelight for a moment. "I hate you and your kind more than you will ever know. The Comanche killed my woman and smashed my baby boy's head against a tree because he cried too much. If I was half the man I ought to be, I'd have already wiped them from the face of the earth."

When the captain was gone, Red Wing shifted her focus to Jim Pockmark sitting wrapped in his blanket. There was a smile on his face and a smirk at the corner of his mouth.

"Don't let the fat captain bother you," Jim said. "The commissioner laughs at him, the Indians laugh at him, and the Tejanos laugh at him. He is an old fool with a bellyful of lies. He thinks he is the man he tells us he is, but all can see the truth. Right now he is going for the whiskey he keeps in his saddlebags."

The Delaware's words didn't comfort her. In fact, the look on his scarred and pitted face scared her more than the captain's venom. His dress was a mixture of both the white man and the red, as if he'd taken all the savagery of both worlds for his own. The white cotton shirt belted over his breechclout, and the Mexican straw sombrero atop his long braids might make him seem more trustworthy to some folks, but she felt the renegade in him. It was plain in his calculating gaze, and the cold stillness of his monstrous face.

"I could get you away from these men," he said.

"Oh?" Despite wanting nothing more than her freedom, she was sure she wanted no part of what was working behind his glittering eyes.

"Do you doubt this?" He chuckled softly and smiled at the other two Delawares around him, as if any question of his prowess were laughable. "The fat captain will be drunk before long. I could slit his big belly open and choke him with his own guts before he even knew I was there."

The other two scouts didn't laugh with Jim, but they didn't say anything against the idea either. Red Wing found herself looking into the dark for signs of the commissioner's return.

"If you stay with these fools, maybe you die or maybe you end up back with the Comanche. I say you go with me."

She glanced out of the corners of her eyes to where Agent Torrey was snoring. He was no match for the three Delawares, but maybe just his being awake would temper the mutinous scheme Jim was working himself up to.

"Don't even look at that little man. I haven't made my mind up yet, but if you wake him I will take his nutsack for a tobacco pouch." Jim was enjoying trying to scare her.

"Would you take me back to my home?" She stalled for time.

"You come with me, and if after a while you still want to go home, I'll let you."

He hadn't risen, or even taken his arms out from under his blanket, but the threat of him was so great that she felt like he was looming above her. She rose quickly and walked into the night. The direction the commissioner had gone would have taken her right by the Delawares, and instinct told her that she needed to be far away from them. Her plan was to get out of the firelight and circle until she was near where the horses were tied. Surely the commissioner or the captain had gone to stand guard over their mounts

The timber along the riverbank was thick and she felt somewhat protected by its cover. When she heard somebody coming behind her, she tried not to panic. If she remained still in the dark, surely they could not find her. She debated shouting for help but feared the Delawares might be counting on her to do so. The commissioner and the captain were the only protection she had, and leading them into an ambush would seal her fate. She waited behind the trunk of a hackberry tree, her ears straining for the slightest of sounds.

Her pursuer was very near. She plainly heard his moccasins brushing against the grass. Her foot bumped against something at the foot of the tree, and she knelt to feel in the dark. Her hand found a thick, broken branch and she wrapped her fingers tightly around it. The stick and the knife in her pocket were all that she had to defend herself with. The sound of slow, stealthy footsteps came again, and she stood with her club at ready. He was so close she could smell him, and he was going to come on her right. Her pounding heartbeats made seconds seem like hours, and she willed herself not to strike too quick.

Chapter 20

Red Wing swung her club with all the power she could muster. She felt the half-rotten limb break as it struck solidly into flesh. She drew back the broken remains of her weapon for another swing. The shadow before her lunged against her and knocked her backward to the ground. His weight pinned her among the underbrush and she could feel the heat of him and his foul breath upon her face. She bucked and writhed under him and struggled frantically to get at the knife in her pocket. Something struck her jaw and another blow grazed her chin and sunk into her shoulder.

She felt the keen edge of a knife against her throat and she went still while the night swirled with splotches of color before her eyes. She tried to maintain her hold on consciousness and to will her numb right arm to fend off the knife before her throat was cut. The moon was just big enough to silhouette the Delaware against the stars overhead. The black shadow of him laughed, and when she cried out faintly and tried to roll away he struck her again. Her struggles pressed her throat ever so slightly against his blade, and she felt the warmth of her own blood spreading slowly to her collarbone.

His hands jerked viciously at the front of her dress and his knee lifted her skirt and fought to force itself between her knees. She had intended to make him kill her or leave her be, but she was too weak.

"You scream if you want to, but I'm going to make a good Injun out of you." Jim's voice was so husky with passion and exertion he might not have been human at all.

He pressed the knife into her more than he intended to while he fought her skirt, and the edge bit into her skin again. She made one last weakened effort to find his face with her fingernails. He hit her again so hard that the rebound of her head against the ground was as bad as his fist, and she felt her lips split beneath his knuckles. Something was wrong with her vision and she could barely see his shadow anymore. He was no more than a panting wisp of smoke in a nightmare.

The night exploded and was lit up with a brief flash. The knife against her throat slid lightly off her neck, and Jim Pockmark's lifeless, smothering weight covered her. She pushed wildly at his torso and squirmed from beneath him. Her breath was coming in ragged gasps and she scrambled away on hands and knees. She threw a wild look back over her shoulder to see if she was being pursued and ran into something in the night.

She pushed herself away at arm's length and knelt to look up at the tall shadow above her. Her fumbling hand found the knife in her pocket and she lunged forward with it, seeking to bury it in her attacker. A rough hand grabbed her wrist and pinned her arm wide while another hand took the side of her face and bent her head backward until she was looking up at her new assailant once more.

"It's me, Red Wing. It's Will," the voice said as if out of a dream.

She screamed again and tried to lunge to her feet. She couldn't break free of him, and fell against his legs, thrashing like a wildcat.

"Calm down. It's all over. You're all right."

This time something about the voice registered with her, and she ceased to fight. She felt the knife taken gently from her hand and the soft touch of fingers brushing back the hair from her face.

"Is that Jim Pockmark I shot?" the commissioner asked.

For the first time she truly recognized the voice and realized that she was crying. She wiped at the blood and grime caking her face and dared to look back at the still form lying on the ground.

"Yes." She sobbed.

He pulled her into his legs and she wrapped her arms about his knees and pressed her cheek against his thigh. She needed to feel safe, and his hands were comforting rubbing into her shoulders and stroking the top of her head.

"He won't bother you again. He won't bother anybody," the comissioner said quietly. "Let me help you back to the fire."

For a moment her legs refused to work, but she finally managed to stand and lean against him. He encircled her waist with one strong arm and started her slowly back to their camp, pausing when she needed him to. They passed close by Jim Pockmark's body with its cold, cruel face staring up at the stars with a bullet hole in the forehead, and its mouth wide open as if in shock or to accuse. But she didn't look down at him, she wouldn't.

"Oh, Will," she said as she pressed herself into his side, needing and trying to bury herself in the strength she felt in him.

"I'll protect you." He pressed his face into her hair and held her tight until he felt her body grow stronger again.

The walked slowly into the firelight. Agent Torrey was sitting up and rubbing his sleepy eyes. The other two

Delawares were just where they had been before, and for all appearances they might not have even blinked since she left.

The commissioner held her with one arm and placed his free hand on the butt of the other unfired pistol in his sash. "I killed that damned Jim Pockmark."

The Delawares stared at Red Wing and the commissioner with blank faces. One of them lay down and rolled over until his back was to them and the fire. The other grunted and nodded his head.

"Jim, he think all the time. He thought he'd maybe take that woman to Mexico and sell her for many horses. I told him that his thinking would get him killed," the sitting Delaware said.

"Well, he won't be thinking anymore. Have you got a problem with that?"

The Delaware looked shocked. "Me? No, I just want to go to sleep."

He did just that, and soon the two scouts at least appeared to be asleep, neither one of them showing the slightest concern or curiosity about their fellow tribesman's corpse. The commissioner sat down, and Red Wing kept close to him. She realized that his arm was still around her, but she couldn't make herself move away. She hated the weakness she felt. Despite all the things she held against him, she felt safe and protected in his embrace.

The gunshot and the commissioner's brief conversation with the Delawares seemed to have finally gotten through to Agent Torrey's sleep-fuddled brain. He jumped to his feet with his shotgun in hand and marched a half circle around the sleeping forms of the scouts. He looked as on edge as a cat in a yard full of snakes, ready to jump back at the slightest sign of life from the two Indians.

"What happened? Did I hear you say you shot Jim?" he asked.

The commissioner frowned and cast his eyes down at Red Wing's head on his shoulder. "There's a bit of coffee in my saddlebags that I've been holding back. I think Red Wing could use it now."

Agent Torrey caught his drift and decided his questions could wait until later. It was obvious that Red Wing had been attacked, and he busied himself with making coffee. He tried to appear happy and calm for her sake, but his hands shook and rattled the lid on the coffeepot. He looked an apology at her, and she managed a hint of a smile.

"When you get that coffee on the coals, go see if you can find Captain Jones," the commissioner said.

Agent Torrey had no desire to go out in the night alone, especially considering the latest revelation that even the scouts weren't to be trusted, but he did as he was told. He just hoped that the captain wasn't already so drunk that he mistook him for a wild Indian after the horses.

By the time the coffee was ready Agent Torrey had returned with his charge. The captain's face was flushed and he was a bit unsteady on his feet, but he took the news fairly well. The coffee did them all some good and they enjoyed it quietly until it was gone.

The commissioner tried to get Red Wing to go to sleep, but she shook her head and stared into the fire. Her face was bloody from a deep cut above one eye, and her lips were swollen and split. She had managed to straighten and hold together the top of her torn dress, and to pin her hair back out of her eyes. He thought she was beautiful, even then. There was a softness and vulnerability about her that he had never imagined, much less seen before. He cursed himself for what he was thinking but knew just as well that if she asked him to take her home in the morning, he would.

"What are we going to do for guides now?" Captain Jones finally asked.

The commissioner studied the Delawares in their blankets. "They didn't seem too bothered by it all."

But he was wrong. They went to their blankets late in the night, with Red Wing lying between the commissioner and

Agent Torrey on the far side of the fire and the captain sleeping propped up against his saddle with his rifle cradled in his arm. The sun was well up in the sky when they awoke, and the first thing they noticed was that the Delawares were gone.

Chapter 21

Odell tried hard to interpret the story Son Ballard and Placido read easily from the confusing mix of day-old tracks crossing the sandy wash. The old frontiersman and the Tonk chief discussed the large Comanche camp that had left the sign while Odell tried to improve his tracking skills. However, all he could be sure of after a long study was the fact that Indians on barefoot ponies had headed off toward the river sometime earlier. He only knew it was Indians from the lines their travois poles had etched into the ground and the large number of dog tracks present.

"Do you think they spotted us?" Odell asked.

Son grinned at Placido before answering Odell. "Hell, boy, I don't care how many cold camps that Prussian insists we make. You can't move through the country with this many men without every Injun out here knowing about it."

That was just what Odell feared. There was no way they were going to head off the Peace Commission before the Comanches decided to attack them. The odds were that numerous small hunting bands or raiding parties had already seen them or crossed their trail.

"Do you think we can find the Peace Commission out here?" Finding a girl and a handful of men out on the vast expanse seemed an almost impossible concept to Odell.

Son rubbed his whiskered chin and winced at the question. "We could if we had enough time, but we might have to fight the Comanche every day between now and then."

"Maybe I should just cut north for the Canadian on my own. A man alone might have a better chance of not getting spotted," Odell said.

"There's no guarantee you'd find them on the Canadian. Even if you knew where they were, it wouldn't be easy. If you didn't get scalped on the way, how would you force Houston's men to turn her over?"

"I guess if they wouldn't listen I could maybe sneak her off from them." Odell always felt like a clumsy child around the old man. His pappy had made him feel that same way.

Placido shook his head at Odell's endless questioning and kicked his pony across the wash, leaving Odell and Son alone.

"What's the matter with him?" Odell asked.

Son took a deep breath and pointed at the Tonk's back. "Old Placido has lived in this country longer than any of us. He's fought Comanches and he knows them like we never will. They even say his mama was a Comanche."

"What's that supposed to mean?"

"It means that he thinks you're a damned fool. You wouldn't stand a fart's chance in a windstorm of finding that Peace Commission before the Comanches got you," Son said. "We don't have much chance of finding your gal as it is, but our only hope is Placido's Tonks, or that we run across some friendly Injuns that have spotted who we're looking for."

"If you didn't believe we could stop Houston's bunch, why did you come along?" Odell found Son's pessimistic attitude to be highly irritating.

"Because there's one thing I can guarantee you about this whole trip. That Prussian is going to find him a fight with the Comanches."

"Those Comanches owe me plenty, but starting a war out here is liable to get Red Wing killed or lost to me forever. I came along with y'all to rescue her, and that's what I still aim to do," Odell said.

"You listen well and stay close to me and Placido, and maybe you'll do just that. At the worst you might keep your hair." Son reached out with his pointer finger and drug it across Odell's forehead while he made a cutting sound between his own teeth. "Right now we'd better catch up to Placido and his scouts if you want to learn a thing or two about Comanches."

They loped after Placido, and Odell thought about what Son had told him. All the Texans seemed to set great store by Placido's skills, and there was something about him that made you want to be his friend. But there was also something scary about him. At one moment Odell found himself admiring the big Tonk, and the next moment he gave him the chills. He knew what was bothering him. He didn't know much about Indians, but he had been in Texas long enough to hear some things.

"Are the Tonks really man-eaters?" he asked.

Son grinned. "Sure enough."

Odell let that ruminate in his mind while Crow rocked along underneath him. "You're pulling my leg."

"I'm telling you the truth. They ain't as bad about it as the Kronks, what we call the Karankawas down on the Gulf, but they'll fry up a man from time to time," Son said. "They say after the Plum Creek fight Placido and his Tonks went among their fallen enemies and cut off their hands, feet, and other choice parts. The next morning they ate that Comanche meat like it was fine cuts of fat hog."

"Why the hell are we riding with them then?"

"Lots of Texans despise the Tonks for beggars and

man-eaters, but you take your help where you can find it,"
Son said. "The Tonks figured out a long time ago that they
couldn't whip us, or the Comanches. Being pinned between
the two of us they had to pick sides or get rubbed out quick.
They hate a Comanche as much or more than we do, track
better than we ever will, and never get lost."

"You seem to set store by Placido," Odell said.

Son nodded while he considered that. "I ain't the only
one. The latecomers to Texas might not have any use for
him, but those of us that have ridden and fought with him
consider the man a friend. I've never known him to be
anything but loyal, and there ain't a man in Texas that's
fought the Comanches longer. In fact, he's just about more
Texan than any Texan I know."

"I just don't particularly care for the thought of being
eaten," Odell said.

"Hell, boy. They don't eat Texans, or nobody else real
regular," Son growled. "It ain't any skin off our backs if they
think they can get some of their enemies' power by chawing
on them, or even if they just like the taste of man."

"That still doesn't make it right."

Son's patience was short-lived. "If you're going to understand any kind of Injun, you'll have to forget all your raising.
I count a few of them as friends, but I don't try and make
them fit into my mold either. Injuns laugh and love, and there
are good and bad among them just like us. But at the same
time, they aren't anything like us. They have their own set
of rules. You and I might think they're backward and primitive, but they find us just as strange. That's why one of us
has to win, and the other is going to lose everything."

"If they're just primitive, how come they ain't changed
their ways since we came along?"

"If somebody showed up and right off started telling you
that all you believed in was wrong, would you listen to
them?" Son asked. "You take the Comanche for instance.
His way of life has served him well for a long, long time,

and carved him out a big chunk of country. You might say his way of life suits the where and when he lives. But times are changing, and I'd say the fact that they won't change will be the end of them."

"You sound like an Indian lover," Odell said a little mockingly.

"Hell, no. If it's going to be them or us, I know who I'm rooting for. Those damned Comanches ain't easy to love, and if we want Texas for ourselves I'd say we ought to be glad that there's such a hateful bunch to take it away from. That way we won't have anything to feel guilty about afterward."

They loped along in silence for another mile. Odell was willing to let the conversation go at that, but it seemed to be bothering the old scout.

"You'd better remember where you're at. Texas ain't like no other place. I love her to death, but she's hard and she's mean." Son raised his voice over the wind that had picked up speed throughout the afternoon until it was bending the grass over and blowing up waves of dust. "The Comanches have to go, but you stay out here long enough and you'll start to live more and more like them."

There wasn't time for them to argue more, for Placido had stopped just ahead of them on the edge of a bit of canyon country stretching across the plains. The Prussian's force had finally reached the Clear Fork of the Brazos after three days of hard riding from the San Saba. On their way north they had experienced relatively easy traveling on the prairie divides between one river and the next ever since they crossed the Concho. Their route took them east of the high escarpment of the Staked Plains, and they avoided the canyons and rugged country that footed it. The Tonks had led them to good water for the most part, and scattered herds of buffalo kept them fed even at the speed they traveled. Nobody thus far had to eat their saddles as Son had predicted.

Placido led them out onto an eroded point overlooking

the river. A handful of Tonk scouts had dismounted and were sitting in the shade of their horses, watching the country across the river. Placido and Son got down and loosened their cinches and motioned Odell to do the same. The prairie they had come from dropped off into a rugged area of bluffs and shallow, eroded canyons. A few miles or so across the river Odell could see open country again.

While the rest of them sat and stared at the horizon, Odell leaned against Crow with his arms draped over the saddle seat. He wasn't sure what they were looking for, but assumed they were scouting out possible ambush by the Comanche. He tried to be patient and will himself to a careful study of the terrain, but his stomach was cramping too badly for him to focus properly.

His guts gurgled violently and suddenly, and he walked away from his companions at as fast a pace as he dared while still maintaining control of his bowels. He barely made the privacy of a little clump of salt cedars a few yards away without messing himself. He could hear the Tonks laughing at him while he squatted in the bushes, and knew that his white butt must be visible through the limbs. The diarrhea that had plagued him since the day before was too much misery to worry about his loss of dignity. He finally pulled up his pants and tried to ignore the jeering grins on the Tonks' faces as he made his way back to the group.

"Got the gyp-water squirts, do ya?" Son obviously found Odell's ailment humorous.

"I've been like this ever since we stopped at that little creek north of the Concho. Everything I eat or drink runs straight through me, and I'm cramping so bad I can barely sit up straight," Odell said.

"Mix you up some salt water tonight with a little pinch of gunpowder and drink it. That always works for me." Son pointed to the north. "We can't have you shitting yourself to death before those Comanches yonder get a chance at you."

Odell strained to make out the enemies Son was pointing toward. He expected to see Comanches riding down the river, but no matter how hard he looked he saw nothing. Son noticed and pointed toward a little steep-sided canyon running north out of the river. A thin finger of smoke trickled from it.

"Comanche camp, maybe," Placido observed.

"How's he know it's Comanches?" Odell studied the Tonk chief cautiously. Son's explanation of Indian ways had made some sense to him, but Odell still couldn't quit thinking about Placido being a cannibal, and a man who laughed at white men with the drizzling shits.

Son looked at him like he was stupid for asking a question with such an obvious answer. Had Odell waited a few seconds before opening his mouth, it would have saved him some embarrassment. He promised himself to ask no more stupid questions. It stood to reason nobody else was going to be foolish enough to build a smoky fire right in the middle of Comancheria—unless they had found the Peace Commission at last.

Placido mounted again, and the rest of them followed his lead. They rode back and met the Prussian at the head of the long line of his volunteers. Despite the grassy plain they had come across, all the men were caked in dust, their faces almost white with it except where the sweat had washed it away in streaks. They were spread out for a quarter of a mile at a steady walk with a sort of grim determination about them that reminded Odell of a herd of buffalo on the move.

The Prussian calmly listened to his scouts' report, and then turned back to face the men spreading out behind him. "By *Gott*, the Tonks have found Comanches across the river, and we are going to pay them a visit."

Nobody cheered or chunked their hats in the air, but every man of them went to checking his weapons and gear. Quiet words were passed, and in the matter of a few minutes the party was split in two. Placido and Son led one half of

them to the east, intending to circle around and come on the
Comanche camp from the north. The Prussian held the rest
behind to give them time to get in position.

"I don't see any need in picking a fight here when we're
supposed to be after the Peace Commission," Odell said to
Son as they crossed the river.

"The Prussian isn't going to pass up a chance to kill
Comanches," Son said.

They were within a mile of the smoke trailing up out of
the canyon, and Odell couldn't tell if it was the gyp water
or his nerves causing the butterflies in his stomach. He had
checked the priming on his rifle three times and couldn't
seem to find a comfortable position in his saddle. Talking
helped calm him.

"The Prussian said he wanted to catch a big camp of
them. That's what he promised these men," Odell said.

Son scowled at him for his chatter. "If he passes up this
bunch, he won't have anyone left to follow him. These men
ain't the sort to tolerate a coward."

"But what about all the talk of striking the Comanches
a big blow?"

"Just because there's only one smoke coming out of that
draw doesn't mean we ain't in for a fight. Anytime you're
after Injuns expect surprises. I've seen many the time when
I'd have sworn so many Injuns couldn't have been hidden
in a draw or gully, and they still came boiling out like hor-
nets from a nest."

"But . . ."

"But nothing. Those tracks we ran across were made by
at least forty warriors and their families. If it's them in that
canyon, we're in for a fight. You just keep your trap shut
and pay heed to what I do. Depending on what the Tonks
have to report, our aim is to run off the Comanches' horses
while the Prussian and his bunch come hell-bent for leather
up the canyon," Son said.

One of the Tonks came loping back from the rim of the

canyon and talked briefly with Placido, who soon sent him racing to the Prussian's force. Son left Odell and went to talk with the chief. By the time Odell caught back up to him, everyone was riding on.

"What's the matter? They're all acting like there isn't going to be a fight." Odell kept Crow at a trot to stay along-side Son.

Son somberly shook his head and loped away from him to the front of their party. Odell threaded his way into the single-file column they made as they followed a narrow, switchback trail down the side of the canyon. A tiny, spring-fed stream trickled down the middle of the canyon, and a campfire was smoldering within a clump of mesquite along its bank. As they rode down a broad bench above the canyon floor, Odell noticed the ashes of many fires and the beaten circles were at least forty tepees had stood.

The Prussian and his men arrived at the source of the smoke at the same time, and the entire force gathered at the edge of the mesquite trees. They sat their horses for a long time in silence and studied what the Comanches had left behind. The mutilated, naked bodies of two Mexican men lay like broken, bloated effigies of human beings. The smoke that had drawn the Tonks' attention wasn't from a campfire of the normal sort. The Comanches had built two little fires under the bound prisoners' feet, and nothing was left of the bodies' lower legs but charred flesh falling off the bone. There wasn't one square inch from the dead men's heads to their knees that wasn't cut and hacked.

Odell's stomach threatened to empty itself, and he ducked his eyes away from the sight of the tortured corpses and leaned out of his saddle to retch. When he straightened up and willed himself to look again he noticed that none of the men on either side of him seemed to have noticed his weak moment, or at least they understood enough to act like they hadn't.

"There's a cart back yonder in the thicket." Son Ballard

rode out of the mesquites and jerked a thumb back over his shoulder. "From the looks of things I'd say these men came out from Chouteau's trading post up on the Canadian to hunt meat."

"It's hard to tell what they were by looking at them," the Prussian said.

Odell had never heard anything truer. The blows from clubs and tomahawks had warped the skulls until the faces were hardly human. Both of them had been scalped and had suffered other things Odell hoped he would someday be able to forget. The rest of the Prussian's little army stared at the dead men with tight faces, but Odell tried to keep his eyes averted.

"Let that Injun-lovin' Houston see this and then tell me about peace with the Comanches. Damned their black-hearted souls to hell," Hatchet Murphy swore.

"Damned Injuns," Son said loudly to himself, and then remembered he was sitting his horse beside Placido. "No offense, old friend."

"None taken," Placido said. "I've called you 'damn white men' plenty of times."

"It's just two Mexicans." The Prussian didn't like the depressing turn their morale was taking.

"I remember when we found old man Hazlewood and his son down on Walnut Creek. He and the boy had gotten caught without their rifles while out gathering honey. The Comanches nutted both of them and ran burning chunks of wood up their asses. I found the old man first, and he was still half alive and sitting there like a coon on a stump." Son cleared his mind of the memory with a grunt and a shake of his head.

"There ain't no Hazlewoods left anymore. The Comanches killed them out last year when they got Jim and his family," somebody said.

"No, the Hazlewood men ain't rubbed plumb out. I hear there's another brother down at Seguin," someone else at the back of the group offered.

"There is, but the brother got his nuts crushed by a kicking mule and won't be siring any more Hazlewoods," another threw in.

"What the hell is the matter with y'all?" Odell all but shouted at the men.

He couldn't sit by and hear such idle talk while the Mexicans' bodies lay before him like bloody meat in a smokehouse. The memory of what the Comanches had done to his pappy was still fresh in his mind, and never again would he ever be able to swap lurid gossip about what the Indians supposedly did to their unfortunate victims. He slid from his horse and went to the closest body. He tried to avoid looking at the deceased's accusing and tortured eyes while he cut him loose from the stakes that bound him. Before he knew it, most of the men were helping him free the bodies. All of them had grown even quieter than they had been when they first discovered the Mexicans.

"Sorry, boy. Don't think we're taking this lightly. It's just that talking foolishness can keep a man from losing his mind." Hatchet Murphy's one wild eye had grown wilder looking, and it was plain that he was reliving other such brutal scenes.

"This ain't an easy thing to look on," Odell mumbled.

"And it doesn't get any easier with time," Hatchet Murphy wiped a tear from his leathery cheek.

Odell looked over to see the Prussian staring at him. The man was as calm and cool as he ever was. Odell already knew that the Prussian was a hard man and had even envied that trait at one time. But now he wasn't so sure that he wanted to be like that, if it meant being able to look on such horrors without a trace of emotion. It seemed to him that a man would have to be half dead not be horrified and weakened by such violence.

They buried the Mexican hunters in shallow graves, and led horses back and forth over them to pack the earth. Son Ballard recited the Twenty-third Psalm, or at least what he could remember of it, and then they mounted and started north once again. They rode silently out of that canyon, a funeral procession of violent men grown more violent from the mere passing of such a day.

Odell couldn't quit thinking about Red Wing as they rode. She may have been a Comanche by birth, but any people who could do such things to their fellow humans were capable of anything. It didn't get spoken of much, but everyone in Texas knew what Comanches did to women captives. For all he knew she might already be suffering terrible things at their hands.

"We have to save her," Odell said to the Prussian when they were two miles away.

"We will, Herr Odell. We will." The Prussian kept his gaze straight ahead to where the Comanche trail headed into the distance. He looked as cold and hard as ever.

Chapter 22

Red Wing sat up and held the filthy, tattered hem of her long skirt in her hands and pulled a piece of grass from the tangle of her hair. She looked to the river and the commissioner nodded at her from where he stood at the edge of camp. She could tell by his posture and the look on his face that he meant his presence to comfort her, but she had to make herself rise and go far enough into the timber to be out of sight of the camp. She tried not to think about Jim Pockmark's body lying somewhere downstream.

She carried her valise to the river's edge and knelt and bathed her face and hands and combed at her hair with her fingers. She washed until her skin felt smooth once again, but she still felt dirty. The muddy water offered a poor bath, but she stripped off and waded in anyway. She laid back and let her hair float and listened to the slow sound of the river echoing in her eardrums. She felt for a moment as if her spirit would float away on the gentle current, but the feeling passed.

She dried her hair with the cleanest portion of her torn dress, and then took a fresh one from her valise. She felt better after her bath and change, but noticed there was still a slight quiver in her hands. The sun shone on the riverbank, and she stood there motionless with her hands upon her hips and looked out across the prairie while she soaked up the warmth. She told herself right then that she wasn't going any farther. Her captors were going to have to tie her hand and foot to take her beyond camp. The stubborn strength that she had relied on for so long had been spent in her ordeal with the renegade Delaware, and she had come as far as she intended to go.

The camp was well above the river, and the first thing she saw when she neared it was the commissioner standing in the same spot he had been earlier. She was going to tell him right then what she had decided, but something about the intense look on his face made her pause. He was focused on something to the southeast, and she turned to see what it was that had his attention.

Two Indian braves sat their horses on the far bank staring at the camp. Captain Jones had come down to stand beside the commissioner, and they looked uneasy.

"What are they?" The sun was in her eyes and she could barely make out the two warriors across the river.

"I'm pretty sure they're Comanches." The commissioner gave her a strange, sad look.

The Comanche braves eventually waded their horses across the river and stopped several yards in front of the Peace Commission. The commissioner tried to grant them the hospitality of his camp, but the two refused the offer to dismount and eyed the white people with cautious disdain. It wasn't apparent whether their intentions were peaceful or not, and they seemed as uncertain about the whole situation as the commissioner did.

"Captain Jones, don't you speak a little Spanish?" Commissioner Anderson asked.

"I do," the captain admitted reluctantly.

"They don't seem to speak any English, so try some of that Mex lingo on them. Tell them that we have come to talk with their chiefs." The commissioner was trying to keep his rifle handy without appearing hostile to their visitors.

Captain Jones rattled off a long explanation in halting Spanish. When he finally paused, one of the Comanches pointed up the river and said something.

"He wants to know why there is a dead Delaware lying down there in the trees," the captain said.

"Tell him the truth," the commissioner said.

The captain spoke again, and then listened to the two Comanches' reply. He turned back to the commissioner. "Their Spanish is almost as bad as mine, but they seem to think it's funny that you shot Jim."

"Can they take us to their chiefs?" the commissioner asked.

The captain shrugged and tried again. When he was through, the same Comanche who had asked about Jim's body jerked his chin toward Red Wing and asked another question.

"He wants to know if she is your woman," the captain said.

Red Wing studied the two Comanches from behind the barricade of saddles they had thrown up. Agent Torrey stood beside her nervously gripping his shotgun. It hadn't been so long since she had lived among the tribe that she had forgotten such warriors. Everything about the two Comanches was familiar, from the naked brown bodies covered only in a breechcloth, to the long lances in their hands, and the haughty, cunning stares from behind their high cheekbones.

The commissioner carefully avoided looking at her. "Tell them that she is a Comanche taken from them long ago, and that we have brought her back to her people as a token of our goodwill."

The captain apparently had some trouble communicating her status, but after a long discussion with the warriors he seemed satisfied. The Comanches talked among themselves in their native tongue while they stared up the hill at Red Wing. They didn't seem impressed by her, or totally convinced that she was *Numuunuh*, or of the People. Finally, the talker of the two said something to the captain in Spanish.

Captain Jones looked even more uneasy than before. "They say most of their band is gathering for a big hunt a little over a day's ride south of here."

"Is that all?" the commissioner asked.

"No, they said a bunch of things I can't understand. Apparently, there will be many lodges present at this gathering, and some bigwig named Iron Shirt will be there. I get the impression he's a pretty important fellow among them."

"Can we safely pay this camp our respects without getting killed?"

Captain Jones sucked in a deep breath and looked at the commissioner like he was crazy. "These two are out scouting for buffalo, and they've offered to take us back to their village. I'll let you be the judge of how safe that would be."

"So be it. Tell them we need a little time to pack our things and saddle up," the commissioner said.

The two Comanches said something to each other and pointed at the commissioner and laughed. Captain Jones asked them what they found so funny, then smiled at the commissioner.

"They say you a have a very pretty coat." The captain chuckled.

"They can go to hell." The commissioner looked down at his rows of brass buttons and slapped the dust from the front of his jacket. "But don't translate that."

None of them knew that Red Wing spoke fluent Spanish, and she didn't tell them either. She had listened closely to the conversation, and quickly learned that the captain's

Spanish was as bad as his whiskey breath. While he got most of the details right, the Comanches hadn't meant to just poke fun at the commissioner's fancy jacket. What they had meant was to call him the Pretty Man. Had it not been for her dire situation, she would have found that very funny.

The commissioner went to bring up their horses, and in doing so he passed close to Agent Torrey and Red Wing. The little man wrinkled his nose and looked up at his superior with more than a little trepidation.

"Did I hear you plainly? Are we to ride with those two Comanches?" Agent Torrey asked.

"You heard right. Saddle up."

Agent Torrey sighed. "I was afraid that's what I heard."

Captain Jones took up his saddle and stood before the Indian agent. "Don't worry, Mr. Tom. You can draw the Comanches' pictures in that little book of yours."

Although Agent Torrey had devotedly sketched the various plants and wildlife he had passed along the trail, somehow he had lost his once grand desire to paint the legendary Comanche in his native setting. Not only had he lost the urge, he couldn't remember for the life of him what had led him to want to do such a thing in the first place. He could only chalk it up to naïveté and foolish, romantic notions of the frontier. Days and nights of hearing Captain Jones's horrid tales of Comanche massacres had terrified him, and knowing that the commissioner was about to turn them over into the hands of such savages made his knees tremble.

"Agent Torrey, saddle your horse. We have no choice but to be brave," Red Wing said gently.

Somehow he managed to saddle his horse. He felt as if the Comanches were watching his every move, and his hands and fingers were unusually clumsy. His three companions were already mounted and waiting for him. He could see the impatience written plainly on the commissioner's face, but he couldn't seem to make himself put his foot into the stirrup. The thought of getting on his horse and riding away with the Comanches felt comparable to jumping off a cliff.

"Just think of it this way. You can either ride with us, or try to make it back home by yourself," the commissioner said.

Agent Torrey couldn't deny the logic of that. If he was going to be killed by Indians, he would rather not be lost and alone when it happened. He took his ragged old wool scarf and snugly tied it over his stovepipe hat and knotted it under his chin. The tall crown seemed especially prone to catching the wind, and the commissioner had become angry in the past when they had to stop their travels for him to get off his horse and chase his lid.

Captain Jones held his shotgun for him while he mounted. He had lost his gun sling somewhere along the trail and hadn't gotten around to making another. He had not quite mastered the art of mounting with his shotgun in his hand, and it felt highly undignified to have to give up his weapon to a more competent man to hold for him while he climbed into the saddle. It was at least as embarrassing as having to tie his hat on.

His little mustang was in a good mood that morning and didn't try to throw him or run away with him. He took his shotgun back from the captain and tried to form an optimistic vision of the day to come.

"Care for a slug?" the captain asked.

Agent Torrey looked up from cleaning his glasses long enough to realize the captain was holding out a bottle of whiskey to him. While they all knew the captain was prone to drink, he usually attempted to keep his crutch hidden. However, he seemed to have been imbibing a little more freely as of late, and his saddlebag supply of liquor was in danger of running dry.

"I daresay, Captain, I think you're a little drunk," Agent Torrey said.

"I haven't even begun to drink. Care to join me?" The

captain smiled wryly and looked to him with his red-rimmed, hound-dog eyes. "I find that Comanches, and life in general, are much more bearable with a touch of the spirits warming my belly."

The commissioner was scowling at both of them. Normally, Agent Torrey would have been far too scared of displeasing the commissioner or of getting too drunk and falling off his horse. However, the thought of having to ride all day beside the captain while the man regaled him with tale after tale of their impending horrible deaths at the hands of the Comanches was too depressing for him to bear. He reached out for the bottle and took a healthy slug, and then another. The whiskey burned his chest like a dose of turpentine. He looked to the captain with tears streaming down from behind the thick lenses of his glasses, and gave the man a faked smile.

"That's the way, Mr. Tom. Keep it up and the day is bound to get better," the captain said.

And in fact it did. After following their guides five miles across the country, the prospect of dying a bloody death had lost much of its horror. Remarkably, Agent Torrey found himself scoffing at such trivial matters after several more slugs of whiskey. By the time they had ridden ten miles or so he had grown so bold as to ride forward to generously offer the Comanches a drink of the captain's whiskey. He couldn't remember why they had looked so scary to him earlier, but he felt sure that all of them would soon be the greatest of friends. The two warriors tried to shoo him away with fierce looks and threatening holds on their weapons, but he was having too good of a time to notice. Obviously they were shy sorts, and he felt it his duty to make them feel welcome. At least they weren't so rude as to interrupt his trying to teach them his favorite song, although from their silence he assumed they had no voice for Irish pub ballads.

Red Wing rode between Commissioner Anderson and

the captain. The captain's whiskey had made him quiet, and the commissioner seemed too ashamed to speak to her now that what he had set out to do finally appeared to be coming to fruition. Both of them kept their attention on the two Comanches, and a careful eye on the skyline for signs of any more of the tribe.

She tried to keep her courage up, and to find whatever strength it was within her that had kept her going thus far. She thought the commissioner a fool to trust himself to the Comanches, and the feeling that the expedition was going to end badly for all of them wouldn't go away. Comanches were no different than white men when it came to lies, and their hatred of the Tejanos knew no bounds. She wondered why the commissioner couldn't see that his ambitions were going to ruin all their lives.

She stayed as far away from the Comanches as possible. The two warriors had said little to them since leaving the Washita, other than to relate that they would reach the main village the following day. Her Comanche was coming back to her enough to catch bits and pieces of the quiet conversations they carried on between themselves. She picked up nothing to confirm her distrust of the two, but she feared them nonetheless.

Agent Torrey was staggering drunk by the time they stopped for the night. He tripped and fell while getting off his horse, and was unable to get back to his feet. He soon ceased his struggles and passed out, still holding the rein of his horse and with his tied-down hat squashed like an accordion over his face.

But Captain Jones and the commissioner made it plain that one of them was going to stay on guard. The captain lay down across the fire from the Comanches with his weapons close to hand. The commissioner took the first watch and sat wide awake with his saddle for a chair and his rifle across his knees. He kept a careful eye on the Comanches, who appeared to be sleeping. Red Wing curled up in her blanket at the commissioner's feet, clutching her little knife tightly in her hand.

The Comanches woke early and full of vigor. Apparently, they had slept like babies and were ready for breakfast. Despite the attempt to stand guard in shifts, the commissioner and the captain didn't look to have gotten much sleep. Red Wing knew that she hadn't. She had jerked awake every few minutes to check if the Comanches were still in their beds.

After a quick meal of buffalo meat, they started on their way. They crossed the Prairie Dog Fork of the Red before the sun was well up, and headed across a broad plain. By midday they were in sight of a line of hills rising up to the south. Soon, the smoke from a large number of campfires could be seen. Red Wing's eyes could barely make out the pale gleam of many tepees scattered along the edges of some canyon lands south of the hills.

The village spotted them quickly, and a large group of warriors raced out on their horses to surround them. Greetings and explanations were passed back and forth between the Peace Commission's guides and the newcomers. The welcome the Comanches gave their visitors was a cold one, but they escorted them toward the camp just the same.

The village consisted of at least sixty lodges, and the women and children stopped what they were doing to watch them pass. More warriors stared at them from where they sat in front of the tepees, and the camp dogs raced among the trotting horses, barking at all the excitement. Red Wing met the curious gaze of a woman fanning away the blowflies from the raw buffalo robe she was scraping. She was covered in grease and bloodstains all the way up to her elbows, and kneeling before the stretched hide like it was an altar. Red Wing had seen her own mother in just the same position many times.

Their escort led them to a large tepee near the center of the camp, where a short, bow-legged warrior appeared to be waiting for them with a group of elder men. They pulled up before him, and the commissioner gave the old Comanches a broad wave. The bow-legged warrior slowly lifted his palm in greeting, while the entire camp pressed in around them.

"Try that Mexican talk on them again. Tell him the same thing you told those two earlier, and make us sound impressive," the commissioner said out the side of his mouth to Captain Jones.

The captain spoke loudly, even if he did get hung up often while he searched for the proper words. The bowlegged warrior apparently didn't speak Spanish, and he turned to a wrinkled old man beside him for translation. When the captain was through, the bowlegged warrior gave an equally long speech, and his old friend repeated what he said in Spanish.

"His name is Iron Shirt, and I gather he is some sort of medicine man or chief, or maybe both. He says he will make no promises, but the men of his village will at least hear us out," the captain said.

Iron Shirt stepped to where he had a better view of Red Wing sitting her horse behind the commissioner. He studied her carefully and then said something for his interpreter to repeat.

"Iron Shirt says that the woman we bring him doesn't look like a Comanche. He wonders if we have made some mistake," the captain said.

Commissioner Anderson eased off of his horse and motioned Red Wing to do the same. She studiously ignored him and all about her and kept her chin lifted and her eyes on the top of the tepee.

"Get down and meet your cousins," the captain said dryly.

Red Wing looked at him like he was trash. She held out a bent wrist to the commissioner and lifted her chin higher. "A lady should be given help dismounting."

Agent Torrey raised his eyebrows above his glasses at her demand. She had been mounting and dismounting on her own halfway across Texas, and he couldn't imagine why she needed help. But then again, his hangover was too bad to think properly.

The commissioner smiled wryly. "Nice act. I almost hope you succeed in convincing them that you don't belong here."

He took her hand while she unhooked her leg from the sidesaddle's post and steadied her stirrup as she stepped down. He watched as she tucked her hair in place and brushed down the front of her dress. She walked forward with a grace all her own and eyed the Comanches around her as if she was on a sightseeing trip that she found especially boring.

Iron Shirt said something to her, but she frowned with feigned confusion. He quickly turned away from her with a dissatisfied grunt. He headed for the door of his tepee, saying something to his interpreter in passing. The old man heard him out and scowled at the Peace Commission. He and the captain had a brief discussion, and then he and the rest of the elders disappeared into the tepee behind Iron Shirt.

"I take it that didn't go so well," the commissioner said.

"Iron Shirt doesn't believe that Red Wing was ever a Comanche, and if she was, she has been so long with us that she might as well be dead," the captain said.

"How did he take to the notion of the peace talks at Fort Bird?"

"All he would commit to was to discuss the matter with you. He said that there are many more Comanches who will arrive this evening. Once most of his band is here they will call a council to hear what you have to say. For now, we are supposed to wait."

One of their earlier guides led them to an empty tepee a few yards from Iron Shirt's. He told the captain that it was for them to use and quickly disappeared. Two young boys showed up to take their horses, and the commissioner knew he was too outnumbered to argue about giving them up. They unsaddled and pitched their gear into the lodge and watched their only means of escape led away.

Commissioner Anderson casually surveyed the number of Comanches still watching them. Supposedly they weren't captives, but it still felt that way. Agent Torrey and Red Wing had already gone into the tepee, but he didn't want to appear to be so scared as to hide like a rabbit in a hole. He smiled at the Comanches and took his sweet time going into the lodge.

"Well, we finally found them," he said to the captain.

Captain Jones spat in the dust. "Yes, sir, I'd say we've stepped right in the middle of it."

Chapter 23

Patience was a virtue that Odell wasn't sure he would ever possess. Red Wing was somewhere out there alone and in danger, and every single mile of the long journey to find her seemed more like five. Common sense told him that a horse could only travel so far, so fast, but the nervous energy inside him couldn't be kept down. The only thing that soothed his impatience was the scouting and hunting trips he took away from the column with Son Ballard. There was something about the lonely, wide-open country that Odell loved, and the old scout was a veritable wealth of information when it came to living in the wilds.

Son might grumble and growl about Odell asking too many questions, but he inevitably answered each and every one of them. Odell came to learn that there was a difference between looking and seeing. Months on the prairies and plains had given him a crash course in survival, but Son taught him to observe his surroundings and to interpret what he saw. Reading sign wasn't just the ability to track, but was instead knowing the land intimately.

Water was everything in arid country, and the ability to find it was the difference between life and death. The Indians and the scant few seasoned plainsmen like Son read the minutest details of nature, from the wildlife and vegetation, right down to even the smallest insect. The tracks of wild horses going to water were easily separated from those they made going away. A thirsty herd traveled with a businesslike determination, while one with its bellies sloshing full scattered wider and grazed along at a more leisurely pace. Swallows built dirt nests, and a keen eye would notice that a mouthful of mud meant the bird was flying away from water. Doves drank often, and a scout could follow their flight just before dusk to where they watered. Cottonwood trees required regular moisture, but a belt of green in a distant drainage didn't always lead a man to standing water. And as Odell had already come to know, a waterhole or a stream didn't necessarily mean a healthy drink. Many of the waterings of that country, especially along the foot of the Llano, were so laden with salt and gypsum as to be undrinkable or were not to be counted on to be wet year around.

Fire was as important as water when the weather could seemingly change in the blink of an eye. Wood for fuel was scarce, but dried buffalo chips made a hot fire. Son carried a length of hollow cane with cotton threaded through it, and a bit of the fluff twisted out one end of the stick readily took a spark from a flint and steel. On a rainy day, cloth soaked in corncob ashes or gunpowder and then dried was often the difference between fire and no fire.

Odell had grown up among timbered mountains, and at first sight the open country seemed almost barren—nothing but brown grass and sky—but he was coming to know its bounty. Besides the buffalo, mule deer, and antelope, which were new to him, many of the game animals he had hunted in Georgia and the woods along the Colorado River made their homes on the plains, and it was just a matter of adapting his hunting techniques to different terrain and food sources. Less cover made ambush more difficult for the hunter, but it also made moving game easier to spot. A far-ranging hunter on horseback who knew what to look for usually could put meat in the pot. Instead of still hunting through the dense cover of acorn-laden oak forests as he had in the Southeast, he learned the art of spot and stalk and to accurately guess the range for longer rifle shots.

A day north of finding the dead Mexican hunters, Odell and Son scouted far to the west of the Prussian's force. They skirted the edge of a red-dusted, broken maze of badlands on their return. The day was hot and Odell badly wanted to take a drink, but his canteen was less than half full. He decided to emulate Son, and put a peeled chunk of prickly pear cactus in his mouth to keep it moist.

"Game gets scarcer the closer you get to the Llano except for buffler, and most of the shaggies are already gone north," Son said. "We'd have done better to stay out of these breaks and to have hunted to the east."

Odell squinted into the sun and scowled at the hard bit of tortured earth before him. "Hell must look a lot like those badlands to the west of us in summer, but I like that prairie country you've guided us through."

Son wallowed his chunk of prickly pear around in his cheek like a chaw of tobacco and nodded lazily. "It's a shitty stretch of ground between here and the Llano if you're partial to good water. I've never brought anything back from that country but dust and an empty belly. I froze my pinkie toe off in a blizzard one winter on the head of the Brazos, and I reckon the little bone of it is still lying out there somewhere if the coyotes couldn't digest it."

Son had managed to kill a mule deer buck, and they had a ten-mile ride back to the column. In Odell's mind, talking was the only thing to help pass the time. "I was thinking that a man could make a pretty good home back there before the Brazos forked."

Son came out of his sleepy trance and looked at Odell like he was crazy. "It's a fair country if you can live like an Injun, but if you want to farm, you'd best go back where you came from."

Odell wasn't one to let go of a thing once he got started, and he had spent too much time thinking about the prairie country just west of the Cross Timbers to be thwarted. "You might grow a little along the river, but farming ain't all a man can do with a piece of ground. Placido said those old Spanish priests down on the San Saba used to run cattle around their mission, and Manuel Ortega tells me that his kin raise cattle on far drier country south of the border."

"Just what do you know about cattle? And besides, a cow is worth just barely more than a cold turd in Texas," Son scoffed.

"Well, there are more folks moving to Texas every day, and maybe cows won't always be so cheap."

Son's laugh was like the bray of a mule. "Kid, you figure out what to do with the Comanches and the buffalo, find somewhere with a market for beef, and maybe you could make a go of it."

"The Prussian is always saying a businessman has to think ahead if he wants to get in on the beginnings of a coming thing."

"You'll notice the Prussian still has the good sense to stay east of the frontier to make his money. That's where the people are," Son said. "At the rate things are going it'll be another fifty years before you can live out here without getting yourself scalped, much less build a rancho."

"I'd be there first," Odell said stubbornly.

"If you want to start wearing a sombrero and big spurs you'd be better off to look at that cedar country down the Brazos and east of the Cross Timbers."

"I like it farther west. The country suits me."

"I don't know why I bother with you. Most times you're like talking to a rock." Son tried to ride ahead and avoid any more conversation.

"My mama used to say that you had to follow your heart," Odell said to Son's back.

Son twisted in his saddle to look back. "No offense to your mama, but I'd recommend following something safer like common sense. You'll live longer that way."

"Sooner or later, we'll all die, and I reckon I'll go my own way until then."

"I'm sure you will, but I would just as soon have that dying part later rather than sooner. There's no sense rushing things." Son paused to cock one ear to the wind. "Did you hear that?"

"What?"

"You can't hear nothing with all your jabbering. I swore I just heard a fawn bleating," Son said.

Odell hushed and the two of them listened until they both heard the sound again. It did sound like the bleat of a baby deer or an antelope in distress. The repeated cries were coming from the foot of a series of red, white-capped buttes on the far side of a deep gash in the ground west of them. The meat from the dead buck they were carrying wasn't going to make a dent in their party's hunger, and both of them headed off eagerly toward a chance at gathering a little more supper.

The periodic bleat of the fawn had grown louder by the time they traveled a quarter of a mile along the edge of the steep-sided canyon. They soon spotted a small bunch of antelope on the canyon floor at the foot of the far buttes some three hundred yards away. Both of them stopped their horses and tried to come up with a means of getting closer to their prey. The wind was at their faces, but they were sky-lined and to ride any closer was sure to run the animals off. The bleating continued and the pronghorns all had their heads raised and were working cautiously toward that sound.

"There's your fawn, and he's an ugly devil." Son pointed slowly to a point much closer and below them.

Odell stood in his stirrups where he could look down over the lip of the canyon wall. The first thing he saw was Dub Harris kneeling behind a hump of ground and scraggly grass with his rifle pointed at the antelopes. He was doing his best imitation of a fawn's bleat to bring his quarry closer.

"That's a neat trick," Son said quietly. "I never would have suspected it from Dub. He's as stout as a bull, but he ain't the sharpest tool in the shed."

They sat still and watched Dub draw a bead on the antelope doe in the lead. His mimicry was about to get him an easy shot, and they would go down and help him skin out the meat once he made the kill. It was Odell who first saw the tawny streak bounding through the grass and rocks toward Dub's back.

The mountain lion was just as fooled as the antelope were, and his ears had it convinced that a tender young fawn lay hidden in the grass. The only thing that even gave Dub a fighting chance was the fact that his calling was so good that it had excited the big cat enough to start its charge from a distance instead of stalking close for a pounce. Dub heard his attacker coming at the last minute and fumbled to get his rifle around in time to defend himself.

The cougar was sixty yards away from Dub and closing impossibly fast when Odell finally shouldered his rifle. There was no time for careful aim, and he simply swung his gun barrel through the running cat and squeezed the trigger when its head appeared in his sights. The Bishop gun boomed and the cat crashed into Dub with the force of a freight train, knocking the powerful brawler off his feet.

"That was a hell of a shot." Son hadn't even managed to get his own rifle from its saddle boot. "You're plumb quick when you want to be."

"It wasn't much." Odell was pleased, but he knew that

a snapshot at a running target at better than a hundred yards had more to do with luck than it did with marksmanship.

The mountain lion must have twitched or shown some sign of life, because Dub jumped to his feet and fired another shot into it before beginning to beat the carcass with his rifle butt. Odell and Son rode along the rim until they found an eroded cut leading down into the canyon. Dub's horse was tied there, and they brought him along with them to where Dub stood over the dead lion. All three of the horses blew and shied nervously, refusing to get too close to a predator that was known to have a special love for horseflesh.

"Thanks, Son." Somebody, sometime, had busted Dub's front teeth, and his smile was a snaggled thing.

"Don't thank me. It was Odell who shot that catamount off of you," Son said.

Dub frowned at Odell but managed to mumble something that might have been faked gratitude. His attention quickly went back to the cat, and he studied it cautiously, as if it might come to life again. "I've never heard of a lion attacking a full-grown man in broad daylight."

"He probably never saw you and was just homing in on what he thought was an injured fawn," Odell said.

"Yeah." Dub studied Odell. "He probably would've veered off when he saw me."

"That's if he saw you. Haven't you ever seen a house cat stalking something it hears in the grass? They'll locate the sound and pounce without ever seeing what they're after," Son said. "I don't figure he would've killed you, but Odell surely kept your backside from getting clawed up."

Dub frowned at the lion. "This critter caused me to miss out on those antelopes, but I've heard you old-timers swear that panther meat is the best there is."

Son tried to look serious, but a grin quickly spread across his mouth. "I've told that whopper myself, but the truth is, I've never tasted it."

"Well, meat's been scarce as of late, so get down and help me load him," Dub said.

"Odell's the one that shot the cat. I reckon the hide is his," Son said.

The mountain lion was an exceptionally big tom, and it was plain that Dub didn't like the thought of Odell getting such a fine trophy. "There's two bullets in the cat, and one of them is mine."

"You know better than that." Son examined the carcass and pointed to where Odell's bullet had gone in one side of the cat's neck and out its throat on the other side, breaking its neck. "Dub, you just shot a dead lion, and made a poor shot at that."

"Maybe that's the kid's bullet hole back there in its hip, and mine's the one through the neck," Dub said belligerently.

"You know better than that. You just don't like Odell, and don't want to admit he pulled your fat out of the fire," Son said.

"You're damned right I don't like him. He's too cocky," Dub said. "And I've just about had all of your taking up for him."

Son had his rifle cradled in the bend of his left elbow, but he turned slightly so that the muzzle was near to pointing at Dub's chest. "Now Dub, I know that look you're getting, and I'm too old to go knuckle and skull with you. You give me trouble and I'll split your noggin with a bullet, and not lose any sleep over it either."

Dub's temper was known to be as volatile as a tornado, but he wasn't mad enough yet not to realize that Son would do just what he said. He clenched his beefy fists and stared past Son at Odell.

"You can have the hide. I've killed panthers before," Odell said. He would have liked to have the pelt, but it wasn't worth Son having to shoot the bully.

"You're full of shit," Dub said. "You ain't shot a big cat before."

Odell knew he ought to keep quiet, but he couldn't. "One time back in Georgia I thought my hounds had a coon treed, but when I climbed the tree to find him and knock him out, I found out it was a panther."

"Are you claiming that you killed a lion with a club?" Dub asked.

"I ain't *claiming* anything. That cat wasn't near as big as this one, but I killed him just the same," Odell said. "He wasn't any too happy about me climbing up in the tree with him, and it was a bit of a tussle there for a while."

Dub looked from Odell to Son's rifle barrel and finally laughed. "You two are a pair. Take that damned pelt if you want it. My horse probably wouldn't let me load it on him anyway. That bronc has been trying to buck me off at the least excuse ever since I bought him."

Dub didn't lend a hand while Odell and Son attempted to load the lion on Crow's back. The horse was having no part of it, and kicked the lion out of their hands and pawed a dent in the crown of Odell's hat before they gave up their effort. They skinned the lion and stuffed a few of the choicer cuts of meat into Odell's saddlebags. Dub rode up out of the canyon and left them before they coaxed Crow into letting them tie the bundled hide behind his saddle.

"That was a big cat," Son said as he mounted. "I'd guess him to be every bit of eight foot from his nose to the tip of his tail."

"He'll look pretty good tacked up on a wall."

Son rubbed his whiskers and grimaced. "You're gonna have trouble with Dub. There ain't no two ways about it."

"I figure I can handle him." Odell swung his leg over his saddle and followed Son out of the canyon.

"You'd best just stay as far away from him as you can," Son said. "I believe your story about that cat back in Georgia, but whupping a catamount would be child's play compared to fighting Dub Harris."

"I ain't never been licked in a fistfight yet," Odell said a little proudly.

"Well, you just tackle old Dub if you're of a mind to. I can already see that I can't tell a scrapper like you anything about fighting." Son wouldn't say another word for the whole trip back to the Prussian's evening camp.

Odell settled in for his share of supper around the fire while Son reported to the Prussian. Odell found the panther meat strong and stringy, and settled for his tiny share of the venison. The other men were apparently so hungry that they didn't mind eating meat that tasted like cat piss and praised the manly quality of their meal. More than one of them came to Odell to admire his lion pelt and to hear how he had killed it. Although he downplayed what he had done, Dub still glared at him across the fire. The fact that the men razzed the bully unmercifully for being saved by a kid didn't help matters any. Odell remained quiet and attempted to guide the conversation elsewhere.

Dub tried to fend off the teasing of his comrades good-naturedly, but every time he looked at Odell he got a little madder. It bothered him that so many of the men set store by the overgrown kid. He couldn't understand why they were so impressed by his determination to avenge his grandfather and save his sweetheart, and the fact that he had ridden the Staked Plains alone. The kid just had more than his share of dumb luck, as was evident by his finding of Bowie's knife. Dub thought he saw Odell smirk at him several times, and he was sure that that the boy was gloating over his recent embarrassment of him. And that was what he hated the worst about Odell—the fact that he wasn't scared of him. In Dub's experience, big lunks like Odell always thought they were tougher than somebody shorter.

Odell was scraping a little meat and fat from the lion hide with his Bowie knife, and the sight of two things that Dub envied brought his temper to a boil. He reached out with one foot and kicked the fire as if by accident, knocking sparks all over Odell.

"Watch it," Odell said irritably.

Dub stood quickly. "Are you looking for trouble?"

Odell took a deep breath and pointed casually with his blade at Dub. He didn't mean the gesture as a threat and did it without thinking. "I reckon it was an accident."

"I'll teach you to pull a knife on me." Dub immediately drew his own knife and started around the fire.

Odell lunged backward off the saddle he was sitting on and barely managed to avoid the swipe of Dub's blade. He sucked in his gut with his back arched and his arms thrown out as Dub's backhand stroke cut a long slit in the belly of his leather hunting shirt. Odell stabbed with his Bowie and missed badly enough that Dub caught his wrist. Dub tried to wrench the blade away, and stuck his leg behind Odell in an attempt to backheel him to the ground. Odell skipped over the extended leg and caught Dub's knife wrist as he reared it above his head for a downstroke.

The two of them slung each other around the fire in an attempt to free their knives. Odell strained to pull away from Dub's viselike grip, and then gave suddenly, punching the heavy butt of his knife handle into the other man's temple. Dub was knocked to one knee, but Odell took a deep cut across his thigh for his trouble when he tried to close. Dub got to his feet with blood seeping from his scalp, and the two of them circled slowly while they looked for an opening to kill each other.

The sharp click of a cocking hammer and the cold steel of a pistol barrel pressed against his temple stopped Dub in his tracks. His eyes grew wide and white in the dim light as he looked to the Prussian at his side without moving his head. The man's hand was as steady as a rock and his finger was on the trigger. Son Ballard stepped in front of Odell with his rifle ready.

"Kentucky Bob, you stay out of this," Son said to Dub's brother, who was slipping closer to the fire with his rifle. "I don't want to shoot one Harris, much less two."

"Herr Dub," the Prussian said coolly, "I can't afford to lose a single man, but if there is to be any killing, I will be the one to do it."

Dub released his knife without argument when the Prussian reached for it. Dub knew that Son Ballard might give a man fair warning, but it was a wonder the Prussian hadn't already shot him.

"That goes for you too," Son said to Odell. "Put up your knife."

Odell sheathed the Bowie while he kept an eye on Dub over Son's shoulder. "He came hunting me."

"I was just going to whittle on him a little," Dub said to the Prussian. "You can take your pistol down if you want."

All of the Texans had gathered close. Most of them didn't look too happy with Dub, but there were a few that seemed generally enthusiastic to see a scrap. Odell realized that nobody believed he could whip Dub, and the thought bothered him greatly. He'd been able to straighten a horseshoe with his bare hands since he was thirteen, and there wasn't a man among them that reached his chin except for Placido. He was tired of being treated like a kid, and thought it high time they all learned who the bull of the woods was. If it took whipping a knothead like Dub Harris to gain some respect, then that was what he was going to do.

"Fists are good enough for me. If Dub there wants a licking, then I'll give him one," Odell said.

Dub smiled, but his eyes were crazy. "You've got to come out from behind all these skirts if we're going to hug."

The Prussian scowled at Odell before lowering his pistol and stepping aside. "Let him loose, Son. These men seem bound and determined to butt heads."

Son winced at Odell before stepping away. "I'm telling you, it's gonna hurt."

Odell cracked the knuckles of both his fists and loosened his big shoulders in his shirt. "Don't worry, I like to fight."

"Uh-huh." Son nodded his head and motioned Odell toward Dub with a grand sweep of his hand. "Have at it, Killer."

Nobody was quite sure what Odell expected, but it was obvious that what he got was no part of his thinking. Maybe he thought he and Dub would scratch their feet in the grass, or spit across a line in the dirt before fighting. However, he learned in a hurry that Dub had done all the talking he intended to do. Just as Odell was about to spout off something tough-sounding, Dub charged forward swinging both fists. Whatever it was that Odell was going to say was stopped by one of Dub's meaty, scarred fists planting itself on his cheek. It was as if a mule had kicked Odell in the head; somehow the sawed-off brawler managed to kick him on the knee and slug him in the face once more as he was falling.

Odell hit the ground flat on his back, and he was dimly aware of Dub's boots impacting with his torso. The punishment was mercifully short and Odell was soon left where he lay. His head felt like it had been busted wide open, and everything in his body screamed at him to just stay down. He rose to his hands and knees and turned his head enough to see Dub's boots a few feet away. He knew that as soon as he attempted to stand Dub would be on him again, but his shame was as great as the anger rising up in him.

"Stay down, kid. You don't want any more." There was a hint of laughter in Dub's voice.

Odell managed to get one leg under him and lurched to his feet. Dub immediately closed with him and Odell barely managed to duck enough to take a punch off the top of his head. His brain refused to think properly, and his legs seemed to have lost all their strength. He fell into Dub, trying to smother the swinging fists and to use his size to his advantage. He caught Dub's thick neck under his left arm and grasped the back of the man's belt with his other hand, hurling him across the fire. He staggered through the shower of embers and landed a long, looping right hand to Dub's ear that tore it half off. Dub bellowed like a bull and bobbed and weaved and ducked so that Odell busted his left fist on the top of Dub's head.

Odell had never hit anything that didn't go down to stay, and he cocked his right fist for a mighty blow that would have downed a horse. He intended to end the fight right then and there, but he was way too slow. Dub stepped inside the ponderous swing and hit him twice to the body and head-butted him under the chin. It was as if every time Odell got the space and time to throw a punch, one of Dub's was already hitting him. They grunted and strained in the smoky dust, and Dub's blows landed with dull, meaty thuds. In a matter of seconds, Odell lay on the ground once more with his face in the dirt.

"Stay down, Odell." Son took a hesitant step forward.

Odell heard none of them. He scooted his knees up under him and struggled to push himself up with his forearms. There was something in his eyes that might have been his own blood. He recognized what he thought were Dub's knees and lunged weakly forward. Dub laughed and dodged easily back and let Odell fall on his face again.

"You ain't worth the trouble." Dub dusted off his hands and spit at him.

"We ain't done yet," Odell croaked.

"You just get up again," Dub jeered. "You're going to fiddle around and make me mad."

"He's had enough," Son said. He and the Prussian stepped forward and grabbed Odell's arms as he wobbled to his feet.

"That kid's lucky I didn't give it to him worse. He better walk softly around me from now on, or I'll finish what I started." Dub turned his back.

Odell was too weary to put up much of a fight against

the hold Son and the Prussian had on him, but he leaned out with his battered face jutted forward. "You come back here. I ain't licked yet."

Dub ignored him and walked away. The Prussian and Son guided Odell to his saddle, and the young man slumped down on it with his forearms propped on his knees. Everyone was staring at him, and he wiped the blood and the slobber from his face and stared back. His right eye was already swelling badly, and blood poured from his mouth where he had bit his tongue.

"I guess they're all laughing at me," he said after a long while.

"Nobody's laughing at you," Son said.

"Dub ain't near as big as me."

"Yeah, but he's twice as mean. None of us doubt your grit."

"I sure didn't put up much of a fight." Odell's breath was still coming in ragged gasps, and his sore tongue made it even harder to talk.

"I'd say you made a fair showing. At least you busted his ear. That's something," Son said. "Hell, there ain't a man here that can whip that cranky sonofabitch, as bad as many of them would like to."

Somebody sat Odell's hat on his head, and a few more men walked by and nodded at him in passing. It came as a shock to him, but truly, nobody seemed to be laughing at him. In fact they seemed to approve of something he had done.

"Get up and dust yourself off," Son said, "and don't be trying to hide your marks. You earned 'em."

"I'll get him next time," Odell muttered.

"By *Gott*, I believe you do love a fight." The Prussian chuckled.

Odell examined his swollen face with his fingertips. "I reckon I've still got a bit to learn at that."

"That's the first smart thing I've heard you say since I've known you." Son slapped him on the back.

Odell tenderly ran his finger inside his mouth. "He knocked one of my jaw teeth loose. I hope I don't lose it."

The Prussian propped his foot up on Odell's saddle. He wet the fingertips of one hand and polished at a spot on the high top of his fancy boot. "Herr Odell, you will find that none of life's lessons are free."

Odell twisted his neck stiffly to look at the Prussian. For the first time, the strange foreigner was almost making sense to him.

A large shadow spread across Odell's back as Placido stepped between him and the fire. Odell looked up into the savage face grinning at him.

"Heap big fight," the Tonk chief said loudly.

Odell rose gingerly to his feet with one hand on his ribs. He wasn't sure if Dub hadn't cracked one or two of them, and his tongue had already swollen until he could barely close his mouth. "Yeah, heap big fight."

Chapter 24

Even though the day was warm, the commissioner dropped the sides of the tepee for more privacy. The four of them sat in the dim light around the ashes of the fire pit.

"Is this Iron Shirt a big chief, or a little one?" the commissioner asked.

"I got the impression that the Comanches here set quite a store by him. I think he's a big chief, maybe a head chief," Captain Jones said.

Red Wing laughed out loud at their ignorance. "There is no warrior who speaks for all the Comanche, or even most of them."

"Well, for someone who claims she isn't a Comanche, you sure know a lot about them," the captain said.

She noticed the slight tremor in the Captain's hands. "I know that you're fools if you think getting one camp of the Comanche to come to sign a treaty will mean peace. They are a scattered people. Sometimes camps come together at certain times for dancing, raiding, or for big hunts. A respected warrior may have a great say among his own camp, or even his band, but every warrior is his own boss."

"Are you telling us there are no chiefs?" Agent Torrey asked incredulously.

Red Wing struggled to find the words to explain the Comanche. "Not as you think of chiefs. Other tribes have many religious ceremonies and warrior societies that create positions of power and require their warriors to conform somewhat to participate. The Comanches' religion and his position among his people is a more individual thing. When a warrior wants to take to the war trail, he will let it be known. If he is a good talker and a successful fighter he can get others to go with him. No chief or group of chiefs can order him to do one thing or not."

"How can they even live together with so little political structure?" It was plain the commissioner didn't like what he was hearing.

Red Wing laughed again. "Oh, there's politics. All Comanche warriors jostle with each other for standing. If a warrior is lucky, he comes from a large camp or a powerful band. The larger the camp, the more warriors they have to steal horses. Horses mean riches, and riches can buy respect or wives that will ally you to other wealthy camps or bands. Power in Comanche terms means victory, wealth, and prestige."

"That still doesn't answer the question of how they settle disagreements among themselves," Agent Torrey said.

"When an argument arises or a difficult decision must be made the men will gather in council and discuss the best solution. Most of them will come to an agreement, but those who disagree can always leave."

"So, even if Houston can make a treaty with this bunch of Comanches, none of the warriors, even from this camp, must abide by it?" The commissioner rubbed his temples as if his head were hurting him.

"There is a saying among the Comanche that treaties are only for old beggars who love to talk," she said.

"Will, President Houston didn't send you out here to solve all of Texas's Indian problems. All he wanted was for you to get as many of the Comanches to Fort Bird as was possible," Captain Jones said.

"That might have to be enough," the commissioner said.

Before the conversation could go any further an old squaw appeared in the doorway. She stared at the ground and seemed too timid to speak. After a long moment of awkward silence she unfolded a beautifully tanned deerskin dress and a pair of moccasins. She held them forth in her outstretched arms.

"It seems our hosts come bearing gifts fit for a Comanche princess," the commissioner said.

Red Wing said something in Comanche, and from the look on the old squaw's face it hadn't been what she wanted to hear. The squaw mumbled something and Red Wing grabbed up a handful of dust and flung it at her. Red Wing was angrier than any of the men had ever seen her and she rattled off another testy burst in her native tongue. Her body was trembling when she finished. She stared at the ground and made it plain that she had nothing else to say. The old squaw laid the gifts down on the ground and backed out of the door.

"Remind me to never offer you gifts. I don't speak Comanche, but I'd say that was quite rude behavior on your part," the commissioner said.

Red Wing remained quiet for a long time, still looking down. "Yes, it was, but they have to understand that I'm no longer a Comanche. I told her get her filthy hides and her ugly face out of my sight."

The commissioner risked making her angrier. "Why do you hate those who raised you so much? Was your mother so bitter over her captivity that she planted a bitter seed in you?"

She shook her head solemnly. "I don't hate them. My

mother lived many happy years among them, and there was a time when I was happy too."

"Then how can you choose a life you've led for only a few years over these that should be your people?"

Rehashing old wounds was painful, and she fought back the tears welling up in her eyes. "I once had a Comanche mother and father who I loved very much. I lived among a strong camp, and we had many friends. Then the smallpox came and took my mother, and my father was killed in a fight with the Texans. Our numbers were weakened until we were few, and what was left of us scattered among the Penateka band. An old widow took me in, but she was cruel and I was little more than her slave. When Colonel Moore attacked us and captured me, I thought I would finally die, but I didn't. I was once taught to hate the Tejanos, but the Wilsons were kind to me. Their ways were strange, and it was hard at first, but they gave me back what I had lost before. After a while I had a family once more. I fit myself into a new world and gave them back the love they gave me."

Red Wing wiped at her eyes and then raised her face to them. "You want to know why I won't go back to the Comanches, and I ask you this. If you were born in a foreign land, would you give up all those you love in Texas to go back to a life that you had almost forgotten? I may be neither one of you nor Comanche, but there is no doubt who my family is. I left here long ago, and now you have brought me back. But I want to go back to where you took me from—home. My mother is waiting there for me."

The commissioner's companions looked back to him with shame on their faces. He cursed himself for a coward and a bully and wondered how a man of honor could blindly stoop so low. "I fear we have done you a great injustice. I can't take back my crimes, but I promise I will do all that I can to see that you aren't handed back to the Comanches. I will tell them that I was mistaken, and you were only once a captive Mexican child."

Agent Torrey smiled at her. "That Iron Shirt didn't be-lieve you were a Comanche anyway. Soon, we'll all be on our way back home and we can forget about this difficult journey."

Red Wing wanted to believe that it all would work out for the best, but she had to be honest with them, no matter how they had treated her. "That dress wasn't a gift from the woman who brought it. Iron Shirt sent her."

Captain Jones rose to his feet angrily, but the commis-sioner grabbed him by the wrist. "Captain, I know how you feel about Comanches, but we were wrong to take Red Wing. I've known it from the beginning, but I just wouldn't admit it, even to myself."

"You and that girl are going to get us all killed." The captain jerked his arm away and looked from the commis-sioner to Red Wing. He suddenly looked much older and very tired. "I volunteered for this expedition, but you're asking me to forget who I've hated half my life. If that chief wants her, you and nobody else can stop him. All we can do by holding out on him is to make him mad. Give her to him."

"I'm asking you to do what's right."

Captain Jones pulled a flask from his pocket and held it at arm's length. He took a drink and tossed the empty con-tainer against the wall. "Well, there goes the last of it."

"I've brought us this far. Are you still with me?" the commissioner asked.

"I'll stick by you three as far as I can. Hell, we probably weren't going to make it out of here anyway. I just never thought I'd die for a mixed-up Comanche girl. It doesn't take a drunk to see the irony in that." The captain tried to walk proudly from the tepee, but he staggered slightly at the door.

When he was gone, Commissioner Anderson looked at Red Wing. "They told me before we left Houston that he was a small man and a coward, but I'd say they mis-judged him."

No sooner had the captain disappeared than the people of the village began to shout and the dogs started barking again. The three of them barged out the door and found Captain Jones standing in their way. He was looking to the south at the large bunch of Comanches nearing the edge of the camp. They were stretched out for half a mile, appearing out of a backdrop of dust. Their ponies leaned into the weight of the Comanches' belongings loaded onto the travois they pulled. The warriors scattered out proudly in the lead and their women waved at old friends coming out to meet them from the camp.

The newcomers mixed wildly with the others and laughter and friendly banter sounded throughout the camp. A young brave raced his horse wildly in front of the people and performed several feats of horsemanship while many cheered for him.

"I've never seen such smiles," Commissioner Anderson said.

Red Wing was surprised at his comment. "They are happy to see old friends and distant family. Sometimes it can be long between visits."

The commissioner continued to watch the joyous celebration played out before him, and the Comanches' white teeth flashing and their eyes twinkling with pleasure. "Yes, but I don't know that I've ever been that happy."

"To know the hardships of their life is to know pleasure in the good little things that sometimes come." She remembered many times when she had either ridden in to such greetings or met visitors to her own camp.

"I find myself strangely envious of them," Agent Torrey said.

"Remember too that their life can be hard. There is little mercy out here away from the settlements. The weak die, and even the strong sometimes pay a price for their freedom." She remembered the great losses of her life just as clearly as she had the good times.

"Those are the proudest men I've ever seen. All of them pose and posture like young men going to war." Agent Torrey pointed toward a cluster of warriors catching up on old times.

"They are Kotsoteka, and once they were the most powerful of all the Comanche. They defeated the *Pakanaboo* and the *Cuampes* until they held the buffalo grounds from the Lakota country to the river the Frenchmen call the Canadian."

"That's about the proudest, meanest-looking Comanche buck I've seen yet." Captain Jones pointed toward a warrior sitting a pale yellow horse and talking to Iron Shirt. He wore a buffalo horn hat, and a fresh scalp flitted in the wind from the end of his lance.

Red Wing saw Iron Shirt pointing her way, and she started to go back into the tepee. Just as she reached the door flap the warrior on the horse turned his head and his eyes locked with hers. She stumbled into the lodge with her heart hammering in her chest. She hugged herself tightly and tried to quell her trembling body and to convince herself that she hadn't just seen a ghost.

Chapter 25

The buffalo hunting had been good, and there was plenty of food in the camp. The Comanches feasted and visited throughout the night while the Peace Commission cowered in their tepee. Once they thought they heard a great commotion just after sundown, and Iron's Shirt's interpreter soon came to tell them that more Comanches had just arrived. He told them that there would be a council held the next day to hear the white men out. The four of them passed the night in quiet contemplation about what fate held in store for them on the morrow.

They barely had time to eat the breakfast that had been given them before the same interpreter came to guide them to the council. There was no lodge big enough to hold the number of warriors present, so the meeting was held under the shade of a small group of stunted trees on the edge of a dry streambed. The Comanche men sat in a large circle with an opening at the bottom of it. The Peace Commission was motioned to sit in the gap provided, and all of them noticed

Iron Shirt sitting on the opposite side of the circle. None of them could read the looks on the Comanches' faces, but it was plain that they had already been discussing the white men in their midst.

While he waited to make sure that Red Wing was seated, Commissioner Anderson noticed another warrior sitting near Iron Shirt. It was the Waco chief, Squash, and the hateful look he was giving the Peace Commission sent cold chills up the commissioner's spine.

"I saw him," Captain Jones said before the commissioner could point out Squash.

Once they were seated, a middle-aged warrior with a crooked eye immediately began to talk. He didn't speak long, but he pointed at them several times. When he was through the entire council looked a question their way.

"Stinking Tobacco asks what it is that you want. He says the white man always wants something when he comes to talk," Squash said.

The commissioner got the impression from Squash's cool demeanor that his presence foretold bad things. At least he didn't have to rely on the captain's stumbling Spanish to communicate with the Comanches. He was unsure whether he should stand to give proper drama to what he had to say, but he decided to remain seated just as the crazy-eyed warrior had.

He reached into his pack and began to scatter before him the trade trinkets he had brought. He paused to let them appraise the glass beads, ribbons, hand mirrors, and the few steel knives and pots. Some of the warriors' eyes lit up with the sight of the small offering of plunder, but none of them moved or said anything.

He cleared his throat and gathered himself to give the speech he had been practicing in his head for months. "President Sam Houston has sent me here to speak with the Kotsoteka and all the Comanche who will hear. Long have we Texans and the Comanche fought, but Houston wishes those days to end. There is more than enough land for both our peoples to live in our own ways without killing each other. He asks that you come to Fort Bird on the Trinity in two months to hear his words of peace. He will give many gifts to those who come with good hearts and open ears. These few pitiful things are but tokens of his goodwill."

Squash smirked and repeated the commissioner's words in Comanche. The warriors seemed unimpressed, and the commissioner hoped that Squash had translated him correctly. A fat warrior on the other side of Iron Shirt finally laughed and pointed at Commissioner Anderson.

Squash laughed with the fat warrior before he translated. "Poor Coyote says that Pretty Soldier has many words but forgot to say what the Comanche must give up for the gifts he promises."

"President Houston only asks that you stop raiding our farms, carrying away our women and children, and stealing our horses," the commissioner said.

Poor Coyote crossed his forearms over his round belly and waited quietly for Squash to relay the commissioner's answer. He grunted and shook his head and spoke again when he had heard the Waco out.

"And when there are more Tejanos and they move farther west, are the Comanche supposed to cower in their lodges like children?" Squash asked for Poor Coyote.

"Tell him we have no wish to live out here. It doesn't rain enough to grow crops, and there's a lifetime's worth of better land along the rivers to the east."

As soon as the commissioner's words were heard, a young warrior spoke angrily. Earrings made of mouse skulls hung from each of his earlobes, and they rattled with every angry movement of his head. The wrath in his voice was just as fierce as the look on his face. Without knowing what he said, the commissioner was sure he would never come to Fort Bird to make peace.

As soon as the angry warrior had finished, Iron Shirt

rose on his bowed legs. He wore a strange shirt that appeared to be made of metal. He glanced at the young warrior and then began to speak. He talked as much to the warriors as he did to the Peace Commission, and turned in a slow circle while his hands made signs to go along with the clear lift of his voice.

"I'll be damned, that's an old coat of Spanish chain mail he's wearing," Captain Jones whispered.

Iron Shirt ceased to talk, but he remained standing. Squash waited politely until he was sure his host was finished. He smiled wickedly. "Iron Shirts thinks you a brave man to come and spit in their faces and suggest that the land to the east where you now live belongs to you. But what he wants to know is why he should believe you tell the truth about the meeting at Fort Bird."

"Tell him that my word is good, and that I always speak the truth, just as President Houston does. Tell him I know a man like himself would see through any lies as quickly as a hawk spies a mouse in the grass," the commissioner said.

When Squash had translated, Iron Shirt rotated once again to look at the ring of warriors. There was a sly hint of a smile at the corners of his mouth. He turned back to face the Peace Commission and held out a hand before him. He stood there as if waiting for something.

Red Wing met his steady gaze and steeled herself. She did not move, and he beckoned her forward with his fingers without moving his arm.

"Come to me," he said.

She noticed the commissioner looking at her helplessly, and Agent Torrey staring at her with wide eyes. She knew she was just prolonging the inevitable and rose to her feet on shaky legs. Faking a courage she did not feel, she strode forward and stood before Iron Shirt. She did not take the hand he offered, but he stepped quickly forward and grabbed hers anyway. His palm was hard and calloused and he gripped her tight while he looked into her face.

"Woman, have you come back to the People?" Iron Shirt asked.

She understood him plainly. "I'm not Comanche. I'm Mexican."

"I think you lie."

It was hard to look him in the eye and lie again. There was a power about him. "I tell the truth. I do not know you."

He held her arm outstretched for a full minute while he stared at her. Finally, he dropped her arm and turned away. When he had walked back to the far side of the council circle, he turned back and pointed his finger at her. "She is not of us. I do not know her."

"What'd he say?" the commissioner asked impatiently.

She took her seat again and tried to breathe normally once more. "He agrees that I'm not Comanche."

Commissioner Anderson looked away from her just in time to see the angry warrior who had spoken earlier leaning forward tensely, as were many of the council. Iron Shirt noticed too, and he held up his hands to ask for patience while he studied the commissioner calmly. His speech was short, and when he was through he strode out of the circle and headed straight for his lodge.

Squash had pleasure written all over him when he finally translated Iron Shirt's last words. "You do not tell the truth. All the warriors here know that you have come to trick us. Many Tejanos are camped a day's ride south of here and they wait to strike the village."

The commissioner and Captain Jones jumped to their feet, and Red Wing stood behind them. Agent Torrey stayed on the ground with a bewildered, disheartened expression on his face.

"You know that isn't true. We came here to his village alone. Why didn't you tell him that?" The commissioner threw at Squash.

The Waco remained seated. "I told him you weren't to be trusted. I told him how my wife was getting better from her sickness until your four-eyed man put evil medicine inside her and she died."

"Agent Torrey tried to help your wife," Red Wing said, shocked and angry at the same time.

"Another lie. Three others in my village who were not as sick as my wife got worse the day you left, and they soon died too. Iron Shirt is wiser than I was to see your wicked hearts at first glance."

"Are the Comanche so low as to murder their guests?" the commissioner shouted at Iron Shirt's back.

Squash chuckled. "An enemy is never a guest, and nobody asked you to come here."

The entire circle of warriors was on their feet and pressing close. The commissioner and the captain put hands to their guns, but both of them knew that to lift them was to die right there. The three white men were roughly disarmed and their hands bound behind their backs with rawhide straps. Somebody struck Captain Jones a nasty lick on the head, and when the Comanches finally drug him back to his feet there was a deep cut on his forehead. The warriors marched the prisoners toward the tepee where they had spent the night. Red Wing wasn't bound but was made to come along.

"What are they going to do?" Agent Torrey's voice sounded lost and far away.

Captain Jones reared back his head to try and keep the blood running down his forehead from getting into his eyes. "I reckon they're going to kill us, Mr. Tom."

Squash was standing halfway to the tepee waiting for them to pass. "They're going to spend all afternoon killing you, and then they will feast and dance tonight. Come morning they will ride out and kill those Rangers across the river."

Red Wing spit on him as she walked by, and the Waco chief was brushed aside by the Comanche warriors before he could react. He wanted to kill her right then, but she belonged to his hosts. What was about to befall the white men could happen just as easily to him if he crossed Iron Shirt. The goodwill he had created by lying about the Peace Commission might protect his village from the Comanches for a year or more, and perhaps Iron Shirt would bring his camp to the Brazos to trade horses for corn.

Squash's woman had truly died, but she had been a hateful hussy and no great loss. The fact that he was sure that Agent Torrey had nothing to do with her death hadn't fit with his plans. The death of a few Tejanos was meaningless to him if it served him well. He had hated the white man ever since Jim Bowie's treasure hunters had whipped sixty of his warriors and shot off his brother's bottom jaw on the San Saba many years earlier. He couldn't believe Red Wing had dared to spit on him and embarrassed him in front of the Comanches. She had always been too sassy and proud to suit his tastes. He knew he should be riding back to his village before the Rangers got any closer, but he was going to enjoy seeing her well raped and beaten.

Chapter 26

The old lobo wolf came trotting out of a draw about a hundred yards away. He was a big, rangy devil with outsized feet and a hide the color of dull steel. He had his nose to the wind, but he traveled without a care in the world. He stopped from time to time to piss on a bush or sniff around for packrat nests and rabbit holes as he made his way toward where Odell, the Prussian, and Placido lay on their bellies on the lip of a canyon.

Odell eased his rifle forward and found the lobo in his sights before a large brown hand clamped around his double barrels and blocked his view. He looked up to see Placido shaking his head with a stern look on his usually unreadable face. He held on to the gun until Odell eased his hammer down.

"Sorry, do you think there are Comanches about?" Odell asked.

"Tonkawas don't kill wolves for sport," the Prussian said while he studied the rough breaks of the Pease River with his spyglass. "They call themselves the Wolf People, and only use their hides for warrior ceremonies and to grant them power in battle."

"Wolves chose my people long ago." Placido didn't seem mad at Odell, but he kept his eyes on him long enough to make sure that the young man had heard what he said.

The lobo must have winded them, for he stopped in his tracks and looked up in the direction of where they lay before he bolted away. Odell would have liked to have had the lobo's pelt. Placido wore a tanned wolf hide over his head and down his back, and Odell thought it looked pretty fetching. The Prussian had a sword and Hatchet Murphy had his hatchet. Odell had the hatband he had made out of the rattlesnake that bit him and the Bowie knife, but felt it wouldn't hurt if he had something more to make him look equally fierce. He thought that maybe his lion pelt might make a fine-looking hat or robe.

"What do you think that is between the river and those hills to the north?" The Prussian offered Placido his spyglass.

"Many tepees," Placido said without taking the Prussian's optics.

Odell found it hard to believe the big Tonk could see so far with his naked eye. The area the Prussian pointed out was at least six or seven miles across the river. "I don't see anything."

"Do you see those hills?" Placido asked.

Once the rough breaks of the river ended miles to the north, there was nothing but a flat plain leading all the way to the horizon. Four low, cone-shaped hills rose up out of that plain.

"Placido told me the Comanches believe those hills are magic," the Prussian said. "I guess they're medicine mounds, or something like that."

"Big medicine," Placido grunted.

"How many tepees do you see?" Odell asked.

"They are too far to count," Placido said, and the Prussian agreed.

"Do you think it's a big village?" Odell wished he could see as far as the Tonk.

"We can ask the scouts." Placido pointed to the maze of gullies and canyons on the south bank of the river.

After a long search Odell finally picked out the three Tonk scouts ghosting along below them afoot. The Tonks were as comfortable on their own legs as they were horseback, and their wiry, tough bodies and cast-iron lungs could easily keep up with trotting riders on long marches. He was ashamed he hadn't noticed them without having them pointed out. They could have just as easily been Comanches stalking him.

"What do you reckon they've learned?" Odell asked.

The Prussian gave him a sour look. Lately, he had grown very impatient and more than a little on edge. "Herr Odell, you ask too many questions."

Odell too had long since lost what little patience he possessed. He had left his home almost a year before, with nothing to show for it but months of hard living. He had done nothing to avenge his pappy's death, and he was beginning to doubt he would ever find Red Wing in time to save her. It often seemed to him that he was fated to fail those who he loved.

They wormed backward until they were sure they wouldn't be sky-lined atop the canyon rim, and then stood and went to their horses. They loped back to where the men were dismounted for a midday siesta to rest their horses and allow them to graze a little. Soon after they joined the men, the three Tonk scouts came running up. Despite their long journey to those medicine hills and back, none of them even seemed tired.

Placido spoke with the trio for several minutes and then came back to the Prussian. All the men ceased their casual conversation and storytelling to hear what Placido had to say.

"There's a very big camp of Comanches between those hills and the river," Placido said. "There are many warriors."

"How many?" the Prussian asked.

Placido had never quite learned all the white man's numbers, and he was unsure if what he was about to say was correct. "It is the biggest camp we've seen since Buffalo Hump brought the Penatekas down the Colorado years ago."

"Are you sure?"

"It would take three or four of our war party to equal the warriors they have."

The men began to question Placido and to discuss the discovery of such a large Comanche encampment. Before they grew too worried with their own speculations, the Prussian asked them to hear him out. He waited until he had all their attention before he spoke.

"We've found the Comanche village we were looking for, and I say we ride across the river and attack it. We are outnumbered but we are not outmanned. Any one of you is worth ten of those Comanche, and if we fight smart I promise you we will deal those savages a hard lick. What say you?"

Every man one of them had come for a fight, and the Texans all nodded in unison. As for the Tonks, they were already painting their faces for war. They needed no speeches and were impatient to fight and plunder their age-old enemies.

"The scouts say there are white men in that camp," Placido said.

The Prussian snapped to attention almost as if he were on a parade ground. "How many? Could they be the Peace Commission?"

Placido shrugged. "My warriors couldn't get close

enough to be sure of their numbers, but they saw the Comanches beating three white men."

"Did they see Red Wing? Did they see a woman?" Odell asked.

"They saw a dark-skinned girl in a long, white woman's dress," Placido said.

"Well, what are we wating for?" Odell tightened Crow's cinch and swung into the saddle without touching the stirrup.

"By *Gott*, don't go off half-cocked," the Prussian growled. "You follow me."

Odell freed his rifle from the saddle horn and found his stirrups. "If you're going to lead, you'd better get on your horse and ride. Red Wing's over there across the river, and I don't aim to wait for anybody."

"You listen. The odds are those Comanches know we're prowling around their stomping grounds." Son Ballard worked his chew around in his jaw and contemplated a hole in the sole of his moccasin. "If that gal is over there we won't do her any good getting ourselves killed. I don't care how tough we are, we ain't going to whip a whole damned passel of Comanches easily. Rein in a little and let's hear how the Prussian intends to skin this coon."

Chapter 27

The men sat stark naked on the ground in front of their former tepee with their hands bound in front of them and their ankles tied together. All but a dozen of the warriors had left them, and those remaining had built a fire. They had pierced cuts of buffalo meat with sticks driven into the ground at an angle over the flames, and they hunkered over their cooking and laughed at the discomfort of their captives.

Agent Torrey covered his genitals with his bound hands and squeezed his scrawny shoulders in toward his chest until he was half his normal size. "I find our current situation to be highly embarrassing and uncomfortable to say the least. I never imagined that such things happened in Texas."

"It will only get worse," Captain Jones said. "Our death won't be easy."

It was disheartening to hear the captain. Despite the man's cynical personality, Agent Torrey was usually impressed with his dry wit and self-assured demeanor. The agent had come to lean on the more experienced man when the trials of the wilderness became too much. But the undignified nature of their captivity made him appear as someone else altogether. He didn't look like a captain anymore sitting there with his pale, pudgy flesh exposed, and his bald head turning red under the sun. The fear on his face was a match for what Agent Torrey supposed was on his own.

"At least old age has already taken my scalp and robbed the Comanches of that pleasure," Captain Jones said.

"That's enough of that, Captain. Scaring Agent Torrey doesn't help matters," Commissioner Anderson said.

Agent Torrey was surprised that the commissioner still looked important and commanding even though he was as naked as the rest of them. He thought that perhaps it was because the commissioner was not fat like the captain. Slender people looked much more dignified naked, and it seemed to him that they had an unfair advantage when it came to Indian captivity.

"If the Comanches are right, there's a company of Rangers somewhere nearby," Agent Torrey said.

"They'd better come quick, if they're coming at all," the commissioner said.

"You two don't get your hopes up for any Rangers to pull our fat out of the fire. If they hit this village, it's just going to get us killed quicker," Captain Jones said.

"It doesn't hurt to hope," Agent Torrey said.

Captain Jones recognized one of the guards for the quieter of the two Comanches that had guided them to the camp. "You're a fine, trustworthy bastard. Judas hadn't anything on you."

The warrior grinned at him and said something that the other Comanches obviously found very funny. Then the comedian took one of the cooking sticks and held it toward the captain. Only the outside of the steak on it was charred, and the half-raw bit dripped hot, bloody juice. It was plain that the Comanche was offering the captain or his friends something to eat.

"They offer us food? Perhaps they intend to ransom us." Agent Torrey was willing to grasp at any hope, no matter how slim. He still wasn't certain that Squash had told the truth. "Surely the Comanches wouldn't murder emissaries of the republic who brought gifts and offerings of peace."

"To hell they wouldn't," Captain Jones said.

Commissioner Anderson motioned with his chin and held out his bound hands with palms turned upward to let the Comanche know he would take the offered meat. "The condemned man deserves a last supper, and I was foolish enough to pass on breakfast."

The Comanche grinned and flung the meat off the stick, slinging hot grease across his victim. The bit of sizzling steak hit the commissioner's leg and he flopped around wildly to get it off of him. When he was through, there were red specks across his chest and a deep burn on his thigh.

The rest of the Comanches joined in. While chewing their own meals lustily, they would take up a stick and dexterously fling a piece of meat at the prisoners' bare flesh. No matter how hard the captives tried to avoid being burned, the flying chunks hit home. The three men were soon flopping around on the ground like fish out of water while the Comanches laughed as if it were the funniest thing they had ever seen.

"The blackhearted bastards are devilishly good aims," Captain Jones said during a break in the action.

The commissioner was trying to reach a particularly nasty burn on his shoulder with his mouth to cool it and didn't answer him. The warriors seemed to have lost their enthusiasm with the game and had turned to the sole focus of filling their bellies with large quantities of meat. Captain Jones said a small prayer of thanks that maybe the ordeal was over, but it turned out to just be an interlude. The

Comanches went back to their torturous antics just as soon as their hungers were thoroughly satisfied.

The commissioner and the captain sacrificed their hands to fend off many of the hot pieces, or to at least knock them off their skin, but Agent Torrey refused to let go of his genitals. The warriors found his modesty even funnier than his epileptic attempts to dodge, and as a result, he took the worst punishment of the three.

The warrior who had begun the fun and games walked over and took the glasses off Agent Torrey's face. He put them on himself and made a big show of acting dizzy. The rest of the warriors passed the spectacles around, each of them trying them out and going through the same little act to loud laughter. When the new had worn off the glasses, they went back to flinging hot meat at Agent Torrey.

"Dammit, Mr. Tom! Let go of your taproot and protect yourself," Captain Jones said.

But Agent Torrey was far too modest for his own good. By the time the Comanches were through, the agent's body was covered in small burns where the hot grease had burrowed itself into his flesh. He curled up on his side in a fetal position and tried to forget where he was at. He thought that if he squeezed his eyes shut tightly enough, perhaps he could make the Comanches disappear.

The hot sun and their full bellies made the Comanches sleepy, and soon they went off to a brush arbor nearby. Most of them proceeded to take naps, but a few of them began to gamble with a set of carved trinkets thrown onto a blanket. They looked up from their game occasionally to check on their prisoners but seemed content to leave off their torture for the time being.

The commissioner's raw wounds stung fiercely, and the sweat running into them and the constant attack of the swarm of flies buzzing around made the pain worse. He tried to ignore his suffering body and reached out and took a piece of meat from the ground. He brushed away the worst of the grass and dirt and tore off a bite of it. Captain Jones watched him chew for a while, and then found himself a morsel and did the same.

"Agent Torrey, you should eat while you have the chance. We need to keep up our strength," the commissioner said.

Agent Torrey seemed not to have heard him, for he remained curled up in a ball. His two companions felt bad for him and understood his state of mind. Neither of them had any doubt that the Comanches could find a way to break them too.

R ed Wing listened to the men's torture from inside the tepee. She was helpless to aid them and knew that it was just a matter of time before her own trials would begin. The suffering of captives was an old story to her, and she waited to hear the sound of footsteps at the door. She had gotten Iron Shirt to confirm that she wasn't Comanche, but there was a price to be paid for that. Her own stubborn and clever plotting had kept her status as an outsider, but soon some warrior or warriors would come to treat her as such.

The Comanches outside had grown quiet, and she took a quick look out the door. It would shame the men for her to see them naked and abused, but she had to know how serious their injuries were. The warriors wouldn't kill them yet, but that didn't mean that the little games they thought up to pass the time wouldn't be dangerous. She was glad to see that the commissioner and the captain seemed little worse for the wear, but her heart went out to Agent Torrey lying there. Except for the rise and fall of his ribs, she might have taken him for dead.

The cowardly instinct for self-preservation urged her not to draw attention to herself, but the sight of the men suffering under the hot sun worked at her more strongly. She took up the Mexican water jug hanging above her and went out the door before she lost courage. She didn't look toward the

Comanches under their arbor, but she could feel their eyes on her. It was only a few yards to where the prisoners were, but the distance seemed like an eternity. She expected the warriors to stop her at every step.

She went to Agent Torrey first and laid a hand on his shoulder. "Sit up, Mr. Torrey. I've brought water for you."

He flinched under her hand. "Go away, Red Wing. You shouldn't see me like this."

"I only see only a friend lying out in the hot sun," Red Wing said.

He stirred slowly and wouldn't look at her when he finally sat up. She held out the water jug to him, but his bound hands were unable to hold it. Seeing his predicament, she held the rim to his lips and he drank greedily until he could hold no more. He stared at her strangely, and she assumed that he was almost blind without his glasses.

He squinted into the sun and tried to focus on the blur of her face. "I'm not sure you aren't an angel."

"It's just me, Mr. Torrey."

She started to rise, but he laid a hand on her forearm. "Thank you."

She moved on to Captain Jones, who managed the jug on his own. She averted her eyes and knelt by him while he drank his fill. He had nothing to say, and when she felt the jug pressed against her hands, she moved on.

Commissioner Anderson's curly blond locks were tangled with grass and dirt, and burn blisters speckled one side of his face. He never looked away from the Comanches under the arbor while he drank.

"I'm sorry it's come to this," he said when he was through.

She blamed him for their troubles, but she couldn't find her anger. It would have been a lie to tell him he was forgiven, but there was no pleasure in torturing him further. "You have been wrong, but you're a brave man."

He had enough spirit left in him to laugh. "No, we wouldn't be here if I had been braver."

"Look over there and see how those warriors glare at you. It's because they see your courage."

"Appearing brave has almost been a profession with me. Now that I'm to die without anyone to see, it remains to be seen if I can keep up the act," he said. "Agent Torrey cringes and cowers, but I wonder if he isn't braver than I am to be so truthful with himself."

The gambling warriors seemed annoyed enough by her kind attentions to quit their game, and Red Wing got to her feet. "I have to be going. It will mean no good for you if they come over here."

"Had things been different I would have liked to walk with you along the streets of New Orleans, or even Charleston. There are places beyond Texas where a gentleman and a fine lady belong. I see no place out here for beautiful things," he said quietly. "The world here is turned upside down."

Two of the Comanches were coming her way. She left the water jug beside the commissioner and walked quickly back to the tepee. She heard one of the warriors kick the jug away just as she ducked inside.

She sat alone in the shadows at the back of the lodge and wished she could see her mother one last time. Somewhere far across Texas, Mrs. Ida would be sitting on her porch waiting for the boys to come in from the fields. The lightning bugs would be flashing in the yard, and the bullfrogs calling from the river. Red Wing longed to sit at her mother's feet and feel her fingers gently twine her hair. Bud and Mike would make them laugh over supper, and then they would all go back out on the porch to listen to the night and to cool themselves in the breeze.

Her longing was interrupted by the sound of someone at the door. She looked up into the ghostly face she had seen the day before. Older memories came to her in a rush, and all that she had come to believe battled against the evidence before her. The buffalo horn hat was gone, but it was him just the same.

Little Bull stopped just inside the doorway. His fierce face was painted black for war, but there was a slight awkwardness behind the mask. "Hello, Sister."

"I thought you were dead. I saw you ridden down beneath a Tejano's horse."

She couldn't believe what her own eyes told her.

"I thought when the white-haired colonel took you away that I would never see you again," he said.

For an instant she wanted to hug him, but there was a strangeness between them that shouldn't have been there. She struggled to bridge the gap between the man she saw before her and the boy who had been her brother. The flashing eyes, the war paint, and the angry tenseness apparent in his scarred muscles were no part of her memories.

"I have avenged your death many times," he said.

"I never forgot you."

"And yet you come here dressed like a white woman to deny your people?"

"My life has taken me so far away from here that I can never come back."

He paced back and forth in front of her like a caged animal, all the while studying her. "I'm no longer a poor child among a band of beggars. I have many horses and many warriors follow me each time I ride against my enemies."

"I'm proud. Our father would be too."

"Come with me. All will know you're my sister, and life will be good. We will live as we were taught, and honor all that we once lost."

Red Wing stood to her feet and held her hands out wide as if to draw attention to her dress. "Do you see me, Brother? This is who I am."

"You are Comanche."

She shook her head sadly. "No longer."

He came to stand close to her, his face inches from hers. "I see a stranger, but my heart remembers a sister who I used to tease and who could outshoot all the boys with her little bow."

Red Wing shrugged and tears streamed down her cheeks. "I can't be her again. She is as lost to me as she is to you."

"Do you remember what will happen to you if you don't come with me? Do these weak, strange white men have such powerful medicine?"

"I have a new white mother that has loved me for many years. I only want to go back to her," she said. "Come to visit me this winter if you wish to be my brother again. I won't ask you to change."

He drew his knife and held it between them lying on her chest. "If I could cut the sickness from your heart, I would. If I could cut you from my heart, I would."

"Your knife isn't sharp enough."

He started for the door, but she caught his arm. He tensed at her touch and the wild, angry hurt was plain in the clench of his jaw and the weathered crow's feet at the corners of his eyes. But he did not jerk away.

"I'm a prisoner in your camp. Free me, Brother. Free the men who brought me here, and let us go home." Her voice trembled.

He strained to see behind the smoke of her words. He felt like a small, helpless boy again, unable to fight strongly enough to keep the good things that were his. His life had been shaped by loss, and he had willed himself to a place among the Comanche. Now all his strength and prowess wasn't enough to gain back what was right before him.

He straightened himself and once more looked like the stranger who had walked into her lodge. He was a Comanche to fear, and a warrior who kept what he was strong enough to take. "I see our mother's face in yours. I will not see you shamed and raped and made a toy for any warrior who wishes to abuse you. Do away with your white woman's clothes and dress yourself as a Comanche woman should. Then nobody will lay a hand on you."

"If I am your sister, does it matter so much what I wear?"

"Show the camp that you are Comanche."

"I will not. I am who I am."

"You've become a fool."

"What I've become is what you must accept."

"Your spirit is not lost, but you have forgotten. After I kill the Tejanos across the river, I will help you remember." He pulled away from her hand.

She cut in front of him as he started for the door. "Spare those outside. They knew nothing of the other Tejanos. How can men who brought us back together be your enemies?"

He looked at her like she was a child. "They're dead men."

She watched him leave, and her heart was pulled and torn more than she had ever imagined it could be. It was as if she was cursed to never know love without loss soon to follow. She had done all she could to hold on to her new life, but stubborn willpower wasn't enough.

Chapter 28

The tepee door was lifted again an hour later and two squaws entered. One of them was tall and slim with a catty look about her, and despite her beauty, bore the bruises of a recent beating. The fat one held a stout mesquite stick that she patted in the palm of her hand. Both had an air of disinterested determination about them.

"Little Bull has sent us to take you to his lodge," the slim one said.

Red Wing had no words left to argue with. She started by them for the door, but they refused to move out of her way. The fat squaw shook her head and pointed at the buckskin dress and moccasins Red Wing had left lying on the floor. Red Wing looked at the dress and folded her arms stubbornly across her chest. She would go to her brother's lodge, but dressed as she was. The slim squaw shook her head sadly, as if she thought Red Wing had made a very poor decision.

"I am Buffalo Butt, and this is Speckled Tail. Our

husband said you are to wear those things, and you will wear them." Buffalo Butt pointed to the buckskin dress again.

"I will not."

Buffalo Butt frowned and reached out to grab Red Wing's arm. "You are sassy for such a little one."

Red Wing clenched her small right fist and swung it from her hip. Her aim was off, and her punch hit the bigger woman in the shoulder. Buffalo Butt's short, squat body felt like hitting a wall. She shoved Red Wing away easily and whacked her across the arm with the stick. The blow hurt horribly, but Red Wing had no doubt that the fat squaw was holding back.

All the frustration of the past days welled up in Red Wing, and she gladly took the opportunity to vent them. She charged Buffalo Butt with both fists swinging wildly. Most of her punches failed to have any effect, but she did manage to get a strong hold on the woman's hair. She scratched and clawed with her free hand while she tried to bend Buffalo Butt to the ground by the hair. But her strength was no match for her opponent. Buffalo Butt let out a girlish shriek that was no way in keeping with her fierce looks or stature. She slung Red Wing to the ground as if her weight was nothing, and sat on her chest and slapped her viciously.

Red Wing's head rang with the blows, and she bucked and squirmed to no avail. She felt someone tugging at her shoe and kicked out. Speckled Tail grunted painfully and flew across the tepee. Buffalo Butt finally managed to pin both of Red Wing's arms underneath her chubby knees, and Speckled Tail circled around carefully and began undoing Red Wing's shoes.

Spent and defeated, Red Wing went still. The beating was humbling enough, without them stripping her. "Let me up. I will fight no more."

Speckled Tail was still tugging at Red Wing's shoes. "Hit her again, Buffalo Butt. The bitch broke my shell necklace and nearly kicked my tit off."

Buffalo Butt wasn't quite sure Red Wing had given up, and she remained on her chest while she considered whether to get up or not. Finally, she eased to her feet with her stick at the ready should Red Wing decide to fight more.

Speckled Tail scampered to safety behind Buffalo Butt. "She's lucky I don't take your stick and beat her good."

"Shut up, you pimple-titted slut. Little Bull says this is his sister, and all your lusty tricks won't keep him from kicking your bony butt if she's hurt," Buffalo Butt said.

Red Wing did hurt in several places, but she wasn't seriously wounded. Knowing that Buffalo Butt had taken it easy on her just added insult to injury. She rose slowly and stared at the dress the fat squaw held out to her. She hated to admit defeat, but she was no match for Buffalo Butt, much less the two of them.

"Go outside and I will change," Red Wing hoped for at least that much of a moral victory.

"You can take off your dress, or I will take it off for you," Buffalo Butt said flatly.

Red Wing slowly worked out of her clothing until she was naked before the two. Buffalo Butt pitched her the buckskin dress while Speckled Tail blatantly stared at her new sister-in-law with more than a hint of jealousy. Once Red Wing had pulled the dress over her head and fitted the moccasins on her feet, Buffalo Butt drew a skinning knife from her belt and pitched it to her.

Red Wing caught the knife deftly, but hesitated to turn it on her attackers. No matter her fighting spirit, she was sure that if Buffalo Butt had given her the knife, she was confident she could take it away again.

"Cut your hair like a Comanche woman," Buffalo Butt said.

"I will not." Red Wing's beautiful, long black hair was one of her only vanities. Hacking it off in the Comanche style would have taken the last bit of her spirit, and she would have been truly defeated.

"You will, or I will take the knife and do it for you," Buffalo Butt said.

Red Wing raised the knife belly high with the cutting edge turned up. "You will have to kill me first."

Surprisingly, Buffalo Butt laughed. "You're as vain as this Kiowa."

The two squaws stepped out from in front of the door. Red Wing started past them and laid the knife into the hand Buffalo Butt held out for it. She went outside with her new guard and fashion adviser right on her heels.

Speckled Tail was intrigued by the fabric of the dress left on the floor and the high button shoes. Red Wing's valise was nearby, and she weighed its potential treasures with pirate eyes. Buffalo Butt was very traditional, and had little use for the white man's trinkets or those who longed for them. Speckled Tail knew she would be angry for her dawdling over such plunder, but the temptation was more than she could stand. She snatched up the dress and shoes and grabbed the valise in her free hand. She had to run out of the tepee to catch up.

Red Wing noticed that the other prisoners were gone as soon as she stepped outside. She searched for them fearfully as Buffalo Butt led her along. They arrived at one of the largest tepees she had seen, set just across a dry streambed from the rest of the camp. Another smaller tepee, the many curing buffalo hides, the number of steel pots and pans, and the two fine horses staked nearby told her that her long-lost brother was truly an important man.

Just as they were arriving at Little Bull's lodges, a small boy came running from behind one of them. He had an excited look on his face, and he tore through the trio without saying a word. He crossed the streambed in a single bound and kept on running even though Buffalo Butt yelled at him to come back.

Red Wing stopped to watch the boy, and his progress led her vision to the large group of men bunched afoot a long stone's throw out on the prairie. It seemed as if every warrior available in camp was gathered there. She stared until a slight parting of their numbers revealed the three mesquite posts set into the ground. Her heart skipped a beat when she recognized that the three Texans were tied to those posts.

She lurched forward, but Buffalo Butt's hand clamped around her arm like a vise. She wanted to cry out in horror at what she knew was about to happen, but her voice seemed lost to her.

Chapter 29

Little Bull sat on the grass with the rest of the warriors and shared a pipe of tobacco with Iron Shirt. The medicine warrior had power that Little Bull envied. His name was known to all Comanches, and he was richer than any man Little Bull could recall. Although only ten summers Little Bull's senior, it took all four of Iron Shirt's wives, several slaves, and many travois to move his possessions from camp to camp. It was said he could blow away arrows and bullets with his breath, and never had he been wounded in a fight. Little Bull thought the man's success in battle had more to do with the Spanish armor he wore than it did with his medicine, but he couldn't deny the number of scalps or the vast herds of horses Iron Shirt had taken from his enemies.

The other warriors were smoking and swapping lies, and some of the older ones had even sprawled out on the ground to nap. Little Bull tinkered with the idea of trying to trade Iron Shirt out of a horse he fancied, but the man wouldn't stop talking long enough for him to broach the subject. Iron Shirt was a great one for promoting himself, and at the moment he was telling a story about a white otter he had once seen swimming in a river to the east—an event that first foretold his ability to see into the spirit world as few men could. Little Bull politely tried to listen, but he had heard the tale too many times.

Little Bull was an angry, restless man. He could not remember when the anger had not been with him, or the reason for it. Like the burning sickness in his guts, it drove him. Physical exertion was sometimes the only thing that could calm him. The shocking discovery of his sister and her rejection of him made him want to fight. Lounging around with a Tejano war party nearby had him ready to explode.

His vision was drawn to the Tejano captives tied to the mesquite posts. He hated the sight of their pale bodies more than anything, but he could see no need in drawing out their demise into such a formal ceremony. Iron Shirt insisted that it would give the young warriors courage to ride against the Tejano war party, but Little Bull didn't want to ride with warriors who needed games to make them brave. The captives should have already been well tortured and the warriors riding out to fight the Rangers before they chanced too close to camp.

Iron Shirt finally finished his story, and was looking at him as if he knew how impatient he was and was purposely drawing things out. The older warrior had a lot of clout, and as it was his camp, all the others deferred to his ideas of what to do with the prisoners. Some of the warriors had wanted to go to work on the captives immediately without having a dance, and others had wanted to ransom them. Iron Shirt had heard them all out, and then in his crafty way had convinced them all that his way was best.

After an hour of relaxation, Iron Shirt and a few other warriors of importance rose to their feet. The rest of the Comanche men quickly followed suit. Every one of them bore a weapon in his hands, and some of them had two. Steel knives, tomahawks, and flint-edged blades were brandished so casually as to almost mask the deadly intent of their presence. Only the wild paint on the warriors' faces and the predatory way they stared at the prisoners foretold what was to come.

There were over one hundred warriors in camp, but only half of them participated. The rest were old men who were willing to leave such pleasures to their younger counterparts, or members of the Yamparika group that had recently arrived seeking new alliance with Iron Shirt's Kotsotekas. Those warriors were only going to sit and watch as interested bystanders.

Iron Shirt had a Mexican slave whose Achilles tendons had been cut years before to keep him from attempting escape. Unlike many victims of the painful procedure, he had never healed enough to run again, and barely managed a shuffling, wobbly walk. What he could do was to fetch his master's horses and play drums. All the standing warriors held their places until the crippled Mexican began to beat on a skin drum. The rhythm was slow and steady, and not overly loud.

Iron Shirt started forward in slow steps that were more a threatening march than they were a dance. There were no wild leaps or pantomimed fighting moves like many other tribes performed at such ceremonies, at least not yet. The other warriors fell in behind him, and while their steps were individual decisions, all of them moved slowly. Not a sound escaped their lips, and they came forward as ominous mutes. Their moccasins scuffed up a trail of dust, and the scrape of leather soles against the ground provided a counter beat to the drum.

Little Bull was near Iron Shirt at the front of the line and he had the pleasure of being able to see the terror on the prisoners' faces as the warriors approached them. That was part of the purpose for the slow pace and the lack of war cries. For some reason the silence behind the slow scratch of shuffling moccasins and the dull throb of the drum scared their victims far worse than a much louder approach. The quiet, restrained procession also emphasized the discipline in battle that a warrior needed to survive.

Three stout posts had been set into the ground, two of them close together, and the other some thirty yards away. The fat white man and the pretty soldier had been tied to the side-by-side posts, and the little four-eyed man with the speckled skin was tied to the odd post facing them across the distance. The line of warriors danced toward the twin posts first.

The prisoners' hands were tied high above their heads to prevent them from falling down, and their ankles lashed to the bottom of the posts. The pretty soldier stood straight and watched the warriors come to him. No matter that he acted brave, his eyes fluttered around in his head like a scared rabbit. Little Bull saw him look to the sky and call on his creator.

The fat man made no attempt to honor his name and was crying like a small child. Iron Shirt approached him first and made one pass across that big stomach with his knife. The fat man groaned, and then screamed by the time the third warrior had cut him. As each warrior passed by him they slashed and hacked. All of the strikes were purposely meant to cause pain but not to kill. Several warriors mocked scalping him before they added to his wounds. Each one of them went on to do the same to the pretty soldier as they snaked by, curving back toward the four-eyed man. By the time the entire group had passed the first two posts those prisoners were cut from head to toe and screaming and groaning with pain, terrible pain.

The warriors moved on toward their next victim at the same monotonous pace. The four-eyed man was the last of the three captives Little Bull would have expected bravery from. From his first arrival in camp he had never met the eyes of a single warrior, but now he seemed fearless. He wrinkled his nose and strained against his bonds to squint hatefully at his enemies. He had to have seen his companions' treatment and heard their screams of agony, but not a single tremor of fear ran along his pale, speckled flesh.

Little Bull had assumed that the loss of his glass eyes would have robbed the man of any medicine they might have possessed, but that didn't seem to be the case. Little Bull had tried the glass eyes on himself and had found that they made the world a blur. It seemed the little man had been blinded by his magic eyes, and without them he was not the coward he had first seemed.

The first warriors passed by the man with weapons flashing, yet their victim went unscathed. Instead of bleeding him well as they had the other two prisoners, they only mocked attack. Their knife edges slid within a fraction of an inch from his flesh, and yet the white man did not flinch. It was if he knew no fear at all.

When Little Bull made his pass, he didn't even raise his knife. He didn't trust himself to hold back his wrath. For some reason the pathetic-looking Tejano's cool courage made Little Bull hate him even more. He looked for the tiniest hint of fear in the pale eyes and saw none. Amazingly, the little man smiled at him. Little Bull wondered if the Tejano had lost his mind in the heat, or if he was a witch like the Mexican traders claimed existed among their people. He didn't think about the matter long before he was sure the entire camp was being mocked by their captive. Iron Shirt was a fool for not killing him.

The pompous medicine warrior had said that killing odd numbers of white men in such a ceremony would bring bad luck to the tribe, and it had been decided that the four-eyed man would live to be ransomed for whatever booty the white chiefs could be made to pay. Little Bull had suggested that the pretty soldier looked to be a more important man, and thus the Tejano chiefs would pay more for him. Iron Shirt had quickly pointed out that it would be wrong to let a soldier live to fight them again, when the pitiful, laughable four-eyed man would never be a threat to them. Iron Shirt had come off looking wiser than ever and managed to make Little Bull look foolish at the same time.

All the warriors danced back to their original starting point and the drum beat ceased. They all sat down on the grass and began to visit with each other again. They watched the bleeding captives carefully to measure their handiwork, but the conversation soon turned to the four-eyed man and his strange bravery. The entire purpose of such torture was to strike fear into the captives and to make them suffer longer mentally, as well as physically. It was the slow, silent pace of the dance that usually created dread and had many captives crying out before the first blows were ever struck. If the four-eyed man was scared to see the warriors coming with their knives, he hid it well.

"It's a shame we can't cut the four-eyed man to see if his courage is real," Little Bull said.

Iron Shirt acted like he had been thinking the very same thing and regretting his decision to spare the man. "No, I had a vision long ago that we should never torture three enemies at the same time."

"Maybe we could still ransom the pretty soldier. He looks as if he might live if we cut him down." Little Bull already knew that Iron Shirt would never admit to his mistake.

"I think the four-eyed man must secretly speak our language and knew that he was to be spared," Iron Shirt said more loudly than necessary.

Many of the warriors heard his words and it was soon the almost unanimous opinion. The four-eyed man knew he was to be ransomed. Had he been cut like the other two he would undoubtedly cry out and beg for mercy. No such weak excuse for a man could be as brave as the Comanche.

However much they may have told themselves that the four-eyed man was the coward he should have been, Little

Bull noticed that the glass eyes traded owners twice, and the last time for two good horses and three buffalo robes. It was plain that many of the braves wanted the power of the deceiving white warrior who knew no fear.

After another long rest, Iron Shirt stood to start another pass by the prisoners. Little Bull studied their victims while he took his place in line. The fat man had bled badly, and was hanging limply from his arms. The pretty soldier groaned occasionally with pain, but still had enough strength in his legs to stand. Little Bull was impatient to ride out and find the Tejano war party and was afraid that the two white men would take longer to die than he wanted them to. He had seen strong captives drag the dance out for hours.

The drumbeat was slightly faster this time, as was the warriors' pace. Occasionally one of them would let out a soft war cry, or strange sounds that the drum moved them to. Little Bull tried to lose himself in the moment and to think only of his hatred for the Tejanos.

He was working himself slowly up to a fury when he noticed a young Comanche boy racing his horse across the prairie straight toward them. The boy was whipping the horse across the hip with his quirt and shouting something at the top of his lungs. The second or third time he yelled every warrior there understood what it was that he was saying.

The crippled slave quit beating on his drum, and the warriors stopped their dancing. The Tejano war party was just across the river.

Chapter 30

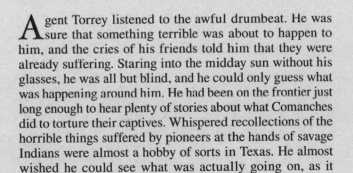

Agent Torrey listened to the awful drumbeat. He was sure that something terrible was about to happen to him, and the cries of his friends told him that they were already suffering. Staring into the midday sun without his glasses, he was all but blind, and he could only guess what was happening around him. He had been on the frontier just long enough to hear plenty of stories about what Comanches did to torture their captives. Whispered recollections of the horrible things suffered by pioneers at the hands of savage Indians were almost a hobby of sorts in Texas. He almost wished he could see what was actually going on, as it couldn't be near as bad as his imagination.

Commissioner Anderson had admonished him to be brave as they were marched out and tied to the posts, but Agent Torrey couldn't remember a time when he wasn't scared of almost everything. It was too late to change and had he not been tied up he would have curled up in a ball again and closed his eyes. Dying well was for men who were concerned about their dignity. He had never felt dignified in his entire life.

Surprisingly, his legs hadn't failed him, even though his heart hammered wildly like a runaway horse on hard ground. But having a little more control of his muscles didn't mean that he had found any peace and calm with the acceptance of his impending death. He leaned forward against his bonds and strained to make out what was going on, but all he could see was blurred images that appeared to be dancing in some strange ceremony. Common sense and habitual pessimism assured him that it wasn't his kind of party.

The heat was beginning to get to him, and his vision became even worse. He could hear the dancers nearing him. As if by magic, a painted Comanche face loomed in front of him like a horrible mirage. A wickedly long and pointed knife waved under the agent's nose, and his body became paralyzed with fear. He felt the uncontrollable urge to urinate, but his bladder was too empty to foul himself. The hot sun was almost unbearable, and his mind couldn't hold on to the present.

The face before him changed to the fat little woman he had once considered marrying back in Baltimore. She floated before him with an airy lightness that defied the weight of her plump thighs and broad hips. Her plump cheeks smiled at him, and her little pug nose was the same as it had been all the long years ago. She stayed with him for a long time, comforting him, and her hands were cool on his face. He couldn't help but return her smile. He felt featherlight himself and about to float away.

She faded slowly and was once more replaced by the blinding sun, watering his eyes. The drum had ceased to beat, and he couldn't tell if it was the lack of music or her leaving him that made him feel so sad.

*   *   *

Somehow the scouts had let the Tejanos get within five miles of the Comanche camp without seeing them first. Little Bull looked across the distance to his tepee and saw that Buffalo Butt was already catching up his war horse while Speckled Tail went inside for his weapons. The word had passed among the camp, and the horse herd was being brought in and children located.

Little Bull turned to Iron Shirt when the drum started pounding again. "Let's end this. There's no time for games with the Tejanos so close."

The drumbeat was much quicker this time, and the dance wilder. War cries went up from almost every warrior. Instead of a winding, snaking path to the prisoners, the Comanches cut a beeline straight to them. The beat sped up even more, until it throbbed like a mad pulse in the warriors' veins. The dance's earlier restraint was gone, and the warriors were in a fury by the time they reached the captives. Knives and war clubs flashed in a brutal flurry. When the drum finally stopped, the white men were dead.

Little Bull passed two warriors dragging the four-eyed man back to camp as he ran for his own tepee. Everywhere women were taking down their lodges and frantically packing in preparation to strike camp. The old men and boys would start them west out of harm's way while the warriors like Little Bull went out to give battle to the Tejanos.

Buffalo Butt held his horse while he jumped on, and Speckled Tail handed him his bow and quiver of arrows. He slung the weapons across his back and took the shield and lance she offered next. The lance was twelve feet long, and two of that was blade. The lance head was made from a broken Mexican cavalry saber, and ground to shape with a rough block of stone. He kept the steel sand-polished to a silver sheen, and its point needle sharp.

Pony Heart was watching him with an eager expression, and already the small bow in his hands had an arrow fitted to it. "Don't worry, Father. I will protect the women."

Little Bull smiled and nodded to the boy, and then he and Buffalo Butt passed a look between them. She laid her hand on his leg, and he put his on top of it for a brief moment.

"Come back to me," she said.

"Take care of our son if I do not."

He rode his horse over to where Red Wing sat in the dust with her hands in her lap. She was staring at the bodies of the captives still tied to their posts in the distance. There were tears in her eyes when she finally looked up at him.

"Sister, if you cry so for two white men, then you will cut your hair and scar your flesh before the sun sets. For the ground will be red with Tejano blood." He rode his horse around her in a tight circle.

She noticed for the first time the silver chain and heart locket hanging around his neck beneath his bison-tooth necklace, and her eyes fell to one of the scalps dangling from his shield. The hair was the deepest red, and it shone like polished copper. Nellie Young had been her friend and neighbor since she first went to live with the Wilsons. Nellie had been a pretty girl, and Red Wing had always envied her beautiful red hair. Nellie's daddy had given her the locket Little Bull was wearing not long before the night the war party slaughtered the whole family and killed Pappy Spurling.

She looked away from him. "There will come a time when your hatred will kill you, and I will weep again as you've made me weep this day."

It seemed to him that he had been battling the world itself ever since he was a boy, and then she showed up just when he thought he might be finally winning. He wanted to strike her with the butt of his lance, to hit her until she was what he needed her to be. "Don't cry for me if I die fighting as our father did. Cry for yourself if you can't live as he taught us."

Before she could answer him he loped away to join the mass of warriors already leaving camp in a long, scattered front. Feathers fluttered in the wind, and the little hawk bells braided into the manes of many of their horses rang the cadence of their strides. Watching him ride away was like looking back over her shoulder all the long years before, when war and misfortune had cleaved them apart with a dull blade until they were a family no more. Her brother was just a memory that she couldn't hold on to, but losing him didn't hurt any less the second time.

Loss, loss, and more loss—her heart was full of more dying than living, and she wanted to live more than anything. She wanted to play her piano again and to read the books that had become her good friends. She wanted to hear her mother softly singing over her cooking, and she missed the sturdy log walls and plank door of the Wilson cabin locking her away against the bad things that trod the earth. Most of all, she wanted to see her Odie again, and to have him look at her the way he always did. He never demanded that she be either White, Comanche, or mongrel half-breed. He asked no more than what she could give, and she needed that kind of love. She was weary of straddling two worlds.

Buffalo Butt took her moccasin toe and nudged Red Wing in the back. "You will help us pack, and then we must be gone."

Red Wing wiped her eyes and rose to her feet. It had been long since she had done such work, but she remembered. Her first mother had taught her well. Little Bull's wives frowned at her and thought her slow and clumsy for one supposedly raised among the People.

But Red Wing's work was purposely slow, for she was stalling for time. The two squaws were obviously scared, and that meant it was a considerably large force of Texans that were coming—perhaps large enough to rescue her.

Seeing the commissioner and the captain murdered had almost broken her, but something inside her wouldn't let her give up, no matter how hard her mind tried to convince her otherwise. There was hope yet, no matter how slim, and she knew she would have to be stronger than ever.

While she worked she cast a glance at the gray buffalo runner tied nearby. The horse looked swift, but it would be hard to steal him with the two squaws watching her. She would bide her time as long as she could, and when an opportunity arose, or the situation forced her hand, she would have to act quickly and decisively.

She had seen Agent Torrey led away alive. No matter that he had been one of the party who brought her to the Comanches, he was the only one of them she didn't blame. He was as much a victim of circumstance as she was, but trying to free him too would only get her caught. The thought of the gentle bookkeeper dying as the others had was terrible, but there was nothing she could do to save him. She was strong enough to face the cold truth, but she hated the decisions survival pushed on her. If she wanted to go back to her family, she was going to have to be as hard and cunning as her captors. To live as a civilized woman once more, she was going to have to think like a Comanche.

Chapter 31

Instead of coming across the plains to the east of the Comanche camp, the Prussian's Texans chose to cross the Pease River at a huge horseshoe bend miles to the south of the four medicine mounds. The maze of canyons and eroded ridges made for hard traveling, but they also offered the chance to possibly sneak up on the Comanches. The Tonks went ahead on foot to make sure they weren't ambushed, and the rest of the party rode slowly so as to stir up as little dust as possible. The men were quiet, and Odell saw them cringe when a shod hoof struck a rock too loudly, or someone's canteen thumped against their saddle swell.

They angled toward the river where it turned north, expecting at any minute to be ambushed or spied out by some Comanche hunter. They purposely held to the roughest, least-likely-to-be-traveled terrain until they finally reached the edge of the plains some two miles from the Comanche camp. Sporadic gunfire began to pop ahead of them, and the Prussian quickened their pace. The Tonks had obviously found the enemy, or the enemy had found them.

The Prussian led them forward at a trot until they came down the canyon to where its broad mouth emptied out onto the plain. A narrow creek cut across their front, east to west, and the Tonks had taken a position behind the high north bank. Just across the drainage from them the Comanches darted back and forth on their horses. The wind carried puffs of black powder smoke across the creek like little clouds as the Tonks tried to keep the growing numbers of the enemy at bay.

"By *Gott*, ride like hell for that creek!" the Prussian shouted.

Not only were the Tonks in trouble, it was plain to all that the position they held was of strategic importance. The Prussian stuck his spurs to his Kentucky horse, and the rest of them followed hard on his heels. They crossed a quarter mile of open ground at a dead run and plunged down the steep banks to join the Tonks at the bottom of the creek bed. The creek itself was only a narrow, sandy trickle, but the channel was forty yards wide and as much as eight feet below the level of the prairie surrounding it. The Tonks were using the north bank as a breastwork and taking occasional long rifle shots at the Comanches. Most of the Texans dismounted and joined them, while others remained to hold the horses.

Odell looked over the lip of the bank at the line of Comanches forming four hundred yards away. The scouts had reported a large camp of them, but he had never envisioned so many. There were at least one hundred warriors formed up, and more still coming from the camp. He had sworn vengeance against the Comanches, but he couldn't help but admire their wild, gaudy trappings of war. Feathers, bells, and beaded strings swung and fluttered in the wind. Even at a distance, the bright-colored symbols and patterns painted on warriors and horses were visible. While some shouted taunts and challenges to work up their courage, other warriors dashed back and forth between the two armies, hanging off the far sides of their running horses and purposely trying to draw the Texans' fire. The whole scene was like some crazy, wicked circus.

"They're madder than a tomcat with his ass on fire," Son Ballard observed.

"Gonna be a heap big fight." Placido had a happy, almost dreamy look about him.

Odell strained to try to make out the Comanche camp a mile beyond the warriors. Although most of the buffalo-hide tepees were darkened by weather, there was still enough contrast between their pale cones and the color of the dry grass to make them stand out. The squaws were taking down some of the lodges as he watched, and boys were catching horses from a huge herd driven to the edge of camp. Odell couldn't begin to number the herd but guessed that there were over a thousand horses milling in the dust their hooves created. It was too far to make out individuals, but he frantically searched for signs of Red Wing anyway.

"They're tearing down their village," he worried aloud.

"Yep, they're getting ready to run while the warriors give us hell," Son said.

The thought of Red Wing being carted away while the braves kept him pinned in the creek bed was almost more than Odell could bear. He had come too far to see that happen. "We have to charge through to the camp."

Both Son and Placido squinted at him like he was crazy. Neither one of them looked especially scared, but they didn't seem willing to charge either.

"Red Wing may be in that camp," Odell said.

Son considered the girl's predicament, if she was indeed a prisoner. He had seen the Comanches kill their captives rather than lose them during retreat. If the badly outnumbered Texans managed to rout them and put them on the run, there was a danger that all Odell would rescue was her body. He decided not to mention any of his thoughts. There was no sense in adding to the boy's worries.

"I agree with the Prussian. The Comanches won't wait long to attack us, and we should fort up here to take their best shot," Son said.

"That Prussian can sit on his sword for all I care. I ain't coward enough to sit here while the Comanches carry Red Wing off," Odell said hotly.

No sooner had the words left Odell's mouth than the Prussian stepped up beside him. A tall black soldier's hat that was more like a flat-topped helmet with a bill was on his head, and a shiny tin skull and crossbones was pinned to the front of it. He glared at Odell and held his saber point just inches from the young man's chest. With his black hat and black silk shirt, all he needed to look like the Devil himself was red eyes and smoke rolling out of his nose.

"Herr Odell, you must learn to curb your tongue or face the consequences of your words," the Prussian said. "If the Comanches do not kill you first, then I will ask for satisfaction for your insults."

Odell studied the sharp blade wagging beneath his nose. "You do whatever you're of a mind to when this is over."

"You are such a fool it won't bother me so bad to kill you." The Prussian lowered his saber slowly.

"Where the hell did you get that hat?" Son asked in an attempt to break the tension.

The Prussian's eyes rolled up to the bill of his hat, as if he had forgotten what he wore and could see it from that vantage point. "First Life Regiment, Death Head Hussars, the finest light cavalry the world has ever known."

"Is that what you've been carrying in that box strapped to your saddle?" Son seemed truly interested in unique headwear.

"Yes," the Prussian said impatiently.

"Well, wearing hats like that is probably why you were fighting all the time back where you came from," Son said.

"How is that, Herr Ballard?" The Prussian spoke better English than any of them when he wanted to, but he hadn't mastered all the nuances of the language. Some things flew right over his head or confused him.

"Ah, nothing. I was just speculating on how it must be open country over there in Prussia, else wise you boys couldn't wear those hats," Son said. "You couldn't get through the brush with that stovepipe strapped on your noggin."

"Are you trying to be funny, Herr Ballard?"

"No, I was just admiring your hat. If that thing doesn't strike fear in the Comanches, then nothing will."

The Prussian scowled as if he were not quite sure whether he should be mad at Son or not. He gave Odell a curt nod. "We'll settle our difficulties at a later date."

"I won't be hard to find," Odell said.

"Those heathens out there might do for us all, and rob you two of your pleasure." Son pointed to the Comanches.

"We can defeat them if we are disciplined." The Prussian went up and down the creek spreading fighting words to the men.

Everybody along the Texan line was counting Comanche heads, and trying to convince themselves that the Prussian was right. While they watched the enemy a Comanche on a dun horse rode out almost halfway to the creek. He gestured wildly and shook his bow at them. He shouted at the Texans while he walked his horse slowly back and forth in front of them. One of the Tonks had enough of the Comanche's mocking insults and took a shot at him. The range was barely two hundred yards, and shouldn't have been that difficult of a shot for a sure-enough shooter with a good rifle.

The Comanche continued to parade back and forth as if the Tonk's bullet had come nowhere close to him. His antics caused several of the Texans to lose patience and fire at him. None of their potshots found their mark, and the warrior stopped his horse facing them and lowered his shield. He reared back his head to the sky and blew a great breath of air out. Red smoke issued from his mouth.

"Iron Shirt has big medicine. He believes he can blow our bullets aside," Placido said.

Iron Shirt continued to taunt the Texans, blowing big puffs of red smoke at them from behind his shield. It seemed as if he could indeed blow the marksmen's bullets aside, for lead kicked up dust around him or flew over his head.

"To hell with him." Odell spent a long time aiming and then squeezed his trigger. His bullet did no apparent damage to the Comanche with the big medicine.

"Danged fools, you ain't going to get a bullet through that bull-hide shield at this range," Son yelled down the line.

"He's wearing some kind of armor," somebody added after another failed shot and a string of profanity.

Odell dropped his rifle butt and began to reload. He had experimented with a heavier load while hunting buffalos, and he poured a premeasured charge down the rifle barrel from a hollow piece of switch cane. After ramming a bullet home he primed his pan and leapt up on top of the creek bank. He knelt and aimed the gun with his left elbow propped on top of his thigh.

"You're a stubborn sort, ain't you?" Son asked.

Odell ignored the remark and focused on the rifle sights on his right-hand barrel. He had increased the powder charge by half again and hoped his gun would hold together as it had with the few test shots he had fired. His earlier experience with the toughness of Comanche shields had taught him that he was going to need a little more oomph. The Bishop hit about three inches high and a little to the right at a hundred steps with the heavy load. He didn't have a clue how that would correlate at over twice that distance, but he took a fine bead a little to the left and to the bottom of Iron Shirt's shield. His right eye was still swollen some from the beating Dub Harris had given him, and he squinted it open and closed a few times to try to clear his vision.

Apparently, Odell had done a poor job of calibrating his crude powder measure, for he was sure his gun had exploded the instant he fired. It was if he had touched a cannon off. His footing on the edge of the creek had been precarious, and the recoil kicked him back down the bank to land on his butt. His ears rang from the concussion, and it took him a count of three to remember just where he was. He stared dumbly at the strange faces looking down at him until he finally recognized Son and the others laughing at him.

Miraculously his gun was still in one piece, but his shoulder and cheek felt like a mule had kicked him. The Tonks and the Texans who weren't laughing at him were cheering wildly and pointing toward the Comanches. He scrambled back up the bank just in time to see Iron Shirt tug himself free of his dead horse.

"By *Gott*, Herr Odell, I swear on my father's beer and my mother's chastity, you are the greatest horse killer in Texas," the Prussian roared.

Odell felt more than a little embarrassed, but the men's enthusiasm soothed some of the sting of being knocked on the seat of his britches by his own gun. He watched as one of the braves led a spare horse out to Iron Shirt. The red ochre dust that the medicine warrior had spewed from his mouth was smeared all over his face, and he looked at the Texans with a dazed expression on his face.

"That'll learn that heathen some manners," Son said. "He won't pull that act again with Odell here to shoot at him."

"I wasn't aiming for his horse," Odell muttered.

"Keep a-shooting, Odell. You'll soon have 'em all afoot," Kentucky Bob Harris called out down the line to him.

Odell's dismounting of Iron Shirt had the Tonks' blood up, and many of them were soon standing on the edge of the creek and shouting taunts of their own and flashing insulting hand signs. A Tonk named Crazy Bug lifted his breechclout to show his bare ass and cawed like a crow at the Comanches. Soon, all the Tonks were up out of the creek bed and joining the ruckus.

For the first time, Odell noticed the white cloth armbands every one of them was wearing, and looked to Son. "What are the white rags for?"

"The Prussian had them tie those on. He figured in the thick of things that one kind of Injun might get to looking like the other to our boys," Son said.

Another Comanche brave rode out alone and called to the Tonks. Odell was surprised when Placido, who had seemed calm to the point of boredom up until that point, went to his horse and started out to meet the Comanche. His massive shoulders were slumped, and his long legs dangled almost comically beneath his little mustang's belly. A small shield was on his left arm and an ancient, battered musket propped up on his right thigh.

The Comanche screamed something at the Tonk chief and let go his rearing, lunging horse to lope a big circle around the battlefield. Placido kept his ugly little mustang to a slow, shambling walk until he pulled up halfway between the two fronts. The little nag seemed to have even less energy than his master and immediately rested one back leg as if he intended to take a nap. Only Placido's head moved as he followed the Comanche's progress around him.

When the Comanche had circled all the way back to his line, he suddenly turned and came straight at Placido at a dead run. He angled slightly to Placido's left and ducked low behind his shield. When the Comanche had neared to within a hundred yards of him, Placido stepped quickly from his horse. The Comanche veered wide at the last moment and fired an arrow in passing. Placido turned the arrow with his shield and spun slowly around to meet the Comanche's next charge from the opposite direction. The Comanche fired another ineffectual arrow and ducked off again.

The Comanche started a third pass, obviously intending to repeat his technique of veering wide with his shield in between himself and Placido's gun. But before he could alter his direction, Placido let go his rein and ran ten steps to his left. His move either forced the Comanche to pass much closer to him, or go the other way with his unshielded side exposed. The Comanche chose the latter and Placido quickly raised his musket and shot him off of his horse.

The Comanche was seriously wounded but not quite out of the fight. He lurched to his feet with a tomahawk in his hand. Placido reloaded and then went to his horse and hung his musket from the saddle. He slipped a massive, stone-headed war club from his belt and stalked toward the Comanche at a jog. The two of them crashed body to body, and their grunts of exertion could be heard between the striking of blows against their shields. In the matter of a few short seconds the Comanche was down on the ground and Placido had taken his scalp.

The Texans cheered as loudly as the Tonks when Placido walked slowly back to his sleepy mustang. He never even looked over his shoulder at the Comanche line, as if he deemed them unworthy of his attention. His ride back to the creek was as slow as his earlier departure.

Placido's victory emboldened his warriors even more. Over the course of half an hour two of them answered challenges to single combat. However, they weren't the wily fighters their chief was, and the Comanches made short work of them both.

"Those Tonks saw old Placido take him a scalp, and now they all think they're a match for the Comanches," Son said as they watched the fighting. "There's nobody more crazy brave than an Injun with his mad up."

"Lucifer's balls, we may have to charge the Comanches before we lose all our Tonks," the Prussian said.

Odell only half heard him. Another Comanche was sitting his horse alone on the battlefield. He called out loudly to the Texans.

"He wants to fight the Running Boy," Placido said.

"Which one is that?" The Prussian was looking to his Tonks to see which one of them was preparing to do battle next.

Placido shook his head. "He asks for the running boy with the powerful gun that knocks down before and behind."

The men that had heard Placido turned to look at Odell, but he didn't notice their attention. He only had eyes for the Comanche. He recognized the same warrior who he had seen back home before his pappy was murdered and the same one who had killed Israel Wilson right before his eyes. Odell lurched to his feet and headed for his horse.

Son blocked Odell's way to the horses. "Don't let that Comanche egg you into going out there. He'll chew you up and spit you out in a horseback fight."

"If he wants a fight with me, he doesn't have to holler twice." Odell brushed by Son and took hold of Crow's bridle.

"Dying proves nothing," the Prussian said.

Odell stepped into the saddle. "To hell it don't. I know that sonofabitch out there, and either him or me has had it coming for a long time."

Before Odell could ride away Son held up two holstered pistols to him. "Take these."

Odell looked down at them impatiently. They were strange-looking weapons, and he hadn't seen their like before. "Keep your guns."

Son thrust them at his belly. "I won these Colt pistols from one of Captain Jack Hays's Ranger boys. They're slow as hell to reload, but there are ten shots between the two of them before you're empty."

Odell held the pistols in his hands and frowned at them. "They don't even have triggers."

"Just cock them and the triggers drop right down," Son said. "There are two extra cylinders for them in those pouches, and all you have to do is knock out the cross pin and pull the barrel forward to change them out."

"I can't take your guns." Odell offered them back.

"Those things are too fancy for an old man like me. I'll stick to old Potlicker here to fetch my meat." Son patted the stock of his long rifle.

Odell took the belted guns and cinched them around his waist. The pistol barrels were almost as long as his forearms, but the weight of them hanging on his hips felt good. He didn't trust weapons he didn't know, but the thought of five shots each without a reload was pleasing. He rode out onto the prairie without another look back. He only had eyes for the warrior in the buffalo horn hat waiting for him.

"That Comanche has Odell plumb pissed off." Hatchet Murphy cackled.

The Prussian watched Odell carefully. "Yes, Odell doesn't forget."

Little Bull had watched Iron Shirt get his horse shot out from under him with some satisfaction, but the humor was short-lived. He recognized the Tejano marksman who had made the shot, and his blood began to boil. It was Running Boy and his big gun.

He raced his horse toward the Texans and pulled his horse to a sliding stop just out of easy gunshot range. He stabbed his lance into the ground and lifted both of his arms high and wide.

"Running Boy, come out and fight me," he yelled.

There was no answer from the Tejanos, and he continued to shout challenges and insults. He remembered how the big Tejano had shamed him twice, and his body shook with anger. Three times over the winter he had dreamed of Running Boy charging across the prairie with his big feet hitting the ground like thunder, and his hands full of fire and smoke. No matter how many arrows he fired, Running Boy kept coming. Little Bull had awakened after each dream in a cold sweat, and his fear shamed him.

It seemed like forever before Running Boy came out of the creek bed straight toward him, but he wasn't on foot like he had been in the dream. Instead, he rode a black horse with the wind under its feet. He was even bigger than Little Bull remembered him, and all the people would sing of the fight to come. He would scalp Running Boy and drag his body by its heels through the village for all to see that he was not afraid of Tejano giants.

He kicked his horse to a run, and was pleased that Running Boy did the same. The distance closed swiftly between them, and he saw that Running Boy had no fire in his hands. Only shamans and weak-minded fools believed such dreams.

Chapter 32

The two horses were close enough that Odell could plainly see the face of the muscled little warrior charging him, and it was like looking into the eyes of a black-faced demon. Odell gritted his teeth and leaned slightly forward in his saddle. He tried to get a bead on the Comanche with his rifle, but the warrior was zigzagging his horse too rapidly make good aim. Odell kept to a beeline course, committing to a game of chicken that could get him killed.

The Comanche snapped a shot from his bow and Odell barely managed to bob to his right enough to dodge the arrow that flew by his left shoulder. No sooner than he righted himself in the saddle than the warrior veered his horse sharply to Odell's left and another arrow ricocheted off Odell's cantle. He tried a snap shot with his shotgun barrel but missed wildly at almost point-blank range.

The Comanche's horse was a runner, but he didn't handle as good as Crow. Odell stopped short, and rolled the good black horse back the way they had come. The Comanche was turning around, but in a far looser turn than Odell had made. For a brief instant the warrior's body was visible without his shield in the way. Odell shot again without thinking and knew instantly that his aim had been off.

The Comanche twisted around and let go another arrow with his bow held crossways over his horse's rump. Odell felt the arrowhead cut across the side of his neck before his mind could even recognize what had just flown by him. The Comanche's rate of fire was amazing, and Odell tensed for another arrow coming his way. He tried to keep Crow in behind and slightly to the right of the Comanche's horse in order to make it harder for the right-handed warrior to get in position with his bow.

Without slowing, the brave hung his bow over his back and snatched up the lance he had left stuck in the ground. Odell stopped Crow and reached for his powder horn while he watched his adversary turning back to him in a tight arc. He managed to get a charge poured home but realized that he was never going to have time to finish reloading. The Comanche was fifty yards off and coming at a dead run with his lance pointing the way.

Odell thumped his spurs into Crow's side and went straight at the Comanche. He thought of his pappy and tried to steel himself against the bite of the lance. The Comanche was going to pass on his left. He waited two more heartbeats and then swung his left leg over the saddle. He balanced in his right stirrup and ducked beneath the lance while he reined Crow hard to the left. The two horses crashed head-on at a dead run, and the impact sent Odell flying through the air. He rolled to his feet well beyond the thrashing animals and picked his rifle up from the ground.

Somehow, the Comanche was still astride his horse, although it was down on its belly and fighting pitifully to get up. Odell took a two-hand grip on the stock of his rifle and charged like a mad bull. The Comanche's horse managed to regain its feet just as Odell reached its side. He swung the rifle as hard as he could. His blow took the Comanche in the shoulder, and he felt the gunstock and the warrior's bones crack all at the same time.

The mighty lick knocked the Comanche off the other side of his mount. Odell fumbled for his knife handle while he tried to come around behind the horse. The frightened, injured animal kicked out and fell back to the ground. One of its hooves struck Odell squarely on the top of his thigh, knocking him to the ground. He fought his numbed leg and somehow scrambled to his feet in time to watch the Comanche fleeing on foot with his left arm dangling limply like a broken wing. The warrior threw one last hateful look back over his shoulder at Odell as two other Comanches raced in to gather him on the back of one of their horses. Odell remembered the pistols at his side and clumsily tugged at the right hand holster. Just as he cleared leather guns began to crack like it was the Fourth of July.

He looked back to the creek and saw the Prussian charging across the prairie with his skull hat on, and his carbine held aloft like some kind of banner. Behind him came the entire force with their guns popping and the Tonks screaming bloody murder. Even the Texans yelled war cries of their own.

The Comanches were coming out to meet the Texans at an equal pace, if not faster. Odell looked for his horse just as Placido rode up with the animal in tow. He couldn't believe he hadn't crippled Crow, but there was no time to check him out. He made his saddle just as the Texans roared by them.

The Prussian stopped his men in a skirmish line and their rifles almost fired as a single volley. The Comanches faltered and pulled up within bow range of the Texans' empty guns. Someone shouted for the Texans to fall back, and Odell and Placido raced in the middle of the retreating men. Arrows flew hot and heavy, and Odell saw the man to his right slump in the saddle with a fletched shaft buried deep in his back.

The Texans poured charges from their powder horns while at a dead run, and spat patch-less round balls down their rifle barrels. After a quick jab of their ramrods, they whacked the butt of their rifle stocks on their saddle horns to make sure the bullet was seated in the bore. A quick dash of powder in their flintlock pan or a percussion cap from a leather strap at their waist had every gun in the force loaded again. The act of reloading from horseback while at a dead run looked fairly simple when viewing it, but Odell knew from experience that it was closely akin to rolling a cigarette while being rolled downhill inside a barrel.

When almost back to the creek, they turned around to face the pursuing Comanches once more. The Prussian shouted for some of them to hold their fire so that they weren't caught with all their guns empty at once. What the Texans lacked in numbers, they made up for with marksmanship. Their rifles turned aside the pursuing Comanches. The mass of warriors split to either side of them, some of them ducking in close to let fly their arrows. Men and horses went down on both sides as the fight grew hotter by the minute.

When the Comanches finally turned back to contemplate things, the Prussian saw a chance for counterattack and charged again. Back and forth across the level prairie this take and give, charge and retreat was repeated. The Comanches tried to overrun the small force, but each time the Texan rifles broke their will before they closed. After ten minutes of fierce fighting the Comanches gathered their dead and wounded and regrouped at a distance. Odell had one of the Colt Paterson revolvers in his hand but had thus far not fired a shot. His targets had been too far away and moving too fast to waste a bullet, and he had held his fire in case he needed to cover the other men while they reloaded.

"Look out, boys, they intend to ride us down this time," Son's voice lifted high and shrill.

The Comanches' horses' hooves drummed the ground,

and nothing on earth could match the terrible war cries issued from the warriors' throats. The Prussian ordered half his men to shoot, and the other half to ride forward when the first group's guns were emptied. It might have been a sound tactic if applied, or if the Comanches didn't have them so outnumbered. More Comanches fell before their guns, but nothing was going to stop their momentum. In an instant Texans, Tonks, and Comanches were mixed together at close quarters. All around Odell was dust and confusion, wounded horses, and dying men. It was a brutal, root-hog-or-die kind of fighting, and a man had to be rabid mean and half crazy to stand a chance of surviving.

Odell stretched out the long barrel of his pistol before him and shot a Comanche at point-blank range. He had no time to gauge the effect of his shot, for another horse almost ran into him as it tore by. In that instant he got a brief glimpse of Son Ballard reeling lifelessly in his saddle with an arrow protruding from his eye socket. Beyond, sunlight flashed on polished steel, and he saw the Prussian slashing right and left in the middle of two Comanches trying to club him from his horse. Odell plunged Crow forward and pressed his pistol into the ribs of one of the Comanches and shot him off of the Prussian's back.

A war club struck Odell between the shoulders and he backhanded with the pistol barrel. His swing only found air, and he nearly toppled from his horse. He wheezed for breath and began firing at the deadly phantoms sliding in and out of the veil of dust. To the right and left of him, his friends in arms had won themselves some breathing room. The slackening rifle fire and the Comanches' receding yells seemed ominously quiet after the hell that he had just witnessed.

He snapped his pistol at a retreating Comanche twice before he realized it was empty. He holstered it and drew the other while he looked wildly around him. Kentucky Bob was down on the ground with a lance stuck through him and the dead Comanche who had wielded it still holding onto the shaft. His brother Dub was sitting his horse nearby, but just as dead with a handful of arrows in his torso. Several more men were wounded, and possibly dying, but surprisingly the Prussian's force was mostly intact.

In fact, the battlefield wasn't littered with the bodies Odell expected. A lame or dead horse could be spotted on the prairie here and there, but the only Comanche corpses visible were a couple in the Texans' midst. Granted, the Comanches made every effort to haul off their dead and wounded, but the casualty count was small for such vicious fighting.

The Prussian stepped down off of his horse and picked up his carbine. He rested for a brief moment against the side of his horse before climbing back on. "Reload, and let's take it to them while they're on the run."

After a little study of his empty Colt Paterson, Odell punched out the barrel wedge with his knife tip and pulled the barrel forward to remove the discharged cylinder. He replaced it with a capped and loaded replacement cylinder from one of the little pouches on his gun belt and reassembled the pistol. He missed his rifle, but he had to admit that while the Colt pistols were underpowered, the ability to shoot so many times between reloads seemed tailor-made for Indian fighting.

The Prussian started them forward at a high lope toward the Comanche warriors assembling near the village. The Texans who could ignored their pain and exhaustion and followed him. Several of the Tonks had been put afoot, but they came along just the same. A handful of men too seriously injured to fight were left in the creek bed.

The Comanches' numbers appeared little weakened, and if possible, they seemed more ready to fight than ever. Half of the camp had already gathered what little it could and was on the move. The warriors fought a rearguard action in random little groups, buying time for their women and children and horse herd to get free of the fight that had turned against them.

Odell stood in his stirrups and looked for signs of escaping Comanches. As the Prussian led them onward, he kept his eyes on the dust cloud worming its way across the prairie a mile to the west. He hoped Red Wing wasn't already being dragged away.

The Texans boiled into the camp with their horses at a dead run. Women who hadn't fled quickly enough ducked and dodged among the remaining lodges with their children dragging behind them, or clutched screaming in their arms. The Comanche warriors were everywhere, sniping with arrows, and smoking trade fusils. A loss of momentum would have meant being surrounded and certain death for the Texans. The Prussian led the run through the gauntlet, with the Texans taking snapshots with their rifles on the fly. They reined their horses through the maze of lodges, leaping them over obstacles, and crashing against the hide walls of the tepees in their wild charge.

They crossed a dry streambed at the far side of the camp and caught a young squaw in the act of trying to mount her frightened horse between two half-disassembled tepees. One of the Tonks had managed to race ahead of the rest of them and he caught her just as she finally swung up on her dancing pony. He wrapped one arm around her waist and pulled her across his horse's withers in front of him.

The Texans were checking up their winded horses to dismount and form a skirmish line facing back the way they had come. Odell saw the fat squaw come out from behind the tepee as if it were in slow motion. Before he could call out a warning, she sent an arrow into the Tonk's back. The rest of the party had seen her too, but she was as quick with her bow as were the men of her tribe. She took aim again and let loose another arrow just as a bullet took off the top of her head.

Her last arrow had missed its mark, but she did shoot

good enough to kill Placido's horse in its tracks. While the men poured fire at the Comanche warriors steadily filtering through the camp toward them, Odell was still trying to get his mind to accept the fact that they had just had to kill a woman. He remembered the bodies falling among the lodges as they had raced through the camp and wondered how many of them had been women too, or even children. He and the other Texans only had eyes for Comanche braves, but there wasn't much time to cautiously pick targets at a dead run under fire.

"Hang in there, men. We just about have the sonofa-bitches beat," the Prussian shouted.

Odell looked past the men to the open prairie, and the black-clad Prussian turned to look with him. Three Comanches burst out of the streambed a hundred yards beyond the camp. They were fleeing at a dead run away from the Texans, and Odell was about to look away when the squaw in the rear turned her head to look back.

Chapter 33

Red Wing heard the gunfire and war cries growing nearer in the distance, but from where she was at the far side of the camp she couldn't see the battle she knew was taking place. Little Bull's son had led in five horses for them, but he was just a small boy, and the sounds of fighting and the frantic goings-on of the camp had the animals nervous and flighty. He led them by neck ropes, and a big blue roan set back on the rope and jerked the boy to the ground. He tried to hang on and keep them from wheeling away, but the rawhide ropes bit into his hands and the horses drug his light body along the ground as if he were no more than a feather. The roan and two others got away from him and stampeded off at a run with their heads held high and wide to avoid stepping on their trailing lead ropes. The two horses he managed to keep hold of and his own mount weren't enough to both pack the household and to carry them all away.

Buffalo Butt immediately accepted the fact that she was going to have to leave behind her home and most of the items that she cherished. She hastily began packing a single, small bundle of necessaries that she could carry with her.

Meanwhile, Speckled Tail was torn between her treasures and the fear of still being in camp if the Tejanos should win a victory. In the end, her treasures won out, and she attempted to roll all her personal belongings, as well as Red Wing's valise, into a buffalo robe.

"You're going to get us all killed if the Tejanos come," Buffalo Butt shouted at the Kiowa. "Our husband told us to be gone quickly."

Speckled Tail ignored the scolding and kept gathering things she couldn't bear to part with. Every time she told herself she was through, she would spy something else that she had to have.

Red Wing stood back and watched it all. While the two squaws argued, she decided to take another look at the gray buffalo runner staked out just beyond the women. She turned to find the boy staring at her. He was obviously worried about the fight and his failure to hold on to the horses, but he made a valiant effort to mask his concern. She remembered another boy who had been much like that at his age—always fierce on the outside and worried on the inside. Looking at the boy was like going back ten years and seeing her brother again as a teenager.

He seemed not to notice that she was studying the buffalo runner and soon lost interest in her and frowned impatiently at his mother and Speckled Tail. "Hurry up. My father trusted me to see you away from here."

Secretly, Pony Heart was torn between the fear he felt among the women of the camp and the need to watch his father and the rest of the warriors fight the Tejanos. He had gone to see the prisoners tortured less out of a desire to see enemies suffer than to lay his eyes on the devils he had heard so much about. Nothing he had seen about the three white men had explained all that he had heard of them, or the concern of his people at the arrival of a small war party of their kind.

Red Wing noticed that the boy was lost in his own thoughts, and she decided that it was then or never if she was going to escape. She ran for the buffalo runner and thought she had passed the arguing squaws without them even knowing it. The boy was slow to react, and she had hold of the horse's stake rope before his mouth could even form a warning.

She tugged the anchor loose from the ground and worked her way up the long rope to the shying horse. Hiking her doeskin dress up her thighs a little, she took hold of the gray's mane at the withers and swung her right leg up over his back. He instantly made two stiff-legged jumps and promptly bucked her off. Before she could get back up and try again, Buffalo Butt jerked the rope from her hands. She stood glaring over Red Wing while the sound of warriors calling out warnings to the camp, and the gunfire of the Texans grew closer.

Red Wing wanted to cry with frustration. She had blown an easy chance by her own stupidity. She had been so long among the white men that she had grown used to mounting on the left side of her horses. Comanches, and most other Indians, used the off side, and many of their wilder horses never learned to tolerate anything different. The gray was obviously no kid horse, and she had startled him by mounting on the wrong side.

She avoided Buffalo Butt's hot gaze and got to her feet. She was dusting herself off when Little Bull rode up mounted behind another warrior. His left arm was bound in a crude sling, and his face was riddled with pain. He leapt off and strode directly for her while the other warrior turned and went back through the camp at a run.

"The Tejanos have beaten us," Little Bull said. It was plain his anguish wasn't all because of his broken arm.

"Here is your horse." Pony Heart offered the buffalo runner's rope to him.

Little Bull went to one of the other two horses and brought it back to Red Wing. "Get on."

She stood stoically and tried to bluff him. "I will not."

He slipped the war club from his belt and brandished it at her. His eyes were crazy with pain. "You'll ride, or I'll tie you belly down on this horse."

"Forget me, brother, and let me be dead again," she said. "Save your family."

"I would kill you myself before I would see you lost to the Tejanos again." He sounded as if he had truly gone mad.

Sweat was dripping off his face, and she saw that both his mind and his body had been pushed to the brink. Delay was her only chance, but she knew he meant what he said. Even injured as he was, there was no way she could fight off the four of them.

She didn't move quickly but got on the horse as he had ordered her. He took his knife and cut a section of the gray's stake rope. He made a one-handed noose and slipped it over her foot and tied her two ankles together under the horse's belly. With an agility that was shocking given his condition, he swung on the gray's back with her lead rope in his hand.

"Come, woman. There's little time," he said to Buffalo Butt.

"Go on. I'll be right along." Buffalo Butt held the last remaining horse at ready, but her eyes went back to where Speckled Tail had disappeared into one of the tepees.

"Speckled Tail!" Little Bull shouted.

The Kiowa finally appeared with her mirror and her comb clutched against her chest. She tucked the items into her buffalo robe and struggled to get the large roll of the hide draped over the horse's back. Buffalo Butt knocked the robe from her hands, and Speckled Tail cried out and went to her knees to dig her mirror and comb back out of the crude pack.

"Get up behind me, and leave that fool!" Little Bull was looking across the village, and he sounded as if the Texans were already upon them.

Red Wing realized that the fight had moved into the camp itself, and her heart pounded with hope. The mix of terror and stubborn courage she felt was the same as the last time she had stood in such a camp just before the Texans had appeared with their guns belching hell's smoke and their big-brimmed hats shading eyes wilder than any Comanche. Only this time, she wanted the Texans to take her away.

Buffalo Butt slapped Little Bull's horse across the rump with the palm of her hand and sent him off in a jump. Red Wing's horse followed by its lead rope and the boy raced alongside them. They turned into the dry streambed and Red Wing looked back to see Buffalo Butt trying to calm her frightened horse into letting her and Speckled Tail mount.

The streambed ran due west of the camp and gradually shallowed until it no longer provided cover for them. Little Bull turned out of it and pointed them westward toward the dust trail of those that had already fled the camp.

Red Wing kept looking back at the camp and saw the Texans overrun Little Bull's lodges and Buffalo Butt shoot one of them before she died. Red Wing started to call out when she recognized the Prussian, but then spotted the tall man sitting his horse a little ways from the others. It was her Odie, and she lifted a hand to him.

Chapter 34

The Texans started back through the lodges on foot like pirates swarming over the side of a ship, and the fighting in the village swiftly turned into more of a wild brawl than a pitched battle. The Comanche warriors continued to linger, but the fight they put up was only a last, wrathful effort to protest the enemy plundering their camp. Odell and the Prussian had spotted Red Wing at the same time, and both of them spurred out of the mayhem in pursuit. Neither one of them said anything to each other, as they raced side by side across the prairie.

Crow was already tired from the battle, but when Odell asked him for speed he didn't refuse. He ran like his lungs were made of cast iron and his heart as big as Texas. There were few horses to match his like, but the Prussian's Kentucky horse ran neck and neck with him just the same. Red Wing's captors had what should have been an insurmountable lead, but there hadn't been enough time for Little Bull's gray buffalo runner to totally heal from his abscess. There

was an ever-so-slight falter to his stride every time the sole
of that hoof struck the ground. That was just enough of a
handicap to make it a race.

Over the course of a mile, they had closed to within a
hundred yards of the two Comanches and Red Wing. They
were close enough for Odell to recognize the warrior he had
fought with earlier, and the wild and pleading looks Red
Wing threw back at him brought on a rage like none he had
felt before. He banged his heels unmercifully into Crow's
belly. The Comanche warrior leading Red Wing was heading for the dust trail on the horizon some four miles ahead.
Odell knew that it wasn't just a race to run the brave down,
but to do it before he and the boy reached the aid of the other
refugees fleeing the camp.

Odell felt how hard Crow was straining underneath him,
and although the horse still seemed willing, he knew he was
running him into the ground. He looked to the Prussian and
saw that the Kentucky horse was lathered and roaring from
the back of his throat with every breath. The Prussian
whipped the horse with the long tail of his harness leather
reins, but it was plain that his thoroughbred was almost
running dead.

When they cut the distance in half over another long
stretch of ground, the Prussian leveled his carbine on the
warrior's back. It was plain that he knew his horse had nothing left to close with, and he was going to take a chance.
Odell started to shout at him not to risk hitting Red Wing,
but the Kentucky horse's front legs buckled and it broke to
a staggering trot and almost fell. By the time the Prussian
regained his seat the Comanche leading Red Wing was already too far away to chance a shot with the smoothbore
carbine.

Odell left the Prussian sitting his wind-broke horse and
continued the chase. He saw that Red Wing was leaning out
over her horse's neck and trying to slip its rope hackamore
over its ears. Crow had brought him to within twenty yards

of the Comanche in front of her, and Odell drew one pistol. A deep but narrow wash cut across their way from the foot of a low hill, and the Comanche hit it at a run. All three riders disappeared over the bank before Odell even recognized what was coming. Crow was running blind and didn't even feel the check of the bit when Odell tried to slow him. They sailed off the six-foot drop and hit in a cloud of silty sand.

The Comanche's gray had fallen on impact, throwing him. Crow came over the lip of the bank at the same time and almost trampled the fallen warrior. Odell twisted in the saddle to fire a shot into the Comanche as he passed, but Crow reached the far bank and stalled halfway up it. He reared high and fell over backward, and Odell was hard-pressed to avoid being smashed by his saddle horn. He pushed himself away from the saddle just before the horse's crushing weight thumped into the ground.

He made it to one knee just as Red Wing rode past him down the wash. He heard her pull up behind him, but he didn't take the time to look her way. The boy had cleared the wash, and there was nothing left between Odell and the warrior except sixty feet of open ground.

The Comanche managed to rise to his knees, and his eyes locked onto Odell. He snarled like the wolf he was and tugged at the long-handled war club at his belt with his good arm. Odell dug his feet into the sand, drew his other pistol, and lunged forward with a gun in each hand. He cocked and fired, cocked and fired, alternating his shots from one hand to the other at a dead run. The crack of the pistols roared in his ears as he charged forward, and he was blind to the rest of the world. He saw only the Comanche's body jerking with the impact of his bullets. Five times he shot, and his pistol barrel was almost touching that hateful, black-painted face when he squeezed off the fifth. He staggered over the fallen Comanche and fell hard.

The Comanche lay lifeless and shot to doll rags when

Odell got back to his feet. He stood over the body with his breath coming in ragged gasps and the pistols in his big fists trembling with fury. He stared long into his enemy's face until all the hate and hurt slowly ebbed from him and was carried away on the wind. The violent satisfaction he had felt moments before was gone, and he only felt hollow and spent.

His mind finally registered the sound of hooves behind him, and he turned to see Red Wing ride up beside him. Of all the ways he had imagined meeting her again, he was in no way prepared for the look on her face as she stared past him at the Comanche lying on the ground. Her tears weren't those of joy at being rescued, and he realized that she wept for the warrior dead at his own hands. He wanted to speak to her, but something heavy and silent settled between them that he had no words to breach.

"Would you bury him?" she finally asked.

He wanted to hug away the pain and the hurt of her and wipe away her tears, but couldn't fathom what cruel trick he suspected fate had wrought. "Who was he?"

"Comanches do not speak the names of the dead, but once he was my brother."

"I didn't know." Odell was at a loss as to how the world could have tilted so.

"No, you couldn't have." There was no accusation in her voice, but she looked at him as if she could see right into his soul.

"He was one of those that killed Pappy and your father." Odell cut the rope that bound her feet.

"I know, but it doesn't make it any easier."

The Comanche boy appeared on the bank above them with his bow in his hand and an arrow nocked. Odell lifted one pistol, but Red Wing rode her horse in front of him. She said something in Comanche and the boy shouted something back. Odell stepped around her horse just in time to see the boy shake his little bow at him and whirl his horse away.

He listened to the sound of hoofbeats until they faded in the distance.

"What'd you tell him?" Odell asked.

Red Wing was still looking in the direction the boy had fled, even though she could see nothing of the plains around them from the bottom of the wash. "I told him to ride on to his people, and that his father's body would be here should he return one day."

"What did he say?" It dawned on Odell that not only had he killed her brother, but he had perhaps orphaned her nephew in the process.

She looked at him sadly. "He said that one day he'll be a man, and he will kill you. He swore that his wrath will never die, and the Tejanos will know this is true and never know a day's peace so long as he lives."

"Will he be all right until he finds the rest of his tribe?"

"He'll find his way. He is Comanche."

Odell knew nothing to say to her that would make it better. Killing the Comanche had felt like justice, but it was also breaking her heart. He dragged her brother's body to an undercut in the sandy bank, and left it lying there while he climbed up out of the wash. He waited for Red Wing to say something, or to instruct him in some burial ceremony, but she just sat her horse and stared at him. He stomped on the lip of the bank until it began to give way, working his way backward until he had caved in enough of it to cover the body well with the little avalanche he created.

He left her alone with her thoughts at the grave and went to where Crow lay on his side at the bottom of the wash. He knelt in front of the horse and laid a hand on his neck. Crow seemed unaware that Odell was even there and groaned and made a halfhearted attempt to rise. The horse only managed to slightly lift its head, and his lungs rattled with every slow rise and fall of his side. Odell saw the blood in Crow's nostrils and the broken bone showing through the torn hide of the right knee.

"Lord Almighty," he whispered.

He thought of all the long miles they had come together and all the one-sided conversations the horse had endured. He remembered how when turned loose hobbled, Crow would sometimes come to the campfire at night to stand by him, as if the black horse too needed the company.

He laid his pistol against Crow's forehead and ran his hands along the horse's neck. He closed his eyes and squeezed the trigger, and felt Crow shudder and grow still beneath his hand. Red Wing rode up and waited quietly.

"He never let me down, not once," Odell said.

"I knew he wouldn't."

"I know you loved him just like I did, and I almost wish you'd never given him to me."

She smiled for the first time, although it was small and faded from her mouth as quickly as it had formed. "He was the only thing I could think of that might bring you back to me."

He thought her more beautiful than he remembered. "I wish . . ."

She cut him off with a lifted hand. "Don't say anything. Just take me home."

He stripped the saddle from Crow and put it on her horse after cutting loose her bound ankles so she could dismount. The animal wasn't used to the rigging or Odell's bit, but was too tired to put up much of a fight. While Odell tightened his cinch, he studied the Comanche's gray gelding standing ground-tied just down the wash. He was a magnificent looking horse, but seemed to be favoring one leg.

"He has a bad hoof that's not quite healed, but when healthy I think he might have even outrun Crow," Red Wing said.

"I don't know what I'd do with a crippled Comanche horse," Odell said lamely, although he had to admit that he was going to need a horse.

"Why, you'd ride him," Red Wing said. "And if you didn't

like him you could sell him to someone in the settlements for a good price."

"Well, it might take a while to heal him up, but I never thought of selling him."

"Mama says that most men never even think a day ahead," Red Wing said.

Odell eased up and caught the rein trailing from the gray's rope war bridle. The horse didn't seem too lame, and when Odell picked up his front right hoof he could see where somebody had whittled a hole to drain an abscess. The infection seemed to be gone, but the hole was deep enough that it acted much like a stone bruise. A leather pad nailed between the hoof and a shoe might cushion him enough for easy travel until he could heal. The more he looked at the horse, the more he decided he would have been a fool to leave him behind. But then again, Red Wing's ideas usually made sense.

He looked out over the lip of the wash and saw more Comanches coming across the plains. The sound of the Texans' gunfire had ceased, and it was a large group of warriors retreating from the camp. He helped Red Wing into the saddle and led the two horses to where the wash was the deepest. He parked them as close to the high bank as he could and waited. He listened for the sound of hoofbeats while he looked up at Red Wing on her horse.

"You run if I tell you to," he said.

She seemed to be paying no attention to the coming Comanches or his instructions. She was looking at him in a way he couldn't get a handle on, and he thought the silence between them was worse than not knowing what she was thinking.

"I don't know how I could have made things any different," he said.

"Odie, I wish there was someone to blame for all of this, but it isn't you," she said.

The Comanches veered south to avoid crossing the wash,

but still came so close that Odell could see their dust. He climbed up in front of Red Wing and started back to the Comanche camp with the gray horse led behind. They hadn't ridden far when Odell felt her arms go around his waist and her cheek settle against his back. His heart felt too big for his chest, and the feel of her against him was more right than anything in long, long time.

They rode up on the Prussian leading his Kentucky horse a half mile outside the Comanche camp. He watched them come with a hand shading his eyes.

"Hello, Frau Red Wing," the Prussian said. "I thought we had lost you for good."

"I brought her back," Odell said.

The Prussian studied how Red Wing hugged close to Odell. "Ah, the spoils of war."

Chapter 35

The first thing Odell saw when he came into camp was Son Ballard sitting on a stack of buffalo hides with a rag tied over one eye.

"Well, kiss my ass. You're the only Texan I know that can find a pretty woman in an Injun scrap," Son said. "And that gray horse ain't too shabby either."

"I thought you were dead." Odell couldn't believe what he was seeing.

Son lifted up the rag to reveal the mangled socket of his left eye and the hoop-iron arrowhead still buried in his brow. "No, but I'm glad to see you back. Nobody's been stout enough to pull this damned thing out of my head."

"That must have smarted some," Odell said.

"It disturbed the hell out of my aim for a while, but I think I'll live," Son chuckled, and then pointed to Red Wing. "Ma'am, won't you step down and have a cup of coffee with me? I ain't as pretty as I was this morning, but I can only stare at you half as much as the rest of these hairy-legged womanizers."

There was a little man with a freckled face and a bad sunburn sitting beside the old scout, and he squinted at the new arrivals as if he wasn't sure they were real. He reached out a hand to Red Wing, even though she was on her horse ten feet away.

"Is that you, Red Wing?" he asked.

"Why, Agent Torrey, I think you are going to have to find you a new hat before you're burned to a crisp," she said.

"I thought you were dead. I thought we were all dead," Agent Torrey muttered.

"We've been through a lot, but we're very much alive," she said.

"Poor Commissioner Anderson and Captain Jones. Mr. Ballard here tells me that they were used terribly, and I can't quite understand why I'm still here." He scratched at the wet blisters on his red cheeks and studied where his bare feet stuck out of the long, buckskin hunting shirt that somebody had given him. Whatever Comanche the shirt had been made for was bigger than the agent, and the sleeves hung past his hands and made him look like some kind of sad puppet when he moved his arms.

Placido was sitting nearby and rubbing some pasty tanning concoction into the raw flesh of a fresh scalp. He smiled a greeting at Odell, and then went back to his work.

Son noticed Odell staring at the scalp. "Placido chased a fat Waco out of camp that none of us saw. He never has liked Wacos, and he's especially proud of himself."

"I wish he would put that scalp up while Red Wing is around," Odell said.

Son cocked his head and considered the scalp in Placido's hands. "Just be glad you don't have to see what's in that bag beside him. I have a sneaking suspicion that he thought that fat Waco was fed out too well to ride off without taking a few cuts of him for snacks later."

Odell couldn't tell if Son was kidding him or not. He could see what looked like blood soaking through the buckskin bag. "He better not cook his dinner in front of me."

As Odell was helping Red Wing down from the horse he noticed a group of about ten squaws huddled together on the ground under the guard of some of the Tonk scouts. They kept their eyes down, and clutched several small children protectively to them. Beyond them, a filthy and ragged white girl sat rocking back and forth with a blanket pulled over her shoulders in an attempt to cover her nakedness. Her blond hair had been hacked off as short as a man's, and the one long leg Odell could see stretched out in front of her was striped with welts and the scabs of healing cuts. She mumbled strange, singsong words, and looked half crazed and even more miserable than the Comanche squaws.

Odell expected Red Wing to sit and rest, but instead she went over to the squaws. The captive Comanche women looked at her with as much fear as they did the Tonks, who were leering at them lustily and telling rude jokes. After much effort, she finally managed to find one squaw who seemed willing to talk. She knelt beside the old woman and began to question her.

The Prussian went straight to the captive white girl without a word to Red Wing. In fact, he hadn't said much to her all the way back to the camp. Odell knew the Prussian had set his cap for her and couldn't understand his complacency. He also knew that the Prussain hadn't forgotten his promise. The man had said he was going to kill him in front of all the men, and a prideful sort like that wasn't about to crawfish on his word and give anyone an excuse to question his bravery or his honor.

"Try some of this if you're hungry." Son pointed to the cast-iron pot over the little chip fire in front of him. "I don't know what kind of Comanche soup that is, but it ain't half bad."

Odell hunkered down and scooped a bit of the stew out of the pot with a buffalo horn spoon. He tried a slurp of the bubbling hot concoction, but he couldn't quit thinking of what might be in Placido's sack. His appetite left him, and he set the ladle aside. He kept watch on the Prussian, because he knew the man's violent temper and wasn't about to be caught unaware.

"I don't think that Prussian is going to be too concerned with you or your woman anymore," Son said laconically.

"Oh?"

"The Prussian doesn't know it yet, but he hit the jackpot when we stumbled on this camp." Son jerked a thumb back over his shoulder to where the Prussian was trying to talk to the captive girl. "There are several men here who swear that pitiful little thing is Susie Smith."

"So?"

"She's Senator Smith's daughter," Son said. "She was stolen away over two months ago, and the senator offered Jack Hays and his Rangers a thousand dollars to go after her."

"How much?" Odell tried to imagine just what that much money would look like. He hadn't seen more than twenty dollars in gold since he came to Texas.

"There's a standing reward out for a thousand to any man that can bring her back alive," Son said.

"That's a lot, even split between so many of us."

Son gave him a wry look, even with only one eye showing. "The Prussian will share the reward, but he'll make sure he's the man who's known for saving her."

"Well, it was his expedition," Odell said.

Son jerked his thumb over his shoulder again. "That man yonder has always had ambitions, and being a hero won't hurt them at all."

Odell looked around the camp. Most of the exhausted men were eating or napping, but he noticed that several faces were missing. "How many men did we lose? I saw the Harris brothers down, but nobody else."

"Three men killed, twice that many wounded, and one that might not make it 'til morning," Son said.

"How many Comanches do you think we got?"

Son frowned. "It's hard to tell with Comanches. They'll do anything to haul off their dead, and you never kill as many of them as you'd like to think. The Prussian will guess more, but Placido says from the blood on the grass and what the men say, that we did for about twenty of the bastards, and two squaws."

"That doesn't seem like much for such a fight."

"Well, it would if you were one of them that bit the dust, or got your eye jabbed out by an arrow."

Odell noticed that the Comanches had managed to haul away very little of the camp, and some of the Texans were holding a good-sized herd of captured horses on the prairie nearby.

"There's a lot of plunder here," he said.

Son nodded his head. "The Prussian's fought Comanches before, and he'll know what to do. He'll take a few of the best horses, shoot the rest, and burn down everything that the men don't want to carry with them on their saddles."

"Shoot the rest of the horses?" Odell asked. The kind of Texans who had followed the Prussian thought a lot of a good horse, and he couldn't imagine them being willing to kill an entire herd of them.

"Don't think we've seen the last of those Comanches. The odds are, they'll follow us and try to steal back their horses. That's a big herd to have to guard at night, and that Prussian is smart enough and hard enough not to remount his enemy if he can help it."

"That seems a shame. There are some good horses yonder, and I'll be danged if I could shoot them." Red Wing's insistence that he keep the gray buffalo runner had gotten him to thinking. He had nothing left back on Massacre Creek but the burned ruins of a cabin. A woman was going to expect a little more than that from a possible suitor.

Son read the way Odell was looking at those horses. "I can't say for sure that the Prussian will do things just like I said, but me and Placido were talking about those horses. If the Prussian and most of the men would settle for all the reward for that Senator's girl, a few of us might gather those buffler robes and the extra horses and take them up to Missouri to sell."

"Why not take them back to Austin, or maybe to San Antonio or Houston?" Odell asked. "We might even take them down to Mexico."

"Naw, half those horses were probably stolen from those parts, and we'd end up having to give too many of them back to their rightful owners," Son said. "They've all got the Oregon fever back in the States, and a herd of good horses might sell for a king's ransom in Independence or St. Joe."

"You've a point there," Odell said.

"What about you, Mr. Torrey? Are you going to throw in with us if we head for Missouri?" Son asked. "I must say that an educated man like you to tell me some new stories would be a welcome change on the trail."

Agent Torrey shook his head vigorously. "No, I'll go with the others. If I make it back to Houston I'm going to catch a coach down to Galveston, and then a fast ship to Baltimore. There's a chubby shoemaker's daughter there, and if she'll have me, I'll gladly wed her. I'll sit in a dark little shop behind a sturdy door and cobble shoes until I forget Texas ever existed."

He rose to his feet and stumbled away from the fire. Odell noticed for the first time that man was naked from the waist down, and he seemed oblivious to fact that the shirt wasn't long enough to completely cover his bare ass and flopping parts. Odell found it highly unsettling that he should parade himself in such a fashion with women in camp.

"Where are you going, Mr. Torrey?" Son called after him.

"I need to find my glasses," Agent Torrey said.

Odell watched him wander off, tottering weakly from one Comanche tepee to another with his eyes squinted tight, and pausing bent far over at the waist to examine everything he came across on the ground.

"Somebody ought to get that strange fellow some britches," Odell said.

"He's a little off his mark right now, but I'd say he would've fit right in with us," Son answered.

Odell's mind was too full of Son's plan to give Agent Torrey any more thought. "Sounds like a few brave men might make some hard money if there's the market in Missouri you say there is."

"Are you game?"

Odell looked at Red Wing among the squaws. "I don't know if she'd be willing to go with us, and I ain't leaving her again unless she makes me."

"I guess you'll just have to ask her," Son said. "She has to have some grit in her craw to have come this far, and I wouldn't be against her coming with us."

As if on cue, Red Wing started over to them, and the Prussian fell in behind her. She looked upset and he had his hand on his sword.

Red Wing started to say something to Odell but turned around when she realized the Prussian was right behind her. "What do you intend to do with those Comanche women?"

The Prussian gave her an impatient look but answered her while he stared at Odell. "I'm going to take them to Austin and see if I can get the Comanches to come in and trade white captives for them."

"Let them go, Karl. Please," Red Wing said.

"Turnabout is fair play. No Comanche ever turned loose a captive unless they were ransomed or taken back from them," the Prussian said.

"Those are women and children and have no part of your war." She tore her eyes away from the Prussian to give Odell a pleading look.

"Frau Red Wing, it is best for you not to worry about such matters," the Prussian said.

She whirled back to him angrily. "If you take those

women, then you are no different from the Comanches you hate. And I've had enough of kidnappers and woman stealers to last me a lifetime."

The Prussian stared at her indignantly and tugged at the front of his black shirt and straightened his gaudy hat. "I can understand your interest in those squaws, but war is never pleasant and is best left to soldiers."

Odell had as little use for a Comanche as the next man, but looking at the squaws, he felt no desire to see them suffer more. "I understand there is a large reward for that captive girl you were talking to."

The Prussian's eyes narrowed and he continued the cold, silent treatment he had given Odell on the way back to the camp.

Odell had never been much of a trader, but the hopeful, expectant look Red Wing was giving him forced him to try. "How about you take the girl, and what plunder the boys want, and I take the rest of the leftover horses and all the buffalo hides?"

"What about the captive squaws? The Tonks may have something to say about them," the Prussian asked.

"Placido can work it out with his Tonks, and we give the squaws a few of the worst horses and let them go," Odell said.

The Prussian smirked. "You've been doing a lot of thinking, haven't you?"

"Some. I was thinking about taking those horses to Missouri."

"And just what makes you think Placido will speak to the Tonks for you, or that any of these men will help you drive horses to Missouri?"

"Count me and Placido and a few others in with Odell," Son said.

The Prussian hissed through his teeth. He liked the fact that some of the men seemed loyal to Odell even less than he liked anyone questioning his command. "And what about you, Frau Red Wing? Will you go with this foolish boy or come with me?"

Odell looked to Red Wing, but she kept her face turned away from him. Odell wished she would hurry up and answer. The waiting made what he feared would come even worse. He had never mentioned to her all the things he had promised himself to do for her if he ever found her again. He knew how badly she wanted to go back to her mother, and Missouri was nowhere near Massacre Creek. Maybe she could never really forgive him for killing her brother or bring herself to forget that he didn't have two bits to his name. She was smart enough to know just how little he had to offer, and the Prussian was going to make her admit it.

She studied the Prussian carefully with a lift of her head, and her little back as straight as an arrow. "I want to go home, but if Odie thinks we ought to ride to Missouri first, I'll go with him."

Odell couldn't believe his own ears. She sounded almost proud and gave him one of the smiles he had missed so badly all the long months he had been alone. He felt his face burning like it was on fire.

"Herr Odell, I never would have thought you so ambitious, or I would've let the Comanches kill you last fall," the Prussian said.

Odell couldn't deny the Prussian had pulled his fat out of the fire the day Israel Wilson was killed, but he wasn't about to yield. "Do we have a deal? I'd reckon you'd be glad to get shuck of me."

"True, Herr Odell, but I don't like to lose." The Prussian's hand went to his sword and Odell was just as fast to grab the handle of his Bowie.

"You're quick." The Prussian smiled a smile that was no smile at all. "You've slandered my name more than once and questioned my leadership in front of the men. I intend to see just how quick and steady you are."

Odell gauged the reach of the Prussian's sword. "I'm waiting."

Red Wing looked from one to the other of them like they were crazy. "You two are neighbors."

"Karl there won't have it any other way, and I ain't going to run," Odell said.

Red Wing stepped in between them. "Karl, if you thought as much of me as you said when you proposed, then you'll let him be just to see me happy."

The Prussian bounced his sword up and down in its metal sheath, and it sounded like an old bayou alligator clacking its teeth together. "I'm going to see if this overgrown boy is worthy of you."

Son Ballard grabbed her and dragged her back. "Girl, this trouble has been brewing for too long to stop it."

"As the challenged you are allowed to choose the weapons," the Prussian said like one way to kill Odell was as good as another.

"I don't need all that gentleman stuff. You just come cutting or shooting when you're of a mind to." Odell took a step back with his hand still on the Bowie.

"A hundred steps with rifles, one shot, and then to the blades if it comes to that," Son said.

The Prussian looked to the old plainsman and then back to Odell. "It seems you have a second. Is that how it shall be?"

Son pitched Odell his long rifle. "Take a fine bead, and old Potlicker will shoot true."

Odell caught the gun by the forearm and turned and started down a long lane running between the tepees. "Karl can count fifty steps the other way."

The Prussian was no fool and wasn't about to go up against a rifle with his inaccurate smoothbore carbine. The men had gathered around to see the show, and one of them had picked up Kentucky Bob Harris's fancy squirrel gun from the battlefield. The Prussian borrowed it and checked the priming on the pan. When he was satisfied with its readiness, he started in the opposite direction from Odell, counting in German as he went.

When roughly a hundred steps divided them, the Prussian said to Son, "You will give the command to fire."

The Prussian turned himself so that his left side faced Odell with his rifle pointed toward the ground at his feet. Odell did the same and dug his worn-out boots into the ground until he felt sure he was planted there. He waited for Son to give them the go-ahead.

Son held Red Wing against his side and looked from man to man with his one good eye cocked to see if both of them were ready. "Fire!"

To say that Odell had cut his teeth on the stock of a gun wouldn't have been too far from the truth. He'd been pulling triggers since he was big enough to hold up a rifle, and never had he thought that any man might be his match when it came to shooting. But the Prussian was quick, real quick. Odell had just found his sights when the Prussian sent a bullet through his side. Odell staggered back a step and tried to catch his wind. He could feel the blood already running down his pants leg. He gritted his teeth and raised his rifle. The Prussian looked grim but held his ground.

Odell put his front sight on the Prussian's chest and laid his finger ever so lightly on the trigger. He held his aim for a long count of five while the Prussian waited bravely for the bullet that would end his life.

"By *Gott*, if you think I will beg, you are sadly mistaken." The Prussian stared unflinching into the business end of Odell's rifle a hundred steps away.

The pain of the Prussian's bullet hitting him had given Odell pause enough to cool his temper and to think a little. Odell grinned and shot the skull emblem off the Prussian's hat, and then grounded old Potlicker and drew his Bowie knife. "You're a stubborn sonofabitch, but I reckon I owed you that much."

It took the Prussian a moment to realize he wasn't dead. He straightened his hat and slowly laid his rifle down. He slid his saber from its sheath but made no attempt to come forward.

Odell's wound hurt like hell, and it felt like the Prussian's bullet had gouged out a ditch in his side. He held the Bowie before him, liking the deadly weight of it balanced in his big fist. Supposedly, its original owner had taken down men armed with swords, and even guns. He knew he was a damned fool for not shooting the Prussian when he had the chance, but it had felt too much like murder. He just hoped he was half the man Jim Bowie had been.

The Prussian made a few practice swings while he smiled at Odell. The blade whistled through the air like a Comanche arrow in flight. Odell tried not to think of the razor edge on that long, curved blade swinging like that at him.

The Prussian sheathed his saber with parade ground flair, and took off his tall hat to examine where the skull had been shot away. He laughed quietly and then put his hat back on and gave Odell some kind of salute.

Odell let his knife fall beside his leg and watched the Prussian walking away from him. "Where are you going?"

The Prussian stopped and turned back to him. "Both our honor has been satisfied. Take your horses and the girl and go."

Odell was too baffled to understand just what was happening. "Well, I'll be damned."

The Prussian laughed again, loud and long. "You very well may be, Herr Odell. You are a brave and reckless man. I think if you stay in Texas long, you might someday be a legend."

Chapter 36

Odell and Red Wing sat their horses at the edge of the river and watched the horses splash across the shallow ford. Placido rode by them leading a string of packhorses loaded with prime buffalo hides. He had a big smile on his face that was no way in keeping with all the stories of stoic Indians.

"The Comanches maybe follow us, and then we ride through the Kiowa and Osage. I'm pretty sure we're gonna have a heap big fight," Placido said in passing.

"I don't know about that Indian," Odell said.

"Wolf People and man-eaters," Red Wing said, but she smiled just the same.

Son Ballard waved the two of them on from the head of the herd. He had a piece of red wool blanket tied over his empty left eye socket that made him look like the footloose rover he really was. He was surprisingly spry considering that Odell had to pull the arrowhead from his skull with a pair of horse nippers and a boot braced against his head.

Odell hefted his rifle and studied the repair job he had done. A little copper wire and some rawhide shrunk around the grip of the stock had made the Bishop gun almost as good as new. The Bowie knife and the fancy pair of repeating pistols fit just right around his hips, and the gray horse seemed just as willing to strike out across the country as he was. If it hadn't have been for the crease the Prussian had put in his side he would have felt as right as rain.

"I told you that was a good horse," Red Wing said.

He patted the gray horse's neck. A pad and a rawhide boot around his hoof had him traveling sound. "He ain't Crow by any means, but he's growing on me."

"It's hard letting go of what we've lost. I think that's half of being happy."

"I'm glad you're coming with me," he said.

Red Wing gave him a stern little frown and fought back the smile she felt when she looked at him. "Why, Odell Spurling, I'm not crossing this river until you ask me what you should have asked me a year ago."

"I thought we had an understanding."

"Do you think you can trade for me or just steal me? I've had just about enough of men dragging me around the country and treating me like the squaw they see."

He lifted one side of his hat a little and scratched at his temple as if in deep thought. "Just how many ponies would you say you're worth? Maybe I can't afford you."

She folded her arms across her chest and her eyes were like the bores of two little shotgun barrels pointed at him. "I can't for the life of me understand what I see in you."

He squirmed in his saddle uncomfortably. "I figured we'd said about all that needed said."

She was like a bulldog when she got something bayed, and wasn't about to let go until she'd shook him a bit. "You just keep talking, and I'll run down Karl. He used to talk sweet to me, and he owns the biggest farm on the upper Colorado."

Odell leaned close to her. "Red Wing Wilson, you're the prettiest girl in Texas, and I'd be proud if you'd marry me."

She patted at the tight little bun of her gathered hair and smoothed her skirt over her bent leg on the sidesaddle. "Hmm. Maybe there's hope for you yet."

He turned in the saddle to watch the black smoke rising from the Comanche camp behind them. The Prussian and those going home were already growing small in the distance, and he could just make out the dust trail of the Comanche squaws and their children making their way west. He almost felt as if he and Red Wing were alone on the face of the earth, and liked that feeling just about more than anything. He sat under the broad expanse of merciless and beautiful sky, and could not put a name to just what poetry it was in the windswept distances that called to him so. It was if the all the living and the dying that was ever contained in the slowly beating and ancient heart of the land whispered a song. It felt like freedom; it felt like home.

"Did you ever imagine anything like it?" he asked.

Red Wing stared into the distance with the wide sweep of country reflected in the deep pools of her brown eyes like a fevered dream. "Nobody ever imagined a place like Texas."

PETER BRANDVOLD

THE GRAVES AT SEVEN DEVILS

BULLETS OVER BEDLAM

COLD CORPSE, HOT TRAIL

DEADLY PREY

ROGUE LAWMAN

STARING DOWN THE DEVIL

RIDING WITH THE DEVIL'S MISTRESS

.45-CALIBER FIREBRAND

.45-CALIBER FURY

.45-CALIBER REVENGE

penguin.com

Don't miss the best Westerns from Berkley

LYLE BRANDT
PETER BRANDVOLD
JACK BALLAS
J. LEE BUTTS
JORY SHERMAN
DUSTY RICHARDS

penguin.com

M10G0610